"I give animals more leeway than . . . trouble-some women."

Shea couldn't stop herself from challenging him. "Me in particular, or all women?"

"Women are all the same, Miss Randall."

"In what way?"

A muscle flexed in his cheek. "Do you really want to know?"

She didn't, but she heard herself saying, "Yes."

He moved toward her, a scowl on his face. When he reached her, he leaned down, and Shea suddenly realized his intention and her mistake.

She tried to move away, but his hand grabbed her arm and held her still. "You know what they say about curiosity?" he said. Then he lowered his head and his lips captured hers. . . .

Relentless

Patricia Potter

BANTAM BOOKS
NEW YORK • TORONTO • LONDON • SYDNEY • AUCKLAND

RELENTLESS

A Bantam Book / May 1994

ISBN 0-553-56226-6

Published simultaneously in the United States and Canada

Bantam Books are published by Bantam Books, a division of Bantam
Doubleday Dell Publishing Group, Inc. Its trademark, consisting of the
words "Bantam Books" and the portrayal of a rooster, is Registered in
U.S. Patent and Trademark Office and in other countries. Marca
Registrada. Bantam Books, 1540 Broadway, New York, New York
10036.

PRINTED IN THE UNITED STATES OF AMERICA

OPM   0 9 8 7 6 5 4 3 2 1

Relentless

Prologue

Kansas, 1863

A bullet in the gut would have been more merciful.

Even hanging.

But nothing in Captain Rafferty Tyler's life had been merciful, and it was obvious that fact was not changing now. Every hope he'd ever had, every dream he'd ever dared dream, was gone. He was no longer Captain Rafe Tyler, respected, decorated officer and gentleman.

He stood there, disgraced. Cashiered. A convicted felon. He wanted to ball his fingers into fists, but he wouldn't give the bastards that satisfaction.

Thief. Traitor. They had judged him a thief and very nearly a traitor. But his exoneration on the latter charge didn't matter. He would carry the stigma of both labels for the rest of his life.

He squared his shoulders, standing alone before the garrison as he was stripped of his captain bars, his buttons, his sword. Stripped of everything that had ever meant anything to him. Publicly stripped of his dignity. His soul.

Drums tattooed out his disgrace, the rhythmic rapping accompanying every humiliation. He tried not to hear them, but he knew they would echo in his brain forever.

And then the branding. A *T* on the back of his hand. *T* for "thief." Public branding was still one of the army's preferred punishments, though not usually for officers. But then he was no longer an officer.

Rafe allowed his gaze to move slightly from the officer directing the punishment. A few army wives and daughters stood on the porches of the living quarters. His jaw tightened as he searched for Allison. He didn't know whether she would watch her former betrothed's humiliation or not. She had been the first to abandon him when charges were filed against him. She hadn't even asked him whether they were true, had only returned his ring by proxy, without comment, while he awaited court-martial in the guardhouse. He'd found he hadn't known her at all, and, Christ, it had hurt.

He shook off the two men assigned to hold him still, and he offered his hand on the forge. He would not wear the mantle of coward as well as thief. But inside he retreated into some dark place where no one else could enter, would ever be able to enter. And he endured this part of the punishment—because he had no choice but to endure.

He tried to blank his mind, but he couldn't. Flashes from the past whirled by, a parade of events that had led to this day, to this ultimate ignominy. That day more than twenty years ago when he had watched his mother and father die, his father scalped, his mother raped before being killed. He had been taken by the Comanches and held captive for three months until he was "bought" back by the army. Little had improved. He had been taken in by a Texas family, but he soon learned it was only because of the work he could provide; he would have fared as well with the Indians.

But he was a survivor. He'd always been a survivor. He joined the army at fifteen and found a home he trusted. A place he belonged.

Eight years on the frontier until the war, working his way from private to master sergeant. Then the war with the South started, and he received a battlefield commission and two promotions. He had found his place in life; leadership had come easily. Because he had been an enlisted man, he understood them and valued their lives. He had known they would go wherever he led, do whatever he told them.

He'd thought he'd conquered his evil star, but now he realized it had just been waiting to strike again. At twenty-five he'd been wounded and assigned to a desk job, away from the fighting he understood and into army politics he didn't. He was temporarily assigned to providing escorts for payrolls headed West. He hadn't trusted his superior, Major Jack Randall; something about the man had rankled Rafe.

Now he stared ahead at Randall, the man who had perjured himself at the court-martial, who had so neatly framed Rafe for payroll robberies Rafe knew now Randall had committed. Rafe had been an easy target, a maverick officer with a Texas accent.

Rafe heard the sizzling of red-hot iron against skin, smelled his own flesh burning, and blessed the momentary shock that kept the pain from immediately rocking him. He stood, his legs braced, as agony filtered through his consciousness, firing the hatred that was fiercer than the branding iron. His eyes never left the face of Major Randall.

The man flinched, and Rafe knew his eyes had promised vengeance. Relentless vengeance.

Randall licked his lips for a moment, then turned away.

Rafe withdrew his hand and, despite himself, despite self-made pledges he would not do so, he looked at it. The *T* was already evident, the skin burned black and raw, the sickening smell hovering in the hot summer sun. He swallowed his own bile to keep from moaning as the pain heightened, assaulting him in waves that continued to increase in intensity.

He was marked now. Forever marked as an outlaw and thief. No matter what he did, he could never rid himself of it.

He could never have a normal life. Not with the brand.

His arms were seized, irons fastened around his wrists, the soldiers unmindful of the burning agony of his hand. He was pushed toward the guardhouse to await transport to the Ohio State Penitentiary where he was sentenced to serve ten years. There were no military prisons, and military prisoners were turned over to whichever state facilities had space.

He bit his lip to keep from crying out in pain, from raging against the injustice. But no one cared. Randall had done his work too well.

If it was the last thing he ever did, Rafe would make Randall pay.

It was that thought, and that thought alone, that carried him through the night, through three days of being chained and displayed like an animal as he was taken by wagon and train to Ohio.

Randall. The name might as well have been burned into Rafe's hand as the *T.* Rafe would never wipe out the stink of burning flesh, the humiliation of being cashiered in front of the garrison he once served, the purposeful, planned destruction of his life.

Not until Randall suffered like a man damned, suffered as Rafe had in the same lingering, irreversible way.

Chapter 1

Boston, 1873

Shea Randall knew her mother was dying.

Guilt mixed with loss. She should have insisted her mother call a doctor sooner, but Sara Randall had claimed over and over again her pain was only the result of eating bad food, that it would soon go away. No sense spending good money for a doctor.

But the pain hadn't gone away. It had increased, suddenly exploding in agony. Her mother now lay on a hospital bed, curled with pain so severe, even morphine couldn't control it.

Despite her frail appearance, Sara had a core of pure steel. She was the most determined woman Shea had ever known. Seeing her now, watching the life drain from her, was like taking a knife to her own heart and exposing it for all to see.

The doctor said Sara Randall's insides were poisoned by the ruptured appendix, and there was nothing he could do. She had simply waited too long before coming to him.

Sara Randall had only a day or two to live, if that much. No more, he had said, and those days would be agonizing as infection invaded and slowly destroyed her mother's body.

Shea held her mother's hand. Sara's eyes opened. "The shop?"

"Mrs. Mulroney is keeping it open," Shea said, fighting back tears she knew would only distress her mother further.

"You . . . should be there. Mrs. Logan's bonnet . . ."

"Mrs. Logan's bonnet is completed," Shea said, telling a lie her mother would despise. Her mother detested dishonesty of any type. A lie, she always said, is the road to perdition. You can never tell just one lie; lies take on a life of their own, reproducing new lies. A lie was like Hydra, a multiheaded monster that grew two heads for each one cut off.

But Shea justified this particular lie to ease her mother. Anything to relieve the pain and worry. Anything. If she could give her own life in exchange, she would. She was rewarded when her mother's eyes closed, and Sara Randall seemed to relax; the next pain, Shea knew, would come soon enough.

Shea didn't want to think of what might happen now. There had always been just the two of them. Her father had died before her birth, and her mother had supported the two of them with the small millinery shop that barely provided a decent living. There was never any money for extras, but Shea and her mother hadn't needed much. They went to free concerts in the park, to church socials, and on occasion, when they had an extra dollar, to the theater.

They had some friends, but no one really close, since they had been too busy with the shop. And there were no relatives. It had always been the two of them against the world, her mother said, and that was a gracious plenty, more than many had.

There had been a few young men, suitors, but none whom Shea cared about enough to marry. Her mother had always urged her to consider several of the suits. Choose a man with honor, she'd said, and you will grow to love him. Don't trust emotions, trust common sense.

And Shea had tried. She had been courted by some she believed honorable, like the father whose tintype image Shea adored. She had been courted by some she believed decent, but none had made her heart sing; there was no intensity of feeling such as her mother must have known to remain loyal all these years.

No, love had eluded Shea, and despite her mother's urging, she refused to settle for less. Now she was twenty-three and thought to be on the shelf.

It was difficult to think of herself that way. She loved her books, she enjoyed drawing, and she knew she was a good designer of hats, particularly whimsical creations that drew customers to the shop. Those inspirations, as well as the caricatures she drew of people she knew, reflected the secret part of a personality usually considered tranquil and sensible. She would never be a good artist, but she had a sense of the ridiculous that she kept hidden to herself for fear of offending people.

But now nothing mattered except her mother. Shea couldn't even think of life without her. Sara Randall had been friend and teacher as well as parent, and Shea felt lost at even the thought of being alone. Although at times she had rebelled against the possessiveness of and strict standards set by her mother, Shea had always felt deeply loved.

And now . . .

Desolation flooded Shea until she heard a moan escape from her mother.

"Can I get you anything?" Shea asked in a whisper. Her mother's soft gray eyes met hers. "I wish . . ."

"What do you wish?"

"Be careful, Shea, be careful who you marry." Sara's eyes filled with tears, and it was almost more than Shea could bear. She had never seen her mother cry before.

"Someone like Papa?" Sara had never said much about Shea's father, and Shea had stopped pressing, thinking that his death had probably hurt her mother too badly. He had been charming, her mother said long ago. Handsome and charming and honorable.

But Sara didn't answer, her mouth contorting as a new wave of pain racked her thin body. Her fingernails dug into Shea's hand until Shea felt blood running down them. And then Sara's pain seemed to weaken.

"I'm sorry, Shea," her mother said in a whisper.

Shea bent down. "There's nothing to be sorry for."

"I did what I thought was best." Her mother was looking into her face, willing her to believe.

"Of course you did," Shea said, not understanding the sudden urgency in the words, or the meaning.

And then her mother screamed. Shea hurried out of the ward to find a nurse. In minutes there was an injection, and Sara's calm gray eyes clouded.

"I did what I thought was best," she mumbled again.

"It's all right, Mama," Shea said. "It's all right."

Sara's eyes closed, and Shea wondered whether she would ever forget the fear that was etched on her mother's face.

He had been so handsome. So charming. So persuasive. Sara saw him now in her fevered pain.

Jack Randall. He had been everything a young girl could want. It had been a miracle when he asked her to marry him and go West.

And then the miracle had turned into a nightmare. She discovered that Jack Randall was an incurable thief. Far more money than he earned showed up in his pockets. For a while she believed his explanations: a wager, a gift, a bonus from a grateful superior. But then Jack would say it was time to leave, often quite abruptly and in the middle of the night.

He always found another position; he could charm birds out of trees, employers out of checking nonexistent references, but then he would tire of his current job, complain it was not worthy of his skills, start stealing and, when he thought he might be caught, move on again.

Like so many women often did, Sara thought at first she could reform him. But stealing seemed to be an addiction with him. He took more and more chances, and then she discovered his participation in a robbery of the bank in which he was a clerk. She had found wrapped bills in his traveling bag following the robbery, just days after she knew she was with child.

He had promised so many times to stop, and she didn't believe him anymore. Part of her would always love him, but she wouldn't raise a child on stolen money. Not as the child of a thief. She might be able to exist that way, but she wouldn't burden a child with that kind of legacy.

And so without telling him of the child but threatening to reveal his part of the bank robbery if he came after her, she left him, telling friends in Boston that her husband had died. She had no intention of marrying again. Shea was born just when Sara's own father died, leaving her a small inheritance, just enough to buy the millinery shop where she worked.

And the lies had started, the lies she had warned

Shea about, because she knew better than anyone how destructive they became. She couldn't let Shea know of her tainted blood, and so she lied and lied and lied, allowing Shea to believe that her father had been an honorable man, a good man.

She knew now what a mistake she'd made. As she emerged again from the foggy, weighted world of morphine, she was terrified that Shea would learn her father was still alive and try to go to him. She couldn't let that happen. Jack Randall would corrupt her as he corrupted everyone around him.

Why had she kept the letters, the money, the newspaper story?

Because you couldn't ever completely let him go. He was her weakness, the kind of weakness she'd tried to keep from infecting her daughter. Perhaps there was still time to burn those few keepsakes of a marriage that had been both paradise and hell.

She looked up at her daughter, who was sitting in the chair next to her, and saw her blue-gray eyes were closed. If only she could go home, she thought just as the pain hit again with agonizing sharpness.

A moan escaped her, and Shea's eyes opened. Such honest eyes. She must never know about Jack Randall. He would charm her with that smile that delighted the heart.

"Mama?"

"There's a box, Shea, a wooden box," Sara said. "In my closet. Go and bring it to me."

Shea shook her head. "I can't leave—"

Sara tightened her clasp on her daughter's hand. "Please . . . it won't take long. . . ."

Shea hesitated. She didn't want to leave, but her mother was growing agitated. She would hurry. "I'll bring it."

Sara's fingers dug into her hand. "Don't open it."

"I won't," Shea said. "I'll get a nurse. . . ."

Her mother's hand dropped as her body arced again with pain. "Just bring . . ."

"I'll bring it, Mama. I'll be right back." She leaned down to place her hand on Sara's cheek, and Sara knew she must look frighteningly ill. "Go," she said.

Her daughter nodded and hurried out the door.

Pain hit again, and Sara felt more of her life draining away with each new onslaught. She must destroy Jack's letters, those few letters that begged her to return, the envelopes of money he'd sent. He had never known about the child, and she never wanted him to know.

Her eyes closed, and she saw him again in her mind, in her heart. Jack had begged her to come back ten years ago. He had said he had joined the army and was now a respected major. He had said nothing about the stealing. He could never admit doing anything wrong, but she knew he was trying to tell her he was through with that. She had been tempted. Dear God, how she had been tempted, and then she read the story in the Boston paper about a court-martial in Kansas and how a Major Randall had testified against another officer accused of payroll robberies. Most of the money had never been found. And she had known, deep in her heart, that it had been Jack who was responsible, not the other man.

She should have contacted army authorities, but then that would have meant revealing her own lies, allowing Shea to know her father was a thief. Still, she had hung on to that clipping. And the money he'd sent. She'd never spend a penny of it. Stolen money. Blood money. She wore an albatross of guilt about that other man.

That clipping . . . in the box with the letters.

The pain was fading now, drowning in a sea of fog. *Hurry, Shea. Hurry.*

Oh, Jack, if only . . .

* * *

Shea couldn't find the box right away. It was well hidden under a number of hatboxes, and she had to go through each one to find what her mother apparently wanted—a lovely carved wooden box with a lock.

She wondered where the key might be. She went through her mother's desk, looking for one. Wouldn't her mother want the key as well?

Almost frantic with worry, she gave up. The key must be either in her mother's possession or at the millinery shop below. Just as she was leaving the house, a neighbor stopped to ask questions, and it took Shea several moments to get away. She couldn't find a rental carriage and started to run, urgency eating at her.

She held the box as if it were a treasure as she ran up the steps of the hospital.

The nurse on the second floor looked away from her when she approached. Feeling a sting of apprehension, she hurried to the room her mother shared with three others.

The doctor was looking down, his face bleak. He saw her and shook his head. Shea rushed toward the bed, fear rushing through her. Her mother's face was pale, unnatural. Shea leaned down and touched her lips; the cheek was cool. Still. Lifeless.

"I'm sorry, Shea," the doctor said.

Shea looked at him uncomprehendingly. Her mother had been fine five days ago. How could this have happened? She looked at the doctor through glazed eyes. She wanted to blame him, but she couldn't. Her mother had resisted Shea's entreaties too long.

Shea knelt next to the bed. She grabbed her mother's hands, trying to get some sign of life. "You can't," she whispered. "You can't go."

Shea willed her to open her eyes, willed warmth back into those hands. All Shea had was her mother.

She felt pain gather behind her eyes, a tightness that threatened to squeeze life from her. "Don't leave me like this," she whispered as tears started to trickle down her cheeks.

She didn't know how long she stayed there before Dr. Sanson pulled her to her feet, the old, often irritable doctor trying awkwardly to give comfort.

"What will you do now?" he asked.

"I don't know," Shea said brokenly. Dully, she looked at the box that had fallen to the floor. It had held importance to her mother, and that was strange. Shea had thought they shared everything.

But that didn't matter. Nothing mattered now except the loss and loneliness she felt. In that state of numbness that protected one from grief too strong to bear, she thought of what must be done. A funeral. Friends to notify. Decisions about the shop.

She leaned down and picked up the box. She would examine it later. Alone.

She watched as the doctor pulled a sheet over her mother. A tear snaked down her cheek, and she brushed it away. Sara Randall had always been strong. Shea could be no less.

Rafe Tyler hesitated outside the walls of the Ohio Penitentiary. The prison-supplied clothes were ill-fitting on his tall, lanky form, and on a hot summer day the wool was uncomfortable and scratchy. But then anything was preferable to the stripes he'd been wearing for so long. Three thousand, six hundred, and fifty-two days, to be exact. He'd counted each one of those days in hell. Ten years gone from his life. Stolen. Just as his honor had been stolen.

He yearned for a cotton shirt, for trousers that fit, for a pair of boots instead of the little more than cardboard shoes he wore now. He longed for a lot of things. A night looking at stars. He hadn't seen stars in ten years. His tiny cell hadn't had a window, and the convicts were locked up long before evening.

Convict. Even if he didn't wear that damning brand, he knew the stench of convict radiated from him. Outside the walls he still found himself shuffling like one; his voice, like that of so many other prisoners, sounded hoarse from disuse.

His marked hand went into his pocket. Abner was there. Abner who helped save his sanity. His finger rubbed the small, contented mouse who liked the wool far better than he did.

Rafe watched as people looked at him warily while they passed him on the street. Some looked through him, as if he didn't exist. He felt a muscle move slightly in his cheek. Ten years locked away, and now . . .

Rafe tried to think of something else, of things small and large he hadn't permitted himself to think about during the past years.

A horse, by God. How he longed to be in a saddle again, to feel control. To go where he wanted.

And a woman. A woman of dubious virtue and no pretensions. Christ, but he needed that physical release. After Allison's betrayal, though, he wanted nothing more from females than a few minutes of physical pleasure with their bodies. He knew damned well he would never trust one again.

But those desires paled in comparison with his longing for revenge. For retribution. For justice, if there was such a thing.

He knew he should feel something more uplifting. Happiness at his release. Relief. But he didn't. Every human feeling had been systematically ripped from him during the past ten years. Pride. Dignity. Everything except hate.

Three years into his sentence, Rafe had been stunned when Clint Edwards had appeared one day. Clint had just heard, he'd said, and knew there wasn't a damn word of truth in the charges.

It had been difficult to comprehend that someone believed him at last, that some human soul gave a tinker's damn. He had seized Clint's offer of help like a drowning man seizing a rope. He had quickly banished his reservations about involving Clint and his brother Ben in his quest for vengeance.

Clint had been a corporal under him during the second year of the war, and Ben a wet-behind-the-ears private. At Vicksburg, Rafe had saved both of their lives. Ben was shot in an open position, and Clint had crawled out to help him. Rafe had disobeyed orders and followed Clint, had given him cover as he dragged his brother back. Rafe had been shot as he turned back to his own lines. Clint and Ben thought they owed him, and Rafe would use anyone to accomplish his aim. Honor was a commodity he couldn't afford. It had been burned away with the branding iron.

Another passerby walked down the street, crossing when he saw Rafe standing in front of the prison. He knew he had changed, that his face had changed. Hate was an ugly emotion, and it left ugly trails. Bitter lines etched out from his eyes now, and a sprinkling of gray mixed with his sandy hair. The once-vivid green of his eyes had dulled; they no longer showed any emotion at all. He had learned that in the first year of prison: Never let a guard know what you're thinking.

He'd learned other things: how long a man could exist in the punishment box, a pitch-black cell with no furniture, not even a slop pail. Later, when he'd been transferred into a cell that was three-and-a-half feet wide, seven feet long, seven feet high, he'd learned how many bricks comprised the walls, how many iron strips barred the gate. For ten years his home had been that cell, with the cot attached to the wall, a night bucket, a spittoon. He'd learned to endure, but he'd never learned to accept.

Where was Ben? he wondered, wanting to get away from here, from these walls, from the stench of caged men.

He gazed up at the sky. It appeared different from outside. He had stopped looking upward since his first weeks in prison; it hurt too damn much. He couldn't think of open spaces or he would go crazy, and he couldn't do that. Not and finish what had been started, what he had been planning for years. Only those plans and hatred sustained him through the endless days and sleepless nights.

An hour went by. Something must have held up Ben. The warden had given Rafe ten dollars, but where could he go with ten dollars? Even without the brand on his hand, everyone in Columbus would recognize the prison-issue clothes. No job here. Probably no job anywhere with that damned hand.

He'd saved some money before his court-martial, money he'd planned to use to build a future with Allison. But he had authorized its transfer to Clint to investigate Randall's past and to seed the beginning of their plans.

A horseman appeared down the street, leading another mount. Rafe felt the first tingling of expectation in a very long time. . . .

He'd remembered Ben Edwards as little more than a boy, barely into shaving, but now there was no mistaking the man. Ben's face was hard, tempered too early by pain and war. He and Clint had wandered after the war, driving cattle for a while, scouting for wagon trains. They'd been farm boys before the war, but the fighting had ruined them for that. The Edwards brothers had seen too much of the world to settle on a small plot of earth and take up plowing. They'd left the small Illinois farm in the hands of a third brother who'd stayed home and who loved the land.

They'd gathered others, too, Clint had written him. Men who had been in the ragtag unit Rafe took over when the war started. Men who had never been able to settle down after the war, whose restlessness drove them from one job to another. Johnny Green, Bill Smith, Cary Thompson, Simon Ford, and Skinny Ware. They'd needed another cause, and Rafe's had become theirs, because there was nothing else. Rafe didn't kid himself about that. Still, he was grateful.

Ben reached him and leaned over to shake his hand, searching his face as Rafe searched his, to find all the changes in ten years. Ben's gaze fell to the back of his hand, to the brand, and Rafe heard the indrawn breath.

It was an awkward moment. Rafe had gotten used to the brand, as had others in the prison. He'd realized it would be more difficult outside, but he wasn't prepared for the reaction of someone who expected it.

"Sorry I'm late," Ben said, trying to cover his reaction. "I took the train, and the damned thing was late. I bought the horses here." He hesitated. "I brought you some clothes, and Clint said you would want some gloves."

Rafe nodded as his throat tightened. He was unwilling to acknowledge the scar with words.

"Want to stop first for a drink or anything?"

"I want the hell out of here," Rafe said.

Ben grinned. "Well, I brought a flask just in that

event. You'll find the gloves and clothes in those saddle-bags on the bay."

Rafe nodded and went to the horse, stopping to run his hand along the horse's neck. Christ, that felt good. He had to wait a moment before mounting. Ten goddamn years. Suddenly, it was almost too much. He was paralyzed by the feelings that flooded him.

"Captain . . . ?"

The word revitalized him. Revitalized his purpose. "Not captain anymore, Ben. Just Rafe."

Ben hesitated. "I think of you that way."

"Don't." It was said too sharply, and Rafe knew it. But the reminder hurt. Rafe felt the ache of loss, the diminishment of his manhood, the erosion of who and what he once had been and could be no longer, as he swung up on the bay. He sat there in the saddle, feeling the animal's muscles underneath him. He fought back the despair and tried to relish this moment alone. He concentrated on it, fed on it, letting it block out all the other feelings.

He lifted his face to catch the dry, hot wind, unblocked now by the high walls of the prison. His eyes caught some lazy clouds drifting overhead, and his legs tightened around the sides of the horse. He was free.

Christ, he was free!

His mind couldn't comprehend it, couldn't accept it. Not yet. He would wake up in the tiny dark cell, the three walls of brick and the door that was grated with iron bars.

No, he would never be truly free again. Not as he once had been.

But vengeance would help. Randall's destruction and his own vindication. And then squaring the account with Sergeant Sam McClary, who had also been involved in framing him.

He looked at Ben. "Which is the best route to Colorado?"

Ben's eyes met his. Understanding was there. Not pity, thank God. "The way I came."

Rafe didn't say any more. He turned his horse and pressed his heels into its side, prompting it to a canter.

He was finally on the road to redemption.

The funeral was small. Quiet and dignified, which was the way her mother would have wanted it.

The burial expenses took all the money they had saved. Shea had the millinery store, of course, but she didn't know whether she could run it on her own. She didn't know whether she wanted to. She had enjoyed the creative part, but she had no liking for the business end. Her mother had handled that.

Still, she had to do something.

The shop itself was not worth much. They had rented the space, and their only asset had been Sara's hard work and Shea's imagination.

She found it so difficult to make a decision, which was unlike her. But she was cloaked in a cloud of disbelief, of loss. She was floundering, and she knew it—and didn't like it.

Shea said all the proper things. She heard herself as if from a distance. She was present, yet she wasn't present.

The last guest finally left. The lawyer had read the will, which left everything to Sara's "beloved" daughter.

Shea wandered through their empty rented rooms. Her gaze went to the wooden box on her mother's desk, the box she hadn't had the heart to open.

Why had her mother wanted it so badly, so badly that she had died alone?

And where was the key? In her need to do something, anything, Shea became obsessed with the box. Shea found a knife and started working on the lock. When it resisted her every effort, she worked around it, trying to dig it out, scarring the lovely wood, but she couldn't stop. She had to open it. Now.

The room had darkened before it came open, but she didn't stop to light an oil lamp. She lifted the lid, and what she could see of the contents stilled her. She sat there, drinking in the implications.

Shea finally rose and lit the oil lamp, then returned to the box. Money. Lots of money. New bills wrapped in paper with the name of a Kansas bank. Used bills.

And letters. She picked one up and saw the name at the bottom. Jack Randall. Her father. She looked at the date. Ten years ago. Her hand shaking, she picked up another letter. Three years ago. There was a Colorado address. A town named Rushton.

Other letters. A total of ten. And beneath them a clipping from a Boston paper. She quickly read the story. A court-martial. A Major Jack Randall was the main prosecution witness, the man who had discovered and caught a traitor involved in army payroll robberies. There were drawings of the convicted man and of Major Randall. She glanced at the former, caught for a moment by the handsome angles of the man's face, but then she moved quickly to the latter. Ten years ago. She would have been thirteen at the time. Why hadn't she seen this before? And if she had, would it have made any difference? Randall was a common enough name.

But that, with the letters and money, posed unsettling questions. Dear God in heaven, what did it mean? She read the letters. At first they asked her mother to return to the writer in Kansas. And then they merely hoped Sara was well and stated that money was enclosed. They said nothing about Shea. Nothing at all.

Shea closed her eyes, trying to think. The major had to be her father. Her birth certificate listed a Jack Randall as her father. Thoughts whirled in her head like flying debris in a tornado. She tried to remember everything her mother had said about him. Honorable. The clipping she'd read seemed to verify that.

Why had her mother left him? Why had she never told Shea he was alive? And why had she never spent the money when they'd so often needed it?

Why had her mother lied?

Suddenly, Shea's whole existence seemed a lie. The foundation, once so solid, quaked and wavered, and she felt she would fall through the flimsy flooring.

Who was she?

Shea knew she had to find out. She had to find Jack Randall. She had to find her father.

Chapter 2

It took Rafe and Ben three weeks to reach Casey Springs, Colorado. Three weeks in which Rafe tried to accustom himself to freedom. He had thought it would be easy. It wasn't. His mind was still caged by the past, by feelings of anger. He'd lost part of himself: the old confidence, the simple enjoyment of basic things.

The first night of freedom had been the best and worst. Every sensation struck him with poignancy. They'd ridden all day before stopping, and despite Rafe's having spent nearly twenty years on horseback, his muscles rebelled, reminding him of how long it had been since he last sat atop a horse, how much time he had lost.

Aware of how rusty he'd become with a gun, he practiced shooting. He had a long way to go to regain his former familiarity with a gun. When darkness made practice impossible, he tried to sleep and found himself unable to.

The night sounds were strange to ears used to curses and moans and restless movements, to the screeching of iron doors and the beating of guards' batons against bars. Serenity had become more jarring than gunshot. Every star mocked him, instead of pleasuring, and the moon . . . Hell, he'd started adding up the number of new moons he'd missed. Nothing was satisfying, only teasing, reminding, torturing. He thought of the nightmares that wouldn't go away, that sensation of waking in a coffin, in that prison box, away from light and sun and everything that gave life.

Only after getting blind-drunk on the whiskey Ben had brought with him did Rafe finally drift off, and then he woke up abruptly to find Ben hovering over him. He knew he must have been yelling. His blanket was wadded up into a tight ball, and his body was drenched in sweat. He wondered what he'd said but didn't ask. He pretended, as Ben did, that nothing had happened.

Abner crept out of Rafe's pocket, and Ben raised an eyebrow. "A friend?"

"A friend," Rafe confirmed. In truth that mouse had been his salvation at times.

"Hell of a lot better than a rat," Ben observed with a twist of his lips. Rafe shrugged as if indifferent, but in prison he would have welcomed even a rat.

The following morning Rafe demanded they leave at sunrise and ride until the horses were exhausted. Ben was a good traveling companion, mainly because he didn't talk a lot. Rafe merely absorbed: the sun, the countryside, the feel of the wind, and the cool of the night. He drank it all in, the way a thirsty man drinks water, not with enjoyment but with raw, aching need.

When they did speak, they spoke about Jack Randall.

"He's been in Colorado since after the war," Ben said, "buying up one little spread after another. Nothing dishonest, as far as we can learn. He paid good prices, and now he's the largest landowner in the area."

"With army gold," Rafe said bitterly.

"Since Clint got hired on as assistant foreman two

years ago, he hasn't been able to find a damaging thing about him," Ben continued carefully. "Randall's worked at respectability, but Clint got a detective to check out his past. Before he joined the army, he had to leave every job he ever had in a hurry. He was in Kansas when the war started, manager of the store there, and he helped the town fend off an attack by Quantrill's men. The militia elected him major because of that. No one apparently ever checked on his background."

"Nothing lately?"

"Doesn't seem to be, but it's a matter of time, if his past is any indication. It seems whenever he gets in financial trouble, he steals. But he usually disappears before anyone discovers something's wrong."

"We need to make sure he gets in financial trouble then," Rafe said.

Ben grinned. "That's our thought." Then he added thoughtfully, "Randall seems to have avoided violence of any kind."

"Men were killed when that last payroll was taken," Rafe said, his voice harsh. He didn't have to look at his hand to know another kind of violence had been committed because of that robbery.

Ben nodded.

"There is another man, a Sergeant McClary," Rafe said slowly. He would never forget McClary, whom he'd once disciplined and who had discovered part of the army payroll in Rafe's quarters. He had also been one of the soldiers who'd escorted him to prison. The man had taken every chance to humiliate him during the journey. Rafe had wondered about the man's antipathy, but that had always been overshadowed by his hatred for Randall. Randall had sent Rafe out the day of the payroll robbery and then denied it. Randall had been instrumental in the court-martial and subsequent punishment. Randall had to have been the brains behind the frame.

"How does Clint feel about Randall?"

Ben shrugged. "Clint knows he's a thief and coward." He hesitated. "But people in Colorado don't, and everyone in the territory likes Randall. He's a damn hard man not to like, but that doesn't change the fact he's a thief, or that he stole from the army during wartime while we were dodging bullets."

Four days after they left Cincinnati, they stopped in a town. Rafe had been wearing the leather gloves Ben brought, but he found them awkward and wanted another pair from which he could cut away the fingers and leave the rest to cover the back of his hand.

After purchasing that and a few other items, they found a whorehouse. It was Ben's suggestion; Rafe would have ridden on. The coupling had been emotionally cold and unmoving, although Rafe's body had reacted immediately. As with all his attempts to restore normalcy into his life and rekindle feelings, he found little joy in the act. He kept thinking about Allison, lovely Allison who had so quickly turned her back on him, and thus, his performance, while not cruel, had been rough and impersonal. He had only taken, when once he'd been considerate. He coolly noted that new lack in himself, only too aware it dimmed his old enthusiasm for making love.

Another goddamn mark against Randall.

They didn't stop again at any town. A volcano was rumbling deep inside Rafe, and it was best to keep away from people.

Even now they decided to skirt around Casey Springs, instead taking a well-worn trail up a mountain pass. Ben stopped, and Rafe looked down at the valley below. A long, graceful log house sat in a clearing. To its left was a large barn, and a long building was located to the right. "That's Randall's place. The Circle R," Ben said.

Rafe's gaze moved slowly across the buildings to cattle far beyond. "Neighbors?"

"The nearest is ten miles away. And then there's a small trading center south of here. An old trading post that's become a town of sorts. Rushton. It's named after a creek that runs through this area."

"The law?"

"Rushton has a part-time sheriff appointed by the territorial governor. Man named Russ Dewayne. He's also a rancher. Casey Springs has its own law."

"Much mining around here?"

"Some placer claims. Most of the gold around here has played out. But Green, Smith, Ware, and Thompson have had some luck while they waited for you. Nothing big, but enough to buy supplies and then some."

"You and Simon?"

"Some hunting. Odd jobs here and there. Gives us reason to move around."

"Tell me more about the cabin."

"Clint found it when trailing some rustlers. Pure luck. He heard some cattle bawling. Otherwise he never would have found the small valley. Perfect hiding place. There's only one entrance from this side of the mountain, and it's through what appears to be solid rock. It was used apparently by some mountain man long gone. We find traps occasionally. But it's safe. I had trouble finding it even after I'd been there a couple of times."

"The rustlers?"

"They won't be back," Ben said.

He pointed at a cluster of oddly shaped rocks. "That's the turnoff. Try to memorize the way from here on up." He moved quickly to the lead, and Rafe followed him into a forest of pines and aspens.

The smells were sweet here, the scent of wildflowers mingling with the tangy one of the pines. The tops of the trees nearly blocked out the sun, casting dancing shadows across the carpet of needles.

The way suddenly became very steep, and the horses struggled to keep their footing.

"There's another route," Ben explained, "but it comes out on the other side of the mountain. During the winter we had to use it several times. But it's a hell of a long way."

"I hope to be gone before winter."

"It can snow early here," Ben said. "Real early. We built a shelter for the horses and supplies."

"Ben . . . ?"

The younger man turned to him, a question in his eyes.

"I don't want you and Clint involved any further. Or the others."

"You need us."

"No."

Ben reined in his horse and stopped. "None of us would be alive if it weren't for you."

Rafe looked down at the horse and saddle. "That was war. We all took care of each other."

"We're still taking care of each other," Ben said, his jaw setting. "When Johnny got in trouble . . ." He hesitated, then turned away.

Rafe frowned. "Johnny Green?"

Ben shrugged. "He got himself mixed up with a gang down in Texas, was involved in a robbery and almost hanged." He gave a small smile. "None of us are exactly welcome down there now."

Rafe was silent. Ten years of prison and bitterness hadn't prepared him for the response he felt. Gratitude?

He didn't know whether he wanted to feel that. It was easier to feel nothing at all.

"Captain, they're not going to let you do it alone," Ben said.

"I don't want anyone else involved now. It's my fight."

"We are involved, whether you like it or not. No way we're going to back off now," Ben said.

Rafe's mouth thinned, but he accepted. He'd already drawn them in too deeply. But he could make sure they weren't hurt. He nodded curtly and moved his gaze to the line of trees they were following.

Chapter 3

"Lady, you don't want to go there alone."

Shea looked at the man at the ticket window of the Casey Springs stage station. "I can't wait a week," she said, trying her best to stare him down.

"I'm telling you there ain't no coach for another six days, and it ain't safe traveling alone, not since them outlaws started robbing coaches and stealing payrolls and attacking everything that moves."

"But I must—"

"Now, miss," said the clerk patiently, "you can wait at the hotel or boardinghouse. Ain't no one going to rent you a horse or buggy to travel alone to Rushton or the Circle R, not these days."

Shea set down her valise in disgust, and her fingers tightly gripped the art case she held at her side.

When she'd decided to come West, she'd sold everything back home. She'd made her decision, and it meant she had to leave the past behind.

That past was a lie that seemed to undermine everything she'd ever believed. She had always accepted life as it came, had always been able to meet it on its own terms, but now . . .

She didn't even know who she was. It left her vulnerable, afraid, when she'd never been afraid before. Everything she knew, believed in, was unreal, and she didn't know how or why.

But she knew she had to find out.

She had looked at the clipping so many times. Looked at her father. How many times had she wished for a father? Dreamed of having one? But for some reason her mother had kept him away from her, and her away from him.

And every time she looked at the piece of newspaper, she also saw the man her father helped convict. A thief and perhaps even a traitor.

He hadn't looked like a thief, not from the sketch. His face was strong and arresting, and she was struck by the contradiction between the strength she saw there and the charge. She wondered whether there could be extenuating circumstances. A Reb fighting in his own way for his cause? But then why had he kept some of the money?

It was a riddle she would never solve, but perhaps she could solve the one of her father.

Why, dear God, had her mother lied to her? Shea had considered a number of reasons. Perhaps Sara Randall had hated the West, or perhaps she and her husband hadn't been able to live together.

The more Shea wondered, the more she needed answers. The only way she could get them was by going to the source, but that was frightening. Had her father not wanted her? Had he not known about her? Would he believe her? Every time she considered the trip, she felt herself shiver with both anticipation and misgiving. Did she really want to know the answers? She wasn't sure. What she did know was she *had* to find answers.

She tucked a falling lock of hair under her bonnet as she glared at the clerk, wishing for one of the rare times she looked more intimidating.

She had a pleasant enough face, but certainly not one that sent hearts afluttering. Everything about her was ordinary. Plain brown hair with remarkably little curl. Blue-gray eyes, which were wider than she would have preferred, although people often said they were her best feature. She'd never cared overmuch about clothes, preferring reading and drawing to fussing over appearances.

Serenity was her most distinctive attribute, her mother had often said. And because that quality seemed to please her mother, the person she loved most, she quieted the hunger inside her for adventure.

But her mother had been wrong. Serenity indicated a lack of passion, and Shea was passionate about many things. She was fiercely protective of those people and things she loved and felt deeply about injustice. She just kept those feelings to herself, hiding them under a cloak of surface practicality. They were too personal to share with others, even her mother.

But now serenity was getting her no place. Neither was impatience nor passion.

She glared again at the clerk. A week seemed a year. She tried to explain. "My name is Randall. I . . . have to get to Jack Randall's ranch."

The stationmaster's face softened. "You kin?"

Shea wasn't sure what to say. She had blurted out the previous information mostly from frustration. Her father may not even know about her. Or believe her. Or maybe there had been some terrible mistake. But the Randall name seemed to have an effect, and she obviously needed an effect.

She lifted her chin. "His daughter."

"Well, jumpin' guns, I didn't know Mr. Randall had a daughter."

"I've been back East," she said.

"Well, wish I could help you, Miss Randall, but that don't change nothing."

She felt the tension behind her eyes magnify. Almost blindly, she reached down for her valise and turned toward the door. She had to find a way.

She reached the porch outside and paused, trying to decide what to do next, when a man came out the door. She had barely noticed him inside, a tall man leaning against a wall.

"Miss Randall?" he said, taking his hat from his head in a gesture of courtesy.

She nodded.

"I heard you say you wanted to go to the Circle R. Perhaps I can help."

Shea studied him. He was tall and fit-looking, with steady gray eyes and an aura of competence. She judged that he was just a few years older than she, but something about him made him seem centuries old.

"Sir?"

He smiled at that. "I work for your father, miss," he said. "It is miss, isn't it? I heard you say Randall."

Shea felt a slight blush. "Miss," she confirmed. "Shea Randall."

"Well, then, I was just here to check on a telegraph, but I'm heading back tomorrow, if you would like to go with me."

Shea wasn't sure she should accept. Traveling alone with a man wasn't allowed. Yet this wasn't Boston, and she'd been treated with nothing but respect by the men she'd met, including those drinking in the coach she'd taken from Denver. Code of the West, she'd been told. Besides, this man did work for her father.

And she didn't want to wait a week, couldn't wait a week.

"You say you work for my father?"

He nodded.

"And you're going tomorrow?"

"Yes, ma'am."

"How long a trip?"

He looked at her, as if weighing her abilities. "By horseback, nearly a day."

She groaned. "I haven't ridden much." That was an understatement, but she didn't dare tell him she had ridden only a few times, and those only walks in the park.

"I'll find you a gentle mount."

He waited. That's what decided her. He didn't push. He was merely being accommodating.

"What's your name?"

"Ben, ma'am. Ben Smith."

She smiled. "You'll have to let me pay you."

He nodded again. "Where are you staying?"

She didn't know. She looked around at the town that seemed little more than a scattering of ramshackle buildings. There was a bank, a sheriff's office, and a place called the Golden Nugget. She'd been told in Denver that Casey Springs was struggling to become a major trading center now that the area's gold was almost panned out, and she had expected more.

"Gold Nugget's 'bout the most suitable place," he offered. "It's not much of a hotel, but the rooming house is full of miners and railroad workers, and sometimes they get a bit rough."

Shea thought about her money. She had put her father's money in a bank in Boston, not knowing whether to use it or not. What she had from the sale of the shop was going down rapidly, and she still didn't know what kind of reception she'd get from Jack Randall.

"The Nugget's also the safest place," Ben Smith added quietly.

Shea smiled. He was concerned about her safety. Any lingering concern she had about her decision dribbled away. "The Golden Nugget then." Tonight, she would have a bath. A good night's sleep on a real bed. And tomorrow, her father. She gave Ben Smith a bright smile.

"I'll help you with that," he said, casting a look at the valise.

"Thank you, Mr. Smith. You're very kind."

As he stooped to get the valise, she saw something odd flash across his face. Regret perhaps. Maybe a second thought about being burdened with a woman.

She felt a slightest tingle of apprehension run down her spine but promptly dismissed it. She was tired, that was all. Just tired.

Ben looked at the woman riding next to him and wondered whether he was making a mistake.

But he had been handed a weapon, just handed it, by God, and he was never one to turn away from opportunity.

Randall's daughter. He hadn't even known the man had one. He didn't think the captain did, either. Strange the way he kept thinking of Rafferty Tyler as captain. Three weeks traveling together would usually break down formality, but not with Tyler. Not that, or the two months since their arrival at the cabin.

Although Captain Tyler had been a strict officer, uncompromising in discipline and training, he'd also been a man with a quick smile and ready compliment when a man did well.

There were no smiles or compliments now. Rafe

Tyler was as contained a man as Ben had ever seen. Sealed up. Talk had been at a minimum, as if Tyler no longer knew how to converse. Question-and-answer. Then silence. That was all there had been.

Both he and Clint had discussed it, and they finally figured that Randall's exposure was the only thing that would help dispel the blackness that hovered around Tyler. The sooner, the better.

They had been making progress. Two holdups now, both taking Circle R payrolls. Randall was hurting financially, hurting bad. But it was just too damn slow. Ben saw the captain's restlessness, his impatience.

And so the encounter with Randall's daughter had seemed a unique opportunity to speed the process.

But after several hours with the lady, Ben was having second thoughts. Her eagerness was cloaked in dignity, which was very appealing. She didn't intrude on him, but when they stopped, she asked questions. Intelligent questions. It was downright disconcerting.

This morning he'd handed her a pair of boy's pants and shirt.

"We're going riding over a mountain, Miss Randall. If you've never ridden sidesaddle before, I don't advise it now," he added, looking at her skirt.

A becoming blush colored her cheeks as she apparently debated proprieties.

"I won't take you if you don't use good sense," he said, and she'd hurried back to her room, the clothes clutched tightly to her. No complaints, no exclamations of horror. He liked that. He didn't want to like it, but he did.

During their last stop, he'd watched her carefully as she untied a case from her saddle and opened it, taking out a pad and leaning against a tree as she sketched. He wondered what she was sketching, but he didn't ask. He wanted to keep conversation at a minimum. He took the opportunity to place a stone under one of the mare's shoes. That was an hour ago. She would start limping anytime now, and he would take Miss Randall on his own horse. She would realize damn soon they were not going where she thought they were going.

They had nearly reached the turnoff to the cabin when the mare started to limp.

"Mr. Smith."

He turned, knowing what he would see.

He dismounted and went to the mare, picking up the hoof from the ground and giving it a superficial look. "You'll have to ride with me, Miss Randall."

Her eyes widened, and he noted a flicker of apprehension. He held out his hand, and she hesitated, making him wonder whether she suspected something. But then why should she?

She finally took his hand and slid off the mare. He mounted and helped her up behind him. A mile later he left the trail and turned into the woods. "A shorter way," he explained.

Her arms tightened as they climbed upward. For a novice she was doing well.

And then they stopped. He took off his bandanna and turned around in the saddle. "I'm sorry, miss, but I'm going to have to blindfold you."

Her body went rigid, and she swallowed. "I won't hurt you," he said, "but this is . . . necessary."

"I don't understand."

"You don't have to. We're just taking a small detour."

"You don't work for my father." It was an accusation, not a question.

He didn't say anything, just tied the bandanna around her eyes. "Now keep your arms around me," he said. "It's a steep ride."

"If I don't?" The voice trembled just a little.

"I'll tie them there."

She was silent, and he took that for assent. "You won't be hurt," he said again.

"Then why . . . ?"

"Good reasons, Miss Randall. Now you just hang on."

Shea didn't know how she stayed so still, except she was too frightened to do anything else.

It seemed she had been riding behind Ben Smith for hours. She had no idea where they were, even if she could escape.

Think! Dear God, think!

His gun. He wore a gun on his hip, as did every man she'd seen in Casey Springs. If she could reach down and grab it . . .

And then what? She had no idea how to fire one.

She tried to contain the shudder that ran through her. She wouldn't show him she was afraid. But why did he want her? Where was he taking her? She could think of only one reason, and yet he didn't seem the type for rape.

Good reasons, he'd said.

What kind of good reasons?

Her father. Ben Smith had heard her say Jack Randall was her father.

According to everything she'd heard in Denver and Casey Springs, he was a respected man, a good man who'd given money to build a school and church. Everyone seemed to like him.

Money then? Ransom? The clerk at the ticket office had said there were outlaws in this area.

Her throat tightened. Why had she been such a fool? Why had she accepted this too-convenient offer?

Because she'd been so expectant. So eager. So stubbornly determined to get to the Circle R Ranch.

And now she would bring trouble to the man she'd wanted to impress. If that was what Ben Smith had in mind. Or was it something uglier?

She suddenly didn't want to touch the man in front of her. Her hands started to slide from around his waist.

"Put them back." The voice was rough. "Clasp them together. And don't even think about the gun."

Or else . . .

The unsaid words hung between them.

"You won't like being tied."

Her hands clasped around him. This way, with her hands free, she still had a chance to escape.

She didn't know how long they continued to ride. She ached all over now, her muscles sore from riding on the backbone of his horse, her body stiff with tension.

They finally came to a stop, and she let go of him, expecting another order, but none came.

He lifted her down to the ground, and she reached for the blindfold, frantically tearing it off, just as two men came out of a log cabin.

"What the hell?" she heard the tall one say in a deep, harsh voice.

Her eyes were riveted on him. It was a familiar face, one she could never forget. It was the face she had studied in the newspaper clipping.

He was older. Harder. But undeniably he was the man who had betrayed his country and stolen from it.

The man her father had sent to prison.

It was the face of Rafferty Tyler!

Fear had been building in Shea for the past few hours. Now that fear turned to terror, something she'd never felt before. Her already unsteady legs threatened to give way, and she found her hand going to the saddle for support.

But she couldn't keep her gaze from the man's face. It was an artist's dream—or a captive's nightmare. His eyes were a vivid blue-green, like clean water playing over white sand, and his thick sandy hair seemed brushed with gold dust. Nothing else about him was poetic, though.

His face seemed carved from rock. Lines etched away from his eyes, and she knew they weren't caused by laughter but by harder, unpleasant emotions. None of the features—the eyes, the mouth, the jaw—gave anything away as he studied her with cool indifference. He turned to Ben. "Why in the hell did you bring her here?" His voice sounded hoarse, almost rusty.

"She says she's Randall's daughter."

Like a fly caught in a spider's web, Shea watched, fascinated, as the man closed his eyes for a moment, as if trying to digest a particularly difficult piece of information, and then opened them.

He studied her closely, but with no definable difference in expression, and she wondered whether that granite face was capable of revealing anything. "He doesn't have a daughter," he finally said in that rusty whisper.

Ben shrugged. "She said she was. She was trying to get to Rushton. I thought it was too good an opportunity to pass up."

Shea hated being talked about as if she weren't there, like an object of curiosity rather than a person. But she stayed silent, still transfixed by the face that came as close to stone as one could.

The blue-green eyes turned back to her. "How can you be Randall's daughter?"

"The usual way, I imagine," she said, surprising herself with the tart reply.

"You're a liar." The accusation was stinging, like the sharp crack of a whip.

Shea stiffened. She didn't lie. She had never lied. Her mother hadn't permitted lies. But then, she thought with sudden bleakness, her mother had told the biggest one of all. She thought about defending herself and then stayed silent. She owed this man no explanation, no answer.

Ben stepped forward as if to give protection, but she couldn't trust him. He had brought her here.

Shea looked at the man next to Tyler. He looked a little like Ben Smith, and she wondered whether they could be brothers. He also looked more approachable than Tyler. But then almost anyone would.

"I . . . I don't know what you want, but I have some money. . . ." A revealing quaver was in her voice.

"What's your name?" the man next to Tyler said.

Shea didn't know what to say. She didn't exactly know who she was, not anymore, or what these people wanted with the man she believed to be her father. She wasn't sure she knew anything anymore. But that was something she wasn't going to admit. She couldn't show weakness, not to Tyler. He would jump on weakness, use it. Her only defense was a show of strength, no matter how difficult it was, how much she had to hide the tremors that shook her. She balled her fists to keep the shaking from showing.

"Damnation," Tyler said. "Who in hell are you?" His voice held a hint of impatience.

Shea's chin went up.

"Why did you say you were Randall's daughter? Or are you one of his whores?" There was contempt in his voice, and Shea knew an anger she'd never known before. *He* was judging her father. He was judging *her*.

She was grateful when her anger exploded, eclipsing the fear. "What right have *you* to ask anything?"

"Oh, you know who I am?" Softness crept into his voice, a softness that she sensed was deceptive.

But she couldn't stop. She was too angry to be cautious, too angry to be afraid. She wouldn't be afraid of a man who betrayed his country during war. "A traitor," she said unwisely.

He fairly purred as he moved toward her. "Your . . . father tell you that?"

There was something menacing in the graceful way he walked. She stepped back, but the horse prevented no more than a few inches retreat.

She tried to jerk her gaze away from his eyes, which seemed to impale her. "You have no right—"

"I have every right, if you are who you say you are." He stopped in front of her, and she had the impression of barely contained anger. She was tall, but she felt inconsequential in front of him. He was several inches over six feet, and his cotton shirt and denim trousers did nothing to hide a very hard, lean body. But it was the cold austereness of his face that really was intimidating. Intimidating and, in some primitive way, mesmerizing. She felt shivers snake up and down her back.

Suddenly, she was awash with conflicting sensations. She was afraid of him, but something in her was reacting to him in a way she had never reacted to a man before. Awareness. Perhaps that was it. She was aware of him, drawn by him as if he were a magnet.

His eyes gave no indication he felt anything at all, but she sensed fury, the way one senses a death-dealing storm.

Deep to her toes, she could feel the rage radiating

from him. She was the one who should be angry. She was the one who had been kidnapped, terrified. But she perceived she could never come close to the emotion that seemed to rack Tyler with such intensity.

He moved around her and went to her horse. With a gloved right hand he took a knife from a back pocket and quickly cut her valise and drawing case free. He placed the drawing case on a log stump before opening it.

Shea wanted to stop him. She felt violated by his actions, but she knew it wouldn't do any good. She would only be overpowered and look foolish. She was no match for these three men. For this one man. The good Lord knew she had been foolish enough already. Better to save her anger for the right time. Let them think her docile. For the moment.

Shea watched as he picked up the newspaper clipping. He turned to her.

"Why do you have this?" He sounded indifferent, but she somehow knew the question was not an idle one.

She wasn't sure what to answer. How could she possibly explain? How could she explain finding out she had a father only after twenty-two years? How could she explain holding on to that likeness, the only one she'd ever had?

How could she explain having *his* likeness? Or a story condemning him?

Silence seemed to make his question echo.

"You don't have much to say for yourself, do you?"

Shea had never felt at such a loss. Whatever she said, whatever she did, might bring more trouble, might hurt her father, might put her in further peril. She felt she was sinking in quicksand, and there was nothing to reach out for. Her legs trembled as his eyes seemed to bore into her, trying to rip out answers.

But then he turned back to the case, as if she were of no importance. He helped himself to several letters and read them, oblivious to her privacy or her feelings. He picked up her drawing pad, riffling through it until he found the sketch of Ben Smith.

"Christ," he said, handing it Ben. "Bringing *her* here was the most damn fool . . ." He stopped. Hesitated. But the *her* still hung in the air. It was said with such disdain, even something close to hate. She shivered in the bright sun.

He turned back to her, a muscle working in his cheek. It was the first visible sign of emotion she'd seen in him.

Ben looked apologetic. "I thought maybe a trade . . ."

"For what?"

Ben shrugged. "A confession, perhaps."

"Randall?"

Ben gave him a small smile. "It just seemed . . . opportune."

"Beware of gifts, Ben," Tyler said without a smile, then turned back to Shea. "They never come without strings, and I think this . . . lady has a damn long one."

Ben shifted on his feet, like a small boy being chastised.

"It looks like you'll have to stay here a while, Miss . . . Randall," Tyler told her.

"No. I'm going to the Circle R."

He was staring at her, and she wished she saw something in his eyes. The nothingness was frightening. It was like looking at a blank piece of canvas.

"Sorry, ma'am," he said, but she knew he wasn't sorry at all, at least not in her behalf. The tone, rather than apologetic, was mocking. "Your . . . talent makes that impossible. I can't have pictures of Ben all over the territory."

"You can keep it," she said hurriedly.

"Ah, but you have too good an eye," he said. "I expect you could draw it again."

Shea swallowed, her silence confirming his words. She didn't know how to lie or hide her feelings. She'd never had to learn, but now she regretted it. She resented his invasion into what should be hers alone. But he was right. She had a memory for faces, especially interesting faces, and Ben Smith had one of those. Though it didn't compare with Rafferty Tyler's for complexity.

"I promise—"

"I wouldn't take the promise of a Randall if it was wrapped in angels' wings."

"Why?" she asked. "Because he helped bring you to justice?"

He snorted.

"You just want . . ." She stopped, not wanting to express the thought that was becoming more and more clear.

"I just want what?"

Why did those eyes fascinate her so? Why did they compel her to say more than she should? "Revenge."

He smiled. She'd never thought a smile could be so menacing. "Very perceptive of you, Miss Randall, or whoever you are."

"I won't let you use me."

"Oh, you won't?" Amusement crept into his voice. "And just how do you think you will prevent it?"

Shea balled her fingers into a fist. It had been another foolish statement—she was in no position to challenge him—but then she had been incredibly foolish since meeting Ben Smith yesterday. "He won't care."

"Oh, I believe that," Tyler said. "Randall's never cared about a damn thing in his life. That's why I don't think much of Ben's bringing you here."

"Then let me go. I don't even know where I am."

"I believe that too," he said. "Unfortunately, you've seen some faces you shouldn't have, and even more unfortunately you apparently can draw them. So you stay here." His voice hardened. "Believe me, I don't like the idea of having Randall's get around any more than you want to be here."

"You can't mean . . . to keep me here."

"Now you're getting the idea, as distasteful as it may be to both of us."

She felt numb, uncomprehending. How could this happen? She had been safe her whole life, safe and comfortable and well liked. She'd never had an enemy, and now this man, who obviously hated her father, and therefore her, was threatening to hold her captive in these mountains. She knew her terror was probably reflected in her eyes, and she turned away so he wouldn't see it. She didn't want to give him that satisfaction. "You'll hang," she whispered.

He laughed. "I would have welcomed the noose ten years ago," he said. "Now I don't give a damn one way or the other, as long as Randall joins me on the scaffold." His voice lowered. "And he will, Miss Randall. He will." It was like a blood oath, and Shea felt a cold wind blowing across her, though the trees were still.

Shea swallowed. Dear God, she believed him, and what could she say to a man who didn't care whether he lived or died?

His words echoed in the silence. She had to break it, no matter how inadequate she sounded. The silence made the words stronger, more invincible.

"How long do you think you will keep me?" She turned back to him, trying to make her expression indifferent, like his, but she knew she failed miserably.

"Think?" His raised eyebrow seemed to mock her.

Shea glared at him, terrified at spending any time with this man who hated so strongly. The thought of it alone sent worms of apprehension crawling through her body. "If you hurt me . . ."

"Oh, I have no intention of hurting you. You aren't worth the effort. But you will obey me."

Oddly, she believed the part about his not hurting her. She should still feel terror, not just for the father she'd never met but also for herself.

"You can't keep me here," she tried again. "People will be looking. . . ."

Tyler looked at Ben Smith, who shrugged. "There was no one to pick her up. I don't think she was expected."

"Just dropping in?" That smile again. The smile that was no smile. "Miss Randall—if that's who you are—I want some answers."

"What for?" she retorted indignantly. "You already read my letters."

"They say damn little, and nothing about a daughter. So I ask you again. Why are you here?"

"It's none of your business."

"Everything to do with Randall is my business."

"Because he testified against you? Because he did his duty?"

"What do you know about it?" His voice was hard now, some of the hoarseness gone, and his eyes were glittering.

"I . . . the clipping . . ."

"What did *he* say?"

She tried to step back again as she felt the intensity of him.

"Oh, no, you don't," he said, his right hand grabbing at her arm. The touch seemed to burn her, through the cotton of her shirt and the leather of the glove. But as she tried to shrug the hand aside, it tightened around her arm like a vise, and she felt herself tremble. Heat moved from the arm through the rest of her, an unwelcome burning heat she didn't understand. She didn't think she could move. Something strange was happening to her, to her senses. They were overwhelmed by him.

In desperation she lowered her eyes to his hand. The clipping said he'd been branded. Was that why he wore a glove on that hand?

She knew immediately the thought was a mistake. She knew he read it.

He suddenly let her go, as if releasing a snake. "Would you like to see it?" He was taunting her now, and she saw a flash of anger in his eyes.

She shook her head.

"Ah, the lady has sensibilities," he drawled in that hoarse whisper. "My hand's not fit for such tender eyes?" His anger was obvious now. "I think you should see what Randall is responsible for." He pulled off the glove.

Shea turned her face away, but his other hand went up to her chin. "Look," he commanded, "so you won't have to wonder."

She wanted to close her eyes, but she knew he would force them open in some way, by the very strength of his will, if necessary. And she sensed his will was very strong indeed. She had no choice. She looked.

The scar was livid on his hand, the *T* emblazoned there forever. She sucked in her breath, suddenly overwhelmed by an emotion she didn't understand. It wasn't pity. No one could ever pity the man standing in front of her; he wouldn't allow it. The emotion was something more like compassion, and resentment of what had been done to him, no matter what he had done.

She couldn't imagine what it would be like to be marked like that. She forced her gaze up and met his eyes. They were blazing now, and she wished for the emptiness again. She had never seen such violent emotions—raw fury and blinding pain.

Words would mean nothing. Less than nothing. They would be insulting. She knew that, so she remained silent. She didn't think she could speak, even if there was something to say. She was too stunned by the enormity of her own reactions—to him, to the brand.

She couldn't look at him, either, for he would see those reactions, and she couldn't allow that. He would hate them, but he would use them in some way. He would use anything to get back at her father. She understood that too.

She was aware of his putting the glove back on, aware of the other two men looking on. She wanted to step toward the older one, but she realized it would do no good. Rafferty Tyler was obviously the leader; the others might have sympathy, but that was as far as it would go.

"What do you want with me?" she asked in a whisper.

"I want nothing from you," he said, "except for you to do what you're told until I'm finished here."

"Finished with what?"

"Destroying Jack Randall," he answered flatly. He turned away from her. "You'd better be getting back, Clint," he said to the man who had been so silent.

"You sure about keeping her here?"

"I'm sure we can't let her go now, unless you both want to end up in prison. And, believe me, you don't want that."

Clint hesitated, and Shea wanted to run over to him and beg him to take her away. But then he nodded.

Tyler's mouth went up in a cynical smile. "She'll be safe enough. I have no interest in any spawn of Jack Randall, even after ten years in prison."

"I still don't believe it," Clint said. "I traced him back thirty years. No indication of a child."

"But there was a wife?"

"For a short time."

"See a resemblance to Randall?"

Clint turned to her, and Shea suddenly felt like a horse being very carefully inspected. "Could be. The eyes are similar. But the hair is lighter." He shrugged. "Hell, I don't know."

Tyler also shrugged. "It really doesn't make any difference. Now she's seen you two, we can't let her go."

"I'll try to get back in a couple of days," Clint said, and Shea's mouth went dry. She felt safer with Clint here. She felt safer with Ben, even. She might even feel safer with the Devil.

Rafferty Tyler turned to her. He took off his bandanna, and before she realized what was happening, he'd pulled her hands behind her and tied them. "Go in the cabin. The door's open."

Shea stood still. She would be horsewhipped before she'd do anything he told her, particularly when he did it with such assurance that she would comply. Pride wouldn't allow it. Stark fear wouldn't permit it. She still held a shadow of hope that the other two might object, might take her back with them after all.

She turned to Ben. "You can't leave me here."

He looked uncomfortable, then shrugged. "He said he won't hurt you. He won't."

"Please." She'd never begged before, not for herself. She hated doing it, particularly in front of her captor.

Ben dropped his glance and turned away from her. She appealed to Clint, looking at him with a plea in her eyes.

He merely shook his head, and Shea reluctantly looked back to Rafferty Tyler, who was eyeing her speculatively. "Go inside," he said again.

"No."

"Then I'll take you." He picked her up in his arms, and she felt the hard strength in them. Heat darted through her again. She smelled the sweat mixed with soap and leather, she heard the beat of his heart, the swift intake of his breath when their bodies met. He cursed, and then he was moving swiftly toward the cabin. He kicked the door open and strode to the bed, dumping her rather than setting her down.

"Stay here, dammit," he said, scowling. "I'm not going to play games with you."

He disappeared out the door, slamming it shut, and she struggled to sit up on the bed. She instantly knew why he had tied her hands. There were guns all over the place. On a table, lying against the wall.

She tried to loosen the bonds but couldn't. She stood and looked around. There was a fireplace with a kettle hanging over ashes. A table littered with books. Several boxes stacked in the corner. The bed, little more than a cot, was neatly made up, unlike the rest of the interior.

A knife. Look for a knife. She could tuck it away someplace and use it later. After the other two men were gone.

Her eyes carefully went over every surface of the cabin. There was a cabinet up on a wall, but she couldn't reach it with her bound hands. Frustrated, she moved to the table, looking at the books. Shakespeare. Dickens. Hawthorne. Thoreau. Surprising selection for a thief.

She heard the sound of hoofbeats and with a sinking

heart realized that Clint or Ben, maybe both, had gone. She moved quickly back to the cot and sat down. Heart in her throat, she waited.

She heard the door start to open and felt a sudden chill, a cold wind blowing away the safe fabric of her life.

Chapter 4

Rafe hesitated at the door of the cabin. He wished the woman had screamed or cried, or even fainted. He could handle that easily. He could handle anything but that quiet dignity that was so unnerving.

Despite himself, despite the fact that she might be Randall's daughter, he felt a glimmer of admiration. She had a hell of a lot more guts than her father.

But that didn't mean she wasn't every bit as devious and treacherous as Jack Randall.

He understood Ben's thinking in bringing her here, but Rafe's quarrel was with Jack Randall, not a woman. He wouldn't use substitutes. Not the way Randall did.

Clint had said the woman's and Randall's eyes were alike. Rafe didn't remember the exact color of Randall's eyes, but he didn't think they could be that soft, that color of blue-gray, like the sky at dawn.

Except for that brief visit to a whorehouse, he hadn't been with a woman. In prison he'd blocked out that kind of memory, that kind of want, and he thought he'd brought them under control. But now they were tormenting him, like tiny devils stabbing his lower region with pitchforks.

Not that the woman was so pretty. She was not his type at all. Allison had been startlingly pretty, with black hair and green eyes and a figure that was all curves. This woman was tall and slender, boyish in a shirt and trousers. Her light brown hair was carelessly bound in a loose braid that hung halfway down her back, and her eyes were calm, even restful, except for those few times when sparks seemed to ignite in them. Mainly when he had said something about Jack Randall.

Loyalty? In a Randall? That was absolutely incomprehensible to him. Any decent quality must be foreign to a Randall. She could, for all he knew, even be a spy. Hell, he wouldn't put anything past Randall. The thought stoked his anger and lowered his admiration to a controllable level. It made things a hell of a lot easier.

He opened the door and strode in, noting that she was sitting on the cot. He suspected she hadn't been sitting there long. The bottom of her trousers was edged with dust that had settled on the floor. His eyes swept the rest of the room. Nothing seemed to have been disturbed.

"Stand up," he ordered curtly as he moved toward her.

She shied away from him.

He shrugged. "All right, stay tied the rest of the day."

She bit her lip for a moment, looking vulnerable, and finally stood, presenting her back to him. His fingers deftly untied the knot that bound her wrists.

She turned and looked at him. She seemed to flinch at the expression in his face, but her back straightened and her chin lifted as she met his gaze straight-on. "Have the others gone?"

It was clear that she hoped they had not. That bothered him for some reason, and his eyes narrowed as he studied her. Either she had lied about being Randall's daughter, or she *was* Randall's daughter. Either way, he wouldn't trust her farther than he could toss her.

Rafe chose to ignore her inquiry and made one of his own. "What's your name?"

She didn't answer. He was getting accustomed to her silence. Hell, he understood it. How many times had he used silence as a tool, especially when he knew insults or curses would only result in punishment? She learned a hell of a lot faster than he had. "All right, I'll call you Joe," he finally said.

She searched his face, and he knew she was looking for a flash of humor. There was none.

"I've got to call you something," he said, surprised at himself for explaining anything to her.

"Shea," she said finally.

"Shea Randall?"

She fell silent once more.

"Let's try something else," he said. "Where did you come from?"

She searched her mind for reasons not to tell him and could find none, except she didn't want to cooperate with him. She didn't want to give him that satisfaction. So she turned away and went to the door, looking out, hoping to see the other two men, but there was only an empty clearing, and she knew she was alone with this . . . outlaw.

"It won't work," he said from behind her. "I'll find out everything."

She whirled around, the anger she had been trying to cage threatening to spill over. She didn't want that to happen. She couldn't let that happen. She suspected he would enjoy it, that he was trying to provoke it.

"Why are you keeping me here?"

"Not for your charm," he said. "So rest easy in that regard. Ten years of prison or not, I'm not desperate enough to take Randall's get. Or his leavings, whichever you are." He uttered the last sentence in a taunting low voice.

She hated his mockery, the contempt he didn't bother to hide. It was the last insult she was going to tolerate. Despite her vow that she would pretend obedience, she found her left hand starting to swing, only to be caught in a viselike grip.

"So the lady does have a temper," he observed. "What else does she have? Tell me, Miss Randall."

"Let me go," she demanded, looking down at his fingers on her wrist.

He laughed bitterly but loosened his hold. "You should know the bite of iron, Miss Shea. Cold. Hard. Cutting. My hand can't come close to that feel."

"I would prefer it to you," she spit at him.

"Obey me, or you'll have the opportunity to find out," he retorted.

She felt the blood drain from her face. "You wouldn't?"

"I'll do whatever I must to finish what I've started."

"And what's that?"

"Your father, or whatever he is to you, has a certain debt to pay."

"Because he testified against you?"

"Oh, that's only one of the reasons," Rafe said.

"He was just doing his duty."

"Was he?"

His cold green eyes suddenly blazed, and she felt the heat from his anger. There was something else in those eyes. Something very frightening. She stepped away. "What are you planning?"

"That, Miss Shea, is none of your business."

"It is," she insisted.

"No," he said flatly. "And you'll stay here. In this cabin."

"And you?" Shea tried to keep her apprehension from showing.

"Lady, I don't want to be anyplace close to you."

"I can't stay here." She hated the plea in her voice.

"You don't have any choice. And if you're smart, you'll do as you're told."

"I'm obviously not, since I was foolish enough to trust Ben Smith or whatever his name is."

"Let's see if you're a fast learner then," he said, glancing around the cabin and then picking up all the weapons. He stopped midway to the door and turned back to her. "I don't make war on women. But be clear on this—I'll do what I must to finish what I started. If it means confining you in here, even chaining you, I'll do it. I won't like it, but I'll do it. In the meantime you don't have to worry about your safety. I have no interest in you, other than to make sure you don't interfere in my plans. Do you understand?"

She defied him silently, her hands clenched at her sides. Her wrist still bore the print of his hand, her skin its heat. She couldn't take back anything, not that foolish trust in Ben Smith, not the words that gave Rafferty Tyler a weapon against her father. She could only try to escape, to get to her father, to warn him.

Outlaws, the clerk had said in Casey Springs. She wondered whether her father knew who led the outlaws, or the hate that drove them. It was like a live thing, that hate. She could feel it vibrate in the room, and it made her shiver.

"Do you understand?" he said again.

She nodded without accepting.

He didn't say anything else; he just walked toward the door without giving her another glance. He kicked the door shut behind him, and the light in the cabin dimmed. After several seconds she heard metal against metal and knew he had placed a padlock on the door. There was one window, through which light filtered, and with a sinking feeling she waited for him to rob her of that too. She didn't have to wait long. Shutters closed, and she heard the slam of a bar holding them in place.

She was alone in darkness now, alone in these forested mountains with an outlaw who hated her father, a man she didn't even know. She didn't understand Tyler's hatred, and she couldn't minimize it. Or her own danger. No matter what he said, he couldn't help but see her as a weapon. She tried to keep the rising terror at bay, to submerge it under other thoughts.

She searched for a weakness in Rafferty Tyler, and the artist in her recalled every feature of his face, every harsh line. She wondered what his face would look like at ease, if it had ever been that way. And she remembered the way he'd spoken of the ten years in prison, of the feel of iron—with tightness in his voice and tension in his body. She relived that moment when anger radiated from him as he'd showed her his scarred hand.

And he blamed it all on Jack Randall.

Unjustly. Rafferty Tyler had brought on his own problems by stealing army payrolls. The punishment did seem barbaric, but it was his own fault, she told herself, trying to dismiss those moments of sympathy for him. That she could feel any softness toward him made it even more essential that she escape.

She just had to.

* * *

Rafe prowled the woods like a wounded panther.

He felt cut to the core and knew his soul was as mutilated as his hand.

He kept seeing those soft blue-gray eyes: widened with terror, glinting with defiance. When he'd locked the door, they must have reflected the feelings he'd had when a cell door first closed on him.

What kind of man was he that he could terrify a woman? What had he become?

Damn Ben. And yet, Rafe might have done the same thing Ben had, given the opportunity. Randall's daughter. He still couldn't believe it was true, but part of him was willing to admit it was a possibility.

Could he really trade the daughter for a confession, instead of going through with the current plan: forcing Randall against a wall, bankrupting him until he did something stupid?

But no one knew about a daughter, so she couldn't mean much to his enemy, certainly not enough to go to prison. Dammit all to hell. What was he going to do with her?

If only she hadn't seen Ben and Clint . . .

But she had, and now their lives and futures were at risk, particularly those of Clint, who was involved too deeply now to unravel himself. It had been Clint who had helped with the first robbery six weeks ago.

An eye for an eye. The woman shouldn't bother him. He wasn't going to hurt her. And God knew he would keep her only as long as necessary, certainly nothing like the months and years he'd spent in prison because of her father. Just a few weeks. Perhaps months.

Christ, how could he handle that?

How could *she* handle that? Despite her gallant attempt at bravery, she had to fear the worst, that he would rape or kill her. There was no reason for her to think otherwise.

He'd thought he'd lost all emotions except the need for revenge, and he bitterly resented the guilt that now nibbled at him.

But it was not enough to change his mind. He had survived mutilation, the worst kind of abasement in prison, and loss of nearly one third of his life only by promising himself that Randall would pay for every moment in kind.

He couldn't let the hate go. The penetrating, consuming, relentless need for revenge was too much a part of him, had been for too many years. He would do what was required to satisfy it.

And then? He couldn't think further than that. The beyond didn't exist. Desolation wrapped around him as if he were whirling down a black bottomless hole, speeding toward a nothingness that was more frightening than any kind of physical pain.

He reached out, anchoring himself by touching a tall pine, forcing his mind back to the woman. He had no idea how to alleviate her fears. Christ, he didn't know how to talk to anyone.

Except perhaps Abner, who demanded little. Suddenly wishing for its company, he put his hand into his pocket, and then he remembered he'd left the mouse in the cabin.

He wondered how Miss Randall felt about mice.

He should go back, but he couldn't force himself yet. He had wanted to touch her, to wipe away her fear. That had surprised him. It had been so damn long since he'd touched anyone with tender human feeling.

That the woman in the cabin had stirred him that way was something he couldn't bear to contemplate, not if she was Randall's kin. He had no compassion left, no pity, dammit. He would never be used again, not by anyone.

His body shuddered as he thought of his imprisonment. He wished he could let that go, but he couldn't. He still slept outside now, even on the meanest nights. He couldn't stand waking up in the small cabin, and even outside he would still awake to nightmares, to the times he'd been stripped and thrown in the punishment box without so much as a bucket for dignity. He'd turned into an animal, living in darkness in his own waste.

He'd lost something then he would never regain, just as his keepers planned. They broke spirits because then prisoners were easier to handle. He found he would do anything, say anything, be anything, to keep from going back to the box, and he'd hated himself for that weakness. He could never totally regain his self-respect, but perhaps vindication might mend it a little.

He'd learned to control his rage, to direct it. But sometimes it still ran away with him, like an untamable wild horse, and he'd have to force himself back in check, to be patient. But, Christ, it was hard. Slowly, he was chipping away at Jack Randall. The Circle R was strapped for cash. Randall's hands would desert their employer if they weren't paid soon; promises went just so far. As did loyalty.

He'd discovered that years ago, when Allison and men he thought were friends so readily believed the worst of him, so completely abandoned him. So had the army to which he had given his life. He couldn't even entirely trust Clint and Ben and the others now; the suspicion that they had their own reasons kept nagging at him. Any belief in justice or loyalty or friendship was smashed ten years ago. Abner was the only creature in the world Rafe allowed himself to care about. The mouse required so little, just the amount Rafe had left to give.

Unwillingly, his thoughts returned once more to his prisoner. Shea. An unusual name. Soft and quiet-sounding. It suited her. And then he cursed himself. He couldn't think of her that way. She was Randall's daughter, nothing more. He had to keep telling himself that. The get of a viper was still a viper.

He started back, moving with his usual caution. The trapper who'd once lived in the cabin had set traps throughout these woods, and Rafe had already found several. Some held dead animals, and he'd felt an infinite sadness for them, a certain kinship. He'd sprung the live ones. He suspected there were more traps, and he always walked warily. The last thing he needed was to be caught in another trap.

Or maybe, he thought as he considered the woman in the cabin, he already was.

Tears had dried on Shea's face. Useless, foolish tears that didn't accomplish anything. She was angry at herself for expending that energy, and even more so at the thought that her captor might see evidence of her having cried.

She was thirsty and hungry and dirty. And so alone.

She'd never been alone like this before. There had always been her mother and friends, customers at the shop who'd oohed and aahed over her hat designs. There had even been the occasional young man.

But that was all gone. She didn't even know who and what she was.

She pushed aside her despair and concentrated on escaping. She would have to plan carefully. The best scheme was to disarm her captor, make him think she had accepted her situation. And she had to get a horse. She'd have no chance without one, not up here, where she could be in more danger from nature than from the man who held her.

She wondered where Rafferty Tyler had gone. She had hoped fervently he wouldn't come back, but now she worried just the opposite. In the darkness she had searched the cabin and found matches and a few candles. She could try to burn the place down, but she might kill herself in the process. Yet that remained an option if he didn't return.

She lit one candle and peered around more closely. There was a box in a corner, and she opened it. Several tins of crackers. Canned fruits and meat. She'd never eaten canned meat, but she was ready to try anything at this point. She had no way of opening the cans, though. She opened the cracker tin and ate half of one. It tasted like chalk.

Shea swallowed, feeling the dryness of her mouth. In disgust she went back to the cot, taking the candle with her, wondering whether she should put it out or not. But she didn't like the darkness. It increased her fear. Somehow she could cope if she had light.

Something moved at the end of the bed, and she flinched. There was no telling what creatures inhabited the cabin. She moved the candle and saw a small mouse on the end of the cot, regarding her as curiously as she watched him.

It sat up on his haunches and put its two front legs together as if begging. It obviously had no fright of her.

She'd seen big, ugly rats in the streets of Boston, but this mouse was small and appealing.

Shea remained still, wondering whether it would come closer or scamper off. She wished she had her sketchpad, but that was outside on the tree stump. So she concentrated on the tiny animal, willing it to come closer.

She tried talking to it. It was better than talking to

herself, and hearing the sound of her own voice was reassuring somehow.

"You don't know a way out, do you?" she asked, as the mouse continued to regard her curiously. "Of course you do, or you wouldn't be here, but I suspect it would be much too small for me."

The mouse came a few inches closer, and Shea reached out her hand to the creature, surprised when it crept forward and then investigated her fingers with its tiny mouth. It flicked its tail and sat back on his haunches again with what Shea thought was disappointment. Fascinated, she wondered if she should fetch a cracker. What if it disappeared while she was getting the tin? That thought was excruciating.

She heard a noise at the door, and she tensed. The mouse didn't move, and she knew she had to protect it. She reached to pick it up, surprised when it didn't flee from her. She thrust it underneath the cot, hoping that it would stay in the shadows.

The door opened, and the bright light of the late-afternoon sun almost blinded her. Her eyes were drawn to the large figure in the doorway. Silhouetted by the sun behind him, Tyler seemed even bigger, stronger, more menacing. She had to force herself to keep from moving back away from him.

He hesitated, his gaze raking over the cabin, raking over her. He frowned at the candle.

She stood. It took all her bravery, but she stood, forcing her eyes to meet his, looking for a crumb of remorse or regret or reprieve. All she saw was a certain coolness.

"I'm thirsty." It came out as more of a challenge than a request, and she caught a flicker of something in his eyes. She was hoping it was conscience, but that hope was quickly extinguished by his response.

"Used to better places?" It was a sneer, plain and simple, and Shea felt anger stirring again.

"I'm used to gentlemen and simple . . . humanity."

"That's strange, considering your claim that you're Randall's daughter."

"I haven't claimed anything to you."

"That's right, you haven't," he agreed in a disagreeable tone. "You haven't said much at all."

"And I don't intend to. Not to a thief and a traitor."

"Be careful, Miss Randall. Your continued good health depends on that thief and traitor."

"That's supposed to comfort me?" Her tone was pure acid.

His gaze stabbed her. "You'll have to forgive me. I'm out of practice in trying to comfort anyone. Ten years out of practice." She heard no apology in his voice, only bitterness.

"So you're going to starve me?"

"No," he said slowly. "I'm not going to do *that.*"

The statement was ominous to Shea. "What are you going to do?"

"Follow my rules, and I won't do anything."

"You already are. You're keeping me here against my will."

He was silent for a moment, and a muscle moved in his neck, as if he were just barely restraining himself. "Lady, because of your . . . father, I was held against my will for ten years."

She wanted to slap him for his mockery. She wanted to kick him where it would hurt the most. But now was not the time.

"Is that it? You're taking your . . . grudge out on me?"

The muscle in his cheek moved again. "No, Miss Randall, it's not that. You just happened to be in the wrong place at the wrong time. I don't have any more choices than you do." He didn't know why in the hell he was explaining, except that her last charge galled him.

"You do," she insisted.

He turned away from her. "Believe what you want," he said, his voice indifferent. "Blow out that candle and come with me if you want some water."

She didn't want to go with him, but she was desperate to slake her thirst and to take care of a personal need. She blew out the candle, hoping that once outside he wouldn't see dried streaks of tears on her face.

Shea didn't have to worry. He paid no attention to her. She knew she was plain, especially so in the loose-fitting britches and shirt she wore and with her hair in a braid. She should be grateful he was indifferent to her, but a part of her wanted to goad him, confuse him . . . attract him.

Shea felt color flood her face. To stop her train of thought, she concentrated on her surroundings.

Her horse was gone, and her belongings were propped against the tree stump. There was a shack to the left, with a lock on the door. That must be where he'd taken the weapons and where he kept his own horse. The keys had to be in his pockets. He strode over to the building and picked up a bucket with his gloved hand.

She tried to pay attention to their route, but in the forest of pine and aspen and bushes, everything looked alike. She thought of turning around and running, but he was only a couple of feet ahead of her. He'd have no trouble catching her.

He stopped abruptly at a stream and leaned against a tree, watching her.

Shea had never drunk from a stream before, yet that was obviously what he expected her to do. The dryness in her mouth was worse, and she couldn't wait. She moved to the edge of the stream and kneeled, feeling awkward and self-conscious, knowing he was judging her. She scooped up a handful of water, then another, trying to sip it before it leaked through her fingers. She caught just enough to be tantalized.

She finally fell flat on her stomach and put her mouth in the water, taking long swallows of the icy-cold water, mindless of the way the front of her shirt got soaked, mindless of anything but the water.

It felt wonderful. And tasted wonderful. Colder and purer than she'd ever had before. When she was finally sated, she sat up and turned around, her gaze instinctively going to Tyler.

His stance looked lazy, but his eyes, like fine emeralds, were glowing with green fire, and she felt a corresponding wave of heat consume her. She couldn't move her gaze from him, no matter how hard she tried, as if they were locked together.

He was the first to divert his gaze, and his eyes assumed their usual icy indifference.

She looked down and noticed that her wet shirt clung to her, outlining her breasts. She swallowed hard and turned around. She splashed some water on her face, hoping it would cool the heat suffusing her body.

Shea lingered as long as she could. She didn't want to go back to the dark cabin. She didn't want to face him or those intense emotions she didn't understand.

She kept expecting him to order her away, but he didn't. She didn't dare look, but she felt his gaze on her and knew she should feel fear. He had been in prison a very long time. Yet she instinctively knew he wouldn't touch her in a sexual way.

Because he despises you.

Because he despises your father.

She closed her eyes for a moment, and when she

opened them, a spiral of light gleamed through the trees. She wanted to reach out and catch that sunbeam, to climb it to some safe place.

But there were no safe places any longer.

She watched that ray of light until it slowly dissipated as the sun slipped lower in the sky, and then she slowly rose.

"Ready?" he asked in that hoarse whisper of his.

The word held many meanings.

Ready for what? She wasn't ready for any of this.

But she nodded.

He sauntered over and offered his gloved hand.

She refused it and moved away from him, stunned by how much she'd suddenly wanted to take his hand, to feel that strength again.

And Shea realized her battle wasn't entirely with him. It was also with herself.

Chapter 5

Rafe didn't know why he'd held out his hand to her. Particularly when she so openly expressed her disdain for it. Because of him? Because of the brand?

What in hell had he expected, anyway?

But she'd looked so wistful caught in the stream of light. The sun had bounced off her soft brown hair, making it appear a halo. He'd wondered why he thought her plain. She looked extremely pretty at that moment.

And fearful, when he'd walked over to her. He disliked himself heartily for causing that fear. But there was no help for it.

He had to keep her more afraid of him than anything, or anyone, else. That's why he hadn't searched for Abner in the cabin. Who, for Christ's sake, would be afraid of a man who kept a mouse as a pet? He would find Abner later and keep him either in his pocket or in the stable.

He scowled at her, allowing her to see his displeasure. "Don't get any ideas about following this stream," he said. "It goes up into the mountain on one end and travels downstream over steep falls. You can't get out either way. And these woods are full of animals—bears, wolves, mountain lions, rattlesnakes—and traps. There's no place to run."

Despite the lingering wariness in her eyes, her voice was almost steady when she spoke. "Are you going to let me run?"

"No," he said bluntly. "But I don't want you to even think about it. You'll leave when I want you to leave and not before."

"I think I prefer a good honest bear."

"That's because you've never met one."

"But I have met *you*," Shea retorted bitterly.

"And anything would be better?" His smile mocked her, but her gaze remained steady as she silently agreed with the implied answer.

"I wouldn't put it to the test if I were you," he said in that agreeable voice that she was beginning to hate. "I don't tear most of my . . . captives to pieces."

"What do you do with them?"

"Tame them," he said with the slightest quirk of his mouth, but again she saw no sense of humor there. Only menace.

"I don't tame."

His voice hardened, and there was a dangerous edge to it. "Anyone can be tamed, Miss Randall."

Shea knew she was on dangerous ground, but she had to pursue what had been started. "Including you?"

"We're not talking about me. We will never talk about me. Now you . . . that's a different matter."

Shea hated the insinuation in his voice, the reminder that he was in control, the rough mockery that meant to provoke and sting.

And it did. But she wouldn't give him the pleasure of seeing that if it killed her. She lifted her chin. "Do you always starve them too?"

"Sometimes," he said. "It goes along with my bad

character. After all, what can you expect of a convicted thief and branded outlaw?"

Despite his light tone, she sensed anguish, a raw pain that drained some of her anger. Did he realize he had revealed something he most likely wished to keep private? That piece of knowledge could be a weapon against him, but she would probably never use it.

She shook her head to dismiss that moment of weakness. She had to use whatever she could to escape.

He was watching her, apparently waiting for an answer to his question.

"Nothing," she finally retorted. "I expect nothing."

"Good, then you won't be disappointed," he drawled. "But I *will* feed you. You look as if you need a good meal. I don't care for skinny women." His taunt made it clear he *was* aware that he had revealed his pain to her. And he was punishing *her* for that.

"Then I'll starve," she shot back.

He shrugged. "Your choice."

He went down to the stream and filled the bucket, averting his face from her. She wanted to run more than anything, but as before she knew he would catch her easily enough. He knew it, too, and his casual attitude toward her infuriated her. His confidence was galling. More than galling.

Humiliating.

He straightened, and she wished he weren't so striking. His clothes molded to the muscles of his body, and there was a suppressed energy about him that electrified the air. Electrified her, for heaven's sake.

Shea swallowed. She couldn't believe she was thinking such a thing. More handsome men had called on her, but she'd always felt little when she was with them, and relief when they left. She'd worried about herself, the way she had remained so cool to them, even when she'd tried hard to feel something.

Whatever Rafferty Tyler was, he did not leave her cold.

He turned, and his startlingly blue-green eyes met hers. She wondered how they would look alight with laughter, rather than shuttered by that flatness that stopped anyone from looking inside.

"You're still here?"

"You would like me to try to escape, wouldn't you?"

"It might be interesting."

"Well, I have no intention of providing amusement for you, Mr. . . ." Her voice trailed off. She had no idea what to call him.

"You *do* learn fast, Miss Randall," he said. "I'm surprised."

"It depends on what you want me to learn," she said, unable to let him think he had cowed her altogether. "I know when to pick my opportunities, and I suspect now is not one of them."

Something like appreciation crossed his face, but whatever it was, it lasted just a fraction of a second, and he was scowling at her again.

"There will be no opportunities, Miss Randall. I wasn't just trying to scare you when I said these mountains are dangerous. I'm your only defense at the moment."

"Is that supposed to reassure me?"

"No," he said. His mouth quirked slightly, but it wasn't a smile. She wondered if he was even capable of a smile. "Stay afraid of me, and we'll do fine."

"I don't want to do fine."

"I don't give a damn what you want, Miss Randall. You can make this hard, or a little less hard. Those are your choices."

"You're a bastard," she said, gritting her teeth.

"Remember that," he said. "If you need to use those woods out there, do it now. And keep your head in sight."

She blushed down to her toes. Bodily functions were something one didn't discuss, particularly in such a cavalier fashion, and especially between a man and woman.

"You aren't going to watch?"

That mouth quirked again. "Only your head, Miss Randall. I don't trust your good sense quite yet."

Sheer necessity quarreled with pride and modesty. Necessity won.

"I hope my father . . ." She stopped, not entirely sure what she wanted.

"Will kill me?"

"Sends you back to prison," she said recklessly.

"You believe that's preferable to dying?" he asked, a peculiar light in his eyes.

It should have warned her, but she plunged ahead. "Far better."

"Perhaps a taste of it will change your mind," he said bitterly.

Shea swallowed. "I haven't done anything."

"And *I* have?" he asked, that glint in his eyes even more ominous.

"I know you've been robbing payrolls here."

"You know that, do you?" He was taunting her again. "And how do you know that?"

Shea started to answer, but she stopped. How did she know? Because he was a convicted thief? Because the clerk in Casey Springs had said there had been robberies in the area? Because he was holding her here against her will? But what if her captivity had nothing to do with the robberies?

She had leaped to conclusions. Had that happened to

him before? Had he been innocent? Was he innocent now?

But then his mouth quirked again, and she knew better. He had played her for a fool. He had seen her doubts and led her right down the path she wanted to take. Now he was enjoying himself at her expense; now he was letting her see that he was every bit as bad as she had thought.

"You did rob those coaches," she finally said in an uncertain voice.

"Of course I did," he replied easily.

She felt anger prick at her again. She had never wanted to commit violence before, but she thought she might be able to do exactly that right now. "Why did you let me think . . . ?"

The pretense of a smile left his face. "It doesn't matter, Miss Randall. Now I'll give you exactly four minutes before we go back to the cabin."

As he watched Shea head for a thick clump of brush, Rafe regretted his cruelty. He hadn't intended it. He had thought she would throw his past conviction in his face when he'd asked her how she knew he had committed the robberies. And then that damned doubt flitted through her eyes, touching him in ways he didn't even want to think about. It had almost made him feel human again, had made hope bubble up inside him. But he didn't want her doubts as to his guilt. He didn't want her pity. Not from a Randall.

And so he had stepped on her, as he would step on an insect, carelessly and without thought. And he'd hurt her.

He kept his eyes on her head, on the fine brown hair that looked like silk. He kept his eyes there as a kind of punishment to himself. He didn't think she would take this time to try to escape. She was too clever for that. She would wait until she had a head start, and then, wilderness or not, he suspected she would take off.

Rafe cursed himself, cursed that integrity and vulnerability about her that kept him off-balance. He told himself it was just an act, but he really didn't believe it. Christ, he wanted to know about her relationship with the one man he despised above all others, and she wasn't telling him. Because she knew he would use it to hurt Jack Randall.

He closed his eyes for a moment, trying to avoid an unpleasant truth about himself. He would use her or any other human being to bring about justice. He wouldn't, couldn't, think beyond that, especially not the fact that this time he might be the one corrupting justice. Any doubts he had were dispelled when he glanced down at his hand.

Rafe sensed her approach. His senses tingled, just as they had ever since she arrived. He didn't look at her, just picked up the bucket and started toward the cabin, knowing she had no choice but to follow.

Shea watched him as he moved restlessly around the cabin. She sensed he didn't like being in here, and she supposed it was because of her presence. She looked nervously at the one cot in the room, and she wondered what he was planning for sleeping arrangements.

Tyler paid no mind to her as he quickly chose several cans of food and unsheathed the knife at his belt. He had opened the window, but it was dusk, and he was wrapped in shadows, which made him seem even more distant and enigmatic than ever.

She wished she could read him better. She had never seen anyone so contained, so infernally elusive. Very little showed in his eyes or face or expression, and she had always been good at ferreting out qualities and feelings of those she met. A couple of times she thought she'd seen a wisp of humor, but then he had tamped it immediately. She wondered whether she'd just imagined it because she wanted to see some lighter emotion in him to temper that deep, seething anger he made no attempt to hide.

He was certainly making no attempt to mask it now. She had the impression of an angry wounded tiger, just waiting to turn on a victim, as he knifed open the cans, then set them down much too softly, as if he had to keep himself from doing it in a more violent way. He produced a spoon for her, offering it to her with a mocking bow. He then took a couple of additional cans in his hand and whirled around, stalking outside.

The cabin still seemed full of his presence, and she felt dwarfed by it, by the anger that surrounded him. A part of her wanted to follow him, to keep loneliness at bay, but her pride wouldn't let her.

To brighten the darkness, both real and emotional, she lit a candle and placed it on the table, and then sat down. He had opened two cans of peaches and a can of beans for her. There were also some dried strips of jerky.

She loved peaches and would normally have found them wonderful, but now she ate merely to keep up her strength so she could ultimately outwit and outmatch her captor. But she felt sick inside, wondering about tonight, wondering about him. So much had happened in the past twelve hours, so much had changed since the time she'd thought she was on her way to see the man who had fathered her.

She wondered where the mouse was. Maybe she would just leave the food here for him. Or was it a her?

Shea went to the open door and looked out. Only a pink glow remained of the sun, which had already set. She didn't see her captor, but she did see her valise and drawing case. The door to the other building was open, and she wondered whether she should try to escape now.

She moved to the valise and picked it up, still undecided. The day had turned cool. It would get even colder tonight, and she would need something other than the lightweight shirt she wore. Just as she thought she might make a dash for it, no matter what, he sauntered out of the other building, as if he had been waiting for the moment when she would make up her mind.

"Going someplace?" he drawled.

"I'm cold," she said. "Do you object to me wearing my own clothes?"

"Not if I see what's in there first."

The thought of him riffling through her undergarments was intolerable, but she knew better than to wage a war she couldn't win.

"If it gives you pleasure," she said, and this time she was taunting him, though she knew she shouldn't.

His brows arched together with displeasure, but then he shrugged. "Think what you want."

"I don't carry guns with me."

"A mirror could be just as dangerous," he said.

"In your hands, perhaps," she said acidly.

"You don't like violence, Miss Randall?"

She wished he wouldn't purr like that, like a full-grown tiger ready to spring. She always had that impression of him, that sense that he would pounce at any moment.

She set her jaw. "No."

"Then we shouldn't have any problems," he said.

"But you still intend to . . . invade my clothing."

"As I said, I have a difficult time believing a Randall."

"Why?"

He leaned back on his heels. "Do you really not know your father?"

Shea hesitated. She didn't know whether the truth would hurt or help her case, make her less or more of a weapon to Tyler. If he thought Randall didn't care, didn't even know she existed, perhaps he would let her go. But then, that wasn't why he was keeping her. He was keeping her because of that foolish sketch of Ben, and nothing was going to change that fact. But perhaps it was worth a try.

"No," Shea said.

"No, what, Miss Randall?"

"No, I don't know him. I've never known him, and he doesn't even know I exist and probably cares less."

"Would you like to explain that?"

"No."

"Oh, yes. You don't start something like that without finishing the tale. An old law of the West."

"But you don't believe in laws," she snapped back.

"I do when they benefit me," he said lazily. "Now tell me more."

"There's nothing to tell."

"I think there is, Miss Randall. A daughter who's never seen the father she claims, who travels thousands of miles to see him."

"I don't even know he is my father," she said desperately, very sorry she'd opened this Pandora's Box. She didn't want to explain her life to him, or her mother's. "I just think so."

"Why do you think so?" He was relentless in his questioning, just as he obviously was in his hatred.

She felt helpless before it. "Because of the letters. And you've seen those," she added with no little resentment.

"That's all?" he asked incredulously. "You traveled that far just on the basis of a few letters?"

"There was money." At the sudden narrowing and hardening of his eyes, she regretted saying those words.

"How much money?"

"It doesn't make any difference."

"It does to me, Miss Randall."

"Why? I don't have it with me. You can't steal it."

"I can steal other things if you continue to try me," he said in that hoarse voice again, his lips barely moving.

Shea knew she had gone too far. She leaned down and picked up her sketching case. His hand stopped hers midway. "There are a few rules, Miss Randall."

She looked up at him. She wished he weren't so tall. She wished he didn't have those vividly colored eyes. She wished he didn't make her feel like a . . . a wanton. She wished she knew where these odd, heated feelings were coming from. Fear, she fervently hoped. It had to be fear.

"What rules?"

"No more sketches of the men who come here."

"What about you?"

"You want a remembrance?" He grinned at her.

"I want to see you hang," she said recklessly. "Maybe a picture will help."

"A few moments ago you wanted to see me in prison," he mocked.

"That was a few moments ago."

"I thought you were against violence."

"You're making me reconsider."

He shook his head. "Such fragile principles."

"At least I have some."

"You lose principles in prison, Miss Randall."

"I think you lost a lot more than that," she said. His jaw set, and a muscle throbbed in his cheek. He was reacting as if she'd dealt him a body blow.

"Very perceptive, Miss Randall. Tell me more about myself."

That was the quickest road to hell, and Shea knew it. So she remained silent.

"Caution again?"

He said it in such a smug way, she wanted to slap him. He was waiting for that, waiting for a reason to retaliate. She didn't know why he felt he needed an excuse, but apparently he did.

"Isn't that what you want? An obedient prisoner?"

He scowled at her. "I don't think you're a damn bit obedient."

"Why is that?"

"Because I've been where you are, lady. You're thinking of escape. Every moment you're thinking of it, and you'll risk everything for it."

"Did you?"

He didn't answer. He didn't have to. She already knew enough about him to know he had. It must have been devastating to him to fail.

"You're comparing me to you. I'm not like you."

"Aren't you?" he asked. "Don't you feel a little bit desperate?"

She did. More so than before, because he apparently knew everything she was thinking. "Does that give you pleasure?"

"Like going through your belongings? Not much. I like my pleasures more direct."

Her face flamed again at the innuendo. Other parts of her were also on fire, and she had no control over the sudden surge of heat. The air between them was magnetic, full of storm winds blowing temptation.

He felt it too. She knew he did. He didn't move, seemingly locked in place as she was. A muscle throbbed in his cheek, and she felt a throbbing of her own deep in the most private part of herself, a throbbing she'd never known before.

The longing it created in her was bittersweet. And terrifying. Of all the men in the world, this one should be the least likely to stir such vivid and exotically painful feelings.

He reached up and touched her cheek with his left hand, and the feelings magnified, the longing more compelling. She wanted to touch him, too, to see whether she could ease the harsh, bitter lines on his face, but she knew she couldn't or she would be lost. It would be an invitation to him, and there were only the two of them up here in this mountain clearing. No safety anywhere. No one to interfere. No one to tell her how unwise she was.

She had to tell herself, and nothing in her life had been more difficult. Using all the willpower she had, she wrenched away from his touch.

He dropped his hand quickly and stepped back, his face still impassive, but there was a brilliant glitter in his striking eyes. She didn't know whether it was from anger or desire. She didn't think she wanted to know.

"Ex-convicts not to your liking?" His body was tense, and she had the sudden impression that she had wounded him. Which was ridiculous.

"Kidnappers are not to my liking," she retorted.

"I didn't kidnap you."

"But you're holding me here against my will."

Some of the tension seemed to fade from him. "Let's just say I don't want anything to happen to you in these mountains."

"You don't care what happens to me," she charged, terribly confused by her own mixed emotions, that moment of regret that she might have caused him pain. She ought to cause him as much pain as she could, as he had done to her.

He hesitated at her charge, started to say something, and then clamped his lips together. He finally shrugged. "Continue to believe that, Miss Randall, and we'll get along just fine."

"I don't want to get along with you."

"You'll have to. Unless you want to stay in that cabin day and night. I don't intend to waste time arguing with you. You do exactly what I say or you stay in that cabin . . . without that sketchpad."

She looked down at her case, still clutched in her hands. "You didn't say whether I could sketch you."

"I don't give a damn. I want Randall to know I'm here. And," he added with a careless shrug, "as you know, there are other pictures of me."

"Will you pose for me?" Shea asked. She had gone this far. She might as well go further.

"Now that, Miss Randall, is asking too much."

"You have an interesting face."

"Really?" he said wryly. "And how is that?"

"I don't know," she said slowly, thoughtfully. "Which is why it's interesting."

"I'm sure you'll tell me when you know." He turned away, as if weary of the conversation.

"I . . ."

He turned back to her. "What?"

"I don't know what to call you."

"*Mr.* Tyler will do," he said. "Or sir."

She looked him in the eyes. She had lost some of her fear of him, knowing she had goaded him and had survived. "Go to . . ." She stopped, unwilling to finish what she had started to say, not out of fear but propriety. "Hades," she finally finished.

"You asked. That's what I called the guards in prison. Now I'm *your* guard, Miss Randall, and I think we should observe the proprieties of such an arrangement."

"Fine," she said. "*Mr.* Tyler." She made it sound as obscene as the way he said "Miss Randall."

He smiled mirthlessly. "Now you have the idea." He turned to leave again, and this time he didn't stop until he disappeared into the other building.

Chapter 6

Rafe left open the door to the shack to let in the last remnants of light and as a reminder to the woman that he was watching.

He should damn well keep her locked in the cabin so he wouldn't have to concern himself, but he'd found he couldn't do that.

He might have been able to if she'd had tantrums, if she had screamed invectives at him, or had collapsed in tears. That dignity, however, touched a conscience he hadn't realized still survived.

The simple fact was that he understood her fear, the terrible sense of helplessness and powerlessness, and therefore he sympathized in ways that cut to the core. The damn woman reminded him of himself ten years ago. He remembered cloaking himself in stubborn pride as his soul was systematically destroyed at the court-martial and subsequent parade-ground ceremony. He remembered trying to feign indifference as chains were riveted around his ankles and he was marched out, in front of Allison and former comrades, to a waiting wagon for transportation to prison. And he recalled masking despair with defiance as the cell door closed on him for the first time, knowing it would be another ten years before he knew anything else.

He saw all of these things—despair, pride, and defiance—in her, and he respected her for challenging him and for wisely realizing exactly how far she could go.

He knew she would try to escape, because he had tried it. Christ, he had thought of nothing else. In the fort guardhouse he had thought of making his break on the way to prison, but the irons on his ankles, linked together by a short chain, made that impossible.

He had tried twice to escape from the penitentiary in Ohio. The first attempt was betrayed by a fellow convict. The other attempt, involving a tunnel he had worked on for months, was foiled after a similar escape was successfully carried out by Confederate general John Morgan and some of his officers, who had been held in an adjoining cell block. As a consequence all cells were thoroughly searched and repaired. Rafe's tunnel was found, and he spent even more time in the box.

His hands went over the bay Ben had purchased in Ohio. It had filled out, and its coat was now thick and rich. Rafe had been working with the animal daily, teaching it intricate maneuvers and to anticipate his wishes. He'd always had a special knack with animals, and working with them was one of the things he'd missed most in prison. His hand ran down the horse's flank, and the animal turned its head around to nuzzle him.

Rafe rubbed the nostrils. "Lonely, old boy? We didn't get our workout today, did we?"

The horse whinnied softly. "We have a visitor," Rafe said. "A guest." He glanced out the door and saw her sitting on the tree stump, her graceful form as still as a statue, her hands on the sketchpad.

Her long braid fell halfway down her back, and he wondered what her hair felt like. Probably about as soft as her cheek. He didn't know why in the hell he'd touched her, and he had immediately regretted it. His brief, unplanned gesture had obviously offended her, despite that fleeting moment when he'd thought . . .

Hell, he'd been in prison too long. He was even imagining things now, imagining that she might welcome his touch. The caress of a branded convict! He had made a fool of himself, but he didn't plan to do it again.

Trying to suppress his self-contempt, he plunged his hand into a sack of oats and held them out to the horse. He hadn't named it yet, hadn't found that right monicker. Not like Abner. Which reminded him that he had to liberate the mouse from the cabin. He didn't think Miss Randall and Abner would coexist very well.

He gave the horse one last pat and went out, carefully locking the door after him.

She was still sitting stiffly, her eyes fixed on the starfilled sky as though her life depended on it. He suddenly realized that Shea Randall was probably worried about tonight's sleeping arrangements. There had been a time when he could have had nearly any woman he wanted. Now, who, other than a whore, would sleep with a man branded as a thief and traitor?

Not even the daughter of a man who was both of those.

As he got closer, he saw her face clearly by the light of the nearly full moon. His voice was gruff when he spoke. "I'll get my bedroll. I usually sleep out here. You will sleep inside."

Those wide blue-gray eyes met his. They were full of relief, which did nothing for his already decimated pride.

She nodded.

"I'll lock the door but keep the window open," he said, trying to keep his mind away from the way she looked, soft and rumpled and appealing in the moonlight.

"I'll sleep outside the window, and I'm a very light sleeper."

If she heard the warning in his voice, she didn't acknowledge it. He shrugged, wishing he didn't feel as discomfited as she looked, and he went into the cabin. After closing the door slightly behind him, he whistled lightly, and Abner crept out from under the bed, his little beady eyes bright.

Rafe gathered up his bedroll and a heavy wool shirt, then reached down and picked up Abner. He glanced around the cabin. A partially nibbled piece of dried meat sat on the table. Shea Randall had apparently left it there, and Abner had taken advantage. He grinned at the thought of her returning and finding the partially eaten tidbit, but then dismissed the thought. There was no advantage to him in scaring her more than she already was, despite the brave face she wore. He tucked both jerky and Abner in the heavy wool shirt and went out the door.

She was standing now, looking uncertainly at the cabin, and he bowed slightly, one hand extended to the door, inviting her inside.

Inviting?

Ordering.

Shea stifled her resentment and marched inside, her drawing case in her hand. She glanced at the valise, but he shook his head. Damn him.

Just a tiny bit of night-light filtered into the cabin, and she lit a candle, just as he brought in the valise. She watched as he opened it, and his hands went through her clothing. She resented it tremendously, particularly as he touched her underclothing, and she felt a now-familiar heat.

"Satisfied?" she finally asked.

His eyebrows lifted. "Hardly," he said, insinuation back in his voice. He eyed her deliberately, his gaze moving up and down, almost undressing her with an intimacy that made every one of her senses tingle. "I wonder what you look like in one of those dresses."

She decided then and there to continue wearing the shirt and trousers, no matter how dirty they became or how she tired of them.

His lips turned into a wry line, and she knew he could tell what she was thinking again. Then he turned and left, closing the door and locking her inside.

She glanced around the cabin, looking for the mouse. The piece of dried beef was gone. The bucket of water was inside, and a tin cup.

Shea went to the window and looked out. His bedroll was laid out a few feet beneath the window, but she didn't see him. She moved away, not wanting him to see her but not wanting to lose the sky either. That, at least, was familiar.

Still, the loneliness she had felt earlier deepened.

She didn't understand anything, not these raw new feelings, or the mysterious cravings inside, or even why she wasn't more afraid.

Angry, yes, but not afraid, and that didn't make any sense at all. She should be very afraid here in the middle of nowhere, alone with an outlaw who so obviously hated the man who probably fathered her.

She heard some rustling noises and wondered whether he was stretched out. She walked to her sketching case and took out a pen and her pad. She quickly sketched what she remembered of him, the stark lines of his face, the lines that gave it so much individuality. She tried to find the essence of him in her mind, but it eluded her. He had given very little away, except for the bitterness that hovered just beneath the surface. She finally gave up.

After deciding against changing into a nightdress—it

would make her so vulnerable—she blew out the candle and lay restlessly in the cot. There were two blankets on the end, and she pulled them up over her, finding comfort in them. She could curl up and hide, as she sometimes had done as a child when something at night had frightened her.

But she couldn't sleep. Not in this strange place, with her enigmatic captor outside. Not in the midst of mountains she didn't know or understand. Not in this small cabin where she had no freedom.

She wondered what it had been like for him, those years in prison. She couldn't even think about it, comprehend it. She thought she would go crazy those few hours this afternoon.

That thought didn't comfort her. Perhaps he had . . . lost his reason. Perhaps that was why he blamed everything on Jack Randall.

She wished the mouse would appear again. She needed something friendly. She needed . . .

And Shea realized she didn't know what she needed.

Rafe smoldered inside. The problem was, he didn't really know if he still smoldered entirely from anger.

It had been easy to hate in prison. Christ, it had been easy. He'd had to hate to get through it, to obey guards who considered him less than dirt.

He turned to stare up at the sky. He did that nearly every night. Even when it rained, he often stayed outside, feeling the cool, clean moisture until the rain got too heavy, and then he'd rig canvas above him. The cabin, when closed up, was too much like a jail cell.

That's why he'd left the window open.

He mistrusted that tiny bit of compassion in himself. And he didn't understand it.

He shouldn't give as much as a flea's damn for the daughter of Jack Randall. He should revel in the knowledge that she was experiencing just a little of what he had. But he only felt sick in the gut at the thought.

He tried to turn his thoughts to other matters. Ben had found out that another payroll would come through in six days on the next stage. Ben would get word to the others to gather here then. But there were still six days to spend alone with Miss Shea Randall, and then he would have no choice but to lock her in the cabin while they robbed the stage.

He'd have to keep his distance. He'd have to avoid those eyes that looked at him with a mixture of curiosity and trepidation. At least most of the fear was gone. He didn't like the thought of being fearful to women and children, even Randall's daughter.

But then he thought of his hand and knew he would always be fearful to them. For a few hours he had almost forgotten. He'd almost forgotten the horror on Miss Shea Randall's face when she had seen the brand.

And the hate flooded back.

"What are you doing here, damn you?" Jack Randall asked as he paced the room. He was tall and large but not fat, still handsome in his late forties with a smile that could lure rabbits from the safety of their holes right into his traps. That smile, wide and sincere, had always opened doors for him. And cash boxes. And safes. But he wore no smile now.

Sam McClary casually lifted his legs, setting mud-caked boots on an antique desk. "Tyler's out, you know. I thought he might head here. And I wanted to protect my . . . investment."

Randall knew exactly what kind of investment Mc-Clary meant. Blackmail.

Anger rushed through him, and fear. He'd known that someday Rafe Tyler would come after him. His eyes had promised as much ten years ago. He'd believed that promise then. He believed it today.

McClary gave a gloating smile. It was a particularly ugly expression. "You should have made sure he hanged. You were a damn fool to lose your nerve."

"I didn't lose my nerve," Randall shot back. "I told you I wouldn't let him hang. God, the branding was bad enough. I never thought they would do that."

"That colonel just plain didn't believe he wasn't connected to the Rebs," McClary said. "If he couldn't hang him, he was damn sure determined to get his pound of flesh." He smiled. He had enjoyed the ceremony that day, and he'd relished taking Tyler to prison even more. He'd even volunteered for that duty when no one else had. He'd never liked the bastard with his soft Texas drawl and the easy way he'd had with his men, the way he had reprimanded McClary when McClary had disciplined the troops. Always interfering.

And then there was that pretty Allison whom Sam had always coveted from afar. He'd envied and hated Tyler when the two courted and were betrothed.

He'd planned carefully to frame Tyler, slowly enticing Randall into the scheme. It wasn't difficult. Randall was already up to his neck in the payroll robberies and had little choice. But Randall was weak; he'd never understood the violence that was necessary to get rich, and he'd been guilt-stricken when a number of his troops had been killed in the last robbery. McClary, though, had never let him off the hook, regaling him with word pictures of how it felt to hang, what it was like in prison. They could push the blame on Tyler. The Texas captain was strong. Tyler could take it. Tyler was a Southerner, in any event. A traitor to his own people.

Jack Randall closed his eyes as he remembered Tyler's punishment ten years ago. Hell, he could never forget it. It haunted his nights, as well as his days. He could never forget Tyler's vivid accusing eyes as the man was branded. Randall had known then that he'd finally made a mistake he couldn't rectify or slide away from.

He'd panicked when McClary had told him that Tyler was getting too interested in them, that they would soon be exposed and then both of them might well hang. And to his own eternal damnation, he had listened, had agreed to McClary's plan to frame the young captain.

Randall should have just deserted and taken off, run as he'd always done before when suspicion came too close to him. But McClary had said he could solve their problems, and Randall had actually believed that because of Tyler's heroic military record he would be shown mercy that Randall couldn't expect. He'd justified it all in his own mind, just as he had justified so many things.

He'd even considered confessing after the court-martial, but a lifetime of survival stopped him. He was a coward. He'd always been a coward. Even his acclaimed bravery when a Kansas town was raided by Reb guerrillas was a lie. He had organized everyone else to fight so he wouldn't have to. He hadn't even fired a shot. But he had been elected an officer, and he hadn't been able to refuse it. He'd been delighted when his troop was assigned to a backwater post, assigned to organize supply routes. Perhaps one reason he'd agreed to McClary's scheme was Randall's resentment of Rafe Tyler. The man was everything Randall had wanted to be but wasn't and could never be.

He'd lost Sara, the only really good thing in his life, because he'd always taken the easy path, and that often meant taking money that was not his. With Tyler's conviction Randall had lost the last of any self-respect that remained.

He'd tried to make amends in his own way. He couldn't help Tyler, not without risking his own life, and his guilt wasn't quite that strong, but he vowed never to steal again. After his release from the army, he'd found this fine valley in Colorado and bought land, leaving the army and McClary behind. He'd tried to get Sara back, but she'd read an account of the court-martial and had realized he must have been responsible. She'd asked that he never write again and not to send money. He'd kept doing both, hoping against hope that she would understand he'd changed, but she never responded, and he hadn't had the courage to go see her, to see that sad contempt in her eyes. He had promised so many years earlier when she had left that he'd not follow her; it was one of the few promises he'd ever kept.

He'd tried to help others in this valley, had donated money to the building of a church and school to make up in some way for what he had done, but now he knew his past wouldn't go away.

He thought about the robberies of his own payroll. The first one occurred six weeks ago, and there had been another since then. Now that he knew Rafe Tyler had been released from prison, he realized Tyler wouldn't stop until he'd ruined the man he believed primarily responsible for his conviction. The look that day in Tyler's eyes had promised as much.

And now McClary had appeared again, the third visit in as many years. Each time he'd stayed for at least a month, wandering the mountains. Randall suspected McClary was wanted by the law and used him as a temporary refuge in addition to demanding money.

Randall was already short of cash, having invested so

much in land and cattle, and Tyler had evidently discovered his weakest spot. Now McClary was trying to drain him further. Jack didn't know how to handle either problem.

He looked at McClary. God, Randall disliked the man. But he feared him too. McClary knew too much about him, and Randall couldn't just chuck him off the Circle R as he would like to do. McClary was smirking, actually enjoying the fact that Tyler was apparently here. But then Randall realized only too well the former sergeant had hated the captain.

Randall suspected that was why McClary had chosen this particular time to reappear, that he had kept track of Tyler and had seized this moment to turn the screws on both Randall and Tyler.

"What do you want?"

McClary leaned back. "You say you don't have any money. So I have another suggestion."

Randall eyed him warily. It wouldn't be a suggestion at all, he knew.

"We know it's Tyler taking your payrolls," McClary said. "I think his activities should be expanded to some of the mining claims around here, perhaps a few more stage robberies. Apparently, he's been most selective so far, from what I hear." He gave Randall a wolfish grin. "Very undemocratic of him."

Randall felt as if he would puke out his guts. "I won't help you."

"Yes, you will. You'll find out what I need to know, and I'll stay at the Circle R."

"No! I won't help you frame him again."

"We won't be framing him at all. He's already robbed the stage twice. He's an unrepentant outlaw," McClary said smugly. "And if you don't cooperate, I'll drop a few rumors here and there, maybe even a telegram to Washington. . . ."

"You would be implicating yourself."

"I know how to hide. Do you? Are you really ready to give this up?"

Randall wasn't. He still had hopes of bringing Sara here. He had built this place, and it had been the first time he'd accomplished anything honestly, even if the foundation was built on someone else's back. But once under way, the Circle R had flourished under his management. He'd discovered he was good at ranching, and he relished the respect it brought him. He'd never really felt he was good at anything before, which was one of the reasons he'd stolen. Jack Randall had never thought he could make it on his own, that he was smart enough. He'd simply thought he was good enough to fool people for a short period of time, as his father had before him. His father had been the consummate confidence man, until he'd been caught and killed by an enraged mark. Jack Randall had been fourteen at the time, raised with the philosophy that anyone easily parted from his money had no right to it.

He didn't say a word as he thought of all this, and McClary took his silence as consent.

"It's settled then, old friend," McClary said, emphasizing the last two words as he watched Randall's lips tighten.

"You can stay here," Randall practically bit out. "But I won't participate in any . . . robberies, or blaming them on Tyler."

"Don't you want to see him caught?"

Deep in his bones, Randall didn't. He damn well didn't have the stomach for it. He'd done enough to Rafe Tyler and preferred to outwit him rather than help apprehend him. He would use different routes for his payrolls.

Different precautions. Perhaps Tyler would decide he'd had enough and disappear. It was a weak hope, but it was all Randall had at the moment.

But he wouldn't admit any of that to McClary, who would think him even weaker. He shrugged. "I'm sure he will be."

"But much faster if the miners are also aligned against him," McClary said.

"I wouldn't think you would want him captured too soon."

"Oh, I'll get mine first," McClary said. "I hear some of those miners do real well, and they don't trust banks."

Randall tried not to show his anger, his distaste.

"Ah, well," McClary said. "I'd really rather not share, anyway. All I need is a place to stay. A respectable place. Someone to vouch for me, such as a respectable rancher like yourself."

Randall wanted as little to do with him as possible. "I won't help you." But he was conceding as he always had, and he felt sick inside.

McClary stared at him coldly. "Don't think you can wash your hands, *Mr.* Randall. They're as dirty as mine. I'm just not a hypocrite about it." He started for the door, then turned around. "Any women around here?"

Randall ground his teeth together. "No, I've had to let them go since the last robbery."

"Well, I'll see what I can find in town then. Rushton, isn't it, *Jack*?" McClary said.

"I'm warning you. . . ."

"I'm real scared," McClary said as he sauntered out, leaving Jack Randall clenching his fists in helpless anger.

Chapter 7

It still seemed a miracle to Rafe to see open sky when he woke. He had not yet accustomed himself to it: the softness of dawn, the tranquillity that made him anguished and angry and aching, all at the same time.

So much missed. So much that could never be recovered.

In an effort to throw off the melancholy, he stretched his body slowly, savoring the cool, dry air that was so invigorating. He always slept lightly and woke early. In prison such habits were not a blessing. It was hell to wake to the small cell, to hard brick and iron, to unbelievable heat and stench, or, in winter, pervasive damp cold.

But dawn was glorious now, the air clean and fresh. Rafe sat up, watching the sun as it peaked over the mountains. A cool breeze ruffled his hair and brushed lightly across his skin.

His sitting up startled Abner, who had found a comfortable, dark spot in Rafe's wool shirt, which lay next to him. He had placed it there for that purpose. Abner, he knew, liked familiar scents, familiar warmth.

He imagined the woman, too, wanted something familiar. She was probably scared as hell, though she did a damn good job of disguising it.

He didn't want to think of her, much less in sympathetic terms. Yet he would have to deal with her, would have to feed her, hell, guard her, and that was the most distasteful thought of all. It made him a prisoner, too, unable to wander off as he liked.

Rafe was still trying to accustom himself to the choices of freedom. He'd been told what to do for so long, it seemed to him that part of his thinking processes had closed up. He couldn't decide what to eat, and during the first week on this mountain he seemed to do nothing but sit and contemplate choices, without ever making any.

It was frightening, this indecisiveness that had never been part of him before. The destruction of Randall, of course, was still his primary goal, but nothing else solidified for him, no definite wants. He felt as though he were walking along a beach, the sand washing away under his feet, pulling him into currents too strong to resist.

The woman must feel a little like that now.

His lips firming in a grim line, he stood slowly and scooped Abner up, putting him in his shirt pocket. Maybe he'd go fishing this morning, catch some trout for breakfast. He'd have to close that damn window, again, if he did. He listened; there was no sound coming from inside the cabin. He wondered whether she had slept. It had taken him a number of nights before he'd been able to sleep in captivity. He'd thought it would be different, that he would sleep to escape reality, but it didn't work that way. Perhaps because every time he woke, the nightmare had deepened.

Rafe went over to the window and closed the shutters, dropping the bar. He'd wondered why the previous occupant had placed the bar outside, rather than inside, but apparently whoever had built it had no fear of external enemies. It had been easier to hinge the shutters outside rather than inside, and the barrier had been designed to protect against weather rather than predators.

He knew, though, the shuttering of the window turned the cabin into a cage. A dark and lonely place. Despite that, he wasn't going to take her fishing with him. Not Randall's daughter. Not and break the peace of this morning.

Why in the hell was he giving her any thought at all? She had more than he'd had. Water. Food. Books. Candle. A better bed than his iron prison cot.

He folded his bedroll and took it to the stable. The horse nickered softly in welcome, and Rafe went over to him, running his hand down the horse's neck. "We'll have a good work session today. Sorry about yesterday. A bit of trouble, but nothing we can't handle." He wondered whether he was reassuring the horse or himself.

Rafe checked the water; there was plenty. He fed the horse a handful of oats, then went to a corner of the stable where he kept his makeshift fishing pole. He decided he wouldn't think of *her* again.

Shea slept in fits, each time waking and experiencing a quiet but intense desperation. The man outside haunted her dreams, the darkness in him overwhelming her, smothering her.

Several times she rose and went to the window silently on stocking feet and looked out at him. Even in sleep, he was disturbing. She thought about trying to climb out the window, but she'd have to step down just about where his hand lay. He'd said he was a light sleeper. She didn't think he'd lied.

When she woke up the next time, no light at all streamed through the window, no breeze. She looked up and saw that the window had been closed. She tried opening it and knew she'd been locked in once again.

She told herself not to panic. He'd come back yesterday; he would return this morning. But the closeness of the cabin was stupefying. She found the matches and lit a candle. There were some logs and kindling in the fireplace, and simply for something to do, she started a fire, taking comfort in both its warmth and bright flames.

Shea wouldn't give Rafferty Tyler the pleasure of thinking her afraid.

To keep busy, she heated water in a pot for washing, wondering whether the iron container could be used as a weapon. But it was too big, too heavy, too bulky, for her to swing with any accuracy, and she suspected he was quick.

She hunted for the mouse again but couldn't find it. Loneliness crowded back, and she tried to banish it. She'd always been content with her own company before, with her sketching and her books. But then she'd always felt safe before, had always known there was a mother and friends if she'd felt the need for companionship. Now there was no one. No one but herself. Even the mouse had deserted her. She felt tears gathering in back of her eyes, but she refused to allow them to fall. That would be weakness, surrender.

Why had she been such a fool to accompany Ben Smith?

But regrets didn't help. Shea mentally made a list of things to do. Wash first and brush her hair. Eat. There were crackers. Maybe they would satisfy the gnawing in her stomach. Then a book. Or perhaps she would try to sketch Tyler again. Or even that mouse. Perhaps she could bring it back in that manner at least.

She hated the desperation in that last thought.

She wondered how long the window had been closed. What time was it? Glimmers of light filtered through the cracks in the cabin, but was it morning? Noon? She swallowed, that overpowering hopelessness closing in again.

She wondered whether *he* had felt the same way. She wished she didn't think of him so much, but then she supposed it was natural. She was totally dependent on him at the moment. But there was something else . . . something she hated and didn't understand: a coiling need inside, an inexplicable fascination with something dangerous and unpredictable in a life that, up until two months ago, had been totally predictable.

She had taken the pot from the fire, washed her face, and was brushing her hair when she heard the key in the padlock on the door, a short knock, a pause.

At least her captor proved to be somewhat of a gentleman. She'd thought he would just come in.

There was another knock, and then the door opened, and sunlight suddenly flooded the dark cabin, nearly blinding her and shadowing him.

Her hand stopped in midmotion, frozen for a moment before she let it slide down. She was sitting on the cot, her hair tumbling to her waist.

She felt terribly vulnerable, terribly defenseless.

Her eyes grew accustomed to the light, and while he didn't shrink in size, he didn't seem quite as threatening, especially when she saw two large trout hanging from a string in his hand. Her mouth watered. She didn't want it to, but it did. She wanted to ignore the fish, but her eyes were riveted on them. It had been two days since she'd had a satisfying meal.

"I saw the smoke," he said as if needing an excuse for entering. His stance seemed every bit as stiff as she felt graceless, dressed in wrinkled, dusty clothes. He looked as striking as ever, like a desperado with bristles covering his jaw. His sun-streaked hair was mussed as if fingers had combed it, and his shirt was open at the neck despite the cool mountain temperature.

But then the temperature in the cabin seemed to rise suddenly as bolts of awareness ran between them. She watched his jaw set and knew he felt it too. The silence was awkward, pregnant with unexpected but compelling attraction, made even stronger by the fact that she knew how forbidden, how foolish, how impossible, it was.

He hated her. He hated her father. He was holding her against her will. He was the opposite of everything she held dear, everything she valued. Honesty. Honor. Loyalty.

She hated him for making her feel unwanted things, for stirring a part of her that no one ever had before. Her hand made one more sweep with the brush down her hair as she forced her gaze away from him, the action dismissing him with a contempt she didn't believe words could.

But he only looked amused at that bravado, apparently seeing it for the fraud it was. "Interesting, Miss Randall," he said. "I thought for a moment you might have inherited some honesty from someone other than your father. I see you didn't."

She glared at him. "I don't know what you mean."

"Don't you, Shea Randall?" His eyes were cold. Calculating. Deliberately baiting her. Distancing. She suddenly realized that he didn't like that odd attraction any more than she had. He was trying to provoke her again, to turn the sparks of awareness between man and woman into anger between captor and captive.

It was working.

"No," she said curtly.

He approached her. She noticed his right hand, the one holding the trout, was gloved again. He saw the direction of her gaze, and a grim, bitter expression appeared on his face.

"You're a liar," he said. "Are you denying you feel something other than the fear that you should feel?" The hoarseness seemed to be disappearing from his voice, replaced by a kind of low, taunting assurance.

Shea was struck speechless that he had put into words something she had been trying to deny. She didn't know how to defend herself. She *had* wordlessly denied those moments of awareness. She refused to think of it as attraction, as sensual. She chose to attack instead. "That's the second time you've accused me of lying. Judging me by your standards?"

His eyes seemed to bore into her. "Let's just say I've had a lot of experience with Randalls who lie."

Everything went back to the man she believed to be her father. She stiffened her back. "Do you always blame others for what you've done to yourself?"

"You're changing the subject. You're denying that moment of, shall we say, interest." He was relentless in forcing her to expose herself, in making her humiliate herself.

"The same interest I'd have in a rattler," she retorted.

"Rattlers have some fascinating qualities, Miss Randall."

"All repulsive."

He raised an eyebrow. "And dangerous. Remember that."

He turned around, as if weary of the conversation. "I'm going to clean the fish," he said. "You can go out if you wish." Without waiting for an answer, he left the cabin.

Shea wasn't sure which she disliked more. His attention, or indifference, as if she weren't worth a moment of thought. But she craved the outside now, the feel of sunlight, and she also had to take care of personal needs.

She quickly braided her hair and tied the end with the blue ribbon in her valise. She hoped he wouldn't think she was adorning herself for his benefit. Her hair was very fine, and without being bound, it would fly in a million different directions.

Shea looked longingly at a clean dress but decided against it. She felt safer in the shirt and britches. And if there were a chance to escape . . .

After the exchange today, she felt the need more than ever.

Rafe sat on the stump, took his knife from the sheath on his belt, and gutted the fish, trying to keep unwanted thoughts at bay.

He'd made a mistake, and he knew it. He shouldn't get into conversations with his prisoner, and he especially shouldn't acknowledge that odd electricity between them. He didn't understand why he bothered to duel with her. He should just ignore her, pretend she didn't exist.

But for a few moments after he'd entered the cabin and watched her brush her hair, he hadn't felt quite so alone, quite so empty. Her hair, caught in the joint light of candle and sun, had rippled with gold and fell in silky waves across her shoulders and down her back. She had looked very fetching. And he'd found himself aching in places he thought immune to tender feelings.

And so he had baited her.

Dammit.

He reminded himself that his quarrel was with Jack Randall, not a woman who accidentally wandered into the middle of his private war. He would have to make some allowances. *If* she would cooperate. He just didn't know how far he could trust her.

Rafe finished cleaning the fish and was threading them through the spit he'd taken from the stable when she came out.

He stood. "I'll make a bargain with you, Miss Randall."

She looked at him with suspicion.

"I'll give you five minutes of privacy, no more, and hope you have enough sense to know these mountains are far more dangerous than I am."

It wasn't a question. It wasn't even a bargain that she could see. Not until she knew what was expected in return.

"You said a bargain?"

"Your word you won't be foolish enough to try to escape."

"You said you wouldn't believe me if my oath was wrapped in angels' wings," she reminded him, not knowing exactly why. She should accept. She should give her promise and then ignore it. A promise to a criminal was no promise at all.

But it was. To her. *How did he know that?*

"It's really quite simple," he said. "If you are that foolish, I won't have to worry about you at all. You will never survive these mountains." His words quickly dispelled any notions that he had softened in some way.

"Then why worry about me escaping at all?"

"It would inconvenience me, Miss Randall. I would feel duty-bound to save you from your own foolishness. I might, or might not, succeed, and I don't like failure." He regarded her thoughtfully. "Are you foolish, Miss Randall?"

He'd spoken so chillingly, it was clear he didn't care

about her, only failure. There were several warnings there, she knew.

Why was she even arguing with him? Why didn't she take his offer and escape?

"I don't think so," she said finally, "but why did you change your mind?"

"Why would I trust you for five minutes?" He shrugged. "It's not very long, and I suspect you might be hungry," he said. "Call it a little test. If you pass, I might give you more freedom." He was holding out two prizes: food and a better chance later to escape.

Five minutes. Long enough to get a head start. Long enough to get lost. Long enough perhaps to get away from this disturbing man who sent so many conflicting emotions slithering through her, who even now made her breathless, who made her want to reach out and touch. She ached to do that, to see what she would find under that harsh exterior.

She stepped back in reaction to that last ungodly urge.

He tipped his head slightly, those sea-colored eyes regarding her steadily, as if trying to steal her thoughts. She'd thought his eyes empty when she first saw him, but now she knew that wasn't true. They weren't empty at all but ruthlessly controlled.

"Well?"

She nodded reluctantly, hating her own surrender, but necessity was now upon her.

"Your word? Say it." He was insistent, demanding even more surrender. She knew then how well he was controlling her. If she did try to escape, he would never accept her word again; if she didn't, he would take it as total compliance.

"Go to hell," she said suddenly, surprising even herself. She hadn't thought she would ever say that to anyone. But she was furious. Furious because a part of her had started to expect more of him. Furious because of the way he made her feel, and the way her body betrayed her. Furious because he used and twisted every private feeling to his own advantage.

"Such language," he drawled. "I thought young ladies from Boston were raised to be more demure."

"They never met you," she retorted bitterly.

His lips crooked in a half-smile, then he shrugged. "Five minutes," he said in a bored voice. "No promises required. But be assured, if you try anything, you will spend every successive moment in the cabin. If you live that long."

Just then a mouse popped its head out of Rafferty Tyler's pocket, looked around curiously, and then ran up to perch on his shoulder.

It was *her* mouse.

Shea recognized it by size, by its inquisitive and unafraid nature. She watched in astonishment as her captor, her heartless, ruthless captor, very gently took it in his right hand and stroked its back with the bare fingers of his left hand.

Tyler looked up at her. "Abner," he explained.

She stepped closer to him, watching as the mouse snuggled into his glove. She swallowed. "We've met."

It was his turn to look surprised. "He doesn't mean to frighten anyone."

"He didn't frighten me."

"Does anything really frighten you, Miss Randall?"

"You do."

"Do I?"

Before she could answer, he spoke again. "I *should* frighten you, Miss Randall. Don't let Abner mislead you. I found him in prison. In prison you take anything you can find. Even a mouse."

That didn't explain the gentleness of his hands, the tameness of the mouse. That took a great deal of patience, a special ability. Animals, she'd always observed, were rather selective in whom they liked. They simply didn't take to just anyone, particularly timid creatures like mice.

But Rafferty Tyler? And a mouse?

"I give animals more leeway than . . . troublesome women."

Shea couldn't stop herself from challenging him. "Me in particular, or all women?"

"Women are all the same, Miss Randall."

"In what way?"

A muscle flexed in his cheek. "Do you really want to know?"

She didn't, but she heard herself saying, "Yes."

He tucked the mouse in the wool shirt that lay on the ground and moved toward her, a scowl on his face. When he reached her, he leaned down, and Shea suddenly realized his intention and her mistake.

She tried to move, but his hand captured her arm and held her. "You know what they say about curiosity?" he asked.

His head lowered, and his lips captured hers, hard and demanding. Shea tried to twist away, but she couldn't and, worse, she found herself responding. The part of her that had responded to him since the first time she saw him was betraying her, humiliating her as he meant to humiliate her.

She found her lips meeting his, found her body moving toward his. She felt the heat that always came from him, and it penetrated her, binding them in ways entirely new to her.

Shea had been kissed before, light, fanciful kisses but nothing like this, nothing that burned, dominated yet pleasured. Her lips softened for his, and she felt his gentle for a second and then harden again, as if he regretted the momentary lapse.

But it didn't matter. Nothing mattered except the feelings fomenting in her body, as if she was finally experiencing the true essence of being a woman. It was wonderful, and it was terrible.

His arms went around her, and she felt his arousal, and that ignited more explosions. His kiss deepened, his tongue invading her mouth. She should protest, should struggle, but she no longer had a will of her own. Her legs were weak, her stomach in turmoil, her heart pounding. It was as if something, or someone, else had taken over her body.

Dear God, what was she doing? He was trying to punish her, and she, she . . .

Shea wrenched away and turned from him, not wanting to see him, not wanting to watch victory spread over his face.

She felt him behind her, felt the whisper of his breath on the back of her neck. She heard his low, hoarse words. "I'm . . . sorry. I said I wouldn't . . . hurt you if you behaved. That . . . shouldn't have happened. It won't again."

Shea sensed pain in his voice and turned to face him. "Give up your vendetta against my . . . father."

"No." Harshness was back in his voice, as were the grim lines in his face. "Don't take my apology for anything more than it is, an apology for one moment that shouldn't have happened. It changes nothing."

"Why?"

"That's something else you don't want to know," he said. "Remember the response to your last question."

"But you said it wouldn't happen again."

"Perhaps not that, but I wouldn't mind locking those

questions away in the cabin." His voice was hard now. "Don't test me any further, Miss Randall."

She swallowed, needing to get away from the intensity of his presence, of her own reactions. "Five minutes?" she asked, referring to his offer from what seemed hours ago.

He looked at her thoughtfully, and for a moment she wondered whether he had changed his mind.

He had. "I think I want your promise, after all," he said. Her feelings must have been obvious again. All she wanted to do now was run and run and run. Because of that kiss. Because of the confusion he stirred in her.

And she would do anything, promise anything at the moment, to do that. "Just this one time?"

His mouth quirked again, and she knew he found her battle between expediency and honor amusing.

"All right," she said ungraciously. "And when I get back?"

"You will stay with me, or locked in the cabin."

She wanted to say she would prefer the cabin, but she didn't. Who could prefer darkness to light? Candles to the sun?

Except she wasn't sure whether the darkness inside wasn't preferable to the Devil in the sunlight.

Chapter 8

Rafe put the trout on the spit and placed them over the fire in the cabin and went back out. He had given Shea Randall five minutes. How many had gone by? Four minutes. Perhaps five. He didn't see her.

He wondered whether he had been a fool. Prison must have affected him more than he'd imagined. Otherwise, why in the hell was he attracted to the daughter of Jack Randall?

But he was. He couldn't deny the way he had responded to her.

He could have controlled it, had it been only physical, but when he was kissing her, other feelings had almost swallowed him. He'd wanted to calm her fears, wanted to run his fingers along her face. He had needed gentleness. He had needed to give it, and receive it. He hadn't known how much he hungered for that rare commodity until that moment.

He'd meant what he said about feeling a certain responsibility to keep her safe. He'd been here nearly three months, and he respected these mountains; he knew they were treacherous.

Six minutes now? Seven?

Cursing under his breath, he headed toward the woods.

Shea hesitated. She'd finished what needed to be done. Now she had a decision to make.

Go back or hide in the woods. The decision should have been easy. Pure terror of captivity—or was it of her reactions to a man she should hate—dictated that she try to escape.

She had given her word, though. But then hadn't he violated his when he'd kissed her? A kiss she'd liked too much. He'd said he wouldn't touch her, wouldn't harm her. And he had . . . in the most humiliating way, in provoking a response.

She didn't have any time to consider such things. She had to make a decision now, if she were to have any hope at all. Hope of what? Getting lost in these mountains?

Shea remembered what he'd said about traps. About animals. Snakes. A lie? She had no weapons, no food, and she was already hungry. She thought of the trout cooking over the fire.

But then she thought of him, of the magnetism that attracted her in ways that were so confusing, so destructive to her. Could anything be more dangerous to her than Rafferty Tyler?

She looked back in the direction she had come from. She could see the cabin through the aspens and pines. Should she wait for another chance? A better one if she could somehow get the horse?

Shea still felt the heat radiating from him, the way she had melted for those few moments in his arms, the tenderness he'd showed the mouse with the absurd name of Abner.

He was using her. He was using her to get to the only family she had left. And he was doing it in the most insidious way.

She darted into the underbrush, just as a squirrel started chattering, and she heard the sound of something moving. The wind? A pursuer? Had it been five minutes?

Shea knew it would be a mistake to run. He would hear her and rapidly overtake her. Or she could step out quite innocently.

She did neither. She saw a log and lay next to it, trying to make herself as small as possible. Berry bushes and brambles provided some cover. If he went on, perhaps then she could circle him, go back to the clearing and get the horse. Perhaps he hadn't locked the stable.

Apprehension ate at her. She tried to stay still as she listened for every little sound. But now the forest was quiet. Very quiet.

She waited for what seemed hours and then lifted her head slightly and carefully gazed from tree to tree. Nothing. He was gone.

Shea rose as silently as possible. The squirrel was chattering again. A bird flew from a tree to the ground, apparently in search of something edible. Everything seemed so peaceful. She looked at the mountain peaks and wondered whether they were as unforgiving as he'd said.

She wasn't a fool. She knew she could get easily lost in this land of gulches and canyons and mountain ledges. She knew there were wild animals. But that kiss, the violent, tender kiss, and the way she responded to it, seemed the greater danger at the moment.

Shea waited a few more minutes. No noise other than that expected of a forest. The distinctive sound of woodpeckers, the sweeter one of humming birds. Ordinarily, she would have been enchanted, but now . . .

She started moving, trying to slip quietly through the clump of trees and brambles. Rocks scattered under her feet, each sound louder than the last, and she thought she heard the pounding of her heart. Could he hear it too?

Which way? Right or left? She stopped, trying to orient herself. Everything looked alike—the trees, the jutting red rocks.

Think, she told herself. Don't panic. But she felt like panicking.

She couldn't be far from the cabin. She could venture a certain number of steps in each direction, watching for an opening in the pines.

And where was *he*? She froze again, listening for something that would give a clue as to his whereabouts. There was nothing, and she felt infinitely alone.

She selected a direction and started moving again. She didn't recognize the outcropping of rocks, the slender aspens and pines. She retreated, wishing she had a knife to mark them, but then she would be marking them for Rafferty Tyler too. She turned in the opposite direction, and remembering her captor's warning about snakes and traps, kept her eyes to the ground.

She retreated to her starting point, then turned in another direction. She wondered whether she was hopelessly lost. Part of her wanted Tyler to find her. She fought down rising fear, and then she saw the cabin through the trees, and she moved cautiously toward it.

Rafe had seen her soon enough, just a couple of minutes after he'd gone after her. He smothered his sense of relief, buried that glimmer of apprehension for her.

The blue ribbon had given her away. Her light

brown hair had blended in with the fallen log, but the spot of bright color hadn't. He'd almost gone over there, and then he'd hesitated. He wanted to know what she was going to do, what kind of skills she had, what reasoning she would use, what he could expect. Know thy enemy, he'd told himself.

He was surprised that he felt a sense of betrayal. She had given her word, even if he had coerced it from her. But then what did he expect of a Randall?

She owes you nothing.

Part of him knew that. Yet another part was undeniably disappointed. *What did you expect?* He damn well didn't know as he watched her go deeper into the woods.

Before the war he had served on the frontier. He'd also been raised in one of the most dangerous parts of Texas, the northwest where Comanches roamed almost at will. He knew tracking, and he knew how to move silently.

Old skills had returned during these quiet months in the mountain. It wasn't difficult to keep her in sight without her knowledge, and he felt a surge of admiration as she moved forward, then retreated without panicking as most women would. Most men too.

He realized she was trying to find the clearing. Why, when she had hidden from him?

The answer came quickly enough as he put himself into her shoes. She probably thought he had gone in search of her. She was going back after the horse.

He'd made sure the stable was locked before he left, and his right hand now fingered the key in his pocket. He debated about catching up with her now, or letting her run her tether. He decided on the latter; he wanted to know exactly how much ingenuity she had.

She reached the clearing, looked cautiously around, and then made for the stable, her hands trying the door.

She then searched the ground, found a rock, and turned back to the padlock on the door.

He stepped out and moved soundlessly to where she stood and took the key from his pocket. "Looking for this?"

She whirled around, eyes wide and startled, like a trapped doe.

"I thought . . ."

"Yes?" His voice was dry and cool. "You thought . . . ?"

She hung on to the rock, her hand tightening around it. She didn't answer.

"You thought you would break your word?" he nudged gently.

She stiffened, and her jaw set rebelliously. "I got lost."

"Not too lost," he said.

"How do you know?" Then she realized she had never lost him at all. "You were there all the time?"

He shrugged. "I warned you."

"You let me think . . ." Anger shaded the words.

"I wanted to see what you would do."

"And now that you've seen?"

"I know you're your father's daughter."

Her chin went up. "I take that as a compliment."

"Don't, Miss Randall. Treachery is not admirable."

"Neither is kidnapping."

He ignored the words and held out his hand. "The rock."

She clung to it.

"I'm not going to ask again."

"You weren't asking," she said stubbornly. She knew she sounded like a petulant child, but she didn't want to give up without a fight, no matter how feeble. "You were ordering."

He had to hold back a smile. "Don't try my patience, Miss Randall."

"And if I do?"

He held out his left hand and moved it down her arm in a sensuous, suggestive way that had nothing of the momentary gentleness of his earlier touch. It was meant as a threat, plain and simple, but he hadn't expected the shudder that ran through his own body, a need so strong he was almost consumed by it. His voice was hoarse as he spoke. "I've been in prison ten years, Miss Randall. I don't know whether you realize what that means to a man." She blinked, and her face drained of color. "I see that you do."

Her face suddenly flamed with color, and she tried to turn away from him, but his hand stopped her. "Look at me."

Shea did. She had no choice. His brilliant eyes were mesmerizing in their intensity, and she wanted to believe that anger sparked that intensity. She was too afraid to consider the cause might be something else. Her hand clenched the rock even tighter.

With his gloved hand, he gently pried the rock loose from her fist. The feel of leather against her skin was pleasant, and apprehension drained from her. Still, she didn't know what to expect from him, what he might do next.

As always, he surprised her. "It would have taken you a very long time to break that lock." He paused. "Are you a good rider, Miss Randall?"

She wasn't, but she wasn't going to admit that to him. She was grateful, however, to leave the previous conversation, the threat in the air between them.

"I wouldn't like it if my horse broke a leg because of you."

"And if *I* broke a leg?"

He sighed. "At least you would stay put then, but I stopped being lucky a long time ago."

His indifference to her possible injury irritated her immensely. He cared about the horse being hurt, but not her. "I'll try to escape again," she said in one last spurt of defiance.

"And I'll stop you again."

Their gazes met and locked. Shea felt a sizzling heat start inside and spread. Her fingers still tingled with his touch. She balled them into fists. She didn't want to respond to him this way.

He broke the contact first. "We did accomplish something," he said in cool words that quenched the heat quicker than any water could. "I know exactly how far I can trust you. And your word."

It was calculated cruelty. She should be getting used to it, and yet it still hurt her. Perhaps it wouldn't have, if she had not fought her own conscience on the matter. She hated the aching regret the words created in her; even more she hated feeling like a chastened child.

She struck back. "*You* said you wouldn't touch me."

He smiled slightly, but it wasn't pleasant. "Ah . . . the kiss. I didn't get the feeling that I hurt you, Miss Randall. For a moment you seemed to even enjoy it. But maybe your objection wasn't over the kiss at all. Maybe it was me. Am I . . . unworthy of your high standards? An ex-convict too base to touch you?"

"That's exactly it," Shea countered, furious at his mockery. "I don't owe you anything. You're a thief and a kidnapper and a . . ."

"Don't stop there," he said smoothly, but something in his eyes warned her. They had darkened, and she felt she was about to plunge headlong into something far beyond her ability to control. She swallowed. He was so still, so watchful. She sensed from him that quiet, desperate pain again, that anguish stored up inside him.

His expression suddenly changed, as if he'd seen something in her eyes, something he wanted to banish. The faint smile disappeared, and his lips firmed in a grim line. "You must be hungry," he said abruptly. "All that stalking around."

"I didn't stalk," she said indignantly. But she was hungry. And the frightening thing was, she felt hunger for something other than food.

He took her chin between two fingers. "I wanted to see what you would do, Miss Randall. You kept your head, but you underestimated me, and you overestimated yourself. I wasn't lying when I tried to explain how dangerous these mountains can be. A mountain lion could have easily heard or smelled you."

She remembered that moment of loneliness, that almost overwhelming fear she had fought down. She wondered whether she would ever completely feel safe again. She didn't want to go back in the woods alone, but neither would she feel safe here. With him. With those eyes that were cold and hot at the same time, aloof and needy. Threatening and understanding. She didn't know what to expect of him. Nor of herself. Everything that was happening was so foreign to what she knew.

His fingers lingered on her chin, but then, as if regretful to do so, he moved away. "The trout is in the cabin on the spit. Eat what you like."

She hesitated. "What about you?"

"I thought you didn't care for the company of a thief and kidnapper," he said, sneering, "and . . . whatever else you think I am."

"Don't forget convict," she said. She was angry with herself for that moment of consideration for him.

"Oh, I don't forget that, Miss Randall. I never forget

that." He headed for the stable but turned back suddenly to see her still standing there, as if rooted to the ground. "And you'll stay in the cabin until I say otherwise."

She walked away without saying another word, her back stiff with resentment and defiance. He wished he didn't feel a sense of loss as she disappeared inside the cabin.

Chapter 9

Rafe tried to stay away from his prisoner the rest of the day, leaving the trout for her to eat alone. He'd lost whatever hunger he had after that acrimonious conversation, and he knew he couldn't eat. But she needed to.

He consciously shoved thoughts of her from his mind as he worked with the bay. Finally, in late afternoon, guilt overwhelmed him. As he'd told her to do, she'd been staying in the cabin—much to his surprise. He had expected her to defy him. The fact that she didn't worried him. He finally knocked on the door.

The trout was gone. Both of them. Her appetite apparently hadn't been affected as much as his. He allowed her outside, although he warned her to keep at least part of herself in sight as she saw to her needs. She did, her back so stiff, he thought it might break if he touched her.

And then, without asking, she went inside the cabin, retrieved her drawing materials, and came back out, seating herself on the tree stump with a look that dared him to object.

He didn't. He ignored her as much as possible, continuing to work with the bay.

He kept all his attention on the horse, teaching it to obey voice as well as touch commands. Training a horse was a matter of patience and concentration, and God knew he needed concentration to keep his mind from the disturbing woman.

The sketch of Ben had been damned good. So good that it could condemn him. Rafe suspected she was now sketching him, with those quick, darting looks at him and then rapt attention to the pad she was holding. He should take it away, but it really made no difference. She would undoubtedly be able to draw him from memory.

And he really didn't care much what happened to him beyond this one quest to even the score. He would merely exist until he died. With the brand on his hand, he had no prospects other than death. No dreams, no hopes, and he wasn't fool enough to allow himself to even consider them.

He *did* care, however, about what happened to the men who rode with him. He'd already burned the drawing of Ben in the fireplace. But he had little doubt she could re-create it, as well as produce a drawing of Clint.

Which made things very complicated indeed.

He would have to let her go eventually, but only after Ben and Clint left the territory. His stomach heaved. In his quest for vengeance he had accepted help. Now he fully realized the price the others might pay. He had always thought they could remain . . . remote, unknown, but they were not remote any longer.

Because of a brown-haired girl with eyes that seemed to look right into him, and wince at what they saw. Dammit all to hell.

He focused his attention back on the horse, moving back and calling softly, gratified when the horse moved with him. There had been times in his life when such a trick had been very, very important to his continued existence. He took out a dried apple and fed it to the animal, his hand running gently down its neck.

They had become friends, he and the horse, on the trip West. That relationship and the one with Abner were the only ties with which he'd felt any ease since his court-martial.

He certainly didn't feel any ease with the prickly lady sitting on the tree stump. Nor should he.

The thought made him feel even more alone than he had in prison. There was something about being physically close to someone but millions of miles distant in other ways that was disconcerting.

He glanced her way again. She was still dressed in the trousers and shirt, her hair braided once more. The long braid had fallen over her shoulder and lay alongside her right breast. Her head was bent over the pad, her hands moving gracefully but with purpose.

She was . . . attractive with the sun sparking streaks of gold in her hair, her face so intent. He'd never known a woman like her before, one apparently content with herself, able to occupy herself. She was so completely different from Allison, who had always been the center of attention, who constantly flirted and was unhappy unless she was surrounded by a crowd of people. He'd mistaken her vivacity, her demand for all his attention, for love. He hadn't realized how shallow her feelings were, that she was more enamored of his uniform than of the man inside.

The horse nuzzled him for another apple, and Rafe longed to mount him. He didn't need a saddle, not since he was little more than a tadpole when he'd climbed from a fence onto the back of a horse. But he couldn't ride these mountains as he had the past few weeks. He couldn't leave *her*.

But damn, he was restless. He hobbled the horse, so

it could graze on the rich mountain grass, and made his way over to the woman. He looked down at the pad and saw a version of himself glaring back at him.

Rafe wondered if he really looked that way, that . . . soulless. Perhaps he did. Perhaps he was.

"Are you going to destroy that one too?" she asked.

He shrugged. "It's not very complimentary."

"Did you expect it to be?"

"You obviously don't believe in currying favor."

"It wouldn't do any good, would it?"

He smiled grimly. "An intelligent woman."

"When are you going to let me go?"

"When I'm ready."

"And when might that be?"

"I don't know."

"You can't keep me here forever."

"I can damn well keep you as long as I want."

She shot a cannonball of a glance at him. "I need some privacy."

"We've been through that conversation. You proved you can't be trusted. I go where you go."

"You surely didn't think I wouldn't try to escape?"

He arched an eyebrow. "I really didn't know. I've discovered I know damn little about women."

There was the same deep bitterness that had been in his voice when he'd said he expected little of women. She hated herself for wondering why. For wanting again to reach out and touch him, to erase a little of that hopelessness she sensed in him, that oddly endearing hesitancy when he spoke as if debating every word, as if he weren't quite as certain of himself and his ruthlessness as he wanted her to believe.

She wanted to believe that, anyway. She had to. That was her only chance to get away from him, to find Jack

Randall, to warn him about the man who intended to destroy him.

"You didn't answer my question," she finally said.

"Which one?"

"My drawing. Are you going to steal it too?"

"I told you before, Miss Randall, I don't give a damn about that. Just don't draw my men."

"You don't care if you get caught?"

"Do you always ask so many questions?"

"Yes."

"So I'm not the only one who suffers?" Dammit, he wasn't going to start this again. He'd decided to stay away from her, but something kept drawing him back. He didn't want to think it was loneliness. Or attraction. He didn't know what in hell it was. Perhaps the challenge she posed. Perhaps because he couldn't quite connect this feisty, independent woman with Jack Randall.

The thought of Randall cleared his head. He turned and started for the horse.

"Ah . . ." Her voice stopped him.

He turned. "Remember," he said, "Mr. Tyler or sir." Christ, he needed that distance when he looked into her blue-gray eyes.

He could almost see her count to ten as she deliberated whether to ask something of him. And then she turned around, her back to him, as she obviously decided against it.

Rafe disliked himself at that moment, disliked the humiliation she must feel over having to ask anything of him. He knew about systematic humiliation: how much it hurt, how it crushed the spirit if not the soul.

He moved over to her. "Rafe," he said. "You might as well call me Rafe if the others are too hard to stomach." He hesitated. "What did you want?"

She turned, and those solemn eyes examined him

slowly, as if to see whether he was just tormenting her. His opinion of himself plummeted even further. "I . . . I would just like some exercise. A walk, or . . . something."

The "something" interested him, but he knew that what the word brought to his mind was the last thing on hers. "All right," he said mildly, although he felt anything but mild. He didn't want to spend more time with her, and yet neither could he lock her back in the cabin. His conscience was warring with that deep burning need for redemption that had consumed him for so many years, and he wasn't comfortable with the battle. Christ, he hadn't even thought he had a conscience any longer. The realization that it was there, lurking around in a dark place, was not comforting. He did not want to deal with it now.

And he suspected her of ulterior motives. Most likely she would be very observant during the walk, hoping to find a way out of the valley and mountains. He didn't want her to try it on her own again. Still, her request was small enough, reasonable enough.

"Stay with me," he ordered.

She did. A little to the left, a little to his back so she didn't have to walk with him, he noticed. Which suited him just fine. She still had the pad under her arm and was clutching it as if her life depended on it.

He walked quickly, needing the exercise, too, the quiet of the woods. He didn't need her, and all the turmoil she created in him. So he pretended she didn't exist except for an occasional glance to make sure she stayed with him.

He followed no trail. He knew the valley by now; he had prowled it enough. There was a waterfall, protected by heavy growth, about a mile from the cabin, and that was his destination. He had discovered it by accident one day when he'd been especially restless and found it a fine place to drink from the pool and sun on a rock. He bathed there now and then; sometimes he just sat for hours, watching animals come and drink or frolic along the water's edge. They had become used to him, tolerant of his nonthreatening presence. It was a rare kind of acceptance, one he valued and told no one about.

He didn't even try to fathom why he was taking her there—except he knew instinctively that it would give her pleasure. After everything she'd been through in the past two days, he inexplicably wanted to give her that.

They finally came to the pool, surrounded by wild raspberry bushes and tall pines on one side, rich red rock on the other. He stepped back behind her, letting her take in the water as it tumbled from multicolored rocks high above. He felt the slightest satisfaction at her exclamation, and then she turned around, a real smile on her lips, and it was enchanting. She was suddenly beautiful.

He forced himself to lean against a tree, to keep his face expressionless, his eyes indifferent and cold.

"It's lovely," she said with pleasure, her eyes drinking in the spray from the waterfall, the deep blue pool that reflected flashes of late-afternoon sunlight filtering through the foliage.

After placing her sketchpad on dry ground, Shea stooped down and scooped up a handful of water, bringing it to her mouth and splashing a little on her face. A bird trilled a song, and another answered; there was a stirring in the woods to her left, and Shea looked up suddenly.

"We've disturbed their world," Tyler explained as she looked toward him. "If you come here at dawn, you can see deer drinking from the pool. I've seen a mountain lion, wolves, bears. They seem to have a truce here."

"And you sit and watch?"

"Sometimes."

The peaceful scene should have clashed with him, Shea thought, with that violence that hovered around him, with the chill that made those startling eyes forbidding, but it didn't, and she didn't understand why. He meshed into it as if he had been born to it, as if he himself was one of the wild creatures he'd just described. She thought of the way he had touched the mouse and had so patiently worked with the horse earlier today. There was an inherent gentleness in him for creatures other than human—none, it seemed, for her kind.

It was a contradiction that fascinated her.

"Thank you for bringing me here," she said suddenly, surprising even herself.

"I thought you could wash up," he said roughly, and turned away from her, walking into the woods.

But she could have done that in the stream not far from the cabin.

She knew he wasn't going far away. What she didn't know was whether he'd retreated out of respect for her privacy or because he didn't want to be in her presence. In any case she decided to take advantage of his withdrawal. She took off her boots and her stockings and dangled her feet in the pool. The water was freezing but as clear as glass. Though drops of spray from the fall struck her with stinging regularity, she enjoyed the refreshing coldness of the water, which quickly dried in the hot sun.

She didn't know how long she would be allowed to stay, so she rinsed her face, arms, and legs and found a rock where she could sit and dry in the sun. She quickly sketched the waterfall, wishing she had something more colorful than the dark charcoal stick. When she was finished, she used a corner to sketch Rafferty Tyler again.

Rafe, he had told her to call him. But she couldn't. It was too . . . familiar. Still, as her hands moved across the pad, she saw differences from the man she'd drawn earlier, the one with cold, angry eyes and cynical set of his mouth. This Rafferty Tyler had a slightly softer cast, a more whimsical twist to his mouth.

She stared at the sketch for a moment, then tore it out and crushed it into a ball. Her first version was the truth. She wouldn't be fooled into believing anything else. She closed her eyes, absorbing the soft rays of the sun, and waited for him to return. Exhausted from a restless night, she soon felt drowsy, and she allowed sleep to come.

She looked so vulnerable. And pretty. Very pretty.

Rafe had emerged from the woods, where he'd checked for traps. He hated the goddamn things. He'd found one and snapped it shut. The sound of the steel jaws being rendered useless gave him some badly needed satisfaction.

And then he returned, reluctantly. He'd just spent an hour or more telling himself his reaction to Shea Randall —the heat in his loins, the gentling of a nature that could not afford to gentle at this particular time—was nothing more than the result of ten years of abstinence.

Unfortunately, the sight of her sleeping, resting against his favorite rock, did nothing to decrease the need building in him. What in the hell was he doing, anyway? Why didn't he just keep her locked in the cabin?

But he knew the reason. As far as he could tell, she was an innocent. A guiltless party. And he couldn't do to her what had been done to him.

Goddammit.

He leaned against a tree and just watched her. Her hair was wet, and the tiniest patch of dirt contrasted with the rosy glow of sun-tinged cheeks. She was sleeping deeply as if she hadn't had any rest in days. And she probably hadn't.

He wanted to touch her. He wanted to run his finger along her cheek, and his mouth along the back of her neck. He wanted to see another smile, like the one he'd seen earlier when they'd arrived at the falls.

Randall's daughter, for God's sake! Unless there was some mistake, he thought with a faint glimmer of hope. Even she didn't seem entirely sure, and apparently she'd never met the man she believed to be her father.

A pillar of the community was Jack Randall now. A pillar built on betrayal and theft, but she didn't know that.

Even without those complications, he had no business thinking of her as a woman. He certainly had no future. He'd be a fugitive the rest of his life, a marked man easily identified by the brand on his hand; the others could blend into normal lives. He never could.

He wondered whether Randall knew who was causing him problems. Rafe was not ready to reveal himself, for then Randall might turn more cautious.

Another reason he couldn't let the woman go. Yet.

He lowered himself to the ground. He would let her sleep.

Shea opened her eyes and shivered slightly. A cool breeze had replaced the warmth of the sun, only a portion of which still remained above the western peaks. Pines were swaying slightly above her. The sky directly overhead was still vivid blue, but at the crest of the mountains it was streaked with crimson and violet. Wispy clouds now took on robes of scarlet. For a moment she was enraptured with the peace of it. And then her gaze shifted to Rafe Tyler, and she remembered everything.

He was sitting cross-legged, like an Indian, and he

was as still as one. But his glance went quickly to her, as though he sensed immediately when she'd awakened.

He put a gloved finger to his lips and rose sound-lessly, making his way over to her and offering his hand. She hesitated, and his eyes narrowed. He shook his head in warning, and she knew he was telling her to obey and be silent. Reluctantly, she reached out and took the hand, realizing as she did so that much of her reluctance re-sulted from the tingling that ran throughout her body whenever he was close.

Even through that leather glove, his hand seemed to burn her as he helped her off the rock, led her along the pool, and up an embankment to another group of rocks. He stopped and motioned for her to lie flat on the ground, then took a similar position beside her. She followed his gaze toward the pool and waited. She knew there was a reason for this, just as there seemed to be a reason for everything he did. She didn't know how long they waited. The birds continued to warble, a squirrel chased another, leaping across trees. And then she saw them: a black bear approaching the pool, followed by a frolicking cub.

The bear seemed hesitant, standing up on two back legs and sniffing the air cautiously; it waited a moment, then grunted and waded into the pool, staring intently into the water. Shea watched as the bear, one moment so still, suddenly jerked its paw with a speed Shea could barely comprehend, and a fish came flying out of the wa-ter, landing directly in front of the cub, which proceeded to play with it before gobbling it up. Three more fish emerged from the pool in the same quick sequence of motions, the big bear keeping the last two for its own dinner.

Both bear and cub then drank from the pool, rolled contentedly in the dirt, and lazily sauntered off.

Rafe waited for several minutes, then sat, a slight

smile on his lips. He was very attractive that way, Shea observed, much more so than when he wore his usual sneer.

Shea wondered if she was as wide-eyed as she felt. "Didn't they know we were here?"

"I come here often. They're used to my scent," he explained. "I've watched them several other times, sometimes even closer." He was quiet for a moment, then added, "I think they know when someone wishes them no harm."

Shea felt disquieted. It seemed as if he were trying to reassure her in a certain way and, in doing so, was revealing something of himself he usually kept private. She didn't like the sudden warmth that stole into her, the liking she felt toward him. How could she? An outlaw. A convict who had made no secret of his bitter quest for revenge.

She turned away, trying to hide her eyes from him. He always seemed to see too much. After a moment of silence she'd sorted her feelings back to where they should be. She swallowed, trying to think of something to say to break the tense silence between them, and turned back to him. "The cub is . . . enchanting."

He nodded. "But don't ever try to approach it. Mother bears are notorious about protecting their young ones. Just one of the dangers in these woods."

A warning again.

"I've never seen a bear catch a fish before."

"There's some deer that water here too," he said. "Even some fawns, but they usually visit around dawn."

For an instant she forgot she was his captive and he her captor, and exclaimed, "Can we come and watch?"

She saw a muscle flex in his cheek. He hesitated, then nodded, his eyes showing the first warmth she had seen, but it disappeared so quickly, she wondered whether she imagined it.

He stood and turned away, this time not offering his hand but obviously expecting her to follow. Shea stood, brushing away dirt and leaves from her clothes, and retrieved her sketchpad from where she had left it next to the rock.

He was several feet ahead now. Disappointed and angry, she trailed behind him. He had seemed so human for a moment, so approachable, so . . . attractive, and then he'd turned back into a relentless outlaw, expecting her to be at his heels like a trained dog.

He kept doing that to her. Disarming her with a small slice of magic and then rebuffing her as if she were lower than a . . . a slug. All his contradictions confused her, that appreciation of animals and his hate for Jack Randall; his tolerance for her, and then his rejection. She didn't understand any of it, and she hated him for the constant turmoil it created in her.

She should hate him. She *did* hate him, she told herself as she struggled to keep up with his long strides, resenting with every step the fact that another emotion also simmered deep inside her.

Clint Edwards carefully adjusted his string tie and ran a hand through his dark hair.

He wasn't sure going to the dance this evening was a wise idea, but then he had never been cautious. Living from day to day had become a way of life.

But since he had met Kate Dewayne, he had occasional thoughts that some peace might be nice for a change.

Courting the sheriff's daughter was not a way to accomplish that particular goal. *Any* courting now was definitely not wise. He had been playing with fire since he joined the Union Army twelve years ago, but now he was jumping in the middle of it, just begging to be consumed.

But like a moth, he couldn't keep away.

Pretty Kate.

He couldn't keep away from her, even though he had promises to keep first, promises that placed him and Kate's father at opposite ends of the law.

Clint had never cared much for the law. Perhaps because only one thing had mattered during the four years of war: loyalty to men who fought alongside him. It seemed crazy to him that he could do things during the war that would now condemn him.

Still, Clint's conscience gnawed at him. He wondered whether the reason was Kate, whether she had shaken his insides, rearranging his heart, soul, and conscience.

So many things were pricking at him now: the woman up at Rafe's camp; the lies to Kate's father, a man Clint liked and admired, even the purposeful betrayal of a man who employed him.

Clint pulled on his coat in his private room in the bunkhouse. The foreman, Nate Kerry, would be coming, too, tonight, along with Mr. Randall.

The dances were monthly affairs, held at the school that Mr. Randall had built in Rushton. All the ranchers, town people, and some miners attended, as much to exchange information as to dance and socialize. This dance would be of particular importance. There would be talk about the robberies. There would be discussions on what to do about them.

Clint hoped Randall's guest wouldn't tail along. McClary was one of the most disagreeable and demanding men he'd ever met. Clint didn't know why Randall tolerated him or made his men cater to him. McClary had been at the ranch on previous occasions, each time making enemies of all the hands.

Clint reminded himself to tell Rafe about McClary when he rode up to the cabin tomorrow. He'd already told Randall he planned to be gone all day, out hunting for a pack of wolves. Ben, Skinny, and the others would also be at Rafe's cabin tomorrow, making plans for the next stage holdup.

Clint wondered briefly how the woman was doing. He knew Rafe well enough to realize that he wouldn't harm her, but that look of fear in her eyes, of pleading, had stayed with Clint. He understood the necessity of holding her, but he didn't like it any more than Rafe obviously had.

He thought of Kate being in the same position, and he felt a sudden tightening in his heart. Damn his brother.

The town dance was considerably more somber than usual. There were many more small groups of men talking quietly than there were couples dancing.

Clint had trouble concentrating on Kate as he danced with her, his feet unusually clumsy as he tried to listen in on various conversations.

In fact, he'd had trouble concentrating on anything since he'd arrived and heard that first scrap of information: "A miner was murdered last night. Must be the same outlaws that's been attacking the stagecoach."

"Clint? Is something wrong?" Kate's voice was low, concerned.

He tried to smile, but he feared it was only a poor attempt. *What in hell was going on?*

"I'm sorry," he said, as he tried to focus his attention on his partner. She looked very pretty, her taffy-colored hair pulled back and tendrils softly curling around her face. That face came alive with animation when she spoke, and she had a happy laugh that always seemed to light a room. Her green eyes had been sparkling earlier, but now they were concerned as they studied him.

Kate was twenty-one, an age at which a girl was considered an unlikely prospect for marriage. It was not that she'd not had opportunities; Clint knew every unmarried man in the valley courted her, but she'd seemed content enough to keep house for her father and two older brothers. She was unlike any other girl he'd met; she could discuss ranching with the most veteran of old hands, and she rode a horse as well as her father and brothers.

After the dance, he guided her to where her father, Sheriff Russ Dewayne, and brothers, Ed and Michael, stood.

"I'm thinking about putting a posse together," Russ Dewayne said, "but Jack doesn't think that's such a good idea."

Clint turned toward his employer, lifting an eyebrow in question. He would have thought Randall would have been the first to demand a posse since it was his payrolls that had been robbed, but he had been curiously quiet about it.

Randall shrugged now. "I just think it would be useless. There are a thousand hiding places in these hills."

"What would you suggest?" Dewayne asked.

"More guards on the next coach," Randall replied. "The others have been easy targets with only a driver and Old Pete riding shotgun."

Dewayne hesitated, looked cautiously around him, and then said in a lower voice, "What about an ambush? We know where they struck last time. We can get there early. Your new payroll is coming on the next stage, isn't it?"

Randall hesitated. "I'm thinking about sending several of my men to bring it back."

"What worries me," said Ed Dewayne, "is this attack on the miners. I think we all hoped that those stagecoach robberies were committed by outlaws just passing through."

Randall's eyes moved to the couples dancing, and Clint sensed his employer wanted to change the subject. Why? Did he know who was responsible for the stage robberies? Even more important, did he know anything about the attack against the miner? It hadn't been Rafe, Clint knew that. A bullet in the back wasn't Rafe's style. But Rafe sure as hell was going to be blamed for it. Along with everyone who rode with him.

He felt Kate's touch on his arm.

Clint looked down at her and saw the concern in her eyes, and he swallowed a sudden rush of pleasure. It was a new experience for him, watching a woman's eyes deepen with caring, and he didn't quite know how to handle it. Particularly now, when he was bound to hurt her.

He smiled feebly, knowing that he would probably be seen as troubled by the recent robberies and murder. Acting a deceitful role did not come easily to him. He didn't like lying to men he liked and respected. Or to the first woman who had made him feel like settling down.

Clint turned his attention to the man who had just spoken. "Maybe the robberies and murder aren't connected."

Russ shook his head. "They have to be. We've never had trouble like this before, not since the war, when we sent those Rebel raiders running. I don't believe in coincidence."

Clint was silent for a moment. Neither did he believe in coincidences. The murder could, of course, have been unintended. A dispute between two miners. A drifter coming upon opportunity. But somehow he didn't think so. Still, he knew that none of his friends would have shot a man in the back. That left Jack Randall.

Yet he'd been watching Randall, and his boss seemed as shocked as anyone at the news.

Clint glanced down at Kate, then up at her father again. "What do you intend to do?"

"Jack's right about these mountains being full of hiding places. I'm going to ride into Casey Springs tomorrow and see whether there've been any other, similar robberies in the area. I'll ride back with the stagecoach."

Randall, who hadn't smiled during the evening, visibly relaxed. "Then I'll send my payroll that way. I'll give you authorization to pick it up."

Clint hid his concern. The last thing he wanted was Kate's father riding shotgun on the coach. He wondered whether he could persuade Rafe to pass this one up and knew immediately he couldn't. Everything hinged on depriving Randall of cash. He must be down to rock bottom now, and he'd already sold off the spring herd. He would have to sell more of his breeding stock to raise cash to pay his hands or resort to something else.

Or perhaps he already had? Perhaps Randall had found a new source of revenue in the vulnerable miners?

He looked toward Randall, studied his face, and all he saw was the same indecision and frustration he saw on the other faces.

The small group started to break up, one of the men captured by his wife, and Kate looked at Clint expectantly. Damn, but she was pretty.

He offered his arm, trying to concentrate on her. He was not a good dancer, never having had much practice, and he had to work at the waltz. He felt terribly clumsy, saved from disaster only by her own grace and agility in avoiding his missteps. It didn't help that he was disconcerted by the way she looked at him, as if he were someone special, and the thought of the trip up into the mountains the next morning.

Chapter 10

The seven men helping Rafe all appeared around noon the next day. Clint and Ben Edwards, Johnny Green, Bill Smith, Carey Thompson, Simon Ford, and Skinny Ware.

Shea Randall was locked securely in the cabin, the one window closed. She wouldn't see any more of his men.

Through sheer force of will, Rafe had remained distant and cool toward Shea Randall the night before and the next morning. She hadn't mentioned making the dawn trip to the pool again, and he hadn't offered. He had ignored her searching look when he'd locked her in the cabin for the evening after opening several cans of food for her. He'd taken several for himself along with a few crackers for Abner and a dried apple for the horse, and sought refuge in the barn with creatures he understood.

He sure as hell didn't understand her. Or himself.

He needed all his concentration for the meeting. The next strike against Randall. He couldn't be thinking of a woman. Particularly *that* woman.

But he did, dammit. Damn *him*.

Clint arrived first, a tense, worried look on his face.

He dismounted and approached Rafe, who was working with the bay.

Rafe cocked his head slightly. Clint usually was even-natured, easygoing.

"A miner was killed two nights ago," Clint said. "It's being blamed on the same riders who held up the stage."

Rafe stared at him without speaking.

"And there's more. You mentioned a McClary. He showed up at the ranch several days ago. He'd been here before, but for some reason I didn't recognize the name when you first said it. Perhaps because we didn't see much of him, and what we did see, we didn't like."

"Sam McClary?"

"Yep. Tall, thin as a rail, yellow hair."

Rafe nodded, waiting for more.

"He was also gone the night the miner was killed."

"How do you know?"

"I asked around the bunkhouse whether anyone had taken out a horse. A man remembered McClary because he'd ordered the hand to unsaddle and rub down the animal when he came in near dawn. Everyone else takes care of their own horses, even Randall, but Randall told us McClary was a guest, that we should do what he said. Didn't sound happy about it."

"A reunion of thieves," Rafe said. "Wonder whether it has anything to do with me?"

Clint shrugged. "I've been doing my damnedest to listen in, but they always close the door when they're together."

"Seems like we might be making progress."

"Or *they* might," Clint said grimly. "Russ Dewayne is thinking about forming a posse." He hesitated, then continued. "Russ and his sons will be riding with the stage, so Randall said he would send the payroll by stage after all. He had been planning to send some of his men for it, along a separate route, which would have been perfect."

"Russ?" Rafe furrowed his eyebrows together in surprise at the friendly way Clint mentioned the name.

Clint met his eyes directly. "I'm seeing his daughter."

"What do you think of the father?"

Clint hesitated. "I like him."

Rafe was silent for a moment, regretting again that he'd drawn the young man into his own battle. "You're out of this, Clint. Both you and Ben."

"No," Clint said. "We've worked on this for five years. I'm not leaving. Besides, the woman has already seen both Ben and me." He glanced toward the closed cabin. "How is she?"

"Angry but safe." Rafe was the one who was no longer safe.

"There's been no mention of her at the ranch. Maybe she was lying."

"From what she says and the letters she carries, I don't think her father—if he is that—even knows she exists."

"Then that explains why I've never heard anything of her," Clint said.

Rafe nodded.

"Someone's going to find out she was asking questions at the express office," Clint said.

"I know," Rafe said. "That should bother Randall some. Everyone in the territory knowing he has a daughter he never acknowledged. Should damage that respectable image of his." He couldn't hold back the bitterness in his words.

Just then the sound of hooves against earth interrupted their discussion, and Ben along with Johnny

Green, Bill Smith, Carey Thompson, and Simon Ford appeared.

They rode up to the two men and dismounted. "Skinny?" The question came from Clint.

"He'll be along," said Johnny, a short, pudgy man who many people underestimated. He was the fastest among them with a gun. "He's at a meeting with the miners. They're talking about a vigilante committee."

Rafe closed his eyes. A posse and a vigilante committee. And he damn well couldn't get it out of his mind that Randall was behind the killing. This time, though, Randall wasn't going to succeed.

"We suspected he would do something if we pushed him," Ben said.

Clint was silent. Rafe looked at him. "Clint?"

"I keep wondering about McClary. Although he's a guest, Randall doesn't seem to like him much."

The five new arrivals looked toward Clint, who quickly told them about McClary's arrival and his role in Rafe's court-martial. Apparently, Ben had already told them about the woman, and they had darted curious looks toward the cabin but discreetly said nothing. Each had noticed he had not been invited inside for a drink.

Johnny sprawled down on the ground. "Got any whiskey?"

Rafe nodded toward the barn. "Clint, it's in the far corner of the stable."

When Clint disappeared inside, Rafe turned toward the others. "I think it's time you move on. I can take it from here."

"Just when it's getting interesting?" The question came from Carey Thompson, a tall, thin man who had a talent for rustling.

"Ain't no way we're showing our back," Bill Smith said. "It's not just you, Rafe. Don't think it is. We went through hell those three years, and I don't like the thought of a yellow belly benefiting from the war."

The others nodded. "What did Clint say?" asked Simon Ford.

Rafe's silence answered the question.

"You're stuck with us," Simon said. "We haven't got anyplace to go, and that small claim is paying my keep. I don't like the idea of someone out there killing miners." He didn't say he filed for the claim simply to justify his presence in Rushton, or that its yield didn't even come close to what he had been making as a top horse hand.

"Hell, you're all a bunch of fools," Rafe said. The words had been difficult to say. It had been a long time since he'd known this kind of loyalty.

He looked at them helplessly as Clint returned. Clint looked around and grinned. "They're not buying it, either, huh, Rafe?"

Rafe gave him a disgusted look. "I don't want to be responsible. . . ."

"You won't be," Ben said with a crooked grin. "We were all damned bored. Things were becoming too tame."

"Is the woman pretty?" asked Simon, the womanizer of the group.

Rafe scowled. "She's a damnable nuisance."

"That means she's right pretty." Simon grinned. "Can we take a look?"

"Not unless you want your face on a poster," Rafe growled, and then was saved from saying anything else as Skinny Ware rode up.

Clint passed around the bottle, each man taking a swallow, as at ease with each other as they had been ten years earlier before a battle. More, in fact. Now they knew what to expect and how the others would respond. They were a family, like brothers. Rafe knew they wouldn't leave him now, no matter what he ordered.

How did everything get so damned messed up?

Clint told them of the possible posse and the sheriff's escort of the stagecoach. Until now the stagecoach robberies had been carefully planned, and there had been no shedding of blood. A boulder or tree had blocked the road; six masked men with guns prevented any reckless action. Both driver and escort had quickly surrendered each time; neither was paid enough to die.

But Clint knew Russ Dewayne and his sons wouldn't give up without a fight.

"We'll have to take the payroll before it's placed on the stage," Rafe said.

"Rob the bank?" Clint asked with surprise.

"The express office," Rafe said. "Didn't you say the money is usually transferred to that safe the night before, since the stage leaves so early?"

Clint nodded. "It has been."

"Randall's payroll will be marked, won't it?"

Clint nodded. "It should be. Randall's arranged for a loan, but it might be the last one he gets. He's just about run his credit out, according to the foreman."

"Does the money belong to Randall or the bank?"

Clint grinned. "Randall's already signed for the money. He was talking about it at the dance; that's why he was thinking about taking special care of it. It's his, all right."

Rafe stood. "Anyone know about explosives?"

Skinny nodded. "I've worked with them in mines."

"We have two days to get dynamite."

Skinny shrugged. "No problem. I can buy some, say I need it to clear some rock."

"Sure it won't be traced back to you?" Rafe worried.

"Miners are always buying dynamite. 'Sides, I can get it here at the general store. No one will connect it with an explosion in Casey Springs."

Rafe nodded. "I've learned a little about picking locks. We shouldn't have any trouble getting in." They all looked at him. "The last year I was in prison," he explained, "the man in the cell next to me could open any damn lock, including the cell doors, and he taught me. Since I had just two months left to serve, I decided to wait and leave the legal way."

"When will we go?" Simon's eyes were gleaming in anticipation of action.

"You don't, Simon," Rafe said. "The fewer, the better. Skinny, because I need his expertise, Ben, and myself."

"Dammit," Johnny Green said. "I didn't come here to sit on my hands."

"We may need you for an alibi for Skinny and Ben," Rafe said. "Both you and Bill. Go into the saloon in Rushton, make it clear you're meeting Skinny and Ben later.

Disappointment clouded Simon's eyes, then they brightened. "I could stay with the girl."

"The wolf guarding the lamb," Ben said wryly, saving Rafe from saying it. They all laughed.

"I'll check on her," Clint offered. "She's already seen me, anyway."

"No one will miss you?"

"Hell, I'll say I'm going up into the north pasture. There have been reports of a wolf pack there killing calves. That's the excuse I'm using today."

Rafe nodded. "If all goes well, we'll be back at dawn." He grinned at Simon's crestfallen face. "She has a tongue that would slice you to pieces, Simon. "I thought you liked your women friendly and enthusiastic."

"Yeah, Simon," Ben said. "She's not your type at all. She's a lady."

"Go to hell, Ben," Simon said good-naturedly.

"What about the miner's death, the one that's being blamed on us?" Ben asked.

Rafe's smile had a hard edge. "Ironically, the woman provides me with an alibi." He looked over to Clint. "Try to keep an eye on McClary. Follow him if he leaves in the evening or at night."

Clint nodded, and together they carefully planned their next move against Jack Randall.

Shea moved restlessly inside the cabin. She'd heard the sound of approaching horses, of muffled laughter.

She had been locked inside since breakfast without explanation. Of course, as a captive, she obviously wasn't entitled to one, she thought rebelliously.

She found herself pacing, and again she wondered how Rafe Tyler had endured ten years of imprisonment when she couldn't stand even a few hours. But he'd deserved it. He'd betrayed his country for money. And she . . . all she had done was try to find a father.

Shea tried sketching. She tried reading. She tried petting Abner—Rafe had left the mouse in the cabin with her. It might have been compassion, but she doubted it. He wouldn't know what the word meant. She'd been a fool to think otherwise yesterday at the waterfall. He'd been cold and contemptuous since the return to the cabin and this morning had simply locked her in like some troublesome . . . mouse.

She would sell her soul to find out what was going on outside. Well, almost. She found the crumpled piece of paper she'd stuck in a pocket yesterday, the sketch of Tyler in which she'd softened some of the hard lines of his face.

With a few strokes she changed it, trying once more to find the real substance of the man but failing miserably.

He showed too many outward contradictions, and he kept too much of himself well hidden.

She tried to occupy herself with plans to escape. She'd paid attention yesterday when he'd taken her to the waterfall. She'd noted their route, the position of the sun. But she wasn't any wiser at which direction to take to get out of the valley.

Refusing to let that dishearten her, she squirreled away some crackers and jerky in her valise, to take if she ever did get a chance to escape. She looked longingly at the two clean dresses inside the valise, even the one she hadn't had a chance to wash in Casey City. The shirt and trousers she still had on were becoming smelly and dirty. Yet changing to a dress seemed to be a kind of surrender, an acceptance of a condition that was unacceptable.

How long would she be locked in here? She looked at the pail of water and soap he'd brought her this morning and decided she would wash her shirt at least. It was something to do.

After changing into a tan skirt and matching blouse, she took a cup and filled it so she would have drinking water, then plunged the shirt into the pail. She started scrubbing, using the shirt as a substitute for Rafe Tyler.

It would probably be the cleanest garment she'd ever worn. If there was anything left when she finished.

Rafe watched the last of the men go, feeling a certain regret as he did so.

There would be little now to keep his mind off the woman.

Ben had brought a few more supplies, including a haunch of a deer and a sack of potatoes. Perhaps some stew tonight would break the monotony of the diet. A hot meal might make her more . . . more, what?

He reluctantly approached the cabin and unlocked the door. She was sitting on the bed, reading by the light of the candle. He noticed she was wearing something different, a blouse and tan skirt, and she looked extraordinarily pretty, her head bent over the book, her light brown hair caught in the glow of the candle as it fell over her shoulder. When she looked up, he found himself inwardly flinching from the silent accusation in her eyes.

"Are your . . . friends gone? Or do outlaws have friends?"

Good question, one that Rafe wasn't willing to answer for her. "Let's say we have a commonality of purpose."

"My father," she stated.

"Your father," he confirmed.

"I still don't understand . . ."

"You don't have to, Miss Randall. It has nothing to do with you."

"How can you say that when you're keeping me here?"

He shrugged. "It's unfortunate."

"Unfortunate?" She glared at him, a blue fire burning in her eyes. "Unfortunate?" Her voice had risen slightly.

He lifted an eyebrow. "How about extremely unfortunate?" Self-defense had forced mockery back into his voice. The angry flush on her face deepened.

"You're despicable."

Rafe shrugged. "So I've been told." His glance automatically went down to his gloved hand, and he wished it hadn't. It showed a weakness he didn't want to display. Not to her.

Her eyes followed his, and something flickered in them. He damned sure didn't want it to be sympathy or pity.

He turned abruptly away from her. The shirt she had been wearing was hanging over the chair, and he knew from its damp look that she had washed it. He walked to the fireplace. Only ashes remained from the fire last night. He stacked some wood and kindling in the hearth and started a fire.

"I'm going to get some water," he said finally. "Do you want to come with me?"

"Or you'll lock the door again?"

"That's right," he said evenly.

Rafe watched her consider. He found himself fascinated again with the expressiveness of her face as she obviously fought a battle between continued resistance and the need to get out. He understood. Christ, he understood.

Her gaze warred with his a moment, letting him know she wasn't surrendering but biding her time. No one, he thought, could say so much so eloquently without words.

He went to the door and opened it, standing back politely as she passed through it. Then he led the way to the stream. It was midafternoon, and the sun was bright and warm. Perhaps this evening he would take her to the waterfall. If he completely lost his senses.

He filled the bucket he brought and leaned against a tree, watching her. She'd always seemed graceful to him, but now she was especially enticing as the skirt swished against her legs, and the blouse hugged a figure the oversized man's shirt had hidden.

Rafe found himself swallowing deeply. Once he had been an officer and ostensibly a gentleman. But the last ten years he had been little more than an animal, treated like one and thus reacting like one. He'd never been well-versed in the niceties of courtship, not even with Allison. He had never thought flowers important, or small gifts, and he had been awkward with such rituals when he realized Allison expected them.

Now he felt more awkward than ever, wanting something that he couldn't have, that he should never even consider. But he did want this woman, and he tried to tell himself it was only because of deprivation. There was a gnawing in his belly, a burning in his loins, and a loneliness in his heart. But he had given in once, and he had no intention of making the same mistake twice, particularly with Randall's daughter.

He'd experienced treachery from a Randall and a woman, and Shea Randall was both.

He looked up, and she was standing a few feet away. "Can I have some privacy?"

He knew how much that question cost her, how much it cost her each time she uttered it. Christ, he wished the hurt didn't go so deep, didn't bite so hard.

Rafe nodded.

She watched him carefully, and he knew she was waiting for something else.

He finally complied. "I don't have to warn you this time, do I?"

She looked at him steadily. "Are you going to follow me?"

"Have you learned anything yet?"

"I think so."

Damn, he wished those eyes weren't quite so clear, so direct.

"I damn well hope so, Miss Randall," he said, "because next time you try anything, you'll spend the rest of your time here in the cabin with a bucket." His voice was harsher than he intended. Her face flushed red, and he felt like the schoolyard bully. But his choices were gone. He had to live with the ones he'd made, and by God, so did she. "Do you understand?"

"Yes."

"Do you believe me?"

"Yes," she repeated, her eyes flashing rebellious fire again.

"I'll wait here then," he said. "Don't make me regret that trust."

"Such as it is," she said bitterly.

"Do you deserve any more?"

Her eyes seemed to burn through him now. Angry. Combative. "I don't owe you any."

"No," he agreed mildly. "You don't."

He knew his answer surprised her. He didn't understand why he kept battling with her, why he didn't just ignore her as he should.

But he did know. He was so damned lonely. He thought he had conquered and caged those feelings, just as he had been caged, but he hadn't. Except for Ben and Clint, he'd not had a prolonged conversation with a human being for ten years. And except for that very brief coupling in the whorehouse, neither had he been with a woman, even to talk. He hadn't realized the depth of his need until he was attracted to the daughter of his enemy, a woman who despised him and had every right to do so.

As that understanding flooded over him, his anger toward her father grew even deeper, even more bitter. His freedom had been taken, his pride, his self-respect, his future. Now he found even his will had been twisted into something he no longer controlled.

A cloak of darkness seemed to smother him, keeping out any light that had found its way into his consciousness. He could never have a woman like Shea Randall, never whisper endearments in the night, or create children, or stand beside a wife with pride. He hadn't understood before. And now he realized that the enjoyment he'd felt sitting with her yesterday and watching the rapt attention on her face as the bears approached had been born of the need for normalcy. For simple companionship.

He heard her approaching, and he turned away. He didn't want her to see the mist in his eyes. Hate, he reminded himself. Remember hate. Something had to fill that hole inside him, and it could never be love.

It had to be hate. There was nothing more for him. Randall had ensured that.

Rafe scooped up a pailful of water from the stream and headed back to the cabin. He ignored the tight knot in his throat, the aching need to look at her.

Chapter 11

Rafe welcomed the prospect of action after so many days of inactivity. He met Ben and Skinny Ware five miles from Casey Springs, and they rode toward the town side by side.

There was a half-moon revealed by drifting clouds that hurried through the sky as if chasing an elusive phantom.

He also welcomed escaping from the growing tension between him and his prisoner. In the past two days they had said little to each other, Rafe trying to build an unbreachable barrier between them.

His only lapse had been taking her back to the waterfall yesterday, knowing that he would have to keep her locked in the cabin while he was gone. The mother bear and her cub had been there again, and Shea had watched with the same bewitching eagerness as before, turning to him once with such a delighted smile that he couldn't help but respond with a slight smile of his own. She'd looked startled, then confused, and returned her gaze suddenly to the animals.

They had both been silent on the way back to the

cabin. He'd dished himself out some of the last of the stew Shea had made two days earlier and retreated outside to eat. She found a spot under a tree and read a book. He'd glanced her way occasionally, mainly, he'd told himself, to make sure she was still there, and sometimes found her gaze on him. But it had always turned away so quickly, he couldn't read her expression. Dislike, most probably. Contempt. Anger. Distrust.

Later that night he had crafted a lock pick from a spoon in the cabin. And now, with the pick in the sheath hanging from his belt, he turned to Ben. "You know what to do?"

Ben nodded. "The old mine just outside town. I'll set the dynamite off at exactly four, then the shack on the other side of town fifteen minutes later. And then I'll meet you behind the express office." He took out his watch and adjusted the time to correspond exactly with the one he had purchased for Rafe.

Rafe nodded. "Skinny and I will blow the safe when you dynamite the shack. Hopefully, most of the town will have gone to the mine to investigate and won't know where the second blast came from."

He had debated whether it was best to create a diversion or risk one lone explosion at the express office and get out before anyone came. But he wanted to be sure he found the right strongbox, and that might take several minutes. He and the others had settled on confusion as the best tactic.

The town was quiet. The saloons closed at 2:00 A.M., sometimes later if there were enough customers. Four, they knew, would find the streets empty.

As the buildings of Casey Springs came into sight, the three men parted, Ben going toward the abandoned mine and Rafe and Skinny heading for the express office in the center of town. There was no back door, but there was a side window that led to an alley in back. It was their escape route.

The sheriff's office, located several doors down, was dark. Rafe dismounted a short distance from the express office and gave his reins to Skinny, who would take both horses to the alley and tie them there. Rafe kept to the shadows as he made his way to the front of the express office. From the sheath on his belt he took out a knife and the lock pick. He only hoped it would work as well on this door as it had on his cell.

He tried the knife first, trying to dislodge the lock before resorting to the longer process of actually picking the lock. The knife failed, and Rafe took a quick look around the streets. Still no movement. No light. He stooped and gently inserted the pick into the lock, feeling for the catch. After several moments he heard it click, and he tried the door. He let out a breath of relief as it opened, and he slipped inside, keeping it open a sliver as he waited for Skinny.

Skinny appeared seconds later, his slight frame and dark clothes blending into the night. After Skinny entered, Rafe relocked the door from the inside.

Ben had drawn a map showing where everything was, and both he and Skinny had memorized it. They moved toward the back and found the safe. Rafe lit a match. He looked at the combination lock with disappointment, wishing that he had knowledge of that kind of safecracking, but there were no safes in prison. It would have to be dynamite.

He looked at the watch. Two minutes to four. They waited, and then they heard the first explosion, then another. There was noise outside. Someone tried to open the express-office door, then left after finding it locked.

About five minutes passed. Rafe didn't want to light another match yet. They both waited another minute. Then Rafe lit a match, covering the flame with his hand, and checked the watch again. Two more minutes. Another match. Fifteen seconds left.

Skinny had already placed the carefully prepared dynamite where he wanted it and arranged several saddle blankets around it to act as a buffer. He motioned for Rafe to move back, well away from the blast site. At Rafe's signal he lit the short fuse and dashed under cover. They heard an explosion in the distance and their own, almost simultaneously. Rafe hoped that, to the townspeople, the blast in the express office sounded like an echo of the first.

The safe door hung by the hinges. Skinny lit a match while Rafe quickly checked inside. Several mail pouches. A cash box. Then a small strongbox with Randall's name on it. Rafe nodded at Skinny, who had already moved swiftly over to the side window and pulled away the boards that blocked it. Every movement had been planned, neither of them needing words. There was more noise outside. Shouts. Yelling. After the last slat came from the window, Skinny broke the glass, and Rafe could hear the people talking.

"What the hell . . . ! ?"

"The mine . . ."

"No . . . old Dakker's shack . . ."

Then they heard Ben's voice, planned as a decoy. It was loud and excited. "Men at the bank. It's a robbery." There were more cries as people went down the street.

Rafe quickly exited through the window, Skinny behind him, just as Ben rode into the alley. Rafe and Skinny sprinted toward their horses and mounted, Rafe clutching the strongbox. They spurred the horses, mixing with others riding and running in confusion up and down the street. The three men turned toward the mine as lights went on in the sheriff's office.

Rafe, Skinny, and Ben stayed with the rush toward the mine for a distance, then allowed their horses to fall behind, finally veering off toward the pass leading from town. They didn't slow their pace until they were well away, Rafe holding Randall's future in his hands.

Clint arrived at Rafe's cabin at dawn. If everything went well in Casey Springs, Rafe, Ben, and Skinny should be back around noon.

He had promised to look in on the woman, make sure she was all right. He had brought a sack with eggs cradled in hay and some bacon. He had noticed before that Rafe Tyler cared little about what he ate and could only assume that his friend provided little better for his hostage.

Clint still felt uncomfortable that they were holding Shea Randall, though he knew no real harm would come to her. Although the captain had changed, as any man would after so many years in a cage, Tyler was inherently decent. Clint had sensed that when he visited Rafe in prison; it was why he had felt compelled to try to obtain some measure of justice for him.

But Clint knew there was a high price on that quixotic scheme, for himself, for the others, and especially for Tyler.

And now there was the woman. She had to be terrified, and Clint couldn't rid himself of guilt on that account.

He reached the cabin and found the key where Rafe had said it would be. He knocked at the door before unlocking it, waiting for some kind of acknowledgment.

"Yes?"

Her voice was tentative. He unlocked the padlock and opened it.

She was standing, her face illuminated by candle-light. Her hair was in a long braid, and she was dressed in a skirt. She looked a little disappointed, which startled him. If there was fear, it wasn't for herself. He knew that instantly.

"I'm Clint," he said.

"You were here the first day," she said warily.

He nodded.

"Where's . . . ?"

"Rafe? He should be back later today."

He wondered whether it was relief that flickered across her face.

Then a question appeared in her eyes.

"He asked me to look in on you," he said. "Didn't he tell you?"

"He doesn't tell me anything." There was bitterness in her voice. "I don't suppose you're here to take me . . ."

"To Randall's ranch? No, I'm afraid not. But I did bring you something to eat."

He realized how little that was compared to her hope, and he added, "I'm sorry."

"Are you?" she asked. "Then let me go."

"I can't do that."

"Why?"

"Rafe is my friend."

"Enough of a friend to hang for?" There was a bite to the question, as well as real curiosity.

"Miss Randall," he said patiently, "my brother and I would have died ten years ago if it were not for Rafe Tyler. I don't take that kind of debt lightly."

"How?" She was hungry to know about Rafe Tyler.

To know his weaknesses, she told herself, even though she knew that wasn't the entire truth. He was a mystery she wanted to solve, a puzzle with too many missing pieces.

Clint went on into the room. The mouse was sitting on the table. Clint suddenly grinned. "You've found Abner."

"Abner found me," the girl said. "He's company. And better than some," she added dryly, making it clear she meant Rafe Tyler.

Clint found himself liking Shea Randall. He'd feared tears, screams, incriminations, or worse. Instead, she had stated her case calmly, even with a little bite. He suspected she hadn't given up.

"And now you have some food . . . eggs, bacon."

But Shea was in no mood to be pacified. Or let him feel less guilty. "For the condemned?" she asked grimly.

"Do you feel like the condemned?"

"How would you feel locked in a small room, at the mercy of people you don't know, for reasons you don't understand?"

"Try it for ten years," Clint said roughly.

"If you're talking about . . ." She stopped, not knowing what to call Rafe Tyler. "He brought it on himself by stealing."

"Did he?" Clint deliberately made his question provocative.

"What do you mean?"

Her puzzlement made Clint suddenly want to explain what Rafe Tyler obviously had not. But it wasn't his place to explain. He could only talk about his own feelings.

"I met Rafe," Clint said slowly, "when he was a captain and I was nineteen, my brother sixteen. We'd enlisted in the Union Army, but God knows we were as green as you can get. Captain Tyler was our officer, and he worked tirelessly to shape us up, but the army hurried us into battle before we were ready. Rafe made captain about that time, and we were assigned a new lieutenant, one as green as we were.

"The lieutenant was trying to make a name for himself. He ordered my brother to take out a sniper, and Ben got caught in the open and shot. The sniper kept firing at him. I went after him and took a bullet myself. No one could reach the sniper from our lines. The lieutenant panicked and told the others to withdraw, leaving us out in the open. Captain Tyler was riding by at that time and saw what was happening. He had orders to report directly to General Grant, but he disobeyed them and crawled out to help us. He was able to get close enough to kill the sniper, but not before he, too, was shot."

Clint didn't disguise the intensity of feeling he always had when he remembered that day. "Captain Tyler was the best officer I ever saw throughout the war. Do you really think a man who would risk his life, who would disobey orders to save two enlisted men, would do what they said he did?"

"People . . . change."

"Not that much, Miss Randall."

"He practically admitted . . ."

"Did he? Or did he just refuse to defend himself? No one listened before."

He saw her tremble slightly as she considered his words. "But he's robbing stages now. . . ."

"He's only stealing from one man, Miss Randall. And you happen to be his daughter. Why should he think you might listen when no one else has? Rafe didn't want you here. He still doesn't. He's just trying to protect my brother and me. Again."

There was silence for a moment, then her eyes widened. "If he was innocent . . ."

Clint waited for her to complete the thought in her mind as well as with her mouth. She had seen the clipping reporting that Jack Randall was the principal witness against Captain Rafferty Tyler. She shook her head. "It can't be. Everyone says Jack Randall is a fine man. He's respected and liked and—"

"You don't know him, do you, Miss Randall?"

"No, but I heard . . ."

"And he's your father." Clint said the words gently.

She just looked at him with those disturbing blue-gray eyes of hers, and Clint suddenly understood why Rafe had been so testy the other day. These days, Clint had his own testiness to cope with, and that, too, had to do with a woman.

"I'll cook some eggs and bacon," he said abruptly, letting her draw her own conclusions.

Shea thought back to late last night when Rafe had allowed her out to attend to her needs. She'd realized he was leaving the clearing, that he had been going out to do something that involved her father. For the first time he'd worn a gunbelt, the holster strapped to his thigh. He'd looked lethal and forbidding, so different from the men she'd known in Boston. His mouth narrowed into a tight line, he'd had very little to say to her. He'd made sure she had enough water and food and left an empty bucket.

She had tried all night to find a way to escape, but her captor had taken everything that could possibly be used as a wedge to force open either the window or door.

And while she'd worked fruitlessly at her apparently impossible task, she'd worried about what she would do if he didn't return. And she, incomprehensibly, also worried about *him*. Because she had become so dependent on him for her every need? Or was it something more?

She now seized the opportunity to learn anything she could from Clint, even though she couldn't accept everything he was saying. He was excusing Rafferty Tyler and therefore himself. If Rafe Tyler had been innocent, wouldn't he try to clear himself rather than commit other crimes?

"Tell me more about . . . Rafferty Tyler," she said as he produced a frying pan from the saddlebags he'd carried inside.

Clint shrugged. "That's all I know. He was a damned good officer."

"Then about you," she said, needing companionship after so many hours alone.

He looked at her sharply. "Nothing to tell."

"No wife? No children?"

Clint stared at her for a moment, his gaze suspicious. "It won't work, Miss Randall," he said. "I won't let you go. You will be safe here until we've finished what we came for, and then you can go wherever you want."

"What *did* you come here for?" She kept trying to probe their real intention toward her father, although so far every inquiry produced nothing.

"You ask too many questions." He put some bacon in the frying pan, which he placed over the flames.

"I'll cook that," she offered, wanting something to do.

He nodded and stepped back.

If only she could keep the frying pan here. It would make a weapon.

The smell of sizzling bacon filled the room, and Shea felt her mouth watering. How many days had she been here? How long since she'd had a decent breakfast?

"You didn't bring some coffee?" she asked wistfully.

"No, but I will next time."

Her eyes clouded. "How many next times will there be?"

"I don't know."

She swallowed, suddenly overwhelmed by hopelessness. She felt alien among these men who wore guns, who talked about violence and robbery like Bostonians discussing a concert. She still didn't physically fear them— they'd had their chances to harm her and had not—but she did fear everything they represented. Still, a wayward part of her was fascinated with them, particularly with Rafe Tyler. An ugly fascination, she thought. She couldn't accept the premise that Rafe Tyler was innocent. The courts couldn't commit such gross injustice. And her father . . . her own blood . . . couldn't have schemed in such a way.

If her father was so greedy, why had he sent so much money to her mother all those years? Why would he build a school? Why would he help so many others in trouble, as the people of Casey Springs had said?

But there was still that nagging worry about Rafe Tyler. The mere thought that he might be wounded or hurt was unexpectedly devastating.

She smelled something burning and looked down. The bacon was black, curling up. Her mind still occupied with the enigmatic Rafe Tyler, she reacted instinctively and grabbed the handle of the pan, heat scorching her hand.

She dropped the pan, and grease went splattering over her dress, splashing on bare skin.

"Damn," Clint Edwards said, moving swiftly toward her. He took her hand; the skin was already turning white.

Shea held her wrist with her other hand as the agony deepened, roaring up her arm. She felt tears form in her eyes from the pain.

"Is there water?" Clint Edwards asked.

She nodded toward the bucket of water Rafe had left for her, and Clint led her over to it. She slowly lowered her hand into it, wincing as she did so, but she made no cry at all.

"It will be all right," he said. "Shouldn't be any scarring, but it's going to hurt like hell for a while. Damn, I wish there was some salve."

Shea wished the hand would just stop hurting. She wished she could go home. But she had no home any longer, she reminded herself.

A thought suddenly occurred to her. "Can we get a doctor?"

"No, but I'll bring some salve." A glint of admiration shone in his eyes. "For now keep it in the water."

Shea recalled the brand on Rafe's hand, and she knew her pain must be very small compared to what he had suffered. She couldn't even bear to think about that.

Instead, she closed her eyes and let the tepid water soothe her hand. Her right hand. Her drawing hand. She tried to move her fingers and winced. She glanced up, catching Clint's gaze on her.

"When will . . . your friend be back?" She still felt awkward calling her kidnapper "Rafe." Or "Tyler." Or anything else that had the slightest hint of intimacy.

"This afternoon."

"You sound very sure of that."

"I am," he said with irritating sureness. "How is your hand feeling now?"

"Terrible."

"Perhaps some mud might help. Want to go down to the stream?"

Shea wasn't sure she wanted to leave the bucket of water, the little relief it gave her, but getting outside the cabin sounded good. She took her hand from the water. It was still agonizingly painful. She looked at the frying pan on the floor as Clint turned toward the door. He had forgotten it!

His back was to her, so she nudged the pan with her foot until it was under the cot, just out of sight.

Murmuring a small prayer under her breath, she followed Clint out the door.

Chapter 12

Shea tried to read. But she couldn't concentrate on the book with her hand continuing to throb. Clint had left hours earlier, promising to return with salve later that day. She had tried to convince him not to lock her back in the cabin, but though regretful, he was immovable. He had, however, done everything he could to make her comfortable.

The frying pan was still under the cot. The question was whether she could—either mentally or physically—use it. Even with the mudpack Clint had made her, her hand felt as if it were on fire.

Time crept by so slowly. Shouldn't he be back by now? It had to be afternoon; the candle was getting low. Before long there would be no light at all.

Abner crept up to where she sat on the cot, and he lifted his front paws as if to beg. Shea ran a finger down his back, and Abner bunched up as if in pleasure. She wondered about the man who had managed to tame the mouse. Because he, too, had been unbearably lonely?

But then apparently Rafe was good with all animals. She had watched his patience with the horse, the tolerance of the bears. And then she recalled, word for word, what Clint had said. Rafe Tyler had been the best officer he had ever seen. He had risked his life to save others.

Those two attributes went together, that gentleness with animals and loyalty to men. What didn't match was the charge that he had betrayed his country and stolen from it. Still, the evidence . . .

They had found money in his quarters. Her father had seen him meet with the raiders. And he hadn't denied . . .

No one listened before.

Clint's words. They didn't matter, she told herself. Rafe Tyler had now placed himself outside the law. He was after her father. He was holding her. Innocent men didn't do that.

She thought again of the frying pan, of hitting her captor when he wasn't looking, and then taking the horse. She had to get away from Rafe, from these feelings he stirred in her, from her fascination with the man who had made it clear he planned to destroy her father.

She had to warn her father!

Lost in her own misery and unusual indecisiveness, she was surprised when she heard movement at the door. She hadn't heard hoofbeats, so whoever it was must have approached at a walk.

There was a knock. His knock. It had a certain impatience that she recognized.

She stood, her left hand holding Abner, who seemed altogether at home there, and watched as Rafe Tyler entered. He looked weary, his face rough with bristles and his eyes as noncommittal as usual. Her own gaze was raking him, and she wasn't sure what she was looking for, until she felt relief when she saw he seemed in one piece.

And then she was pierced by his own examination,

by eyes that moved downward from her face, finally stopping at her right hand.

His sandy-brown brows knit together. "What in the devil . . . ?"

Shea felt oddly confused at the concern in his voice. "I . . . I burned myself."

Two quick steps, and he had reached her, his hands —both gloved, Shea noted—extending to take Abner from her left hand. He placed the mouse on the floor, then gently examined Shea's injured hand. The sensitivity in his touch was unmistakable. His eyes asked her about the mudpack.

"Your fellow outlaw," she said, trying to remind herself who these men were.

"He didn't . . . ?" There was disbelief in his words.

She shook her head. "He just tried to help. . . . I burned my hand on a . . . pan that was too hot."

He released her hand, pulled off his gloves, apparently unconcerned now about his ugly scar, and tucked them into his pants pocket. He took her hand again, his fingers brushing away the mud and very lightly running over the surface of her palm. She felt as if a feather were touching it, a feather that made her shiver down to the core of her being. And some of her pain seemed to fade as he led her over to the bucket of water, washing the mud away and then examining the hand carefully.

"I'm sorry," he said. She sensed the apology came with difficulty. "I never meant for you to get hurt."

"It's all right," she said in little more than a whisper.

"No, it isn't," he replied. He closed his eyes for a moment, and Shea wondered at his thoughts. If only she could read them better.

"It . . ." He hesitated, then continued. "The burns shouldn't scar your hand, but I know how much it hurts.

Damn." The last word was explosive, full of anger, and Shea wasn't sure whom it was directed toward.

She felt a sudden need to comfort *him*, even though she knew how insane that was. She should be using the wound to the fullest, demanding he let her go. But for some elusive reason, she couldn't. Perhaps because she sensed the scar on his own hand was his one weakness, the one that went to the core of him, and she couldn't exploit it.

"Clint . . . said he would bring some salve," she finally said, as she watched his face struggle to maintain its usual iron mask. She wished she didn't want to see the man behind it so badly.

He released a long breath. His hand left hers and held her chin in his fingers, forcing her gaze to meet his. Suddenly, his head came down, his lips touching hers in a tentative, searching way that was so unlike him, unlike anything she'd experienced with him.

His other kiss had been violent, angry, hungry, even punishing. With only a moment of gentleness. And even then, she'd responded in some primitive way she'd despised in herself. Now she was responding on another level, with a need so overwhelming that it drained all reason from her.

The kiss deepened, and she felt her arms going around him, even though she knew it was a terrible mistake that could never be taken back. She knew exactly how terrible when all of her responded, her tongue reaching out to meet his, her body swaying against his.

The embers of fire that had glowed between them since the first day flared, enveloping them in a circle of heat that was exquisitely provocative. Painful in deliciously wicked ways that aroused and stung and burned . . . and wanted.

Shea lost herself in his touch, in the feel of his lips

against hers, in the feel of his aroused body against hers. His hands moved along the side of her neck as his mouth explored hers ever so slowly. She sensed he was barely holding on to his control. That fact only made her own need greater, more demanding.

She didn't understand what was happening to her, why nothing mattered right now but an outlaw she should hate. She heard the beat of his heart, heard it race suddenly, and her own senses spun out of control.

Despite her knowledge of who and what he was, despite her disquietude over all the pulsating sensations building within her, she felt the strangest sense of belonging. As with every moment since she had met Rafferty Tyler, her being warred with itself, mind against heart, body against will.

Something in him reached out to her in ways she couldn't decipher, ways she didn't seem able to deny. She felt his hand move to her hair, stroking it with strong, sure movements, then hesitating. His hand fell down to her back, his fingers running along the outside of her blouse, sending quivers throughout her body. His mouth invited hers to open, and it did so readily, so eagerly that she was shocked. She had never kissed like this, never been kissed like this.

But from the moment his lips touched hers, she was helpless to resist, helpless to stop the tingling of every nerve, the aching in the deepest, most private part of her, helpless to keep from giving a part of herself that had never been touched before. She wanted to tame the fury she'd seen in him, wanted to watch him smile, wanted to dispel the bitter wariness that enveloped him.

She wanted *him*! The knowledge was excruciating. She realized from the tenseness in his body that his kiss was as involuntary on his part as it was on hers, spurred by some otherworldly beings who had conspired to bring together two people who should never have met.

But she was drowning in the essence of him. His hair was damp, curling around her fingers. She felt tremors course through his body as his kiss deepened, his tongue teasing and playing, arousing even more unfamiliar feelings in her, speeding the flow of her blood, of her breathing, of her heartbeat.

She whimpered as the pressure inside grew, every part of her, every bone, every nerve stingingly alive, as if fire ants were running wild throughout her. Her hands tightened around him, and their bodies melded together as one. She felt as if she would explode with needs that were still a mystery yet irresistibly beckoning.

He groaned, and then his mouth left hers, and her eyes met his. She saw a muscle straining in his cheek. His eyes were no longer hooded but burning in a way she thought impossible before. She felt his fingers, which had been sensually wandering up and down her back, press into a fist as his body went incredibly still.

And then he released her and moved away, the expression on his face one of such unbearable anguish, Shea thought her heart would shatter from it.

He turned around abruptly, his fist suddenly pounding into a table, a gesture of so much boiling violence that she flinched. His back bowed slightly as he leaned down. So much raw, naked emotion surged from him that the room felt like a storm center, furious currents rushing between them, sucking at the life core of her. Shea couldn't even begin to comprehend the complexity of those currents. She just knew they drained the very breath from her as she watched him fight them.

Rafe silently cursed every perverse star under which he was born. Since the Comanche had killed his parents so many years ago, fate—and man—had systematically destroyed everything he held dear. He'd once thought man made his own luck, but obviously not, if a higher being decided otherwise.

Ten years. Ten damned years lost. And the rest of his life haunted by his scar.

He couldn't let go of those years, or the man responsible for that loss.

And some demon had put that man's daughter in Rafe's way, had made him want her with all the passion still left in his soul. More than that, those searching, sometimes bewildered but always honest blue-gray eyes touched a chord of a tenderness he hadn't known still existed in him.

Choose, the demon said. But there was no choice. The man in him cried out for justice, for vengeance. Hate was stronger than newly discovered need, passion. Ugly, violent emotions like hate and greed and jealousy always overwhelmed the gentler ones. He'd learned that in war, and it was a lesson reinforced in prison.

Passion was all he felt for the woman, he assured himself.

When he'd entered the cabin minutes ago, that brief look of relief—even welcome—on a face glowing in candlelight had been unexpected. Christ, he'd felt like a monster, particularly when he'd seen her hand. But she'd placed no blame on him, instead she'd given him that small smile, the one that said he had been missed. And so he had done what he had told himself he would not do. He had touched her, and touching her had led to something more.

And he discovered he wanted so much more.

He locked the thought away, as he had learned to lock away so many emotions, and slowly turned to her. The glow was gone from her face, and she stood against the wall, as if needing support.

Something in him made him strike out at her. Possibly because if he didn't, he might take her in his arms again, and it wouldn't be possible to let go. He had to make her hate him.

He made his gaze deliberately cruel as it swept over her, his words intentionally crude. "Are you offering to trade your virtue for your freedom? If so, I'm not interested."

Rafe knew he'd succeeded when outrage flared in her eyes. Her burned right hand swung toward his cheek, but he caught it before she could make contact. His eyes went to the blisters already forming there.

"Slapping me would hurt you far worse than it would me," he said mildly.

"You're a . . . a . . ."

" 'Bastard' is the word you're searching for, I think," he said mockingly.

" 'Bastard' isn't strong enough," she replied.

He grinned, though he felt no amusement. "I like that temper."

Sparks darted from her eyes like fiery rock thrown off by a volcanic eruption. He had taken a moment of sweetness and made it ugly. The ache inside him opened like a chasm, swallowing up those very brief seconds of pleasure, of normalcy, of forgetfulness. He was back in prison, the bars not of iron but every bit as confining, as stifling.

He turned away from her. "If you need to go to the stream, come with me," he said carelessly.

He was ripping away her privacy, her pride, just as the prison guards had cruelly shredded his. That first day in the penitentiary he was stripped, searched in the most intimate places, then scrubbed and deloused. He had crawled inside himself then; it had been the only way to survive.

He'd had no choice. Just as he had no choice now.

Too many other lives were at stake. His revenge was at stake.

It was the last thought he had before he heard a noise close behind him. Before he could react to it, pain ripped through his head, and he felt himself falling as darkness closed in on him.

Shea stared down at him. He seemed so big crumpled up on the floor, a spot of blood on the side of his head where the frying pan had struck.

The pan was on the floor too. Shea had used both hands to wield it, her right hand exploding with pain, then dropped it as soon as she'd hit Rafe Tyler.

For a moment she was rooted to the floor, unable to take her gaze away from Rafe Tyler. She leaned down and touched the cut, the skin that was swelling. His breathing, at least, seemed normal.

Go, she told herself. But she hesitated, not wanting to leave him lying there. Finally, she opened the door, having to move him slightly out of the way. His horse, thank God, was still saddled. She didn't know whether she could saddle a horse, particularly with her blistered hand. Then it occurred to her that Rafe Tyler must have been so concerned about her, he'd checked in on her without looking after the horse first.

She looked back at the still form now partially hidden behind the door. How long before Clint returned? How long before Rafe Tyler regained consciousness?

She thought of the kiss, the way she had responded, his mocking comments, and she hesitated no longer. She wished she had a pair of gloves, but she would have to step over him to find his, and she wasn't prepared to do that. Instead, she leaned down, tore a strip of material

from her white petticoat and wrapped it around her injured hand.

Shea walked quickly to the horse, running her left
hand down the side of his neck as she had seen Rafe do.
The horse was still sweaty, and she'd learned enough to
realize he needed a rubdown and rest, but she needed to
escape Rafe Tyler more. She needed to erase the memory
of that kiss, that moment of sweetness that had turned out
to be nothing more than one of his taunts. A punishment
for what he thought her father had done to him.

She bit down on her lip to keep from moaning as she
put her burned hand on the saddle horn and swung up.
She wished she had time to change back into the trousers,
but she didn't dare go back into the cabin, not when he
might wake at any moment.

The skirt and petticoat rode high on her legs, showing white underdrawers, but Shea didn't care. She had to
get out of here. She had to get to her father.

She had to go to the one place that she had been
thinking of as home.

Most of all, she had to get away from Rafe Tyler, from
all those feelings she didn't understand. She had to try to
outrun the poignant ache that already was gnawing a hole
in her. She pressed her heels against the horse's side,
feeling its reluctance to move for her. She kicked again,
and slowly, the bay moved away from the cabin with its
half-open door and the sprawling body beyond it.

Clint Edwards stopped by the Circle R ranch to report he'd killed two wolves in the woods around the
mountain pasture and would be going on into Rushton to
meet the sheriff and the incoming stage.

Jack Randall had already left for Rushton, hoping to

collect the payroll. Sam McClary had also disappeared earlier, according to one of the hands, who was feeding the stock.

Clint quickly changed into a clean shirt and saddled a fresh horse. There should be news of the robbery by now, and he needed to stop by the general store for some salve. He'd then have to find a way to get it to Rafe's valley; he'd been gone too often already. Perhaps Ben could take it; the mining claim where Ben often stayed with Simon was fairly close, and the woman had already seen Ben.

If Ben had made it through last night's attempt to steal the payroll. Clint's stomach knotted. He had faith in Rafe Tyler. He hadn't exaggerated when he'd told the woman that Tyler was the best officer he'd ever seen.

Yet Ben was Clint's best friend as well as brother. It was always Ben and Clint. At times others had been allowed into that small circle—those they'd served with during the war and those who now served the same restless master. Perhaps if there had been a woman, a certain kind of woman who understood . . .

Kate might have understood. But Clint was in direct opposition to Kate's father, a path—now that Shea Randall had seen him—that would lead to deadly collision if he stayed after their task was reached. He wouldn't subject Kate to having to choose between family and himself.

Furthermore, Clint was only too aware that what he and Ben were doing might well result in prison terms. He'd seen what imprisonment had done to Rafe Tyler, the change from confident, well-liked officer to the embittered, driven, withdrawn man he was now. And he wouldn't saddle Kate with that kind of burden.

But damnation, it hurt. He knew from her eyes that she was more than halfway in love with him. And when he was with her, he knew a peace he never thought he could have, a sense of belonging gone since the war.

He had to stay away from her, to keep her removed from his house of cards before it fell in on her. If the robbery last night was successful, this whole mess might quickly come to an end. If they were right, if desperation spurred Randall into doing something openly dishonest, they could leave by the end of summer. Move on to someplace far away, like Oregon or Montana. The prospect was painful. Clint had enjoyed his position at the Circle R. He had learned he was good at ranching, and then, of course, there was Kate.

He dismissed the thought. Other obligations were more important. Loyalty, for one. Justice, for another. He would never let Rafe Tyler down, no matter what the cost. His own losses would be minor compared to Tyler's.

As Clint approached the general store in Rushton, he was aware that excitement permeated the usually quiet town. Jack Randall's buggy was hitched to the rail in front, along with a dozen other horses. Several men talked excitedly outside the doors of the store.

He dismounted, tying the reins of his animal to the hitching post, and walked inside. Randall, his face strained and his mouth grim, was talking to Russ Dewayne. McClary was standing a few feet away, a smirk on his face. Clint felt his dislike for the man increase.

"Mr. Randall. Russ," he acknowledged. "Did the payroll arrive?"

Dewayne looked disgusted. "There was a robbery at the stage office in Casey Springs. They took the payroll."

Clint didn't have to feign the concern on his face. "Were any of them caught?"

"Hell, no," Russ said. "It was the damnedest thing I've ever seen. There were explosions on two sides of

Casey Springs. There was so much damn confusion, no one paid attention to the express office."

Clint was able to breathe again. "Any idea who's behind this?"

"They took only the Circle R payroll," Russ Dewayne said. "That's the peculiar part of it. There was other money there, and mail. It seems someone has it in for Jack here. We've been trying to figure it out."

Clint glanced toward Jack. "Any ideas?"

Before his employer could speak, the sheriff continued. "There's something else odd. A young lady apparently appeared at the stage office several days ago, claiming to be Jack's daughter and inquiring about an escort to Jack's ranch. She seems to have disappeared."

Clint raised an eyebrow. "Claiming?"

It was Russ who answered. "Jack doesn't have a daughter."

Clint turned back to Russ. "She's an impostor?"

Randall hesitated. "I was married once. . . . I wasn't aware there was a daughter. . . ." Randall turned to Russ. "I'm going to Casey Springs and make some inquiries, send some telegrams."

"What should I tell the men?" Clint asked.

Jack Randall put a hand to his face as if to protect it from other revelations. He suddenly looked old and tired. "I don't know."

Clint brushed away the faintest sympathy. "You'd better take my horse then. I'll take the buggy back to the ranch."

Randall's blue eyes met his. They were filled with a gratitude that hit Clint like a hammer stroke to the stomach. "Thank you."

"What about Mr. McClary?" Clint asked. "Will he be going with you?"

Randall shook his head quickly, and again Clint had

the impression that Randall disliked McClary. Then why
was he a guest?

"You and Nate are in charge," Randall said. "I don't
know how long I'll be gone. I'll have to wait for some
telegrams."

"I'll ask the men to be patient about their pay," Clint
said.

Randall's gratitude was hard to accept. Clint had
never been a devious man. He didn't like the role now,
dammit, but he nodded.

Randall started to walk out. "It's the roan," Clint
said.

Randall nodded as if sleepwalking. "Thanks, Clint,"
he said quietly, and disappeared out the door, leaving
Clint and Russ standing together.

"What are you going to do, Russ?"

The sheriff shook his head. "They could be any damn
place, including north of Casey Springs, though I don't
think so. The robbery is in Sheriff Quarles's jurisdiction,
not mine, but still, I think I'll do some looking around in
the mountains. If they really are after Randall alone,
they'll be up there someplace."

"It doesn't make sense," Clint said.

"No," Russ agreed. "But somehow they knew the
stage would be heavily guarded this time."

Clint's stomach clenched. The implication was clear,
and Russ was not a stupid man. There were a limited
number of men who knew Russ Dewayne and his sons
planned to accompany the stagecoach today. Clint was
among them.

But there was no suspicion in the man's eyes. Instead, he smiled suddenly. "Why don't you come to supper tonight? Kate's a damn good cook. And I'd like to get
your ideas on this."

Very much surprised by the invitation, Clint couldn't concoct a reason to refuse. He nodded.

"Seven," Russ said.

"Seven," Clint agreed, hoping his voice didn't convey the sickness he felt in his belly.

Chapter 13

Shea headed the horse into the woods, but she had no idea which direction to take. The valley seemed ringed by ridges and walls, but there had to be an opening. She remembered climbing the day that she was brought to the cabin, and then descending, so she headed toward the highest ground. The horse remained reluctant, continuing to try to turn its head toward the direction of the cabin, and it took all her determination to keep him going in the direction she wanted.

She heard the sound of water, and she knew they were near the waterfall. She didn't remember hearing it when Ben had taken her here, and started to turn in another direction until she thought of the horse. She wondered when the last time was that the horse had had something to drink.

She decided to head for the waterfall. There, she dismounted, and holding the reins tightly, led the horse to the pool. It drank slowly, and she stretched out on the bank to splash cool water on her face. She needed all her wits about her.

The horse suddenly acted skittish, almost jerking the

reins from her hand. She rose and tried to mount, but the horse was shying away, trying to get loose.

And then she heard an agonizing cry from somewhere in the woods, followed by a roar of rage. The first cry was almost that of a child. Pain was evident in the sound, and she felt herself tremble. Something was very wrong. She wished she'd taken the gun Rafe Tyler had been wearing.

She made another desperate attempt to mount, and this time she succeeded, but only by holding on for dear life with her blistered hand. Pain sliced through her. She could feel the horse's agitation, its fear. There was another long-drawn-out moan, and several more roars.

Shea suddenly thought of the bears that had been so carefree a few days ago at the waterfall. The roars must be coming from a full-grown bear, the cries from a cub. She closed her eyes as if that would also shut out the sounds, but it didn't. And then the moan became whimpers.

There's nothing you can do. Go while you can, her mind kept repeating. *Go. Go. Go.*

Run!

The horse neighed plaintively, still fighting the reins, and Shea knew she couldn't leave, not without the cries haunting her the rest of her life. There were traps throughout the woods, Rafe Tyler had said. What if . . . ?

Rafe Tyler would know what to do. But he was back in the cabin. Did she dare go back? What would *he* do?

She swallowed hard and heard the piteous, heart-rending whimper again. She had heard horses hated and feared bears. Even if she could somehow get near the animals, how could she help the cub with an enraged mother nearby?

Rafe Tyler will know what to do.

This time you won't get another chance to escape.

She ignored the last caution and gave the horse its head, knowing it would return to its master.

Rafe felt as if the world had fallen in on him. His head pounded. His hand went to a particularly painful spot, and he winced as it encountered a sizable bump and a trickle of blood.

He sat up slowly, after discovering that any abrupt move only made the pain worse. As he leaned on one arm, he saw the frying pan next to him and realized immediately what had happened.

He looked around, knowing Shea Randall was gone. At least, his gun was still in the holster and the knife in its sheath at his belt. He felt in his pocket. The key to the stable was there, the stable where he'd stored all the weapons and hidden Jack Randall's money.

How long had he been unconscious? And why in hell had he been so careless?

He thought of that damn kiss and swore to himself. If he found her again, he'd stay well away from her. And, if necessary, keep her hog-tied. If he failed to find her, he'd have to reach one of the others who could then alert Ben and Clint.

He stood, his head ringing, his bones feeling like jelly. He leaned against a wall, trying to will strength back into his body. Finally, he walked over to the door and looked out. The horse was gone, but then he expected that.

Ben had told him that Shea wasn't an experienced rider. Rafe thought of her alone in the woods, with a horse that was tired and could be hard to handle. Even if the bay didn't throw her, it could very well stumble in the mountains at night. It was still afternoon. How long had she been gone? It couldn't have been more than a few minutes.

Gritting his teeth against the pain in his head, he made his way to the stable. There, he chose a rifle, checking quickly to make sure it was loaded. He locked the stable again and turned toward the woods. A flock of birds rose from the trees, and then he heard the sound of hooves against hard ground. He quickly moved to the side of the stable, out of sight.

He watched as Shea Randall rode into the clearing. Had the bay turned back? But she appeared in control of the horse. Hellfire, she was returning on her own.

He started to move forward, then stepped back. Were there others behind her?

She slid down from the horse and hurried toward the cabin. She had no weapons in her hands, nor did there seem to be anyone with her. She stood in the doorway, apparently puzzled.

He still thought of a trap. Dammit, why else would she return when she'd risked so much to escape?

But the forest was giving him no warning. The birds had settled back in the trees again; the squirrels, after a brief respite, were back chasing one another across the branches.

He stepped out, the rifle in his hand, and she turned, suddenly seeing him and going still.

Rafe was a master at keeping emotion from his face. But his stalking walk, he knew, expressed his anger. She stepped back, blocked now by the wall of the cabin.

He reached her, but she didn't flinch. Her gaze held steady, and he couldn't help admiring her. Before he could say anything, she spoke, the slightest tremor in her voice.

"There's . . . an animal in trouble in the woods. I think it might be that bear cub."

He saw her swallow, and he believed her. God help him, he believed her. "Where?"

"Near the waterfall."

"Go inside," he said harshly.

"No."

"Don't press your luck," he said, his voice like a growl.

She ignored his warning. "Are you going . . . ?"

"Dammit, get inside before I carry you there."

"You won't know how to find them."

She was the most infuriating woman he'd ever met. Her face was so pleading, so earnest, those soft eyes so determined. Damn, but she got under his skin.

"Look, lady," he finally said. "You can't shoot, can you?"

She tipped her chin up defiantly. "Of course I can," she said, but those unbelievably honest eyes gave her away.

"Christ, you're a lousy liar," he said, exasperated. "If you're right and that little cub's in trouble, the mother's going to be damned dangerous. I can't worry about you and help him."

"What if something happens to *you*?"

He knew her concern wasn't for him but for herself. After all, hadn't she just tried to kill him? He looked at her coldly. "Clint said he would be back. He *will* be back."

She gazed up to the side of his head where blood had congealed and dried. "Are you . . . are you all right?"

"No," he said. "Now get inside."

"If I promise not to leave . . ."

"Miss Randall, don't even suggest it. Don't ask me for a goddamn thing. You want someone to help that cub, then you get inside." His usually indecipherable eyes were raging. She stepped back into the cabin.

"You might pray that Mama bear gets me before I return," he said in a low, furious voice before he slammed the door closed and locked it.

He stood there for a moment. Christ, his head hurt. He hadn't had any sleep in more than thirty hours, and he didn't know how to deal with a woman so unlike any other he had met. She never did what he expected. To risk everything to escape and then return because of a bear cub? He hated the thought that she *knew* he would go after that cub and had returned because of it. At least she'd had enough sense to come after him rather than trying to do something on her own.

Rafe realized the contradictory nature of those thoughts and chalked it up to his exhaustion.

He swiftly unsaddled the horse and put him in the stable. He couldn't take the horse. After getting a whiff of the bear, the bay would be nearly uncontrollable. And God knew what he would find. Rafe had seen what those steel-jaw traps could to do an animal.

Cradling the rifle in his arm, he started through the woods at a slow run. Halfway to the fall, he heard the poignant cries of the cub, the frantic grunts of the mother, and he increased his pace until he saw them directly ahead.

The black bear rose up on its hind legs, its teeth bared. Rafe froze, keeping very still until the bear remembered his scent. Then his gaze moved and found the small cub. Its leg was caught in a trap all right, and it was crying in anguish, moving frantically to free itself, gnawing at its own wounded leg. Blood covered the ground.

Rafe very slowly pulled on his gloves. "It's all right," he said to the mother bear in a crooning low voice. "I'm here to help."

The bear growled, pawing the air threateningly, and Rafe hoped he wouldn't be faced with the choice of killing the mother to save the cub or killing the cub so it wouldn't suffer. He moved a few feet closer, all the time crooning, "I'm a friend."

The mother bear moved closer to the cub, then came down on her four paws. She still made snarling sounds, baring her teeth, but as Rafe continued his approach, the bear gave way, falling back, leaving the way open toward the cub.

"You understand, don't you?" Rafe said in the same calm voice. "You know I just want to help."

But when he was nearly at the cub's side, the mother lunged at him, swatting him with a paw. A claw caught his left arm, and he felt ripping pain, blood running down his arm.

The cub whimpered, then resumed gnawing on its own leg. Rafe would have to kill the cub, and the mother bear too. He couldn't leave the small creature to suffer, and he knew the she-bear would never let him go.

But just as his right hand reached for his Colt, the mother moved to the cub. Her large tongue ran over her young, and then, surprisingly, she moved back, as if she had suddenly made a decision. Rafe took his hand away from the gun and leaned down, his fingers gently petting the cub to show the mother he meant no harm. There was a low growl but no more.

Ignoring the pain in his arm, Rafe reached down, anchoring the trap with his booted foot and taking the steel jaws in his right hand. He pulled with all the strength he could muster, and the trap opened. The cub dragged free its mangled leg and crawled away several feet, whimpering softly all the while.

The mother bear loped over to her cub, her tongue running over the leg, trying to heal it. Rafe watched them for a short while; then he took off his now-bloody shirt and ripped a piece of cloth from it, which he tied tightly around the gaping wound. He swayed for a moment, wondering what to do. He just couldn't think.

The cub cried out as it tried to walk, and Rafe knew the animal couldn't make it on its own. The leg hung at a crooked angle; it needed to be set and splinted if it was to be saved.

But would the mother let him take the cub? And if she did, could he get back to the cabin?

He moved slowly to where the cub sat, still whimpering. The mother watched carefully, but the hostility was gone. "You know I won't hurt him now, don't you?" Rafe said, speaking with the soft voice that had tamed Abner and gentled the bay. He reached out with his right hand and took the cub in his hand, half expecting the black bear to lunge again. It didn't.

He started walking, the she-bear following him at a distance. The cub huddled in his arms, its small, miserable cries spurring him on. A mile . . . maybe more.

Think of Shea Randall, of those anxious eyes. He forced himself to keep going. One step at a time. His arm was all fiery pain now, and his head still ached from the earlier blow. And he was so very tired. He reached the clearing and fumbled in his pocket for the key to the padlock on the cabin door. His left hand was so clumsy, nearly numb, but he finally fitted the key in the lock. As the door opened, he started to fall. His left hand grabbed the edge of the door, and he managed to lower the cub to the floor, but then his body started to crumple. He felt a hand grab his arm. Such a fragile hand. Yet there was surprising strength, he thought as he made it to the cot before everything went black for the second time that day.

* * *

The feel of cool water against his skin brought Rafe back to consciousness. The feather-light touch of fingers tempted him to return into an unwelcoming world of pain. He felt so heavy, weighed down by total exhaustion. His head pounded, and his arm felt on fire. He tried to move, but his body wouldn't obey.

"Rafe." The voice was soft and gentle and coaxing. He couldn't remember when anyone had said his name like that before, and it curled around inside him, warming and soothing, a balm to wounds much deeper than those on the surface of his body.

He opened his eyes to see hers. They were so near, the blue-gray color full of concern and worry. But not for him. Never for him. That wasn't possible, could never be possible. He closed his eyes. His mouth was dry, and he tried to swallow.

"Rafe," she said again. "You have to help me." There was command in her voice now, unexpectedly strong. He opened his eyes again, trying to understand.

"You can . . . go now," he whispered harshly, refusing to believe she would choose to stay. "I can't . . . stop you." He didn't want her to stay. He couldn't permit her to stay, because then . . . it would be her choice, and he couldn't deal with that. As his prisoner, she had been forbidden; he had been able to maintain some distance from her, although at times he'd failed miserably. But as . . .

"Hush," she said softly, her voice seeping through the denial in his mind. "This is my fault."

"The cub . . . ?"

"He's in here. I need your help. I don't know what to do. The mother is outside. She's going back and forth."

Rafe tried to sit. The movement made his head pound even more, and he felt a new surge of pain in his arm. He swallowed a groan but knew his lips had twisted into a grimace. He managed to lean against the wall, his gaze finding the cub cradled by blankets and clothes in a corner.

His gaze then went to his arm. The bandage he'd wrapped around it had been replaced by a piece of white linen now red with blood. His chest, he remembered, had been streaked with blood from both himself and the cub, but Shea had apparently washed it off.

Her eyes followed his. "I . . . sewed that cut up," she said hesitantly, "while you were still unconscious."

His face questioned her.

"My sewing kit." She hesitated, apparently not knowing whether additional explanation was needed. "I'm very good at sewing. My . . . my mother had a hat shop. I helped her."

Rafe tried to assimilate the information. Randall's daughter. Hat shop. Sewing kit. He remembered it then, remembered finding it when he was searching her belongings and deciding to let her keep it. A small needle was no weapon.

"How long was I unconscious?"

"Long enough for me to do that," she said.

"Why . . . didn't you leave?"

She tipped her head slightly and suddenly smiled. It was a breathtaking smile, full of a mischief he hadn't expected in her. "The mother bear wouldn't let me."

"You could have let me bleed to death," he said bluntly. He didn't understand why she had doctored him, nor why she hadn't left when she had the chance. She still could. He couldn't stop a kitten from leaving now.

The mischief left her face. "Do you really think I could do that?"

"Yes," he said grimly. "Anyone with a grain of sense would have."

"Anyone with a grain of sense wouldn't have fol-

lowed a stranger into the mountains," she answered
mildly. "Now what do we do about that little fellow?"

"What you did with my arm," he said. "Sew up that
wound. And a splint. I'll need a splint for its leg. Maybe
we can save it." The "we" slipped out, and he regretted it
immediately. Still, it sounded . . . right.

She nodded. "Can you hold him while I sew?"

He didn't know if he could hold the small bear, but
he would try. He'd gone through too much for the
damned animal to let it die. "Yes."

She left his side and went over to the bear, picking it
up with such care that Rafe envied it for a moment. He
moved his wounded arm to take the cub and bit back an
oath as the throbbing pain flared again into red-hot sparks
of agony. Something must have crossed his face, because
she asked, "Are you sure . . . ?"

In reply he reached out and took the cub, gritting his
teeth against the pain. "Just do it."

She reached down beside him, and he saw the sewing box. He watched as she threaded a needle. "We need
to muzzle him first," he said. "Despite his age, he has
sharp teeth, and he isn't going to understand."

Distress crossed her face, and then she nodded and
leaned down, tearing a strip from her petticoat. It looked
exactly like the one on his arm. He took it and expertly
tied the cub's muzzle closed, then ran a hand down its
back, comforting as much as he could.

Shea washed the leg with water that he supposed
was bloody from her doctoring of him. Then her face
screwed up with concentration, she leaned over her little
patient and started to sew as Rafe held the leg tightly with
his right hand. Her movements were surprisingly deft,
even with the animal flinching. When she had finished
the last stitch and tied it, he glanced up and saw her
anxious expression, her teeth biting her lip, her eyes

glazed with tears for the little bear's pain. Her cheek had a smudge of blood where her hand had brushed away a strand of hair, and it was livid against her skin, which was pale from strain.

Her gaze rose to meet his, and he found himself smiling slightly at her, a wave of satisfaction, of intimacy, passing between them at what they'd accomplished with the cub. A lump formed in his throat, and he couldn't breathe for a moment. She was blood-splattered and sweaty, tendrils of damp hair escaping the braid and falling by the side of her face, yet he thought her the most lovely thing he'd ever seen.

A pleasure he'd never known before snaked around inside him, soothing all the raw, aching places. Since the court-martial, he'd felt as if someone had taken him, ripped him up in pieces, and now those pieces were finally coming together again.

The bear squirmed, and its muffled wail suddenly broke the spell that had mesmerized both Rafe and Shea. Rafe came back to reality, to who and what he was, and who and what she was.

"I need a splint," he said, forcing a coolness he didn't feel into his voice.

She jerked back. "What kind of splint?"

"A piece of wood. Small but sturdy."

She looked around the cabin. She'd used all the wood in the fireplace last night. "I'll have to look outside."

He gave her the cub. "I'll go." He tried to rise. The loss of blood, the blow to his head, the nearly overwhelming weariness, were like a ton of iron on his back, but he couldn't let her leave the cabin with the outraged animal outside. The she-bear knew him and apparently trusted him to a certain extent. Using all his will, he stood and staggered to the door.

The bear was prowling back and forth under the

trees. It eyed him malevolently but made no move toward him as he went to the woodpile and found a branch he could use. He barely made it back to the cabin and fell on the cot, closing his eyes as he willed himself not to lose consciousness again. In a moment some of the dizziness faded. Christ, he needed a drink of whiskey, a good night's rest.

He took the knife from his belt, and fashioned a small splint while Shea crooned to the cub as he had done. He signaled her to bring the animal back, and he tied the splint to its leg. He knew the cub would try to bite it off, especially when the itching of healing began.

When he was through, he leaned back against the wall, and Shea placed the small animal in the makeshift bed she'd made for it. Rafe closed his eyes, immense weariness flooding him.

Something cool touched his shoulder, and he forced his eyes open. He noticed her hand then, the hand that had sewed his wound and the bear's. It had tiny blisters all over it, several now broken and oozing.

"Why?" he said hoarsely as Shea lowered his head to the cot. "Why in hell do you have to be Randall's daughter?"

Chapter 14

Shea sat next to Rafe as he slept.

She couldn't take her eyes from him. Not from the new wound on his arm, nor the old scar on his shoulder, the one he must have incurred when he'd saved Clint and Ben during the war. Two wounds. Both because of his compassion and courage.

Her gaze went down to his hand, to the *T* branded there. She could only guess at the cost of that brand to his pride. She didn't even want to think of the ten years he'd spent in prison.

What if he had been innocent?

Shea Randall now thought that he probably was. She'd suspected it earlier but hadn't wanted to admit it, for that would be condemning the man she believed to be her father. It had been his testimony that convicted Captain Tyler.

But no one who had done what Rafe had just done would have betrayed his uniform. He'd risked his life to save an animal, had shown patience and gentleness even after being mauled. A greedy man, a dishonest man, would have stopped at much less.

The only explanation that vindicated her father was that Captain Tyler had been a soldier for the other side, but she couldn't accept that either. He was too straight-forward, too bluntly honest, to have been a spy, too admired by men ready to sacrifice everything for him.

Captain Tyler was the best officer I ever saw throughout the war. Do you really think a man who would risk his life, who would disobey orders to save two enlisted men, would do what they said he did?

Clint Edwards's words. Words from a man who backed his belief with a loyalty that could cost years of his own life.

Abner had climbed up on the bed and on Rafe's leg. Shea leaned over and swept him up before he could venture across her patient's naked chest and perhaps wake him.

She ran her fingers down the mouse's back. "You missed him, too, huh?" she whispered brokenly.

Lying on the cot, sleeping fitfully, Rafe Tyler looked so . . . so vulnerable. Golden eyelashes sheltered those daunting eyes. Light from the late afternoon sun softened the harsh lines of his face. She thought of his kindness and gentleness to the cub. Despite all he'd suffered, he'd not lost compassion, nor the ability to care about something weaker than himself.

Why in hell do you have to be Randall's daughter? He would never forgive her for that.

She should leave, but she didn't. Any number of things could happen to him. An infection from the wound. A delayed reaction from that blow to his head. The mother bear might get impatient and try to come in. She couldn't leave him helpless like this.

Her mouth was suddenly dry, and she realized there was no drinking water. She had used the water in the bucket to wash his wounds. Reluctantly, she set the mouse down on the bed and went to the door, opening it. The bear had stopped prowling and was sitting not far from the cabin door, its eyes intent on her. It stood up, as if to warn, and Shea slammed the door shut, realizing that she was just as much a prisoner now as she had been this morning.

She couldn't escape if she wanted to.

Rafe's skin was clammy by early evening. He needed a doctor.

He needed more than she could offer.

Several times he had seemed to gain consciousness, but his eyes, bright with fever, didn't see her. He stared sightlessly at the ceiling, a strange calm holding him still when others would have been thrashing from the fever. She realized in a flash of insight that he was so accustomed to controlling his emotions that even now a subconscious part of him was keeping him quiet.

She was thirsty and knew he must be too. She had been cooling him off with the bloody water, and it was getting sticky. She couldn't wait any longer. She had to get water.

Shea had tried the door several times, only to close it quickly against the bear each time. She had to try something else. Perhaps if the bear saw its offspring, it would back off, knowing the humans were only offering help.

Shea was shaking as she leaned down to pick up the cub. It whimpered at the disturbance but then swiped her hand with its tongue. If only the mother had the same gratitude . . .

Shea opened the door slowly and took a few steps outside, keeping the cub in front of her, showing the mother it was alive and, if not well, at least in caring hands. She set the cub down and retreated to the doorway, watching as the mother approached and carefully examined it, sniffing and poking. The mother urged the cub up, and when the cub tried to take a step and fell, the mother looked confused and tried again to nudge its offspring to its feet.

Shea stood watching, sympathy welling in her for the she-bear, for its obvious frustration, but nevertheless eager to get to the stream. As if the bear sensed her need, it gave a low growl and retreated. Slowly, carefully, Shea walked to the cub, picked it up, and carried it inside, then went to the door again. The bear had moved back to the trees.

It was worth a chance, Shea thought. She picked up the pail and cautiously left the cabin, praying with every footfall. The bear stayed where it was, and Shea quickened her pace. At the stream she rinsed the bucket, then filled it to the top with cold water and returned to the cabin.

Rafe Tyler had moved and was now half off the small cot, his leg dragging the floor. Abner had crawled up and was snuggled in the crook of his arm. It was a wonder, Shea thought, that the mouse had not been smothered in her absence. She swallowed hard as she saw the new blood on the bandage on his arm. The cub was also making distressed sounds in his corner.

Dear heaven, where was Clint?

Shea didn't know why Rafe was unconscious. The head wound? Loss of blood? Exhaustion? All three? She poured water into a cup and tore off still another piece of petticoat. She soaked it and then washed his face, distressed at the heat of it.

"Rafe," she whispered. "Please tell me what to do."

His eyes flickered open, and he tried to sit. She saw a muscle move in his cheek, saw the frustration in his eyes as he struggled to rise.

Her hand went out to steady him, and his gaze moved to her face and then to her hand. The expression on his face was confusion, and then . . . something like rage replaced it. He jerked away from her hand as he apparently comprehended his own weakness, his dependence on her.

"I don't need you. . . . I don't need . . . a Randall. I would rather hang, goddammit. Why don't you go?" When she didn't, he snarled, "Get out!" And then, as if the anger had been too strong to sustain, it drained from his eyes, and they closed again.

But his fist balled up tightly, and she knew he was still awake.

She felt his words like a knife in her heart. She'd never been hated before, and now she was being hated for something she couldn't help, because of a man she didn't even know. She retreated to the door, but she couldn't force herself to open it.

She was as puzzled as to how to help him as the mama bear had been about her cub. A part of him had given up when he'd realized he was no longer in control, that he was at the mercy of a Randall. And he needed to fight. He was so weak, and infection was a distinct danger.

She suddenly had an idea, the only one that might work. "What about your friends? Do you want them to hang with you?"

His eyes flew open, fury clouding pain, clouding that defeat. "You wouldn't."

"How do you know what I'll do?" she taunted him. "I'm a Randall, remember?"

He tried to get up but fell back, beaten by the loss of blood, she thought. Or that exhaustion he had defied long enough to save the cub. She knew him well enough now to understand how much he hated showing weakness and pain.

"Damn you," he whispered.

"Even that bear outside had enough sense to know it needed help," she said softly.

His eyes met hers. "You didn't go out . . . ?"

"I showed her the cub, that it was all right, and she seemed to understand we were just trying to help. It was the only way I could get some fresh water," she explained.

"That was a damn fool . . ."

"Not any more than rescuing that cub."

He moved slightly, and she saw the sudden strain in his face, the clenching of muscles in his cheek. "Don't move," she said.

"Why didn't you leave?"

"I told you earlier. Mama bear wouldn't let me." She knew the other explanation—that she was worried about him—would only worsen things.

"But you got water."

She shrugged. "I don't know the way out."

"That didn't bother you before."

"There's the cub."

He hesitated. "How is it?"

"Hurting. Like you."

His breath seemed to catch, and she saw beads of sweat form on his forehead. She dampened the cloth she'd been using and wiped it away. He flinched. "Don't."

"You need help."

"Not from you."

"You didn't do it, did you?" She didn't know why the question exploded from her at that moment. She both needed and feared confirmation of her growing conviction that he'd been wrongly accused and punished.

Instead of answering, he said wearily, "Go away."

"I can't."

"The hell you can't. I don't want you here."

"It's too late now," she said, a lump in her throat making her voice hoarse.

He ignored her denial. "Just . . . just promise you won't mention Clint and Ben."

"You don't believe my promises." Her hand went up to wipe his forehead again, and his wounded hand came up to push it away. His subsequent hiss of breath was loud and filled with agony.

She wanted to tell him not to move, but he wouldn't want even that show of concern.

"If you want me out of here," she said, "then you're going to have to take me. That means you have to get better. And you won't get better without rest." It was the only thing she could think of to make him stop fighting her, fighting his obvious need for her.

His face relaxed slightly. "Clint . . . should be back."

"Sleep," she said. "Get some rest."

"I don't want . . ."

"Until you're better, there's nothing you can do about what you don't want."

His gaze met hers. Rebellious. Angry. And then surrendering as he closed his eyes. It was, she knew, as much an attempt to close her out as to obey.

Rafe tried to block her out as he closed his eyes. He didn't understand why she persisted. Why she hadn't left. Why she was so determined to take care of him. Why she didn't understand he didn't want her help.

You didn't do it, did you? He hated the way he'd felt when she asked that question. But she hadn't really asked. It had been a statement, presented sadly, as if she already knew the answer. He'd felt a quick flare of warmth. Christ, no one had believed him except the small group helping him against Randall. Men he'd considered friends had deserted him, afraid he would taint their own careers. And the woman he'd planned to marry . . . she had been the first to desert him.

He couldn't even remember what she looked like now. In his mind's eye he saw just Shea Randall. And felt her hands. They had been so gentle when they'd touched him. No one had touched him like that before. Allison had touched him with passion, but never with tenderness, never with a soft, caring look in her eyes.

Shea Randall was the last person in the world he would expect to show understanding. He kept telling himself it was a lie, nothing but a lie. A trick.

Or that unlucky star again. He'd felt rage when he had seen her above him, so much bitterness toward whatever fates controlled him. He hadn't wanted that flash of wonderment over her presence, over the concern for him that made her eyes hazy. And he had lashed out at her, daring her to betray him, to prove him right about her.

He kept trying to convince himself that she would do exactly that, even as he fell asleep. There wasn't a damn thing he could do about it, in any event. He had to get his strength back. And then . . . and then he could reason again. Without those damned eyes looking at him, he could think again.

Shea kept the door to the cabin ajar, to catch the light, to listen for any rider and warn that person about the she-bear.

It was almost dark when she finally heard a frightened neigh and realized an incoming horse had smelled the bear. She looked down at Rafe. He was still sleeping, as restlessly as before but at least he was getting some rest. She was worried about fever; his skin had gone from warm to clammy and then warm again.

The rider was Ben. She ran out to him, keeping her distance from the large bear that was only too visible as it kept a careful eye on the cabin.

"What the hell?" he said as he tried to calm his skittish horse.

"You'd better take him inside the stable," she said.

"Where's Rafe?" His voice was suspicious, his eyes wary.

"Inside the cabin. Ill. I think he needs a doctor."

"If you . . ." The warning died as he realized she would have been long gone if she'd been responsible for whatever had happened. Still, his eyes remained watchful as he searched her face. "Why are you still here?"

"It doesn't matter," she said impatiently as the bear rose on its back paws, growling loudly. "Just take the horse inside," she said.

Ben dismounted, led the horse over to the stable, and stopped. "It's locked."

"The key must be on Rafe." She noted the stunned look on Ben's face, and if she hadn't been so concerned about Rafe, the bear, and the cub, she would have been amused at the odd expression. "I'll get it."

He hesitated, but he had no choice. His horse was nearly uncontrollable, and he couldn't tie it to a tree, not with the bear nearby. He nodded.

Shea went into the cabin and knelt next to Rafe. The key had to be in the pocket of his trousers, where he usually kept it.

He had moved again, and his leg had fallen off the side. His breath was not quite so labored, but his skin was still clammy. Thank God, there was some help now.

She searched the pocket that was reachable. Nothing. Her fingers skimmed over his chest, silently urging him to move without waking him. She found her hands lingering against the smooth hardness of his body. He groaned slightly and moved enough that she could reach his other pocket. She quickly searched and felt a key.

Just as she was extracting it, his eyes opened. His hand reached out, clasping her wrist with unexpected strength.

"What are you doing?"

The suspicion in his voice angered her even though the touch of his hand was like lightning running through her. "I thought you wanted me gone."

His hand didn't let go.

Shea tried to pull away, but he continued to hold her. "Your friend is here. And if he doesn't stable that horse, that bear's going to drive it wild," she said.

"Clint's here?"

"Ben."

He released her. "I'm sorry," he said, though he didn't seem sorry at all. But he'd given her as close to an apology as she was apt to receive.

She started to rise, but his question stopped her. "The bear's still out there?"

"She's not going anyplace. Not while her baby's here."

He lifted up on his good arm. "How is it?"

"In the same shape as you."

"That bad?" There was the slightest bit of humor in his voice, but his face was as harsh as ever. She wondered whether he'd ever laughed or joked or, for that matter, even smiled.

Shea looked down at her wrist, still red from his grasp, and his gaze followed hers. His hand touched it, fingers moving softly along the bright red ring, and then they moved to her hand, turning it over. Her palm looked so raw, a mass of broken blisters. She had almost forgotten the burn in her concern for his much greater hurt.

"You need some doctoring yourself," he said roughly.

She shrugged as he had done so many times. "It didn't help when I—" She stopped suddenly.

"Bashed me?" he asked wryly. There *was* humor in him. She hadn't imagined it. It was in his eyes, those gloriously bright sea-green eyes with all their mysteries and secrets and anger.

"I don't think I regret that. You deserved it. I *do* regret sending you out after that cub."

"Lady, you didn't send me. I went willingly. Damn fool thing to do, almost as damn fool as your hanging around and sewing me up."

Lady. It was an improvement over "Miss Randall," said with such disdain. But despite his light tone—light for him—his mouth was grim, lines of strain deepening the crevices of a face already deeply sculpted by hardship. She knew he was struggling for control, control of himself, of her, of a situation he'd almost surrendered to earlier. Struggling with the sheer force of his will rather than physical strength. Whatever weakness, whatever despair, he'd expressed earlier was gone now, overpowered by a relentless determination that awed, even frightened, her. His hand still held hers, not by might, but by another force that was just as strong. Their gazes met, held, mesmerized one another, will battling will even as recognition of something more stretched between them, binding them as no rope or chain could.

Shea had never believed in love at first sight. She had believed that love had to grow, had to be nurtured carefully as any young thing. Her mother had told her that, and Shea had believed her. Her mother had loved, enough to mourn all her life. At least that was what Shea had once believed.

Nevertheless, she'd never been able to bring herself to accept one of the few men who offered for her. There had never been the slightest spark, the slightest ember, of a smoldering great love ready to be fanned.

Now there were sparks. Dear God, there were sparks. Sparks and fireworks. Explosions. Tornado and cyclone, both spawned of powerful, conflicting winds. More than that, there was an intimacy that kept creeping between them, a knowledge of each other that revealed itself in unexpected ways. He had known she would love the waterfall, would enjoy the playful bears. She had known he would go after the cub. He had suffered himself —it had been in his eyes—when he'd seen her burned hand. She had felt the pain of his ripped skin where the bear had clawed him. No matter how little either wanted these feelings, they were there. Destiny? She had always thought people wrote their own destiny. Now she felt buffeted by furious winds over which she had no control.

There was a wild, terrified neighing outside, and Shea suddenly came back to the moment, to Ben waiting outside. How long had it been? Not more than a few moments, but in some ways it seemed a lifetime. She shook off the forceful emotions caused by Rafe's touch. A touch she didn't want to relinquish but must. A tremor racked her body as she pulled away, the key still clutched in her hand.

Rafe sank back on the cot, as if he, too, had been battered by a storm too strong to resist. But that piercing gaze of his didn't leave her, and it took every bit of will she had to rip away from it.

She nearly ran from the cabin. Ben was having even more difficulty controlling the horse as the bear growled, moving restlessly under the trees. His gun was out, and Shea screamed, "No," and ran toward him.

His hand wavered, then dropped as he waited for her to open the stable door, but the key fell from her injured hand. Ben stared at her hand for a moment, then leaned down, picked up the key and quickly unlocked the door. Shea held it open with her good hand as he took the horse inside, calming it with his voice. When the horse finally stood silently, he turned to her. "It took you long enough. I was about ready to shoot that damn bear and come after you. Will you tell me what in the hell is going on?"

"Rafe . . . rescued the bear's cub. . . . It's inside the cabin." She tried not to see the surprise in his eyes at her use of Rafe. The name now came easy to her. Too easy.

He began unsaddling the horse. "You said he was ill."

"The bear clawed him when he was taking its cub from a trap."

Ben didn't seem surprised. "And you. Why are you still here?"

She knew the mother-bear excuse wouldn't work on him. He had seen she wasn't afraid. She shrugged. "I didn't know . . . what direction . . ."

He nearly smiled. "I heard that didn't stop you before."

"I learn quickly."

He finished rubbing the horse down and picked up his saddlebags. "Clint told me you'd burned your hand. I brought some salve and a few other medical supplies. Appears it's a damn good thing."

"He's in a lot of pain."

"That bother you?"

The quizzical expression on his face rattled her. "A hurt polecat bothers me."

This time he grinned. "Then you two have something

in common. I've never seen a man so concerned with critters. Even that little mouse. You know he carried him a thousand miles. . . ."

Shea suddenly felt defensive. "We have nothing in common. He's an outlaw, a—"

"Be careful, Miss Randall," he said, his voice very quiet all at once, "or we might talk about your own shortcomings or those of your . . . father."

"I wish you would," she defended herself. "You insinuate, you make charges, you blame, all the while kidnapping, stealing, robbing—"

He stopped her with a penetrating gaze. "Randall doesn't know anything about you. *If* you are his daughter. He was completely surprised when someone told him a woman claiming to be his daughter appeared at the stage office."

Shea went stiff. She'd realized from the letters, from the absence of any mention of her, that he probably hadn't known. Yet the reality still stung. The mystery deepened. "I have to see him."

"Not until this is over."

"What is *this*?" she said with frustration.

"Rafe will tell you when he's ready," Ben said, giving her the saddlebags, then going to a corner to get a bottle of whiskey.

He moved to the door, opening it and grandly waiting for her to go first.

She did so and then watched as he closed the door and locked it, pocketing the key. A part of her had considered escape now that Rafe Tyler had help. But as she looked into Ben's face, she knew she had forfeited what little chance she'd had. She was a prisoner again, this time with two keepers.

She heard the lonely, anguished growl of the bear

still prowling under the trees. It didn't understand what was happening.

Neither did she. She didn't understand anything that was happening, particularly inside her mind and heart. Dear God, she didn't understand.

Chapter 15

Clint walked with Kate through the rose garden behind the Dewaynes' sprawling ranch house. It was her garden, and it suited her. The roses were planted haphazardly, not in neat rows but with abandon. Reds mixed with yellows, pink with white.

They smelled like her, too, and he thought she probably used rose petals for the fine flowery scent that always seem to cling to her.

Her hand touched his, and he found his fingers closing over hers, despite his intention to do exactly the opposite. He had meant to make it plain tonight that he wouldn't be seeing much of her, that his ranch duties precluded any social activities.

But nothing had worked as he'd planned, not since the moment he stepped over the Dewayne threshold. She had greeted him with that smile that warmed him through and through. Her green eyes had lit just at his entrance, and he felt his resolve fade like fog under a morning sun.

Even more disconcerting was his welcome by the others. He'd been treated like one of the family by her father and two brothers. Worse, he had been asked his opinion on what to do about the new lawlessness in Rush-ton.

Clint had felt so damn small, as if he needed to crawl under a rock. Instead, he had shrugged. "It seems strange they seem to be targeting Jack." He hesitated. "I don't much like that McClary who's staying there. And he *was* out the night the miner was killed."

Russ Dewayne nodded. "Can't say I care for him much, either, but he wasn't here when the stage robberies started."

"Maybe. Maybe not." Clint let the implication hang in the air: Maybe McClary just hadn't announced his presence until now.

"Can you keep an eye on him?" Russ asked.

Again, Clint felt like crawling under that rock. He'd done a lot in his lifetime he wasn't exactly proud of, but he'd never lied to a friend, to someone whom he re-spected and who trusted him.

He nodded, then changed the subject, asking about the Dewayne herd.

"Hell, you know. It's been rough all over; we were hit by winter as badly as Jack. We have to sell more of what's left of the herd than we'd like. But that's ranching; we expect bad weather, drought, wolves, coyotes. What we don't expect is that human carrion circling around here."

Clint inwardly winced. He wished he could explain. Now. But he couldn't, not without betraying Rafe, his own brother, and the others.

"What are you going to do, Russ?"

"Damn if I know. Wait, I suppose. Jack was right about trying to find anyone in these hills. There wasn't a trail after that first robbery. The tracks just seemed to disappear. I feel so rotten about Jack. He's worked hard to build the Circle R. Some of us are talking about advancing him a loan ourselves, but we all have our own problems now. What will his hands do?"

"They're getting impatient. Some are talking about leaving."

"And you?"

Clint was only too aware of four sets of eyes on him. He shifted slightly in his chair and saw Kate's face, anxiety on her face. No one had ever looked at him like that before. He hated to think of how that look might turn to something else, like contempt. "I haven't decided."

"You have a job here if you want one," Russ said.

Clint nodded a noncommittal acknowledgment of the offer, realizing that there was a hint of matchmaking going on here. He had been accepted as a suitor by Kate's family, and while he might have felt pleasure under other circumstances, he felt plain ill now.

Moments later, Russ suggested that the two "young people" take a walk, and Clint couldn't refuse without hurting Kate. That was something he simply couldn't force himself to do, not with her cheeks flushing with embarrassment over the unsubtle hint. He rose and went to her chair, pulling it out for her.

The moon was nearly three-quarters full, gold rather than silver, and expectancy hung in the air, the kind that usually preceded a storm. There was also expectancy between the two of them, a tension relayed by their touching hands, an almost imperceptible squeeze of fingers, a responding tightening of clasp.

"I'm sorry," she said.

"About what?"

"My family's . . . not so subtle matchmaking."

His hand tightened unwillingly around hers. He couldn't say he hadn't noticed. He wasn't good at lying. And that was the whole problem. At least one of them.

"You aren't going to stay, are you? In Rushton?"

How did she know? Clint stopped and looked down at her. She was lovely in the moonlight, a wistful look on her face, a faraway gaze in her eyes.

"No," he said. "My feet are tumbleweeds. They don't stop for long."

"You've been here nearly two years."

His eyes met hers directly. "I'm a drifter, Kate. I've never been anything else, not since the war."

He watched her swallow with difficulty, as if his words choked her. He felt the same thing happening to him. He wanted to kiss her so damn bad. But that was the last thing he should do.

"You never want to settle down?"

Yes. Now. He shook his head slowly. "I don't think I can." That was as direct as he could get.

She nodded, accepting his words, what she believed was his honesty. "I used to think I would like to travel. To go East. Or to San Francisco."

Kate was trying so hard to make it easy for him. There had, after all, been little between them except glances, a few dances, conversation that, up to now, had come so easily to them, and . . . that instinct between two people that tells them something extraordinary is occurring. Clint hadn't known it existed, and now it was too late for him.

"And now?" he said softly.

"Now I know this is where I belong, this land. These mountains."

Clint felt it again, that attempt on her part to dismiss the implications of their previous words, as if she was reassuring him that his decisions were his, his life his.

If only . . .

"If only?"

Clint hadn't realized he had uttered the words. He smiled down at her. "If only you weren't so lovely."

He saw her pleased look, that becoming blush coloring her face again. She truly didn't know how pretty she was, he thought.

He couldn't help himself. He moved closer to her, bent his head to touch her lips. She was like a lodestone to him, a magnet drawing him ever closer.

Her lips were soft, welcoming. Her skin was so incredibly soft, smelling delicately of roses. He wanted her as he'd never wanted anything in his life, had never thought he could want anything this desperately.

His lips played over hers lightly, and her mouth opened slightly to his. Her hand went to his arm, hovering there, as if uncertain what to do. That innocence was his undoing. His arms wrapped around her with gentle possession, and his lips moved along the delicate curves of her face, memorizing the pleasure of each touch, the quiet, satisfying joy of her response.

He rested his cheek against hers for a fraction of a second. "Oh, Kate," he heard himself say.

Her only answer was a slight movement of her face until their lips met again in a kiss so pregnant with promise, yet so bittersweet with understanding, that Clint knew he was lost between heaven and hell.

Jack Randall felt his world crumble as he looked down at the telegram.

Sara was dead!

There was a daughter. A daughter whose existence his wife had kept from him because Sara had so hated what he was.

He crushed the telegram in his hand. He had used what little cash he had left to hire a detective in Boston, adding a bonus for quick results.

It hadn't taken long. A day. A day to find a death

certificate and a birth certificate. For a daughter named Shea. His heart pounded so hard, so fast, he had to grab the counter to keep standing. Sara. Dead. Every hope he'd ever had died with her.

"You all right, Mr. Randall?"

It took a moment for the voice to penetrate his shock. *Mister* Randall. He had worked the last ten years to earn that title, that respect in the man's voice. He had always believed he would someday lure Sara back and show her he had changed.

"I'm fine, just a bit of a shock. A friend . . . died."

"I'm sorry, Mr. Randall. Is there anything I can do?"

Jack shook his head. "No. No, thank you." He turned around blindly, searching for the door, finding it and stumbling out into bright sunlight.

He headed for a saloon.

Sara had despised him so much, she had never told him he had a child. Only one thing in his life had ever hurt more: the day he'd returned to their boardinghouse room and found her gone, a note lying next to the bank bills she'd found.

And now he knew exactly why she had left. Sara would stay with a thief, but she wouldn't allow her child to do the same.

He was indifferent to the others in the saloon, going straight to the long bar. "Whiskey," he told the barkeep, and quickly swallowed the glassful. "Another."

He hoped the liquor would numb the overwhelming pain, but it only made brighter the memories. Sara's startling blue eyes that had once looked at him as if he were a god. He had saved her from a pair of runaway horses on a Boston street and then had charmed her into running away with him when her father had objected to his lack of family and a steady job.

He should have known better. She was as honest as

he was dishonest. He had been raised to see nothing wrong in relieving careless people of their money. She had been raised to see everything in black and white. And he had turned out to be very black indeed.

Until he met Sara, he'd never had a conscience. And in truth one didn't sprout then, either. Stealing had been so damnably natural for him. When Sara had first caught him at it, he'd sworn he would never do it again. But he had. Even then she'd stayed with him until . . . until she was with child.

He gulped down another whiskey. He'd never stopped loving Sara. After she left him, he'd had brief liaisons with women who expected little more than a few gifts, but he'd always hoped he could win Sara back. The army payroll was part of that scheme. It would provide enough money for him to go back East for her, convince her that he had changed.

But she'd seen that blasted article, and though he had continued sending money, he never again received any acknowledgment.

A daughter!

A daughter who had disappeared.

A daughter who had traveled all the way from Boston to see him.

He had tried to find out his daughter's whereabouts while awaiting information from the Boston detective. Someone at the hotel said a man had met a young woman the morning after his daughter's arrival. No one knew more. The description of the man fit a thousand men.

What had happened to her? Why hadn't she reached the Circle R?

Considering the robberies and McClary's information, he had a damn good idea. His hand closed around the whiskey glass tightly. Rafferty Tyler!

Rafferty Tyler had found his revenge.

* * *

Ben stayed overnight. Shea knew it was because he didn't trust her, but she was grateful just the same. The medicine and bandages he'd brought for her were useful in treating Rafe. Ben also had rudimentary doctoring skills Shea did not.

A legacy from the war, he'd explained as his hands had explored Rafe's wound. "There were few doctors, and we learned to do for ourselves much of the time."

He made the remark as he undid the bandage on Rafe's arm. He looked at her with surprise after examining the stitches. "You did this?"

Shea nodded, pleased at the sudden respect in his eyes. She didn't want to question why she cared, except a part of her was intrigued by the bond that linked these men together, by the loyalty that made them risk everything for one another.

Was it the war, which had been over eight years before? Or was it Rafe Tyler himself who commanded such extraordinary devotion?

After he'd finished with Rafe, Ben had turned to her. Rafe had wanted him to look at Shea's hand first, but she had demurred, saying it didn't hurt anymore and that Rafe's injuries were the ones that required immediate attention. Ben had needed little convincing, and Rafe had been too weak to counter Ben's determination.

Ben's lips now tightened as he looked at her hand. He said little as he spread salve on it. "Don't use it," he said curtly.

"I have to. The little bear."

Ben looked over at the corner where the cub was sleeping peacefully. "Rafe doctored it?"

"I sewed the wound. Rafe put the splint on."

He shook his head, as if at the foolishness of two

children. "I suppose I'd better bandage your hand then. It would be better to let the blisters air, but if you insist on using it. . . ."

She held it out to him and was surprised at the gentleness in his fingers as he carefully bandaged it. He then turned to Rafe. "I'll bunk here tonight, since you two can't seem to stay out of trouble." There was the slightest hint of amusement in his voice, and Shea reluctantly found herself liking him as she'd liked his brother.

Rafe sat up on the bunk. "I can take care of things."

"The hell you can. Abner could knock you over, and he doesn't even have a frying pan." Rafe had refused to say anything about the wound on his head, and Shea had had to explain, in a stumbling manner.

Rafe ignored Ben's comment. "Any news about the robbery?"

"None that I know of." He looked up at Shea. "Randall's gone to Casey Springs."

Shea flinched at the ease with which they discussed her father, their plans to destroy him. She still didn't know exactly what those plans entailed, but she knew the two men in the cabin were undeterred by her presence.

Rafe's glance only casually caught hers before turning back to Ben. "McClary?"

"At the ranch."

"Clint?"

Ben's eyebrows furrowed together, and he glanced at Shea as if unsure whether he should say anything. "He was busy tonight."

Rafe moved slightly and winced. "I'll move outside for the night."

"Hell you will," Ben said. "I don't want you getting pneumonia, and that's damn likely with that fever."

Tension rose in the room. Both men turned and looked at Shea, as if she had been created for the sole

purpose of bedeviling them. Well, bedevil them she
would. She was tired of being treated as if she weren't
even present, or a mere inconvenience.

"I'm hungry," she complained, and she found that
she was. She'd had nothing to eat all day.

The side of Rafe's mouth lifted, and Ben looked startled at the reminder that captives took a certain amount of
care.

"And the cub," she added, now that she had their
attention. "And . . . Rafe." She felt awkward using the
name in front of his friend, but it was too late to retreat to
anything else.

Rafe's mouth quirked even more. "I notice I come
last."

Shea ignored him and looked at Ben, who looked
bemused. "Something besides canned peaches and old
venison stew?"

Ben looked at Rafe. "Any ideas?"

Rafe shrugged. "I hung up the rest of the deer, and
it's a sure thing that damn bear has already gotten to it.
You *can* go fishing."

"And leave you alone with her?"

Rafe glanced quickly at Shea. His eyes were as indecipherable as ever. "She could have left before," he finally
said.

Shea felt anger rising again. She had, after all, sewed
him up and nursed him, and she was receiving precious
little credit for either.

Ben nodded reluctantly. "She did hit you. . . ."

For a moment Shea thought amusement danced in
Rafe's eyes, but it disappeared so quickly, she wondered
whether it was merely the glow of a candle.

"I promise I won't turn my back on her," Rafe said.

"You wouldn't have to," Ben said. "A little nudge on

her part would do as much damage now as that damned frying pan."

Rafe ignored the warning. "There's a pole in the stable."

"If I can get past that bear of yours."

A noise came from Rafe that could be interpreted as a chuckle. Shea doubted, however, that Rafe had the ability to do such a thing, even if his rock-hard nature allowed it. Even the slightest movement appeared to cause new waves of pain and weakness. He was wincing now as he very slowly lay down.

Ben took one last measuring look at him, and then at Shea. "I suppose Rafe has told you about the dangers of the woods at night."

"Repeatedly," she said wearily. Her gaze turned toward Rafe. "He even went so far as to give me an example."

"The captain can carry his point to the extreme," he commented dryly, unaware of the wince on Rafe's face at the use of the military title.

Shea noticed it, though. *He was the best officer I ever saw.* How much had it cost Rafe Tyler to lose that uniform? Particularly to lose it in disgrace?

Dear heaven, why did she hurt so much for him?

She turned away from him. She didn't want him to see her face; already he was all too astute at reading it. She had to do something, to take her mind from the hard, lean man who suddenly seemed so vulnerable. He would hate that, hate her for even thinking it.

The cub moved and whimpered. She leaned down and picked it up, cuddling it in her arms. "It's all right," she whispered. At least the bear tolerated her care. "We'll take good care of you."

Rafe shifted on the cot and watched her. Shea. He didn't want to think of her as a Randall now. Only Shea.

As she looked down at the baby bear, her mouth was softened by a smile, her blue-gray eyes alive with concern. She had not changed clothes and didn't seem to care about the stains of blood from both him and the bear.

Shea had said "we" when she'd crooned to the bear. *We* sounded good. Right. Even natural.

Maybe she wasn't Randall's daughter, he thought. But it really didn't make any difference. There could never be a *we*.

He closed his eyes, wishing for the oblivion of sleep, yet fearing the nightmares it sometimes brought. He didn't want her to hear them, to see the drenching sweat he sometimes woke to. Sometimes he dreamed of the branding. Sometimes the punishment box at the prison. But whichever, the dreams were always as real as the actual event.

The crooning from across the room turned into a lullaby, softly sung, filtering into his consciousness, lighting the darkness there. He allowed himself to relax, to listen.

When was the last time he'd heard a woman sing like that?

When he was seven? Before his mother was raped and killed by the Comanche.

The song was faintly familiar. Sweet and sad and lingering. Poignant in the love it invoked. Comforting in the soft, reassuring words. A promise of happiness. How long since he'd been truly happy?

He didn't want to think about it. He just wanted to absorb these sounds, the quiet, if temporary, pleasure they gave him. He wanted to go to sleep with them.

He knew he wouldn't have a nightmare tonight. For the first time in years he knew.

Chapter 16

Sam McClary watched as the miner below gently swished water in the pan and then dug through the residue. He picked something up, held it up to the setting sun, grunted, and placed it in a pouch he took from his pocket.

It was something, McClary thought disgustedly, but probably damned little. He'd discovered the remaining miners in these hills worked very long hours for precious little gold. They weren't really worth his bother, except for a certain side benefit: Rafferty Tyler.

He wanted to see Tyler hang. The superior "hero" who had humiliated and chastised him years ago in front of an entire troop. Rafe Tyler should have hanged years ago and would have, had it not been for that chicken-livered Randall, who interceded.

And in doing so Randall had created a very dangerous man, who was a threat to McClary as well as Randall. McClary had no doubt he would be Tyler's next target.

McClary had considered killing Tyler on the trip to prison but never got the opportunity. He'd been able to take out his frustration on the prisoner though. The fact that Tyler, despite his chains, had viewed him with disdain, had only hardened his hatred.

Now Tyler had help. That much was obvious. McClary didn't know who. He didn't know why. But he did know they weren't amateurs. Which made it very important that Tyler be caught, and caught quickly. The murder of a few miners might just spur on the law, place Randall even more under his control, and earn McClary a few dollars to boot.

He would wait until the miner left the creek and started the trek to his cabin.

Randall would know who did it, but Randall couldn't turn in McClary without revealing his own past. And the same timid streak that saved Tyler would keep Randall from saying a word now.

McClary smiled. He'd been small for his age as a boy and bullied by his schoolmates in the Kentucky hills. But he could shoot. Damn, if he couldn't pick off a squirrel at a thousand feet. This skill had made him a sergeant. But he still hadn't won the respect he so badly craved.

The miner below him checked his pan again and threw away the contents in disgust. He took up the wool shirt he'd discarded on the ground, pulled it on, and tucked the tail carelessly inside his trousers. He then reached for the gunbelt he'd placed next to the shirt, buckled it on, and started toward the cabin a few feet into the woods.

McClary, who was already spread flat on the ground, carefully sighted his rifle, the barrel following the route taken by the miner. McClary's finger slowly squeezed the trigger.

After several minutes he snaked his way down to the side of the miner, pulled the pouch from the man's trousers, and weighed it in his hand. There were several ounces, anyway.

He thought about checking out the man's cabin but decided against that. Most miners carried their pouches with them, afraid to leave the small amount of gold they collected in empty cabins. No sense staying longer than necessary.

McClary took one last look at the miner. Hell of a lot easier than rabbit hunting. He grinned mirthlessly. Another miner shot in the back. That should stir the folks up.

Randall debated with himself whether to tell Russ Dewayne about his daughter's disappearance or go looking for her himself.

He'd had a long ride back from Casey Springs, weighed down as he was by guilt and regret. He kept seeing Sara, accusing him, blaming him. And he felt responsible now for what she apparently had feared most: that he would, in some way, ruin their daughter's life.

The clerk at the Casey Springs express office said the woman who had approached him had light blue eyes, light brown hair, and a lovely smile. Sara had once possessed a lovely smile, quick and easy and guileless.

He would give anything to see their daughter. Even, he knew with sudden clarity, his life.

Would she be killed if he brought in the law?

If only he could talk to Tyler. Discover what he wanted. But he had no idea where Tyler was hiding.

He felt so damn helpless. Probably, he admitted to himself, as helpless as Tyler himself had once felt. What kind of man was he today? What did ten years of prison do to a man who had once been decent and honorable? Randall had avoided thinking about it these past few years, brushing the guilt away, performing charitable deeds that he hoped somehow made up for the one truly evil thing he had done.

Randall made his decision then. He would spend the next three days searching the mountains for Tyler and his daughter. If he found no sign of them, he would then ask the sheriff to form a posse.

And if he did find Tyler? He would bargain his life, his reputation, his freedom, if necessary.

If his daughter was dead? Randall knew he would kill Tyler and hope that Tyler's men killed him in turn.

Shea was sitting outside when Ben returned from the fishing trip. She had taken the cub outside to be inspected again by the mother. Once more the she-bear had urged it to walk, but the cub's clumsy attempts sent him sprawling, and so the she-bear had retreated.

Rafe was sleeping, so Shea, the cub in her lap, waited for Ben and put her fingers to her lips when he'd appeared. He gave the cub one of the fish at her insistence and at the cub's begging, and then built a fire outside to cook the fish.

The sky was breathtaking, the stars so many twinkling diamonds on a deep blue backdrop. Everything out here was so incredibly lovely, so different from the dirty streets of Boston, from the noise and the lights and fog that so often rolled in at night. She felt as if she could reach up and grab a star and clutch it closely to her. She wanted to take it inside and show it to Rafe, to show him there was something besides vengeance.

And then she grew sad, hope fading to a painful, hollow ache that echoed throughout her, when she realized she could never comprehend how he felt, how she would feel if she'd lost so much.

She looked over at Ben. He was watching the cub more closely than he was watching the fish. The baby bear was nibbling on her good hand; her bandaged right hand was resting on its head.

Ben also kept a wary eye on the place at the edge of the woods where the she-bear had paced earlier; it had disappeared, apparently to find its own dinner.

"Why didn't you leave when you had a chance?" He had asked the question before, and she had given him a nonanswer, one he hadn't accepted.

Shea was tired of avoiding truths. "He was hurt because of something I asked him to do."

"The cub, you mean?"

She nodded.

"He would have done it, anyway," Ben said dryly. "During the war . . ." He stopped.

"During the war . . . ?" she urged after a few moments. She was tired of being shut out, of sentences started and stopped.

"We had to kill some horses once. They were pulling caissons, cannon, and the Rebs were about to overrun us. There was no time to cut them loose, and we couldn't let the Rebs take them. Rafe gave the order to kill them, and I'll never forget the look on his face as he did it." Ben looked away. "As you probably know, he does damn little hunting. He hates it."

"And yet he's hunting my father."

Ben's glance cut through her. "I suppose he considers that necessary."

"Why?"

"Same reason you stayed here, I guess. It's something that he feels has to be done."

"And you?" She wondered whether she would get the same answer from him as she had from his brother. "Why are you here?"

"Why not?" He rose as if bored with the conversation. "If you want to know more, Miss Randall, ask Rafe."

He checked the fish and gave a sound of satisfaction. "Why don't you go see if he's awake."

Shea stood reluctantly. Ask Rafe. That's all they said. And Rafe said nothing.

Disgruntled, she walked to the cabin, hesitating just inside the door. The candle was now a puddle of wax without fire. A small bit of light from the moon crept through the window, though, and she could see that Rafe once more had rolled halfway off the cot. She leaned against the wall, watching him as her eyes grew accustomed to the dim light. He looked so uncomfortable, so big for the small cot, so restless for the small cabin. His hair was mussed, and his face, she knew, was thick with a day's bristles. She didn't want to wake him, but he needed to eat.

Still, she couldn't bring herself to disturb him. She very quietly walked to the corner where the cub's bed was at and put the animal down to sleep; then she sat down in the one chair and simply looked at Rafe Tyler. Even in sleep, his face was grim, severe. She wanted so badly to reach out and touch him. She was raw with the emotions she'd felt today: that desperate recklessness with which she'd hit him, the fear that she might have hurt him, the momentary exhilaration of freedom, and then the anxiety while he went to see about the bear. And finally his bloody appearance. Her nursing. Their doctoring of the cub. *We.*

Failure and success. Grief and joy. And now . . .

She was incredibly tired, completely confused. How could she care about someone who hated so fiercely, so relentlessly? But she did, and she couldn't deny it any longer.

Shea had sought a new home, a place where she belonged, and now she felt she had found it. Here in a rickety cabin with an outlaw and ex-convict who thought of nothing but revenge. No, that wasn't right. He'd thought of that bear cub. He'd worried about her hand. He cared about a mouse.

His eyes opened, as if he'd felt the intensity of her thoughts, and fixed on her.

"Your friend has cooked some fish. You need to eat."

Rafe moved, sitting up against the wall with a sigh. Then, carefully, he stood, swaying for a moment, and she instinctively held her hand out to him. When her fingers caught his elbow, he stiffened.

She melted. Touching him always seemed to have that effect on her. She was very close; his chest, still naked, was inches away. His breath was ragged, and she didn't know whether it was because of the wounds or something else. Her breath was also ragged, hard to come by, as it tried to pass through an almost closed throat.

She felt a tremor run though his body, and she looked up at him. His lips so near. "I'll bring you something to eat. You . . . you shouldn't be up."

"No," he agreed, and his lips came closer.

Her own body trembled then. Her strength was seeping away, lost in all those soft, wanting emotions. She felt fragile; her control could so easily be shattered by him, broken into a thousand pieces.

"Ah, Shea," he said. "Why didn't you leave?"

It wasn't a question this time. It was a plea, a surrender that was full of pain.

His head lowered, and she thought he was going to kiss her, but he didn't. Instead, his cheek brushed hers and stayed there a fraction of a moment in a gesture so tender and so sad, she thought her heart might break.

"I didn't thank you for . . . taking care of my arm," he whispered. "I don't know why—" His voice, husky with emotion, broke off.

She pressed her head against his chest, feeling, hearing, living, that strong heartbeat. She let it linger there, relishing the moment's closeness, the smell and feel and touch of him. The gentleness he exuded at the moment.

Then he drew away, and Shea moved back. He took several hesitant steps, then seemed to get stronger. He moved toward the door. "I hate being in here," he said suddenly in a tense, tight voice, and she knew he was thinking of prison again, that his rare moment of tenderness was swallowed by the darkness that usually cloaked him.

He lurched forward and leaned against the doorjamb as he looked up at the sky. He closed his eyes. Remember, he told himself. Remember . . .

But he wasn't sure what he should remember. Not anymore. He heard her steps behind him, and he opened his eyes. A lacy bit of cloud was waltzing across the sky. The wind was cool on his hot skin, and he drank in the mingled aromas of fish, burning wood, and pine. He was assaulted by sensations, overwhelmed by ordinary things that shouldn't affect him.

"Rafe?" It was Ben's voice. Worried.

"I'm all right," he said. "It's just . . ." Just what? He wished he knew.

"It's just that you're damn weak, and you need some food," Ben finished for him. "You haven't had anything since we left yesterday, have you?"

The question puzzled Rafe for a moment. And then he felt Shea sliding out between him and the door. For God's sake, what was happening to his senses? He damn well couldn't think. Not with her around.

He shook his head. "No."

Ben looked sheepishly at Shea. "I don't suppose there's anything we can use for dishes?"

"Just one tin plate, I think."

"That will have to do." Ben's eyes moved from her to Rafe.

That knowing glance jerked Rafe back to reality. He wanted to feel hostility. He wanted to feel anger. He wanted to feel indifference.

He wanted to take her in his arms. He wanted to kiss those cheeks that could flush so hotly, to touch that face that screwed up with such concentration. He wanted to see her smile.

Had he ever seen her smile?

Once. At the waterfall when she watched the bears. Not since then. Not before then.

What in hell had he done?

He had locked her in a place he himself couldn't tolerate. He'd subjected her to terror and hunger, and still she had stayed and helped him. He had truly become an animal himself, and he could no longer blame it on others.

His eyes met hers, and he sensed she'd read some of his thoughts.

"I'll get the plate," she said. "And the spoon." The latter was spoken wryly. He had taken all utensils except the spoon.

Rafe made his way slowly to the fire. "I . . . don't like keeping her here," he told Ben.

"Are you sure that's the problem?" Ben said. "Not that you like it too much?"

Rafe grimaced.

"She's seen both Clint and me."

"I know," Rafe said. "I don't think she'll say any-thing. . . ."

"Why wouldn't she? Especially if she sees Clint at the Circle R."

Rafe couldn't explain it. He just knew it in his gut. But could he risk two lives because of instinct? Christ, he'd been wrong in the past.

"Do you want to give it up?" Ben asked quietly. "Just move on?"

"I can't do that," Rafe said, hearing his own ragged voice, hating it, hating the weakness. "I won't do that," he added, his voice stronger. He looked down at his hand, the lifelong reminder of exactly how much Jack Randall owed him.

Just then Shea reappeared, her face a little pale in the moonlight. Rafe wondered whether she'd heard anything.

Ben took the fish from the spit he'd fashioned over the fire and, after looking at Shea's bandaged hand and Rafe's wounded arm, pulled the flaky flesh away from the bone and offered the plate to Shea, who placed it between herself and Rafe. "What about you?" she asked Ben.

"I already ate," he lied. "Mixed up a pan of beans. I'll go look after the horses." He made his way to the stable, leaving an uncomfortable silence.

As much as he wished differently, Rafe couldn't dismiss the last few minutes in the cabin with Shea Randall. They echoed between them, the feelings and emotions still radiating in waves. He felt like a marionette, whose strings were being pulled by someone else. It was a familiar feeling, one he'd vowed would never be repeated.

Yet the strings were being pulled again. By another Randall.

His gut tightened, and he hurt beyond healing. He was determined, though, not to show it. He forced his fingers to take a piece of fish and eat it. He had to rebuild his strength. Perhaps it was his physical weakness that made him so vulnerable.

He noticed she hadn't taken a bite, despite the fact that she had been the one who'd complained about hunger earlier. She sat there like a statue, staring into the fire.

"Eat," he commanded more curtly than he intended.

"Another order?" Her voice was strained, and he knew she had heard him and Ben talk. Christ, what had she expected? That he would drop everything because of a . . . kiss?

"Call it that if you like," he said, forcing indifference, masking the despair he felt.

"You aren't going to stop, are you?" she asked suddenly. "And you're going to destroy yourself as well as . . . my father. And probably your friends too."

"I'm already destroyed, lady," he said harshly.

"Only if you believe it," Shea said, her words trembling.

He laughed bitterly. "Do you think anyone would hire me? Do you think any community would ever accept me? And that a woman would look at me twice after seeing that brand, look without repugnance?"

"Yes." Her voice was soft but forceful.

He turned and looked at her, his lips twisted in a cynical smile. He didn't try to mistake her meaning. "Up here, when we're alone, maybe. For a few moments. Because you're scared and lonely and there's no one but me. But in town? How would you introduce me to friends? The outlaw? The ex-convict? A man who betrayed his uniform? A man so treacherous and vile, he was branded so everyone would know his dishonor, his shame, no matter how long he lived? Tell me, Miss Randall, would you really look then?"

There was a long silence. Her gaze met his, and he saw tears glisten in her eyes before she gave him the same answer as before. "Yes."

"You're a liar, Miss Randall," he said coldly, and stood. "You'd better eat." He didn't wait for an answer. He walked stiffly, every movement a supreme effort. He hoped like hell there was some liquor in the stable. He couldn't stand seeing those damn tears. No one had ever cried for him.

But he knew he was right when he'd said any feelings she might have would disappear quickly enough when she was free.

He found Ben, who looked at him with a raised eyebrow as he filled a feed bucket with grain for the horses.

"I'm more thirsty than hungry," Rafe said.

"I can tell I'm going to have to make another little pack trip into Casey Springs." Ben grinned knowingly. "That whiskey's going down fast."

"Go to hell, Ben."

"Friend, something tells me you're already there. She *is* rather pretty. More than pretty, really," Ben said as he fumbled in his saddlebags and brought out a flask.

Anguish ran strong and deep in Shea. She knew now that Rafferty Tyler would never give up his vendetta against her father. He would destroy himself and everyone around him first.

You're a liar. She would never forget the rage with which he'd hurled that accusation.

No doubt he thought he had reason. He believed her father was guilty of something much worse than merely telling what he thought was the truth. That meant he thought her father had lied, had deliberately sent an innocent man to prison and worse.

Shea couldn't accept that, couldn't accept the fact that *any*one would do that, much less the man she believed to be her father. Nor did it fit with the picture painted of Jack Randall by people in Casey Springs.

She had to get away. She had to find out for herself. Above all, she had to escape from Rafe Tyler and all the tumultuous emotions he evoked in her. Or he would wound her as fatally as he himself had been wounded.

She ate because she had to eat. The fish, which had smelled so good minutes earlier, was now tasteless to her. Only through sheer will was she able to finish a portion of what lay on the plate. She left the remainder for the two men, placing it on the stump, then went inside.

The cub was snoring gently in the corner. She wanted to touch it, to touch anything to keep at bay the aching loneliness she felt. But she didn't want to wake the cub when it was sleeping so peacefully. She found another candle and lit it and just watched the bear.

She felt something at her feet and looked down. Abner had his paws on her boots, looking around with those bright eyes. She picked him up and cradled him, her index finger running down his back, which she knew he liked. "Abner," she whispered. "Now why were you named that?" It had such a whimsical touch from a man who allowed himself no whimsy.

The mouse made little squeaking noises. "You've been ignored," she observed. "Hungry?"

He sat up, begging endearingly. Coincidence, she thought. He couldn't know what she'd said.

Carefully, she rose, the mouse still in her hand, and went to Rafe's small store of goods, extracting a cracker from the tin. She set the mouse and cracker down on the cot and watched as he daintily ate his supper.

"Do you ever want to escape?" she asked. "Do you think about a little girl mouse? Or adventures? Or have you already had more than you want?" She wondered about her sanity in talking to a rodent, but she needed to hear the sound of her own voice, and she wondered whether Rafe had needed to hear his voice in prison. She remembered his bitter words when she had first come here. "Anyone can be tamed, Miss Randall."

She couldn't imagine Rafe being tamed, but she wondered whether he had tamed her, after all. Was that why she had stayed here when she could have escaped? Because he'd tamed her in ways she hadn't expected?

She sighed. She was tired. So much had happened today. So many emotions expended. She went over to the cot; blood had dried on the blanket. His blood. She thought of that gaping wound again and was almost sick.

Still, she was too weary to do anything about the stains. She lowered her head on the rolled-up blanket that served as a pillow, thinking that sleep would be long in coming. She was mildly surprised when she felt herself drifting off into a dream-shrouded sleep.

Chapter 17

Ben left the following morning after tending Rafe's wound, and for two days Rafe felt very much like the snarling bear that was still prowling outside the cabin. He was too weak to go fishing, too restless to stay quiet. He tended to the young cub, tried to curry the horse before giving up in disgust when his arm rebelled.

He was so damned weak, and he hated that fact.

At least, Shea hadn't played nursemaid to him. He'd managed to care for his wound himself. He didn't think he could tolerate Shea Randall's touch, not after his bitter words that night several days ago. He had revealed all too much then, and he was thoroughly disgusted with himself for doing so.

And thoroughly disgusted with the way his head felt after drinking Ben's whiskey, homemade by one of the miners Ben called friend and strong as the Devil. He'd not drunk that much since the night after his release from prison, when he and Ben had gotten thoroughly drunk. The aftermath wasn't worth the momentary oblivion, and he didn't want oblivion, dammit. He wanted to remember everything. He needed to remember everything. Every lonely, godforsaken day in prison, every look of revulsion when a stranger, even convicts, saw his scar. He needed to feel the waves of hate, the way his stomach knotted when he thought of Randall, by God.

He shouldn't need reminders, but the damn woman was eating into his consciousness like locusts through a cornfield.

She even made him feel guilty for doing what needed to be done. He didn't need guilt. He already had enough anger to fill every nook and cranny of his being.

Shea Randall, however, was difficult to ignore. He found it impossible now to put her in her place as his captive. Things had inevitably changed. If she'd ever had any fear of him, she didn't now. He saw that readily enough. They had become partners of sorts days earlier when she had tended him, and together they had tended the small bear cub.

He still locked her in the cabin at night, sleeping outside the window after that first night in the stable, but it was more a reminder himself that she was captive to his captor rather than fear she might escape.

He wished he knew what she was thinking. Her eyes were watchful, questioning, but not afraid.

Christ, if only the physical attraction between them weren't so strong, so damnably obvious, even to Ben. Rafe didn't understand it, couldn't accept it, not with Randall's daughter, but there it was. Even with his arm hurting like hell, he wanted her.

The tension between them rose steadily after Ben left. He had been a safety valve of sorts, a buffer between them, but once he rode out, the level of pressure between Rafe and Shea rose and boiled, threatening to explode again. Rafe knew he had to do something, but damned if he knew what.

He could only watch her, try to keep his frustration to a controllable level. He'd even tried to read a book.

Reading had been his only escape in prison. Since his release he had asked Ben to buy any book he happened to find and had collected a very small library, which, until Shea Randall's invasion, had engaged him when he wasn't wandering in the woods, exploring his freedom.

Words made him forget. Words freed him, momentarily, from bitterness.

But they didn't have their usual magic today, the third day since Ben left. Rafe felt strong enough to go fishing this morning. The wound had stopped seeping, and for the first time he could move it without agonizing pain.

He looked up as the door to the cabin opened, and Shea came outside with her sketchpad. She was wearing a very simple blue gingham dress that deepened the blue in her eyes; her hair was not braided but pulled back and tied with a ribbon. She sat down on the tree stump with Abner on her lap. She kept looking down at the mouse, and he knew she was drawing it.

A charming picture, he thought, trying unsuccessfully to color it with the cynicism and bitterness that had been his longtime companions.

Where in the hell was the she-bear? It had provided a distraction during the past few days, but it disappeared this morning after sniffing the cub once more and finding it better. A few more days, Rafe thought, and the cub would be able to return to the woods. It was already moving better, learning to balance on its three good legs. He had high hopes for the injured leg.

He supposed the cub was sleeping now. It had consumed all of the crackers, except for a few held back for Abner, and the canned goods were being swiftly depleted by Rafe and Shea. Something had to be done about finding food.

Ben should return sometime this afternoon. Clint had ridden up yesterday to check on Rafe and to tell him Randall· had disappeared the day earlier, saying merely that he was going up into the mountains on a hunting trip. Clint had thought he might be trying to track Rafe, but Randall was not known for tracking skills, and Clint doubted anyone could find this valley. Randall, Clint reported, had said nothing about the daughter, and had been tense and unusually uncommunicative.

There was something else, Clint had said. Another miner had been found dead. Apparently killed a few days ago. There was a meeting called in Rushton tonight.

Ben was mingling with the miners, trying to bring them together for protection rather than to form a vigilante committee that might mistakenly go after Rafe's outlaw band, which they believed responsible for all the troubles in the area south of Casey Springs.

A third piece of news was more welcome. Men were leaving the Circle R. They'd not been paid in months now, and only a few drovers remained to guard what was left of Randall's herd.

All of that was said outside Shea's hearing.

"McClary?" Rafe had asked.

"He was gone again the night the second miner was killed," Clint said. "Unfortunately, he left when I was in Rushton, so I couldn't follow him."

"Randall has to be involved," Rafe said.

Clint shrugged. "Could be." He darted a look at the cabin. "How's the girl?"

Rafe winced. The question should be, how was he with the girl around? Godawful.

"That bad?" Clint tried a smile, but it didn't work. Ben had chortled about the all-too-obvious attraction between Rafe and Shea Randall, but Clint hurt for them. He hurt for himself. He knew only too well now how it felt to want someone he couldn't have.

"I've been thinking about letting her go," Rafe said quietly.

Clint just looked at him.

"I don't think she would say anything. . . ."

"Think? Or know?" Clint asked, and Rafe knew it was Clint's life he would be gambling with, Clint's and Ben's, not his. Clint was gently reminding him of that fact.

"Christ, I don't know anything any longer," Rafe said with defeat.

"We're close, Rafe."

"But what about those miners?" Rafe said. "I didn't want anyone else to get hurt."

"We don't know Randall's responsible."

"The hell we don't."

Clint hesitated a moment. "He might have changed, Rafe."

"Hell, he's always been damn good at covering his tracks."

Clint nodded. He'd never had any doubts about Rafe's story, not after he'd backtracked Randall's past. Still, Jack Randall had been a fair boss. A good one. None of it made sense."

After Clint had left, Rafe felt more alone than he'd had in his life, even in prison.

And now . . . An attractive, smart, warm woman was only a few feet away, and he could do nothing about the raw sexual hunger that ate at his insides, or the fierce, unexpected need for something soft in a life that had never known softness. Her touches in the cabin, when she'd tended his wound, had nearly been his undoing. And those tears. Those damnable tears the other night. The tears for him.

He had to stay away, and that kind of loneliness was so much sharper, so much more painful, than that which came from actually being physically alone.

How much longer could he endure it?

He had managed admirably the last few days, but then he'd been ill and weak. Now his strength—and desire—were returning at breakneck speed, and he wasn't sure he could handle his growing need for her.

As if she knew exactly what he was thinking, Shea looked up at him. "You promised to take me back to the pool," she said. She tilted her head askance, the gesture becoming endearingly familiar.

Rafe knew it was unwise being close to her. But she had asked for little in the past few days.

"The cub?" he asked, wanting an excuse to deny her request.

Her expression softened. "Sleeping off his dinner."

"The irritated mother is still out there," he commented.

"I think she trusts us."

He stared at her. "Don't ever believe that, Miss Randall. That she-bear is a wild animal. So is the cub. They're both unpredictable."

"I'm getting used to unpredictability," Shea snapped back, irritated at his use of "Miss Randall." Whenever she thought they were reaching some kind of understanding, he started snarling again. He made the she-bear look cuddly.

"You don't know the half of it, Miss Randall. So don't bait me."

"Is that what I'm doing?" she said recklessly. "I thought I was asking you to keep a promise."

"Outlaws don't keep promises."

"No?" she retorted. "I thought it was just to women. Or Randalls."

He tried to scald her with his eyes, but she just glared back, ripping him with his own words.

"Didn't anyone teach you not to play with fire?"

"Who started it?" she demanded, incensed at his attitude, his hostility, during the past three days. She'd felt as if she were walking on eggshells, that her belief in him had been thrown back in her face, that . . .

Rafe felt the side of his mouth twitching suddenly. Shea's face was set with determination, those blue-gray eyes luminous with something he couldn't, didn't want to, understand.

He looked down at his hand to remind himself to stay away from her.

"Don't," she commanded softly.

He raised his gaze to meet her eyes. There was so much understanding, so much compassion in her face, it seemed to smother what was left of his anger, the anger he held on to for dear life.

He didn't want her compassion, dammit. Or her pity. He thought about walking away, as he had before, but that would be admitting that she'd hit a raw nerve. Hell with it. He would give her what she wanted, and perhaps then she would stop probing into places she didn't belong.

"Don't say I didn't warn you," he said shortly, and started for the woods. He knew she would follow him.

Though she had won this particular battle, it felt good to be wandering these woods again. It felt . . . soothing to have her with him, even behind him. Just knowing she was near, hearing the soft sound of her boots against the pine needles, was a fine thing, no matter how much he tried in his mind to color it with anger.

If there had been any wildlife at the pool, it had scattered by the time they reached the lake. The water that fell from the rocks above seemed to glisten with sunshine, and the blue seemed purer than before. Rafe wondered whether it was Shea's presence that seemed to make colors more vivid, more fanciful.

She was absorbing them with a delight that never stopped surprising, and touching, him. The simplest of things seemed to make her happy, like a child, and yet there was also a maturity about her that complemented the innocence that mesmerized him. It had been a long time since he'd experienced innocence.

He turned around abruptly. "I'll give you some privacy."

"Don't go." Her voice was soft but determined.

He glared at her. "Don't play games with me, Miss Randall. I've been in prison a very long time. I warned you before what that does to a man."

"Rafe." Her voice caressed the name. He didn't know whether she meant to do that or not, but the effect was the same. It was like lightning running through his veins. It was also like a leash pulling him to her. He fought against it—but in vain.

"What do you want, Miss Randall?" His voice was harsh with wanting, with frustration.

He saw her swallow. "I don't know . . ."

"You'd better decide," he said roughly, "or you won't have a choice in the matter."

Shea felt the lump in her throat swell. She *didn't* have a choice in the matter. She hadn't since that kiss three nights ago, since that flash of agony crossed his face, and she'd recognized his complete loss of any kind of hope or dream. She hadn't entirely understood until then, until that spurt of anguished despair revealed the depths of what had been done to him. He had appeared so strong, so confident, even prideful, that she hadn't realized how much his core had been eaten away by injustice, an injustice she no longer doubted.

She wanted to heal him. That was part of it. But it wasn't all. She had meant what she said about the brand not making a difference to her, not now that she knew him. She ached to have him touch her again, with that same gentleness he had before. She had never known anyone could touch like that, the very restraint vibrating between them, stroking sensations like a fine violinist coaxing music from his strings.

Shea didn't answer but instead moved toward him.

"Shea?" His voice was ragged.

The fingers of her left hand reached up to his mouth and closed off any further protest. She didn't let herself think about what she was doing. Instincts guided her. Feelings. Emotions.

With a groan he lowered his head, and his lips met hers.

They were tentative at first, even though she had issued an invitation. It was as if he didn't believe it, couldn't accept it.

But Shea felt every part of her respond to him. She felt his pain, his uncertainty, his pride. She felt the rawness inside him and made it hers.

She looked up and saw those guarded sea-colored eyes of his, but now they weren't at all guarded. They were desperate and wounded, so full of dark despair that shudders ran through her.

His lips left hers, and he stepped back, as if certain those shudders meant revulsion rather than the uncontrollable response of her body to his. "Don't leave me," she whispered.

"You don't know—"

"I know everything I want to know." That wasn't true. It was, in fact, the greatest lie she'd ever told, but there was no guilt in her when she saw him relax. His lips returned to hers, this time with a need that shook her down to her toes. Heat pooled inside her as his body touched hers, and she felt him harden against her. His hands went down, encircling her hips, pulling her up until the swelling at the apex of his legs matched the crevice at hers, and she felt that heat inside her turn into hot, throbbing rivers of desire, painful in intensity.

Shea had never felt such longing, such yearning, in her life. She wasn't sure what that longing reached for, but she didn't care. She just wanted to touch him, to feel that gentleness that said so much more than he would say.

She heard the quick intake of his breath as his lips pressed hard on hers, taking now, because he sensed that she needed, wanted, this as much as he. But even then, he tempered his moves, the strain of doing so obvious on his face.

"Oh, Shea," he said, his voice breaking as he moved an inch away from her lips, his face taut with wanting. "This is . . ."

He stopped. She didn't know what he'd started to say. That this was impossible or ridiculous or insane or all of these things.

"Right," she finished for him.

"Nothing about this is right," he whispered, but then he belied those words, kissing her again with a desperation that said something else altogether.

Shea put her arms around him, carefully so she wouldn't hurt the wound on his arm. She welcomed the feel of his lips on hers, and she opened her mouth to him under the gentle prodding.

She had never been kissed like this, and she was startled that his exploring tongue could set aflame so many other places in her body. Then she stopped wondering and could only react. Her own tongue instinctively stroked his, and she felt him go rigid as a low groan rumbled from deep inside him.

His hands left her hips and moved up and down her back in sensuous strokes. Her body stretched to feel his hardness against the core of her; astonished at a need so compelling, she couldn't stop herself. She wondered at the way his body, his hands, made her quiver with expectation. She had never thought she would welcome such an invasion, but now she craved more and more and more.

His lips left hers and moved along her face with feathering caresses. She closed her eyes. She just wanted to feel and savor. To memorize. To remember.

Rafe unbuttoned her dress, and his hands slipped inside her chemise. She wasn't wearing a corset; it had seemed foolish to endure the discomfort up here in the mountains, and now she was glad, for his hand easily found and touched, almost reverently, her breast. She felt it swell and grow taut and tingle.

And ache. Dear God, how it hurt. And then the other breast. She thought she would burst with feeling, with all the new sensations ravaging her body. New and wondrous and exciting and needy.

Her body pressed even closer to his, seeking something she didn't understand, seeking to unite. Her hands had climbed up the back of his neck, tickling and playing with his thick, curling hair, twisting it in her fingers.

In response his hands moved from her breasts and tangled in her hair, freeing it from the ribbon holding it back, and she felt it fall over her shoulders and breasts.

"God, you're beautiful," he whispered. The words sounded almost worshipful, and she *felt* beautiful. For the first time in her life she felt truly beautiful.

Mindless of his wound, he swooped her up in his arms, and she linked her hands around his neck. He carried her several feet and then laid her down on a bed of pine needles, soft now from months of exposure. He knelt beside her, his face strained as he watched hers, and she knew he was waiting for her to say no.

She couldn't say it. She didn't want to. She wanted him in a way she'd never wanted anything before in her life. She wanted to see his eyes thaw, and his mouth smile, and the hard, set lines of his face ease. She wanted to hear him laugh.

She wanted to love him.

But that was something she couldn't tell him.

Only with her eyes could she let him know that she wanted him as much as he wanted her.

His eyes didn't relax, nor did his lips smile, or his face ease, as his hands lifted her dress and chemise over her head and tugged the pantalets down. He did all those things with the same intense concentration he'd used when training his horse, or doctoring the cub, or cutting wood. She wondered sadly whether there was any joy left in him at all. As if he knew what she was thinking, his hands hesitated as they pulled the last garment from her.

They rested on her thigh for the briefest of moments, then his right hand turned over her right one, and he studied it. She no longer wore a bandage, and the blisters were healing. It was still sore, though, and he ran his thumb over it so lightly that it teased rather than hurt. "I'm sorry for that," he said.

Shea gazed at the two hands together, hers white and slender, his tanned and large. He was not wearing his glove, and the brand was stark on his skin, but he didn't try to hide it. It was as if he were reminding himself, or testing her.

She hated that mark for what it had done to him. Her hand went down to it, her fingers running along it. She wished that she could absorb some of the pain he must have felt when it was done to him.

She brought his hand up and placed its scarred back

to her cheek, surprised that he allowed it. Her gaze went to his eyes, and they were as frozen as ever, watchful, waiting. She moved his hand to her lips and kissed the scar lightly as if it were something honorable rather than unspeakably ugly.

His fingers tightened around hers, and then his lips were back on her lips, the kiss desperate and hurting and angry, consuming her.

Shea didn't know whether she had done the right thing, whether he was trying to punish her, or forget, or . . . whether he did care for her a little, in spite of himself.

She wanted to make him forget all the bad years, all the pain, all the suffering. She wanted to bury them all, if only for a brief time.

Her response to his kiss tried to tell him that. It seemed as if she had been waiting all her life for him, for this, for the extraordinary way she felt when he touched her, when those probing, angry eyes met and clashed with hers.

His kiss deepened at her response, at her ready acceptance of him, at the way her body gravitated toward his. His tongue was no longer gentle, but hungrily invasive, as if he still wasn't sure whether to be punitive or . . .

Loving. There was a hint of that in the gentleness of his fingers as they ran up and down her body. His arms went around her waist, and he rolled over with her so she was lying naked on his clothed body. She felt the throbbing of his sex and little fires starting to glow inside her. She maneuvered herself to get closer and closer, and then she pulled away from his kiss and started to unbutton his shirt. She wanted his skin next to her skin. She wanted no physical barriers.

When she rid him of his shirt, her hands ran up and

down his chest as his had done with her body. She felt him quiver, tauten. She leaned down and shamelessly ran her tongue along his breastbone.

"God, Shea," he whispered.

"Did anyone ever tell you that you taste good?" she said, smiling to herself at the utter astonishment in his face.

She moved her mouth to his neck, brushing it with kisses, savoring the saltiness of it. She was acting so totally unlike herself, so wanton. She didn't even know how she knew what to do. She just *knew*. She felt so seductively alive, particularly when she saw the way he unsuccessfully tried to hide the desire burning in his own eyes, those glimpses of sheer, startled pleasure.

He groaned, and Shea felt his hands go down to the buttons of his trousers. She lifted herself slightly so she could unbutton them herself and slip the trousers from his hips. And then there was nothing between them, and she felt his manhood press tightly against the now-heated entrance between her legs.

Rafe rolled over so he again was on top, his body hovering mere inches above her, that straining part of him touching and teasing the increasingly sensitive part of her femininity.

For a moment she felt fear, as if she'd roused something she couldn't control. Then his mouth came down, touching her face lightly, with such restraint. His body lowered all the way, and she felt him begin to enter her, slowly.

Fear melted, and she was filled with desire, with need for him, with an aching craving for what was coming. But he felt very strange, very large, and intrusive, and the pain came so unexpectedly that she couldn't hold back a whimper.

"Christ." The word exploded from him, and he hesitated. But despite her pain, the need was still inside her, building, boiling.

"Don't stop," she whispered.

But still he hesitated.

"Please," she pleaded. She needed whatever it was he was giving.

She felt him move again, even more slowly than before, and his lips feathered her cheeks with caresses, as he carefully continued, his muscles taut with control. And then the pain started to fade, replaced by rivers of delicious sensations as he moved inside her.

"Oh, Rafe," she said, astounded at the wonder of what was happening. His rhythm quickened, and she felt the core of her grasp and tighten around him. Her own body was suddenly moving in concert with his.

And then she couldn't think anymore, just feel. Feel and feel and feel. And want to give. She wanted to give him pleasure and joy and happiness and forgetfulness. She wanted to change every bad thing into something glorious, just as he was doing to her.

Suddenly, there was a tumultuous explosion inside her. Pleasure rocked her, going on and on until she thought she could stand no more. She closed her eyes at the miracle that had just happened, and she felt his body relax, settle down on hers with a sigh of contentment.

After a few moments he moved slightly, rolling her to the side, so his weight wasn't on her. His hand reached up and touched her cheek with such sweetness, she thought she might die happy at that moment.

"I . . ." He hesitated, his words obviously coming with great difficulty, and shadowed by regret. "I didn't know . . . that you were a virgin." It was an apology she didn't want.

Some of the joy seeped from Shea. Of course he wouldn't have thought she was a virgin, the way she had responded to him, or perhaps because she was Randall's daughter. But his assumption hurt. She felt her face suddenly flush with humiliation.

And then his hand was touching her cheek. "Don't," he said. "It's just that I've never . . . I've never been with a virgin before," he finished awkwardly. "I'm . . . dammit," he added. "It shouldn't have happened."

"A lot of things shouldn't happen," she said slowly, "but I don't think this was one of them."

He moved away, breaking the joining of their bodies, but his hand closed around hers, keeping it captive. He closed his eyes, as if he wanted to close out this scene.

Minutes seemed like hours to her, and then, without opening his eyes, he said hoarsely, "This doesn't change anything."

The humiliation Shea had felt earlier was nothing to what she felt now.

"You think . . . ?" She couldn't finish the sentence. She couldn't put it in words. She couldn't bear the idea that he thought she was selling herself to save her father, or herself.

"Or have you just been wondering what it would be like with a man who had been caged for ten years? Christ, I couldn't even tell . . ." His ragged, bitter voice trailed off, and she realized that he was blaming himself for what had happened, that guilt had made him turn on her.

"Oh, Rafe," she whispered. "Can't you understand that I just . . . wanted this? If that makes me a . . . a whore . . . then I guess that's what I am."

He was silent for so long, she wondered whether he'd even heard her.

"Why?" he asked. "Why?"

She knew he meant why had she wanted him—a convicted criminal. Her hand ran along his chest again. "I don't know," she lied.

"I don't believe in gifts," he said. "The last time I received one, it was a pair of leg manacles. The sergeant who took me to prison said it was the army's last present to me." He paused, and she knew he was reliving that moment. Dear Lord, Shea hurt for him.

"Your family?" She had to ask. He had never mentioned anyone.

"Killed by Comanches when I was young," he said in that toneless voice that she now knew covered simmering emotions.

"And you?" she urged.

"I was taken captive, rescued a few months later." He shrugged. "I guess you could call it rescue."

"How old were you?" she said, horrified.

He shrugged. "Six. Seven." The familiar coolness settled over his eyes, and she knew he was retreating behind that shell that concealed so much.

He made it clear he wouldn't talk about himself any longer. He was still clasping her hand, though, and she wondered whether he was even aware of his tight grip. She wanted to touch him in other ways, but she was afraid he would misconstrue it, move farther away. So she waited, letting the pregnant silence drift between them.

He cut it first. "Tell me about Boston."

"There's not much to tell. I told you I made hats," she said uncomfortably. Still, she was pleased he hadn't retreated into the usual silence that followed any kind of warmth between them. "My mother owned a small hat shop. I designed the hats for her."

There was a long silence. He had asked few questions of her. It had apparently been enough that she was his enemy's daughter. He hadn't wanted to know more. She was surprised when he asked, "Where is your mother now?"

"She died four months ago."

"So you finally decided to find . . . your father?"

"I never knew about him until she died, and I found . . . those letters. She'd told me he was dead."

"So you decided to come West by yourself and find out." His voice was wry, but there was admiration in it.

"My mother . . . prided herself on honesty. I couldn't understand why she hadn't told me. He had been sending money, so he obviously . . . cared about her. I had to know about him. I had to know why she left him. Why she never told me about him. Whether he's even my father at all."

He withdrew his hand from hers, reached for his trousers and pulled them on. And when he spoke again, his voice was cool. "I'm sorry," he said, a muscle in his cheek working. "You had nothing to do with . . . this. I'm sorry I have to . . . keep you locked up at night."

She shook her head, and her gaze found his. "It's nothing. A few nights. Not compared to . . ." She stopped, not wanting to mention the years he'd spent locked up.

His face tensed.

"Rafe?"

His expression didn't relax at all. He stared straight ahead. Still, she continued, wanting him to share pain as well as pleasure with her. "How could you endure it?"

His jaw clenched, and Shea wished she hadn't asked. "By hating your father."

The earth seemed to still. It was as if every living thing was caught, frozen, in the cold menace of his words. Even the birds had quieted.

She hesitated. She was delving into dangerous waters, but she had to ask it.

"Could it be that he . . . my father . . . just made a mistake . . . thought he saw you?"

"That particular day, he sent me to check on some

settlers who, by some strange coincidence, had moved on. He knew where I had gone. At the court-martial he denied sending me anyplace and testified that he saw me at another location, with someone I've never met. He said— with great reluctance, I might add—that he had no doubt he saw me, that the man I was with was unquestionably one of the raiders he'd recognized during the last robbery. And I sure as hell didn't plant part of the payroll in my quarters." Rafe swallowed, remembering the fury and hopelessness he'd felt at hearing Randall's perjured testimony.

"He knew exactly what he was doing, just as he did when he presided over my branding." Rafe stopped and took a few deep breaths. "Five soldiers were killed during that raid. Jack Randall was one of the few survivors. He was in charge of the escort, but I had planned the route. Your father and I were two of the very few who knew it." He paused. "How in the hell do you think he bought the Circle R? Certainly not on army pay."

Shea knew so little about Jack Randall, she couldn't defend him. Still, she couldn't believe he would purposely condemn someone to a living hell.

He must have seen the doubt on her face because he moved away from her, distancing himself as he had so many other times. It was as if those few earlier moments never existed.

He stood and pulled on his shirt, then handed her clothes to her. He turned and disappeared into the woods, leaving her alone with a body that still tingled and quaked with wondrous satisfaction but a mind tortured by agonizing thoughts and questions.

Chapter 18

Prison must have made him as crazy as a rabid fox. Rafe slammed his fist against an aspen. He couldn't believe what he'd just done.

A virgin, for God's sake.

And Randall's daughter!

He slammed the other fist into the tree, feeling the jolt up through his wounded arm. He wanted to hurt. Hell, he should be shot.

He couldn't undo the last few minutes. The sickening fact was, he wasn't even sure he wanted to.

But, Christ, the complications.

Rafe relived every unbelievable moment of pleasure, the tender strokes along his body. No one had ever touched him like that, and despite his angry words he knew that what had just happened had nothing to do with Jack Randall.

No one could fake that glow in her eyes, or her reaction to his lovemaking. Lovemaking. He'd never thought of coupling like that before. It had always been a purely physical act, a release, nothing more. He'd never made love, or even tried, with Allison, believing that an officer and gentleman just wouldn't do that. And he had tried damned hard to be both.

It did no good to tell himself he could stay away from Shea. He hadn't managed that feat before; he sure as hell couldn't do it now. She was like rain to his parched earth.

Rafe swallowed. He almost believed he was being offered a choice: vengeance or love. But then reality set in. He would always be an outcast. *He* could live like a hermit, always wearing gloves, avoiding army posts or anyone who might know him. He couldn't do that to a wife or child.

A child. He closed his eyes again. What if . . . ?

Unexpected pleasure streaked through him, followed by unbearable loneliness. He shuddered when he thought Shea might one day have to do what her mother had done: lie to protect her child against a father she thought would bring shame to that child.

Shea had to understand that.

She had to leave. He suddenly had an inspiration. He would offer her a trip back to Boston. He certainly could afford to do it with Randall's money. Ben could escort her to Denver, bypassing Casey Springs. In exchange, she would agree to say nothing about Ben and Clint. Surely, she would accept.

He remembered Clint's warning. Rafe would be gambling with Clint and his brother's lives. But Rafe knew deep in his heart that she would keep her word.

He turned around and started back, feeling as if a ton of weight clung to each boot. He couldn't bear to have her around him; he couldn't bear to have her gone.

Jack Randall was dirty, tired, and despairing. He had found no trace of his daughter, Rafe Tyler, or the outlaws. He'd been out three days, used up what few supplies

he had taken. But he might as well be looking for a needle
in a haystack. He had no choice now but to go to Russ and
give him at least part of the truth.

His stomach heaved whenever he thought of his
daughter in the hands of a man who hated him. Hated
him justifiably.

He deserved anything Tyler planned, but his daughter didn't. And now McClary was starting anew a path of
violence and deception that Randall could no longer tolerate. He had done nothing to prevent murder when Mc-
Clary returned. Backbone, he'd discovered, was not easily
built after years of avoiding consequences. But now his
daughter's life was at stake. He *had* to do something.

He reached the ranch and started for the barn.
Where there had been thirty hands, only ten still remained when he'd left. God knew how many there were
now.

A cowhand, who'd been at Circle R for three years,
was leading out a horse. "Came in for a fresh horse," the
man said.

"Anyone here?" Jack asked.

"Mr. McClary is inside the house," the hand said,
"but everyone else is out." He hesitated, then added, "Another miner was killed, apparently a few days ago. Someone just found him."

Jack felt the knot in his gut tighten.

The cowhand cleared his throat. "Three more men
left," he said. "I'll have to leave, Mr. Randall, if I don't get
paid."

Jack nodded. "I understand."

The cowhand turned his horse and rode away.

Jack watched him go. The money didn't matter anymore. He would lose the Circle R, one way or another.
He was resigned to that.

The question now was what else would he lose. The

daughter he'd never known he had and now wanted desperately? His life? His freedom? He had already lost what little self-respect he had regained. He had lost it the moment McClary had reappeared and reminded him of the past, the second Randall had acquiesced to his demands, knowing it meant murder.

Randall rode up to the ranch house, dismounted, and tied his mount to the hitching post. He had something to do, and he had to do it while he still had the courage. He knew what Sara had thought of him, even apparently to her death. He couldn't bear to think how his daughter would react if she knew he was involved in the murder of innocent men.

If she still lived . . .

He buried his head in his hands for a moment, trying to think. He had to get help to find his daughter, and he also had to stop McClary. Even if he went to prison, he had to stop him.

"Sara," he murmured hoarsely. "What should I do?" He knew what she would have said. He should saddle a fresh horse, go after Russ, tell him everything. But then he thought of Shea, who looked like Sara. His daughter.

He knew suddenly he couldn't tell Russ the truth. He couldn't let his daughter know what a despicable man her father was. Maybe later, when she had learned to like him a little. A week. A month.

Perhaps he could convince McClary to leave this territory. He swallowed. The weakling's way out.

But a way out, just the same. Then he could tell Russ that Tyler was just a man bent on revenge. It would be his word against Tyler's, just like before. . . .

He doubled over, emptying the contents of his stomach on the ground. He rose unsteadily. McClary first. Then he would figure the rest. He put his hand on the butt of his gun, trying to reassure himself. He knew how to use it. He was neither fast nor accurate, but McClary didn't know that.

Determined, he headed into the ranch house and found McClary in his office, going through his books with a glass of whiskey in his hands.

"What are you doing here?"

"I heard you went looking for a daughter," McClary said with a smirk. "Didn't know you had one, you old fox. Is she pretty?"

Jack stiffened. He should have known McClary would have heard something. "You heard wrong," he said. "I had business in Casey Springs."

McClary raised an eyebrow. "That so? Trying to raise money?" He looked down at the open books. "I've been thinking. Your books here . . . they don't look so good. I might consider a partnership."

Distaste and anger became rage. Reason started slipping away. He had been a con man, a thief, never a murderer. But now he could easily kill McClary.

"No!" he said.

"You have no choice."

Quietly, Randall said, "You're going to leave."

McClary laughed. "Why would I do that?"

Randall's hand went to the butt of his gun. "Because I'll tell the sheriff you're responsible for those murders."

"You aren't going to do that," McClary said with absolute certainty.

"I'm going to do more than that," Randall retorted with reckless bravado. "I'm going to tell him the truth about Rafe Tyler, about who really planned those robberies." He was bluffing, pure and simple, and he hated the small quake in his voice. He might not be a killer, but he knew McClary was.

McClary merely shrugged. "You'll be condemning yourself."

"You condemned me to hell a long time ago."

McClary laughed. "You didn't object. And I didn't see you turning down the money."

"No," Randall said, fighting down his self-revulsion. "I thought it would buy me back my wife. I was a fool."

"You still are. A yellow-bellied fool," McClary said contemptuously.

"No more." Randall realized that his plan was not going to work. McClary was not going to leave, not on his own. That left only one alternative: to tell the truth and accept the consequences. As devastating as the prospect was, he knew he could no longer allow McClary to continue killing, or risk his doing something to further endanger his daughter.

It was as if McClary suddenly understood something had changed. His eyes narrowed.

"Don't be an idiot. You'll hang."

"I could go to prison. I'll accept that. But I haven't killed anyone."

"No?" McClary said. "You knew what I was doing. You were a part of that robbery in Kansas." His mouth twisted. "I'll have them believing you planned everything."

"I won't let you kill anymore."

"Hell you won't," McClary said. Lazily, he moved his hand to the glass of whiskey.

Randall's anger conquered his fear. Meaning to scare McClary, he went for his gun. In a smooth movement McClary dropped the glass and swept his gun from the holster around his hip.

Randall felt the impact of the bullet. Pain swallowed him like a red tide, and he felt himself fall. He desperately tried to reach for his gun again, but his arm didn't obey. And then his brain exploded into nothingness.

* * *

McClary watched as Randall fell to the floor, his head hitting the corner of the fireplace. Blood was spreading over his chest and the side of his head where it had hit stone.

Had anyone heard the shot?

He looked out and saw Jack's horse. No other.

He went through Randall's pockets, looking for money. Jack was bleeding profusely. He wouldn't live long, and McClary needed to make this look like a robbery. He forced open a locked drawer in the desk and was rifling through it when he heard the sound of riders.

Dammit all to hell.

He looked at Randall and thought about putting another bullet in him, but the riders would hear it and stop his only avenue of escape. He had one chance, getting away before anyone discovered Randall's unconscious body. He hoped Randall bled to death.

He slipped out of the office, closing the door behind him, and went to the front window of the ranch house. Damn. Clint and two other hands, too many to take. He would wait until they disappeared into the barn, then grab Randall's horse.

He watched as the last man went inside to unsaddle and rub down the horses. Then he slipped out the door and took Randall's horse, leading him around in back before mounting and ruthlessly spurring the tired horse into a gallop.

Wearily, Clint emerged from the barn and looked toward the ranch house. Randall's horse had been there minutes before; now it was gone. "What happened to Jack's horse?"

One of the men shrugged, too tired to care.

Clint looked at the ranch house. Something was odd. Coming in from the pasture, he had met an outgoing hand, who'd said Randall had just returned. Surely, he wouldn't have left again on an exhausted horse, nor allowed anyone else to do so. Randall was particular about his horses.

"I think I'll check with Mr. Randall," he said, and walked over to the ranch house.

His knock went unanswered. He stepped inside. The main room was empty, but the door to Randall's office was ajar. He knocked, hesitated when he heard nothing, then pulled the door open, and saw Randall's body sprawled across the floor. His heart stopped beating a moment; his breath caught in his throat.

Clint moved to the body and knelt next to it. Two wounds, a gash alongside the head, a bullet in the shoulder, just an inch higher than the heart. Blood was everywhere.

He felt Randall's neck. There was a slight movement. He put his hand to the man's mouth. There was some breath. He leaned over, his hand touching Randall's right side. "Mr. Randall."

Randall's eyes opened, fogged with pain. He tried to move and then groaned. "Sara. My daughter . . ." And then his eyes closed again.

It had to have been McClary, Clint thought, but it could well be blamed on Rafe. He had to keep Randall alive to talk. He ran outside, shouting for the two men who had ridden in with him. Both came running.

"John, go for Russ Dewayne. Caleb, ride like hell to Casey Springs for a doctor."

"What happened?"

"Mr. Randall's been shot."

"Them outlaws?"

Clint shook his head. "I don't know. Get going."

He hurried back inside and knelt once more next to Randall. What in the hell had happened here?

Randall's color was excessively pale, his pulse weak.

Clint thought back to the war, to what he'd seen done on wounded men, to what they'd had to do for one another.

Loosen clothes, provide fresh air. Dash cold water on face and chest. Compress wound to stop the bleeding. Remove foreign matter.

Clint removed Randall's shirt. The bleeding seemed to have stopped on its own, but bits of the shirt were stuck to the wound; threads were visible in the blood. Randall had been damned lucky. An inch down, and he would be dead. The assailant had probably thought he was.

He went to the kitchen. Randall's cook had left several weeks earlier with her horse-wrangler husband. The men had been foraging for themselves, and the kitchen was a disaster. He found a relatively clean towel, however. He filled a bowl with water from the pump and went back into the office.

Clint opened the windows; it was hot as hell in the room. Stuffy. The smell of whiskey and old tobacco ashes permeated the room. Where was McClary?

He washed away blood from the wounds and plucked cloth from the hole in Randall's shoulder. But Randall needed a doctor with the right instruments. He moved, groaning, but his eyes didn't open.

Clint went upstairs, found some sheets, and ripped one into long strips. He returned to the office, pressed a couple of wads tightly to the wounds, then bandaged Randall's head and chest and shoulder, binding the arm so it would be immobile. He had done all he could.

He washed Randall's face, hoping he would wake

and tell him something before the others arrived. The only thing Clint knew was that Rafe had nothing to do with the shooting. The captain had been clear as to exactly what kind of justice he wanted, and it had nothing to do with a quick death.

He heard several more riders coming in. Nate, perhaps. Clint went to the door and gestured to the foreman.

"The boss has been shot. I need some help."

"Bad?"

Clint nodded. "I've already sent for the doc and Sheriff Dewayne, but I need help getting him upstairs."

Nate dismounted and quickly followed Clint to Randall's side. He stooped and felt Randall's clammy face. "Any idea who did it?"

Clint hesitated. He didn't want to say anything that might give him away, but neither did he want blame to fall immediately on his friends. "Randall's horse was here when we rode in, and several minutes later it was gone. Whoever did it was probably here when we rode in."

Nate nodded. "Mr. Randall say anything?"

Clint shook his head. "He just mentioned the name 'Sara.'"

"Let's get him more comfortable. I wish we had a doctor closer." He shook his head. "I can't help but think it has something to do with those robberies."

Clint felt a noose tightening around his neck. He couldn't claim now that there had been no violence connected with those robberies, not if the law wrongly connected them to the recent murders of miners. He shrugged. "McClary was here earlier, according to one of the hands. I've never trusted him."

"Maybe," Nate said dubiously. "Maybe we can find out from Mr. Randall. Let's get him to his bed."

Clint, who was the stronger, took Randall's shoulders, while Nate took the legs. They had just settled him in the bed when they heard more riders coming in.

"That must be the sheriff," Clint said.

Several minutes later Russ appeared in the doorway, followed by Kate. She gave Clint a tentative smile; it almost was the breaking of him. "I thought I might be able to help. I've taken care of three men with assorted injuries."

Clint nodded, afraid to smile back, afraid to give away the pleasure and despair her presence stirred in him. She was like the sun coming into the room, and he wanted to go to her, to touch her. But he couldn't. It would be too unfair to her.

Russ turned to him. "What happened?"

"I don't know. I returned from the north pasture and found him like this. He mentioned a woman's name, nothing else."

"Any ideas who might have done it?"

Again, Clint hesitated. He couldn't really say what he knew, and yet he wanted Russ Dewayne to believe what he believed, that Sam McClary was behind this, and the other murders. "I think," he said slowly, "you might want to talk to Mr. McClary."

"Why?" The question was sharp. "Do you know any more than you did the other night?" The other night. The night he'd been with Kate. The night he had lied about so much, but not about McClary.

Clint shrugged. "From what I know, he was the only one here this afternoon. He's not here now."

Russ turned his attention back to Randall, whom Kate was inspecting. She looked up at Clint with that blinding smile again. "I think you did better than I could."

Pride and pleasure rushed through Clint as his gaze

met hers. "You learn some in war. But he really needs a doctor. I'm afraid there might be bleeding inside."

Russ's voice blessedly diverted him, but it took a second for Clint to understand what he was asking. "He mentioned a woman's name?"

Clint nodded. "Sara."

"I wonder whether it has anything to do with his trip to Casey Springs. A clerk said some woman claiming to be his daughter stopped by and then seemed to disappear."

Clint hated feeling so damned devious. "He's been gone for three days. Didn't say where he was going. I was coming to see whether he'd discovered anything and found him like this."

Clint's eyes followed Kate as she rose from the bed. "I'll get some water."

"Clint."

He looked away from Kate and met Russ's questioning gaze. "I think it's time to put a posse together."

"Shouldn't we wait to see what Mr. Randall has to say?"

"You're convinced it's McClary, aren't you?"

Clint nodded. "Despite the fact that Mr. Randall said he was a friend, there was a lot of tension between them. I sensed Mr. Randall didn't like having him here."

Russ hesitated. "I'll wait until tomorrow, see whether he returns, whether Jack can tell us anything. But if he doesn't, I'll form a posse at dawn. Can we count on you?"

Clint flinched inside. He hoped like hell Jack Randall would wake up and blame McClary. If he didn't, lawmen and vigilantes would be all over these mountains. "Someone has to take care of this place," he said. "Nearly every hand has quit. I don't want him to wake to find his cattle gone too."

Russ nodded, accepting the explanation, and Clint felt worse. He had to head up and warn Rafe. And Ben.

Kate returned and chased them all out. "He needs quiet. I'll call if he wakes," she said.

The men went into the main room. Clint found a bottle of whiskey and poured them all a drink. And they waited.

"No," Shea said flatly. "I won't run away."

Rafe felt his fingers tighten into fists. He'd expected her to jump at his offer. It had cost him a great deal to make it. He'd had to make himself trust again.

And God help him, he didn't want her to leave. Which made it an absolute necessity that she do exactly that.

Because freedom meant so much to him, he thought it would to her too. He hadn't thought she would hesitate a second before accepting his offer.

At her first refusal he'd felt a rare sense of pleasure, and then he realized it wasn't him keeping her here, it was her father. Jack Randall was the reason she'd refused his offer to take a train back East.

His instinct proved true with her next words. "I came all this way to see my father. I want to see him."

"No," he said flatly. The brief pleasure he'd felt turned to a clump of clay in his throat. Disappointment made him angry, even though he had no right to that anger.

"If you trust me enough to go to Boston, why won't you trust me not to say anything about you and your friends?" The question was reasonable, but Rafe didn't feel reasonable.

"Please understand, Rafe," she pleaded. "I have to know if he is my father. Why my mother left him. I have to know whether he's done what you think he has."

Rafe laughed harshly. "You think he'll tell you? Jack

Randall is a charmer, little girl. He'll make you believe white is black and black is white. And he'll have you telling him everything he wants to know."

"No," she said. "I wouldn't do anything to hurt you. Or Clint or Ben."

"I don't believe that," he said. "I'm making you one offer. Take it or leave it."

"I'll leave it," she said, and those usually calm blue-gray eyes were spitting sparks at him.

In self-defense he attacked. He had to protect himself, his heart, his soul. He wouldn't let her destroy what was left of them. She had to leave. His hand reached out to her, running up and down her arm, but there was no tenderness in the touch, no gentleness. Only ugly insinuation.

"Because you like this?" he said. He spoke as a man did to a whore.

Her eyes widened. "Don't," she said, in almost a whisper.

"Why not?" he said, forcing indifference into his voice. "Prison has made me . . . hungry. Any woman will do. Even a Randall. Abstinence does that to a man."

He was playing with fire and knew it, but he couldn't stop. He had to halt whatever was building between the two of them. He *had* to. For both their sakes.

His hand kept moving along hers, and then he raised it to her hair, pulling it back until she had to meet his eyes. "Last chance, Miss Randall," he said. "Unless you want to become my whore while I finish with your father." He wondered whether those words were hurting him more than her. He tried to shore up the wall around his heart, but her stricken face kept tearing it down.

"Let go of me," she said, trying to jerk free as shock registered in her eyes.

"I don't think I want to do that," he replied coldly.

Her hand went back, and he knew she was going to strike him. He let her, feeling the stinging blow to his cheek. "Feel better, Miss Randall?" he asked.

She just stared at what he knew was a red mark on his cheek.

"That's right," he said. "Hate me. You should hate me, Miss Randall. And if you stay, you'll hate me more. I can promise you that."

She stood her ground even as she blinked back tears. Christ, he admired that stubborn backbone of hers. "I don't understand you. Why do you believe once I get on the train I won't get off and head right back?"

"Because unlike me," he said, "you have an undeniable streak of honesty. Usually a trait I don't particularly like, but now it serves my purpose."

Something flickered in her eyes, and he knew he had made a mistake. She didn't believe him. She was searching his face, seeking something he was afraid to reveal, was determined not to reveal.

"I lied to you before," she said in a shaken but determined voice. "I promised I wouldn't run, and I did. I think I'm as good a liar as you are."

Rafe wanted to smile: She was the world's worst liar. He shrugged. "Take the offer or leave it," he said.

"I'll leave it."

He stared at her with astonishment. "I told you what that means."

She looked at him solemnly for several moments. "Kiss me," she said. "Kiss me and then tell me you don't care."

He didn't move.

She stood up on tiptoes and lifted her head so her lips could meet his.

His mouth came down on hers. He meant to do it with the same disdain he'd used before. He meant to do it with careless cruelty, but the second he touched her, he couldn't continue the charade.

He knew how foolish he was. He was denying everything he'd tried to tell her, tried to use against her, but he couldn't stop. Shea was the first good thing that had touched him in many years; her touch was like a balm to his wounded soul, her giving like nourishment to a starved heart.

God help him.

God help them both.

Shea nestled her body next to Rafe's on the narrow cot. She didn't know whether he was asleep or awake. She wondered wistfully whether she would ever know much about him.

But then his arms tightened around her, and she knew he was just as awake as she, just as aware of the nearness of their bodies.

They'd shared a storm-shaken evening, made even more intense by what had been said. She had felt so betrayed at first, and then she'd known he was lying, for her sake. She'd known it the moment he'd said "Hate me." Those were not the words of a seducer, and they'd been said in such a ragged tone.

She didn't know what she was going to do. He would never marry a Randall, probably would never marry anyone, feeling as he did about the scar on his hand. But she felt drawn to him. He obliterated anything and everything else, and she would take whatever he had to give.

Shea wondered whether her mother had felt like that. She had to know why her mother had left her father. Shea knew she would never willingly leave Rafe Tyler, no matter how deep the abyss he dug for himself. She also knew she was walking into one with him. She'd lied to

Rafe; the reason she wouldn't leave was Rafe, not Jack Randall.

Perhaps if she thought Rafe were really dishonest, really a killer, rather than a man seeking his own kind of justice, she would feel differently.

Had her mother thought Jack Randall irredeemable? Had she tried to change him? And failed?

Was her daughter fated to make the same error? Loving the wrong man?

She heard the cub moving around. It was walking well now, although still using three legs, protecting the wounded one. Rafe said it would be time tomorrow to give him back to his mother.

She would miss the little bear. She could give it the hugs and assurances and unconditional love the man next to her wouldn't allow.

How could she feel so unbearably sad and so . . . loving at the same time?

Shea moved slightly, feeling the friction of his skin against hers, and blood pulsed through her again. Hot and demanding and wanting. She felt him harden against her, heard his soft groan, and she barely held back one of her own. His hand wandered up and down her back, inciting shivers of expectation.

How could she love someone like this? With so much power.

She moved carefully on the narrow cot so she could see him, so their bodies could fit together again. His usually wary eyes were lazy and sensuous. His mouth crooked with the smallest hint of a smile as his hand touched her face. "You play hell with my . . . scruples."

"You finally admit you have some?" she said, hearing the new seductiveness in her own voice.

"Maybe scruples isn't the right word," he amended, the wry smile widening slightly.

She snuggled closer, feeling the hot throbbing of his sex against her and the responsive craving inside. Waves of longing surged through her, so strong that a sound that was part wonder, part plea, escaped her lips.

He kissed her. Long and hard and deep. And desperate. She felt the desperation in that kiss, and she answered it with a passion and strength that astounded her. And him. She saw it in his eyes, that guardedness that meant he expected her to recoil, even now.

He still didn't trust himself. Didn't trust her. And that increased her longing, her need to make him believe she cared about him in ways that eclipsed everything else.

"Pretty Shea," he said hoarsely, moving his mouth from her lips down to her breasts, tantalizing her until she felt ready to explode with need for him. His need for her was in his voice, in his hands, but she knew he would never admit it.

She felt the heat and dampness of his body, the urgency of his sex, and she moved against him, wanting to bring him inside her, to make him a part of her in the only way he permitted. As he entered her, her body arched to meet his, matching his demanding rhythm. Her legs went around his, bringing him even farther into her, allowing her to ride with him, to whirl with dizzying sensations until her body convulsed, and she felt his explosion in her. She felt wave after wave of pleasure flood her, exquisite layers of aftershocks fill her with contentment. Her body quivered with each one, the core of her still clasping him, reluctant to let go, reluctant to lose the feel of him inside her. He shuddered, his breathing labored against her neck as he sought to regain that control he always fought so hard for.

Shea moved her head slightly and touched her mouth to his with all the wonder she felt. It was an exquisitely tender kiss, and he shuddered again, his mouth trembling before he rolled away from her with a groan that was part protest and part pain.

Her hand went up and brushed a lock of hair from his face, the sweat from his forehead. She wanted to say something but was desperately afraid he would reject it. Reject her. So she just laid her head on his chest, surprised when his arms went around her with something like possession.

No words passed between them. No promises. None of the assurances she wanted so very badly. And she knew nothing had really changed. There was a chasm between them that could never be crossed. A chasm named Jack Randall.

Chapter 19

Rafe checked the small bear's leg. The cuts were healing; there didn't seem to be any infection.

He wrapped the injured leg again with the splint, making it tighter than before so neither the mother nor cub could tear it off easily. It was the best he could do.

The time had come for the cub to return to his mother, to the woods where he belonged. The mother was still haunting the cabin area, and it was only a matter of time before she hurt someone. And it wasn't good for the cub to become dependent on human beings who would soon be gone.

Rafe looked up at the sadness in Shea's eyes. She was already very much attached to the small bear. He had watched her cuddle it, sing to it. It was only natural; she had been lonely.

Lonely enough to bed with him. Lonely and scared enough to accept what companionship she could find. He didn't delude himself that what had happened between them was any more than that.

He couldn't let it be, no matter how much he wished differently.

He looked at the cub in his arms. Trouble, he called the small fellow in his mind, but he hadn't said the name out loud. He hadn't wanted to share a name with Shea, to make it more difficult for her to give up the animal. He was a man without attachments. He didn't want them, didn't need them. But Shea wanted them. Her search for her father proved that.

"Do you really think he'll be all right in the woods?" Shea asked, her hand trailing down the thick fur of the cub, which began nipping on her other hand.

"I think that she-bear outside will take very good care of it," he said.

"His leg?"

He shrugged. "The young heal easily."

"I'll miss him," she said sadly. "So will Abner."

Abner had taken up sleeping next to the bear, since the time the mouse had darted in to grab a crumb of cracker the cub had left scattered on the floor. The cub had been asleep, and Abner had crawled up next to it and nestled against its little fat stomach. Now he did it frequently, and the cub made no objections.

"He'll find a new, warm place," Rafe said wryly.

He saw her quick, questioning glance. He was talking about more than the mouse; he was trying to reassure himself that Shea Randall would have a warm place after this, a safe place.

Still, nothing had changed. He wouldn't rest until he received some kind of justice.

The cub's rough tongue licked him. The salt he thought. The salt that remained there from the sweat of lovemaking. The thought made him stiffen again, and he knew he needed a swim in the icy water of the pool.

"Let's go see if the mother will claim him," he said, trying to keep the roughness from his voice.

Shea nodded. She had braided her hair again and

dressed in the trousers and shirt that were so unintention-
ally enticing. She was quiet this morning, attuned to his
own laconic mood.

They went out the door. The mother bear was back,
prowling back and forth as it had every morning, waiting
to see its offspring. Rafe approached cautiously, watching
the bear rear on its legs. He came within ten feet of the
animal and very carefully set the cub down and backed
away.

The bear moved just as warily toward its cub, licked
it, and then nudged it. The cub moved several feet, then
several more. It looked back toward the cabin, but the
she-bear nudged again, and it obediently limped toward
the woods. The she-bear roared and then headed toward
the woods, looking behind to make sure its cub was trailing. It was.

Rafe turned and saw the sheen in Shea's eyes. He
had never met anyone so tenderhearted, so gentle. He
had to keep reminding himself that she really was Jack
Randall's daughter. He didn't want to remember that, but
it was there between them.

"Damned bear nearly ate everything we have," he
said, forcing irritation in his voice. "Ben will have to make
another trip."

She glanced up at him and smiled. He buried the
pleasure he felt at her smile, trying to smother it under
anger. But it didn't work anymore, dammit. He felt buoy-
ant.

"And what will we do about this morning?" she
asked saucily.

He could think of something, God help him. And it
had nothing to do with food. His hand reached out and
touched the braid. "Nothing daunts you, does it?" His
tone was unusually whimsical.

"I could think of a few," she replied with devilish humor. "A furious bear. A glowering outlaw."

He wanted to glower again, but he couldn't. He was lost in the magic of her eyes, the glow of her face, the grin on those much too inviting lips. He let go of the braid and moved his fingers to her face, running them down those smooth cheeks, and then the woods went silent, and he knew someone was approaching.

Automatically his hand dropped to his side, and he realized he hadn't worn his gunbelt. The rifle, too, was inside the cabin. He no longer worried that Shea Randall might try to use it.

Rafe heard a low whistle, and he knew it was Clint. Each of the men had a different, predetermined whistle. "Clint," he said to Shea. "There must be some news."

He felt tension suddenly invade her, as if reality had just stolen back into her life, and she was silent as Clint rode toward them.

Clint looked at them. Rafe was afraid he would see more than he wanted Clint to see. Not for his sake but for Shea's. "I have to talk to you," Clint said. "Alone."

Rafe turned to Shea. "Wait inside." It was more curt than he'd intended, but there was something in Clint's eyes he didn't like. He saw a quiet protest in her eyes.

"Please," he added, wondering when he'd last said that word.

At his tone she turned around and walked to the cabin. Clint dismounted, went to the cabin and closed the door, then drew Rafe away from it.

"Jack Randall's been shot."

Rafe felt as if a bullet had punctured his own gut. "Dead?"

"Not yet, but he may well be now. I found him yesterday. He was unconscious with a bullet wound near the heart and a gash in the head. The doctor doesn't know whether he'll make it or not."

"Did he say who did it?"

"He hadn't regained consciousness when I left, but I put my money on McClary. According to one of the hands, McClary was at the ranch house when Randall returned from his search for you . . . and Miss Randall. No one's seen him since. But if Randall doesn't gain consciousness, you know who's going to get the blame."

Rafe stood stone-still. This was not what he'd wanted. He didn't realize until this very moment how much he had depended on forcing a confession from Randall. Clearing his name—at least that one undeserved blot.

He glanced down at his hand. He closed his eyes, fighting waves of dark pain. He was there again, at the parade ground, everything being torn away from him as Jack Randall watched. He waited for the hate to cascade, shrouding him as it had for so long, but it didn't. He just felt empty. So damn empty.

All of this for nothing. He steadied himself, thinking of Shea. She had come so far to get answers of her own.

He opened his eyes to see Clint's concerned gaze, and not for the first time he wondered what he'd done to deserve this kind of loyalty.

"Will you take Miss Randall down with you?" he said. "She won't say anything about this place or you or Ben."

Clint nodded.

"And, Clint, you and Ben get the hell out of here. You and the others. It's over."

"He may not die."

Rafe gave him a quizzical look. "With my luck?"

"What about McClary?"

Rafe shrugged. He wasn't going say that McClary

was unfinished business. The brothers would insist on staying with him. "He's probably at least a state away from here."

"Russ Dewayne is talking about a posse."

"More reason for you to leave this area. No one's seen you with me. No one knows about you."

"The girl does," Clint said.

"Another reason you should leave. She won't say anything on purpose but she could slip. She's not a very good liar." He saw Clint's bemused look and realized his voice had softened, betraying more than he'd intended.

But Clint only nodded. "I'll wait and see whether Randall survives." He hesitated. "And what Russ Dewayne's plans are."

Rafe heard Clint's reluctance, and that all-too-familiar guilt rocketed around inside him again. Clint had mentioned the sheriff's daughter before. Rafe knew what it must be costing him to lie to people he liked.

"No more risks," Rafe said. "Not for me."

"We've started something. It's hard to let go."

"It's my battle, Clint, and now it appears to be over. I don't want any more casualties."

"I know it's not what you wanted."

Rafe shrugged. It had been a long time since he'd gotten what he wanted. He needed to cut his losses now. Free the men who had followed him. Free Shea Randall.

But if Randall died, Rafe would never be free. He doubted now whether it would make any difference. What was done was done. The brand would remain with him. The memory of prison.

He turned around and headed back to the cabin, his stomach and heart churning. He had to tell Shea that she might never see her father alive, that he was letting her go. It would be his fault if she was too late. He didn't give a damn about Randall, except to regret his death foiled his plans, but he reluctantly admitted he did care about Shea.

And now she would hate him again. And what light there was in his life would be extinguished, just as surely as it had been ten years earlier.

She was sitting on the cot, playing with Abner nervously, as if she knew something had happened, something that affected her. She looked up at Rafe, a plea in her eyes.

"What is it?"

He swallowed. "Jack Randall . . ." Rafe couldn't bear to say the word *father*.

She stood, her body stiff. "What? What is it?"

"He's been shot. He . . . might be dying."

Her shoulders stiffened. "You . . ." Her voice choked suddenly.

He took her shoulders. "It wasn't me, or anyone connected with me," he said softly.

It was clear she didn't, couldn't, believe him, and he understood why. He had let her know how much he hated Jack Randall, how he had made plans to ruin him.

"No," he said. "That wasn't what I wanted."

"What did you want?" she said bitterly.

He turned away from her, his own body tensing. No one had believed him ten years ago. No one would believe him now. Not even the woman who had expressed a certain belief in him hours ago. He had been a fool to think it went any deeper than the moment.

He clenched his jaw and turned back to face her. "I had planned, *Miss Randall,* to force him to do what he always did when he got in financial trouble—steal. Steal and run. Steal and blame it on someone else. And get caught doing it this time. I wanted my name cleared, dammit, even if nothing can be done about . . . my hand. That's all I planned, but I don't expect you to believe that." There was a pause, then he added defeatedly, "Why in hell should you?"

There was a silence. Painful and long. Her jaw trembled, and her eyes filled with tears. She stepped toward him. "Rafe?"

"Clint will take you down if you swear you'll say nothing about him or Ben," he said through clenched teeth, as if he hadn't even heard her. "Swear on your mother's grave."

The air between them vibrated with tension. "You?"

Rafe shrugged. "If Randall's dead"—his voice was purposely cold—"there's no reason to stay here."

"And if . . . he's not?"

"There will be another day, Miss Randall. You can tell him that."

Her hand moved toward him, then fell before touching. "You're leaving here?"

"As soon as you ride out." He watched her swallow. He was lying. He would stay around and see what happened, but he didn't want her coming back here.

The mouse ran up her shoulder and sat there, begging. "Abner?"

"My cellmate?" he said purposely. He held out his right hand to her shoulder, the brand ever so obvious. The mouse ran across it, and Rafe turned his hand, catching the creature in the palm of his hand and holding it there gently. "He comes with me."

"I don't . . . want you to go."

"No?" he said coldly. "The man you were just accusing of having your father shot and lying about it? What then, Miss Randall," he said, his eyes narrowing, making his face even more severe, more daunting, "does that make you?" He wanted to hurt her. He had to hurt her. He had to make her leave and never look back.

"Don't," she pleaded with him.

"Don't what, Miss Randall?" he mocked, steeling himself against those huge blue-gray eyes that looked so wounded. "Or would you like me to stay around and be thrown back into prison?"

She turned away from him, and he knew she was trying to hide tears. He was being a bastard, but she had to know anything between them was impossible. Whether or not Jack Randall survived, Rafe had little future. Together, they had none.

"Swear it, Miss Randall. Swear that you'll be quiet about Clint and Ben, and you can go to the man you've traveled so far to find."

"I swear it," she said, her voice broken. Pain sliced through Rafe. But he had to make her hate him. He had to.

"If you say anything, so help me God, I'll hunt you down and . . . hurt whatever, whoever you care about."

She whirled around. "How can you even think . . . ?"

"I think lots of things. And I know a hell of a lot about betrayal. I've learned not to expect one goddam thing."

"And your friends?" she said bitterly. "Don't you trust them, even though they've risked everything for you?"

He was silent. He had no answer to that question. He was so scared of believing in someone else, yet he had done that out of sheer frustration and desperation, and he was doing it again now with Shea.

But apparently she accepted his silence as a negative answer. "Where will you go?"

"That's none of your business."

She stared at him. "It will always be my business, no matter what you think."

"That's your problem, Miss Randall," he said coolly,

though he felt hot all over. He knew he was successful, though, in hiding that discomfort when he saw her face pale.

She started to say something, but he stopped her. He couldn't hear it, or he might do something they both would regret.

"Clint will help you devise a story that will protect him and Ben."

"What about you?" she whispered.

"I don't give a damn what you say about me."

"Do you *want* to go back to prison?"

"I won't go back, Miss Randall," he said in a tone that said he would die first.

"Rafe?"

The sound of his name on her lips was nearly his undoing. He wanted to take her in his arms, hold her close, feel that warmth that only she had ever given him. He was tearing his own heart out by doing this, the heart he'd thought destroyed long ago. Now he wished he had been right.

He looked at her, trying to appear disinterested, something he'd learned well in prison.

He saw her swallow. He was terribly afraid that she might say what she wanted to say anyway, and he knew that might be the one thing that would break him. "You were a bed partner, Miss Randall. Nothing more."

Tears formed at the edge of her eyes but didn't spill over. "I don't believe you."

"Believe it," he said, "but know that Clint had nothing to do with that particular part of your abduction. He's a good man whose loyalty led him astray."

"Are you protecting me too?" she asked quietly. "It seems you're protecting everyone but yourself."

"I don't need protection," he said roughly. "And

don't romanticize my actions. It looks like I'm through here. I've accomplished what I wanted."

She shook her head. "No, you didn't. I don't know exactly what you planned, what you wanted, but it's obviously not my father's death. You could have killed him any time."

"No one else will believe that," he said.

Comprehension dawned in her eyes. "I'll tell them you couldn't have. You were here. With me."

Rafe knew he had made a mistake. He had revealed something that gave her hope. It was a mistake he had to rectify, no matter how cruelly. "Every second, Miss Randall? And my men? In any event I've been responsible for a few other . . . robberies, and like I said, I have no intention of going back to prison."

"I can't just forget—"

"Consider this, then. I seduced Jack Randall's daughter. I used you. It gave me some satisfaction. Now go back to your own life." Rafe looked directly down into her eyes, forcing her to accept his words.

A tear spilled then, and a fist went up to wipe it away furiously. He wanted to lean over and lick that tear and other ones away, but he forced himself to stay still, to keep an unforgiving scowl on his face.

"You better put on those trousers," he said, turning toward the door. He stopped, looked at the drawing pad on the table, and went over to it, flipping through it, tearing some sheets off and crumpling them in his hand.

Without any more words he went to the door and started to open it.

"Rafe," she said. He stopped dead still and then slowly turned around and looked at her.

She moved a few steps toward him, her face stricken. She stumbled, then straightened, her shoulders stiffening. She gave him one long look as if memorizing his face.

"I love you," she said.

Rafe felt all his defenses crumbling around him. But he managed to keep his face still, his eyes noncommittal. It was the hardest thing he had ever done. Enduring the parade-ground ceremony was child's play next to this. He forced himself to turn and walk out the door, closing it behind him, shutting it on what was brief happiness for him, potential tragedy for her. He walked away, more alone, more hollow, more heartsick, than he'd even been, even when the cell door closed on him for the first time.

She'd had to say it. She had been bursting with it. It stole her pride, her dignity, but she'd had to say it.

Shea was battered by a maelstrom of emotions, still uncertain as to the truth about Rafe. She had never been able to read those guarded eyes. She had been confused by all his contradictory actions. She had been guided only by instinct.

She was silent, huddled inside herself as she rode behind Clint in silence. He had always been kind, but today there was extra concern for her. She didn't know whether it was because of her father, because of the awkwardness at the cabin, or because of whatever Rafe Tyler had told him. She doubted he had told Clint anything. He was a man who'd perfected the art of hiding emotions . . . if he felt anything at all. She'd often wondered if he had any emotions to hide.

After Rafe had left the cabin, she slowly changed from her dress into the trousers and shirt and packed the valise. She didn't bother to check to see what had been censored from her drawing pad. Rafe wasn't around when she came out. He was obviously willing to leave things as they had in the cabin. There was to be no good-bye. No reprieve.

Clint had been standing there, next to his saddled horse, waiting for her. He looked at the valise and shook his head unhappily. "We can't take that."

"Why?"

"You're escaping from your abductors. You would hardly take that with you."

"My drawing pad?"

"Rafe said you could take it, but . . ." He stood there uncomfortably. "I'm . . . sorry about all this, Miss Randall. You got caught in the middle of something, and you didn't deserve that. If there's anything I can do . . ."

She didn't doubt his sincerity. The lump in her throat grew larger. No one could help.

He tried again. "Rafe . . . he's hurting too."

"Is he?" she asked.

"I've never seen him like this," Clint said. "Not even when I saw him in prison. He didn't want to hurt you." There was reluctance in his words, as if he felt he was betraying his friend and yet desperately wanted to help her in some way.

She turned away, on the verge of tears. She knew that once they started, they wouldn't stop.

She took the drawing pad and stared at it for a few moments, then flipped it open. She took several pages from it, folded them carefully, and tucked them inside her belt. She then put the pad in the valise, dropped it on the ground, and swallowed hard, trying to pretend it didn't matter. "He . . . Rafe said my father is hurt badly."

He nodded. "He's lost a lot of blood. The doctor said he has a concussion, and there could be infection."

"How do you know so much?"

Clint hesitated. She was going to know sooner or later. He might as well find out now how she was going to react. "I work for Jack Randall. I live at the Circle R."

"So that's why I was . . . kept prisoner."

He nodded.

Shea tipped her head. "Will you tell me something about him? About Jack Randall?" She had to think of something else, someone other than the man she was leaving behind. Forever.

There was a silence. "You'll have to learn for yourself," Clint said finally as he swung up on the horse, holding his hand down to her and guiding her up behind him.

She had turned as they left the clearing, watching the cabin until the foliage hid it, willing Rafe to appear. He didn't. They traveled about thirty minutes, and then Clint stopped and twisted around, taking a bandanna from his neck.

Shea was still too locked in misery to care. Clint was watching her carefully. "I'm going to say I found you in the woods, that you apparently escaped from your abductors."

He didn't ask for her agreement, but she nodded her head.

"I'm going to have to blindfold you."

"Rafe said he was leaving," Shea heard herself say tonelessly.

"It's for your own sake, Miss Randall. It's better if you say you had no idea where you were." He hesitated. "Rafe said you weren't a very good liar."

"What else did he say?" she asked bitterly.

"He asked me to take care of you," he replied with a small, crooked grin.

"Why do you trust me not to say anything? About you, I mean. Especially," she said pointedly, "since I'm not a good liar."

"You don't have to lie. You *were* abducted. You *did* get away. You *don't* know the way."

"But I know about you," she insisted, wanting a reaction of some kind. Wanting him to take her back. To Rafe Tyler. To the man who didn't want her.

"Will you say anything?"

She looked at his face. It was strong, the eyes honest. She remembered him bringing breakfast to her, his concern over her burn. His present awkwardness told her he obviously hated what he was doing, but he also believed in loyalty and friendship and his idea of justice.

"No," she said finally.

"You're quite a lady, Miss Randall," he said as he blindfolded her.

Shea didn't feel like a lady. She felt hollow, like a shell whose core had been ripped out piece by painful piece. She wished numbness would set in, but it didn't. The hurt was raw, jagged, soul deep, and she didn't think it would ever lessen.

Not even the thought of finally seeing her father helped. Because now she didn't know if he was alive or dead. And if he was alive, what had he done to ruin the man she loved, would always love?

And would never have.

Chapter 20

Shea looked at Jack Randall, trying to see something of herself in him. Trying to find what her mother had loved and what Rafe Tyler hated.

He was still a handsome man and would have been very handsome years ago. She couldn't see the color of his eyes. They had not opened since she'd arrived hours before. He was so still, she had to put her hand to his mouth to make sure he was breathing.

It was the head wound, the doctor had said. He might regain consciousness. He might not. He might remember what happened. He might not. Nothing was certain.

She looked across the bed at Kate, who had been here when she arrived. Shea had liked her instantly, liked her warmth, liked her support when she had hushed her father, who started asking questions. "Later," she had said when she saw the tiredness in Shea's eyes. She had hurried Shea to the room where Jack Randall lay so silently, and Shea had blessed the woman's own lack of questions.

How many hours now? How many since she'd left

Rafe? How many since she'd gazed on the man she believed to be her father? The man who was Rafe's nemesis.

She was part of him, this man. And yet he was a
stranger. Nothing was familiar. She'd thought there would
be a flicker of recognition, a facial feature that matched.
Something. Anything that would tell her the truth. A truth
she wasn't sure she wanted to know any longer.

She looked back at Kate. Shea felt a bond with the
woman who was close to her age. Shea hadn't missed the
glances that had darted between Kate and Clint, the longing in both their eyes, even as Clint made the introduc-
tion curtly. It was a curtness Shea recognized from Rafe.
Because Rafe had cared? Because Clint cared about Kate?
A defense? A wall?

The sheriff's daughter. And Clint was in cahoots
with an outlaw band. No wonder he had been so understanding.

There was a knock on the door, and Sheriff Dewayne
came in. "No change?" he asked.

She shook her head.

"Can you spare me a few moments?"

"Papa," Kate said warningly.

Dewayne shook his head. "There's a big mystery
about you, Miss Randall. In fact, there's any number of
mysteries around here."

Rafe said you're not a very good liar. When was it
that she realized everything Rafe had said had been said
to protect her? He hadn't needed to let her go, especially
not to see a man he despised. He'd known, though, how
important it was to her.

And now she needed to be a good liar for him. No
matter how many times he'd said he didn't care if Randall
knew who was after him, she wasn't going to be the one to
place a noose around Rafe's neck or clang a door shut on
him again. She wasn't going to repeat the story she was

coached to tell. She had simply become lost, that's all. Just lost.

She looked up at Sheriff Dewayne.

"Randall never told anyone he had a daughter," Dewayne said.

"I don't think he knew," she said softly. "I didn't know myself until a few months ago when my mother died, and I found some letters from him to her. She . . . always told me my father was dead."

"Why is that, do you think?"

"I don't know," Shea said. "That's what I came to find out."

"Where have you been? The clerk at the stage office in Casey Springs said you left there weeks ago."

"I . . . got lost," she said.

"That long?" he said with disbelief.

"I found an abandoned cabin. There was some food," she said.

His eyes narrowed. "I was told you left with someone who claimed to be a Circle R hand."

"He changed his mind," she said. "I left by myself. I'm not a very good rider, and my horse threw me, and I got lost. And then I found a cabin by a stream. There was some food. Maybe a miner . . . left it."

Shea saw the doubt in his eyes and knew other questions were coming, questions she wasn't quite sure she could handle. Rafe was right. She was a bad liar. She felt the flush on her cheeks, the strained quality of her voice even when she was trying so hard.

But she was saved from any more questions by a sound from Jack Randall. She leaned down, trying to hear what he was saying, if anything.

That sound came again, along with a slight movement, but his eyes didn't open. Shea dampened the cloth in her hand and ran it gently down his face.

The doctor had gone. He had other patients who needed him, he'd told Kate, and he could do nothing for Jack Randall but what they were doing: wait. Wait and see whether he woke.

Shea had such mixed feelings toward him, so many doubts. Yet love had been building in her since she'd learned of his existence. She felt disloyal to Rafe for having them. She felt disloyal to Jack Randall, the man who might have given her life, for doubting him.

She wished she could feel numb, not hopeful that this man would live, not wishful that Rafe would stay. The two were incompatible.

"Sara." Her mother's name was a groan on Jack Randall's lips.

Immediately, the sheriff stepped closer and knelt next to the bed. "Jack. Jack."

Randall's eyelashes flickered, revealing confused, clouded blue eyes. Shea's mother's eyes were gray, and her own blue-gray.

Jack Randall's eyes tried to focus. They wandered about the room and then hesitated at Shea's face. "Sara?"

The wavering tone penetrated Shea's very fragile calm. She shook her head. "I'm Shea. Sara's daughter."

He focused on her with an intensity that frightened her. "Shea? My daughter?"

Hearing the word "daughter" was nearly her undoing.

"I'm here," she said softly.

"I was . . . so afraid for you. The clerk at the station said . . ." His hand reached out, clutching her arm. "Did anyone . . . hurt you?"

Shea shook her head, hearing, seeing, love in his eyes. Her heart beat faster, harder, against its cage. "I just got lost," Shea told him. "I was frightened."

The sheriff moved in. "Jack . . . what happened here?"

Shea watched Jack Randall hesitate, look around frantically, as if searching for something that would bring back the memory. "I . . . don't know."

Dewayne shook his head. "Try to remember. Who shot you?"

Jack Randall closed his eyes. "I'm . . . trying. I remember . . . looking for . . . my daughter. Coming back. Nothing more." Shea saw him clench his teeth and knew he was in pain. She looked up at the sheriff, who looked thoroughly frustrated.

Dewayne tried again. "Jack, this all started with those first robberies. Then the killing of the miners. There's some connection. Help me, dammit."

Shea watched her father struggle. She didn't think he was faking. He seemed genuinely confused. "I just . . . don't remember." He looked up again at Shea, his gaze devouring her. "Shea," he whispered again. "My daughter." He moved his hand slightly toward her, and Shea found herself taking it, tightening her fingers around his, feeling his respond, clinging to her almost desperately.

Then he looked toward the sheriff. "I'm . . . sorry, Russ. I just . . . remember riding toward the ranch. . . ." His voice trailed off, and his eyes closed, his breathing becoming steady again.

Shea kept holding his hand, holding on to that tenuous connection to her father. Her father. He had been looking for her. He wanted her. His eyes had told her that.

She looked down at the pale face, at the now-closed eyes, and she shook with the realization she was a part of this man. There were so many things she wanted to know. So many questions to ask. So many answers she needed. Not the least among them his involvement in the robbery so many years ago. His face was not evil. His eyes had not been devious.

Rafe had to be wrong!

Dewayne stood. "Hell, that's it," he said, then looked at the two women. "Begging your pardon." Kate just smiled, but Shea couldn't. She was too tied up in knots to do anything but look at him helplessly.

"I've waited long enough," he said. "I'm putting together a posse and combing these canyons if it takes me a year. God knows what happened here, and I'm not sure Jack will be able to help anytime soon."

Clint had been lounging along a wall, watching with intense interest. Shea's gaze went to him and met his quick glance. There was neither approval in it nor disapproval.

"You going after McClary?" he said lazily.

"Him and those damned outlaws who've been deviling Randall," Russ said. "McClary could be dead or kidnapped himself. It's time I got some answers." His gaze went again to Shea, and he was frowning. Shea realized he hadn't swallowed her story. He turned back to Clint.

"Where exactly did you find Miss Randall?"

"Around Rushton Creek, near Casey's old strike," he said. "I was looking for signs of McClary."

"You think he's around the creek?"

"That's where the last miner was killed," Clint said. "You still think . . ."

Clint nodded. "McClary was gone each time a miner was killed. Now he's disappeared again."

"I wish I could be so certain," the sheriff said. "But that doesn't explain the other robberies. There were at least six men involved, and two occurred before Sam Mc-Clary arrived."

Clint shrugged. "Before he publicly arrived," he corrected.

Russ nodded. "That could be. Yet my gut tells me something else. Someone had it in for Randall, and I don't think it's someone he would invite into his home. Damn, I wish he could remember something. . . ."

"The doctor said we could expect this," Clint reminded him. "He might or might not remember certain things."

Russ nodded. "We'll be leaving in the morning, if you change your mind and want to join us, Clint."

Clint shook his head. "I think I'm needed here."

"Nate's here," Russ said pointedly.

"Nate can't take care of the herd alone," Clint said. "Just about everyone else has left, and whoever did this might come back."

Russ nodded. "You're right." He turned to his daughter. "Kate?"

"I'll stay here, make some dinner," she said. "I'll ride home later."

"Not alone," Russ warned, and Shea saw Kate bristle slightly.

"I've been riding alone since I was twelve."

"We didn't have killings then."

"Clint will bring me home," Kate said, turning toward him.

Clint's face tensed, then relaxed. "I would be pleased to."

Russ nodded, then turned to Shea. "I'm sorry your visit has been so . . . unfortunate, but at least it appears that your father will be all right. You'll let me know if you remember anything else? Or if Jack does when he wakes again?"

"Yes," Shea said, uncomfortable under his steady, questioning gaze.

After he left, Kate announced she would go down and find something to cook for dinner. "You stay here with your father," she said sympathetically. She looked toward Clint, her eyes softening, and Shea felt a tug of sympathy for Clint. His jaw had set, a muscle tensing in his cheek. She wondered whether Rafe had any idea of the dilemma his friend was in.

She sympathized with all her heart. She was learning the agony of divided loyalties.

Kate left, and Shea was alone with Clint. Her father was once more in a deep sleep.

"You did well," he said.

"I'm a good liar after all?" she said, hearing bitterness in her own voice.

"Not the best, but you'll do."

"You're pretty good at it yourself." She couldn't contain the accusation.

His lips twisted in a wry smile, but he said nothing. His eyes, however, clouded, and she sensed the regret in him, a dislike for what he was doing.

"Rafe is lucky to have you as a friend," she said suddenly.

"He's had damn little luck these past years," Clint said. "Even now . . ." He shut his mouth, then turned away and walked out of the room.

Shea gazed again at Jack Randall, her eyes fighting to stay open now. She hadn't had any sleep for a long time. Last night . . .

Was it only last night that Rafe had made love to her? So gently. So passionately. She closed her eyes, remembering his touch, her mind erasing the cruel words of this morning.

"Rafe," she whispered to herself, unaware that the name somehow penetrated the half-conscious world of the man so near to her. "I'll always love you."

* * *

Sam McClary cursed his luck as he rode his horse along Rushton Creek. If only those hands hadn't ridden up.

He could only hope that no one had seen him leave, that Randall was dead. But he couldn't count on either one.

There was nothing here for him now, anyway, not at the ranch. No more money to frighten from Randall. No more baiting the bastard.

Damn Randall for losing his nerve. Sam had always known Randall had a streak of yellow. But this thing about Tyler . . . That odd, incomprehensible guilt had destroyed Randall's usefulness. Could it have anything to do with rumors of a daughter? Randall had denied it, but . . .

Too bad. The connection with Randall had been a good thing. Always good for a few dollars when things became too hot for McClary someplace else.

He should leave this place, leave Colorado, but he knew if he did, Rafe Tyler would find him. Just as he had found Randall. McClary couldn't take that risk.

Although he couldn't return to the ranch, he had to stay just a little bit longer in the area. The law would be looking for him and Tyler, but Tyler wore the brand. And Tyler would stay, McClary knew, if the murders continued, if Tyler suspected McClary was still in the area. Mc-Clary would take his chances now rather than wait until the day Tyler found him.

McClary wanted to see Rafe Tyler hang. He wanted it enough that he was willing to risk getting caught. Tyler had become a personal obsession, and not only because of the danger he represented. McClary had hated him ten years ago; he hated him every bit as much now. He would never forget Tyler's contempt, before Tyler's disgrace and even after.

There were plenty of places to hole up here, and McClary had been in the territory enough times to know many of them. Abandoned dugouts and cabins dotted the canyons from the heyday of placer mining. And he could increase his stake. A few more dead miners should give him enough dust to head down Mexico way and tie the noose tighter around Tyler's neck.

But damn Randall. He'd enjoyed the Circle R. He'd enjoyed baiting Randall.

His attention was diverted when he saw what he'd been searching for. He rode up to the flimsy dugout built into the hill that ran alongside the creek. Almost totally hidden by the bushes, it was obviously abandoned. He could stake his horse in the woods to the side.

Sam McClary dismounted and went inside. There was nothing left of the dugout except three log walls, the back being packed earth. Whatever the previous owner had left had been picked clean.

It would do well enough for now for shelter. Then he would go hunting again. For miners.

Rafe Tyler sat on the rocks above the pool. He hadn't seen the bears this afternoon. He hoped the cub was surviving, healing.

He stared at the waterfall, which had given Shea such delight. He tried to concentrate on his next move, but there could be no next moves until he knew whether Randall lived or not.

What had Shea found? The father she'd wanted badly enough to travel half a continent? A dead man? He hoped for her sake, it was the former. But then what?

He had to continue his pursuit. He couldn't throw

away ten years of planning, all the sacrifice Clint and the others had made. He couldn't give up the last hope of being vindicated.

Rafe had put the glove back on today. He didn't want to see the brand. He had purposely left it off the last few days, trying, he told himself, to make a certain point to Shea. But she had not reacted the way she should. The way he thought she should.

He still couldn't believe it didn't make a difference to her.

The woodpeckers drummed out a melancholy song, and it reminded him of the tat-tat-tat of those drums so many years ago. Years ago but only yesterday in his mind. He would go crazy if he stayed here. Tomorrow he would go hunting on his own. He would find McClary and then make the other decision: what to do about Jack Randall if he still lived.

He sensed the sergeant was still around, especially if he'd killed Randall. He would want to eliminate anyone who knew of the connections. McClary would know that he was Rafe's next target.

Rafe took Abner from his pocket and ran his hand along the mouse's back, feeling its shiver of delight. But Abner was no longer enough. He closed his eyes, trying not to think of Shea Randall, of the light in her eyes and then the sadness. He tried not to think of the warmth she'd sent rushing through him.

He looked up. The sky was darkening. Night was coming. An early moon looked transparent in the sky. The temperature was lowering. Before long, it would be cold.

But he was already cold. And he didn't think he would ever be warm again.

* * *

Jack Randall slid in and out of consciousness.

Pain sliced through his head with such agonizing strength that part of him wanted to slip away. But another part, the part that recognized the miracle of finding a daughter, kept him fighting to return.

He felt her hand, and at times he thought it was Sara's hand. And then he remembered Sara was dead, and he'd never had the chance to say good-bye.

Once he'd opened his eyes, and his daughter was there, her eyes closed, her body slumped in a chair. She was asleep, and he'd ignored the pain to watch her. She looked very much like Sara. It thrilled him, but then sadness flooded him for having missed the joys and pleasures of watching his child grow.

He would have changed. If he had known about the child, he would have changed.

He tried to remember everything that had been said, but images started to form and then faded away. He had heard her say she had been lost. Thank God nothing had happened, but then other words crept into his consciousness, tapping at him and then sliding away. *Rafe*. She had mentioned that name. Why?

Jack Randall tried to move, and agony shot through him again, pushing every thought from his head. His shoulder was burning, and he tried to move his arm, only to find it tied tightly against his chest. A moan escaped his lips, and the girl's eyes opened again, his daughter's eyes, filled with concern and sympathy.

"I have some laudanum," she said. "Would you like some? Or a glass of water?"

He swallowed. He wanted oblivion from the pain, but then he would sleep again, and he wouldn't see her, talk to her.

Jack shook his head and held out his hand, which she clasped. "Just . . . talk to me."

She smiled. "About what?"

"Your mother. You. What you've been doing these years. What you like to do . . ." The last words trembled slightly on his tongue as the pain struck again, and he closed his eyes.

He forced them open again after a moment. She was watching him intently. "Please," he said, "just talk."

She started in a low, uncertain voice, hesitating now and then as if the words weren't worth much, but they were worth everything to him. He let them drop on him like diamonds from heaven. "We lived in Boston, in a fine little house there, and we had shop, a hat shop. I designed hats, and I like to draw."

His eyes closed, but her words went on, and he soaked them up like a sponge. They were better than laudanum.

"We used to go to concerts in the park, and we would read. I went to the Young Ladies' Academy and learned all the social graces, although you wouldn't know it now," she said, a bit of humor in her voice. And a sweet guile-lessness he remembered from Sara.

"All my dresses are somewhere in the mountains." She paused, and there was a long silence. He opened his eyes and looked at her and saw wistfulness, even a deep, heartfelt grief she tried to hide.

"We'll buy new ones," he said. But the sadness didn't leave her face, and again something pounded in his head, something he should remember. *Rafe.* The name had been said softly, not hard and accusing, as it had echoed in his mind for years. But it couldn't be. He was mixing up dreams and nightmares. She had only been lost.

Her words stopped. She'd hesitated again, and then those wonderful eyes looked down at him, this time with a question. "Do you remember anything yet?" she asked.

"About who shot you?" There was an intensity in her voice that startled him.

He tried to remember because it sounded so important to her. But there was only the memory of riding, of thinking. . . .

And then it started coming back. Brief, quick, painful flashes. McClary drawing a gun. McClary firing. Holy Mother in heaven. He'd told McClary he was going to confess all.

He looked up into his daughter's face. The daughter he'd just met, the daughter who looked at him with a wonder of her own. And he knew he couldn't explain his past and see the contempt on her face.

Jack closed his eyes. He had to have time first. Time to make her love him. Time to spoil her. Time to know her.

McClary was probably gone for good, especially since he must have thought he'd killed the man he'd blackmailed for so long. And Tyler? Perhaps Tyler would decide the shooting had been vengeance enough. He would realize he would be the prime suspect.

"F-Father?" The word was so uncertain on her lips. So tentative. He had to have time before she realized what kind of man he'd been.

He kept his eyes closed, pretending sleep to keep anything from showing on his face, to keep from answering any more questions. But he kept her words in his mind, like photographs he could take out at will and study. Then Rafe Tyler's face replaced them, his eyes piercing him with hate as they had ten years ago on the parade ground. And he knew Tyler would never let him go.

Her hand touched him so gently. He heard her soft sigh, and then the movement of the chair, her steps across the room, the opening and closing of a door. He opened his eyes, and the room was empty.

Jack Randall tried to move again, tried to sit up. He managed, but only after waves of pain assaulted him. He could see himself in the mirror, and he looked away, hating what he saw there, hating the notion that now kept flitting around in his mind.

He had only one way of holding on to his daughter. And that was to destroy Rafe Tyler one last time.

He only needed to tell Russ Dewayne it was Tyler who shot him.

Jack Randall clamped his teeth together, trying to swallow the leadlike lump in his throat. Rafe Tyler or his daughter. Guilt against his need to know and love his daughter. He already knew which course he would take. Even if it hastened his descent into the hell he'd tried to avoid these past few years by doing some good.

But God knew him, had offered another choice, and Jack Randall knew he would fail again. The Devil had always had the upper hand with him, offering comfort rather than poverty, freedom rather than punishment. Someday he would pay the price, but he'd never been able to resist the Devil's choice.

As he knew he wouldn't now.

He only wished he could remember what it was that kept nagging at him. Words he should remember. His daughter's whispered words.

Chapter 21

Kate made a stew from a chicken Clint had killed. There had been precious little food in the ranch house.

But she'd found onions, potatoes, and salt. She would bring over supplies tomorrow as well as some clothes for Shea Randall. The poor girl apparently lost everything in the mountains. It was a miracle she'd survived.

Kate's father had asked her to try to find out anything she could about Shea Randall and the weeks she'd been missing. It was unfathomable to him that a woman could survive that long alone, but Kate had always had a streak of self-sufficiency, and Shea struck her as the same. There were certainly numerous deserted cabins along the creek and enough wild raspberries for a person to survive a long time.

She had only admiration for the grit it had taken an Easterner to come this far and then to keep going. She had liked Shea Randall on sight, had liked her determination and her obvious concern for a father she hadn't known. Her own father, Kate thought, was just being suspicious.

She turned around from the pot as Shea Randall entered the room. She looked pale and tired, her eyes haunted, and sympathy surged through Kate.

"How is he?"

"He woke for a few moments and then went back to sleep."

"Did he remember anything about the shooting?"

Shea shook her head.

Kate hesitated, not wanting to intrude. "You've had a hard time."

Shea smiled wanly. "It wasn't what I expected when I left Boston."

"But now that you're here?"

"The land is beautiful," Shea said.

Kate had already set the table, and now she dished out two plates of food and filled glasses with water.

Shea sank down gratefully on a chair. She should be starved, but uncertainty curbed her hunger. "Mr. Edwards?"

"Clint, you mean?" Kate said. "He went to check in with Nate, make sure everyone has come in. With all the lawlessness . . ."

Shea took a bite of food and found it tasty, but her questions were building, and there were so few people she could ask.

"I know so little about . . . my father."

Kate smiled. "Everyone likes him. There's hardly anyone that he hasn't helped."

Shea sighed. "Why do you think someone shot him?"

Kate's smile disappeared. "No one knows. My father has tried to talk to Mr. Randall, but he says he doesn't know anyone who has a grudge."

Relief flooded Shea. At least no one knew about Rafe. Not yet. But why hadn't her father said anything about him? Did her father even realize who was behind the robberies?

Kate looked at her sympathetically. "You must be very tired. Would you like me to stay tonight?"

Shea shook her head. "You've done enough. I'm ever so grateful. But I can manage."

"I'll bring you some clothes tomorrow. And a ham."

Shea swallowed. She knew now how Clint felt, being wrapped in the protective warmth of people she couldn't confide in. "Thank you," she said simply.

"You'll like it here," Kate said impulsively. "It's usually very peaceful. And Papa will catch the people who shot Mr. . . . your father."

"I heard there was a man staying here, that he disappeared when my father was shot. Can you tell me anything about him?"

"Just that he came here several weeks ago. He didn't say much, or attend the socials. I know Clint didn't care for him, nor my father."

"Couldn't he have shot my father?"

Kate nodded. "But there have been so many other instances lately . . . That's why Clint thinks he should stick around here."

The way Kate said Clint's name made Shea smile. "You like him, don't you?"

Kate blushed, the matter-of-fact competence disappearing. "I didn't know it showed."

"Just a little," Shea said.

Kate's smile faded. "I wish it didn't," she said. "He says he has tumbleweeds for feet, that he'll never settle down."

Shea reached out with her hand and touched her. "Don't believe him," she said. "Fight for him."

She knew she shouldn't say that. Clint had his reasons, but she'd also seen how he looked at Kate. With pleasure, then wariness. Like Rafe's wariness.

Shea wondered whether she had any right to interfere, but something had made her say the words. *Fight for him.* Because she couldn't fight for Rafe?

Was he already gone? Had he lied about leaving? Why else was Clint still here?

And, dear God, there was a posse forming.

She shivered, and Kate looked worried. "Perhaps we should get the doctor back here to look at you."

"I'm just tired," she said, and Kate looked immediately apologetic.

"Of course you are," she said. "But are you sure I can't stay and help? I don't like leaving you alone."

"I won't be alone. Mr. Edwards said he'll be around, and several of the remaining hands. I'll sleep in my father's room." She was careful to avoid naming Clint, afraid of the familiarity of his name on her tongue.

Kate nodded, rising. "I'll be over in the morning with some clothes. Send for me if you need anything before then."

Shea looked at her gratefully. "I'll go talk to Mr. Edwards a moment. She hurried over to the bunkhouse, hesitating at the door, uncertain whether she should enter. She knocked, and Nate came to the door.

"How's Mr. Randall, miss?" he said.

"Conscious on and off," she said. "He still doesn't remember anything."

"I guess that makes you the boss now," he said.

Shea hesitated. "I understand a lot of men have left. Thank you for staying."

Nate shrugged. "I've been here a lot longer than most. Mr. Randall's always been real fair."

"That's what I keep hearing," she said, wanting to probe a little more, but there was greater urgency in talking to Clint. "Can you tell me where Mr. Edwards is?"

"The barn, ma'am. Taking care of the horses."

"Thank you," she said, and turned away.

"Miss Randall?"

She turned back. "Anything I can do to help," he said, "just let me know. I'm sorry you came here when there's so much trouble. Damn thing, what's happening. The Circle R was . . . is a real nice spread."

Before the robberies. Before Rafe Tyler.

"How bad is it?" she said.

"I guess you have a right to know. We're losing cattle every day because we don't have enough men to keep them out of the canyons where there's not enough grass to keep them alive. It doesn't look like we'll have enough men to take them to market this fall, and even if we did, there won't be enough to meet the note. Mr. Randall's lost three monthly payrolls; none of the men have been paid in four months. Can't blame them for leaving, 'specially when the prospects ain't very good."

Shea nodded. "Thank you for being so honest."

"You need to know in case . . ."

In case her father didn't make it. And then Rafe Tyler would win. He would have destroyed everything Jack Randall had built.

Don't think about it.

But she couldn't help thinking about it as she walked to the barn and opened it. Clint turned around from the horse he was saddling and looked at her warily as she closed the door. They were alone.

"He's still up there, isn't he?" she asked.

Clint's jaw set stubbornly, and he said nothing.

"Are you going to tell him about the posse?"

"If he's still there, he'll find out. Do you give a damn?" His eyes bored into her in the dim light of a lantern.

"Yes," she whispered.

"What about Randall?"

"Can't there be some mistake? Perhaps that Mc-

Clary . . ." She heard the plea in her own voice, a plea that he agree with her.

"Has Randall said anything about the attack?"

She shook her head.

"He won't," Clint said bitterly. "He'll blame it on Rafe."

"He doesn't remember. . . ."

"Are you sure of that, Miss Randall? Are you really sure?"

Shea wasn't sure of anything anymore, not even that the world was round or the sky blue or the sun always rose. "No," she finally answered.

"Rafe can take care of himself," he said, his voice softening.

"And you?"

He stopped saddling the horse. "What do you mean?"

"Kate."

Friendliness left his voice. "What about Kate?"

"She's in love with you."

"She can't be."

Shea just looked at him.

"In any event it's none of your business," he said curtly. "Now if you'll excuse me. I'll see if she's ready to go home." He led the horse out of the stall, and then took a small mare that must belong to Kate out of another. He stopped, turned back. "Thank you for . . . what you said to Russ Dewayne."

"I don't think he believed me."

Clint gave her a wry smile. "I don't think so, either, but there's no way he can disprove it." He started to say something more, but then clamped his lips together and led the two horses out the door, leaving her in the barn. She sat on a bale of hay, feeling very alone and lost, and then she remembered the sketches she'd brought with her. She took them from inside her belt.

The drawing of Abner was there, another of the cub. One of Rafe with the horse. He had torn away the sketch of the fall and pool, of the mountains drawn from the stump in front of the cabin. And she realized he hadn't meant to leave immediately; he had ripped away every geographical landmark she'd captured on paper.

But he'd left alone the sketches of him. And it made her sick inside. *I don't give a damn what you say about me.* He'd already given up on a future. Or maybe, just maybe, he didn't want her to forget, no matter what he said.

And she hadn't given up. She knew she would never give up. Somehow she would make things right. She didn't know how, but she had to.

She heard horses ride off and knew that Clint and Kate had gone. She balled the drawings up, took the lantern down, and went outside the barn. Carefully, very carefully, she burned all evidence of Rafe Tyler.

She didn't need them. She had memorized him in her mind, in her heart. She recalled every expression, every hard line of his face, especially the way it had gentled last night before Clint arrived with his news. That was the picture she held now in her heart.

From a distance lights were visible at the Dewayne ranch. A number of horses were tied to the hitching rail.

The evening was cold, but Kate felt a chill of another kind. She had stood outside on the porch, waiting for Clint and Shea Randall to appear. It seemed a very long time before Clint came out of the barn alone, his expression daunting and visibly warning her to be silent.

Kate had never been jealous before. She had never

fallen in love before. Until she met Clint Edwards two years ago at a dance.

He was a fine-looking man, with light gray eyes and a cleft in his chin that eased the starkness of a face darkened by the sun. He said little, and though he regarded her with interest, he offered none of the compliments her suitors did.

It took a year and many socials they both attended before she'd summoned the nerve to ask teasingly for a dance, since he obviously wasn't going to ask her. He had given her a slow smile that made her heart do strange jumping things, and then he'd admitted that he didn't know how to dance.

They had gone outside, and she had taught him a few steps. He was a quick pupil, and the smile that had appeared so rarely came more easily.

That had been the beginning. Then he'd sought her out. They'd gone for rides on several of the occasions when she'd visited the Circle R with her father, and she'd grown to like him more and more. She even enjoyed their moments of silence, because there was never awkwardness, only a warm companionship. He never said much about himself, or his past, although once he'd mentioned the war.

And every time she saw him, her heart and senses started spinning out of control. When he kissed her, she felt as if she owned all the stars in the universe. But he puzzled her. Her eyes told her he cared, so did that lazy smile of his, but he never said anything, never promised anything, never asked anything of her. He always held a part of himself in check.

She'd never seen him as tense, though, as he was now, as he had been since he brought Shea Randall to the ranch, and uncertainty and jealousy ate away at her.

There had been an intensity in the way Clint had regarded Shea, a personal interest that he couldn't hide.

The silence between them now made Kate feel as if he were moving away from her.

"Shea Randall is very pretty," she finally said, seeking a reaction.

Clint glanced over at her and shrugged. "Is she?"

Kate stiffened at the artificial indifference in his voice. There was an undercurrent there, and she wanted to cry. She knew then she hadn't really accepted his words the other night. Something would keep him from leaving. Someone could stop those tumbleweed feet.

She glanced over at his face. It was hard and set. She swallowed, afraid to say anything that would distance him even further. Feeling very much alone and miserable, she rode to the boundaries of her father's ranch, to where she could see the lights shining in the house, and stopped, turning to face him.

"You don't need to come any farther," she said in a strained voice.

"I want to," he said.

"I think," she said, "you should return to the Circle R. She might need you."

"Kate," he started, then stopped. A muscle moved slightly in his cheek, and his hands tightened on the reins. But just as she thought he might say something, he nodded, turned his horse, and rode back in the direction of the Circle R.

Shea slept on and off in the chair in Jack Randall's room. A dimmed oil lamp sat on a table in a corner. She continuously fueled the large fireplace, waking every several hours as the room chilled, telling her additional logs were needed.

He had come to consciousness several times and, though he recognized her, he remained confused about the events surrounding his injuries. But there was no doubting the sincerity of his pleasure that she was there.

No matter how she tried, she simply couldn't equate this man with the one Rafe and Clint portrayed with their dislike. Though he was obviously in pain, Jack Randall's eyes twinkled when he looked at her. His hand was warm when he touched her, his clasp warm and welcoming. She couldn't stifle her love, which had risen almost automatically. If he had turned from her, perhaps it would have been different. But he'd embraced her with unquestioned affection.

She wanted to ask him about Rafe. She had to know the truth of what happened ten years ago. But then she would have to admit she knew Rafe, knew he was in the mountains nearby, and there was no reason for him to be there unless he was a hunted outlaw.

And so she huddled miserably in the chair between spurts of sleep, wishing she knew Jack Randall better, wishing she knew what he would do if he were aware of the truth of the past few weeks.

She didn't hear Clint return and wondered whether he had gone up into the mountains to talk to Rafe. She hoped so. She wanted him to know about the posse. She wanted him to live.

Jack Randall moved restlessly in the bed, and Shea tried to shake off the weariness drugging her. She moved over to him and touched his face. It was dry with fever.

She wet the cloth in the cool water on a table next to the bed and bathed his face.

He muttered some words she couldn't understand, and she leaned down to try to hear. "I won't . . . let you. . . . No." His movements became frantic. She leaned down, pressing on his good shoulder, trying to wake him.

His eyes finally opened, and he stared at her as if he'd seen a ghost, and then recognition came. "You . . . look so much like your mother." He sighed, and quieted.

Shea rinsed his face with the cloth. "Do you remember anything more? You were saying a few words."

"I don't remember," he said, but his voice lacked assurance.

"Try," she insisted. "The sheriff is forming a posse. They don't know who they're looking for." She paused a moment, then continued with determination. "Your friend . . . Mr. McClary . . . is also missing."

He moved, and pain rippled across his face. Guilt stabbed at Shea. She reached for the laudanum, poured some in a glass, and held it to his lips.

"Don't leave," her father said. "Please don't leave."

She knew he didn't mean now. He meant ever. He wanted her. Rafe didn't. It should be simple. But it wasn't.

She ached for Rafe Tyler. Her heart ached for him, and her mind and her body. She kept seeing him in her mind's eye. She tried to force him out, tried to replace his face with that of this man she'd searched for, this man who had given her life.

"I'll be right here," she said, deliberately misunderstanding him.

He closed his eyes, the laudanum obviously taking effect. His body relaxed, and Shea tried to do the same. But she was stiff and hurting and confused.

Restless and unhappy, she rose and moved through the door down the hall. An oil lamp was lit in the main room, and she quickly lit another in the kitchen. Her eyes kept going to the door of her father's office, the room where he was shot. His office.

"No," she told herself. "I can't." But still her feet moved in that direction. She picked the oil lamp off the table in the main room and slowly opened the door to the office.

Dark brown stained the rich, colorful rug, and she suddenly wanted to run from it. But she couldn't. She had to know the truth. She didn't know what to look for. Perhaps, she thought, she merely needed to confirm the fact that Jack Randall was everything he seemed: a rancher respected by his neighbors and friends.

But what did that make Rafe Tyler?

Shea avoided the stain on the rug and went to the desk. There was a half-smoked cigar on a plate and a ledger. Feeling like a traitor, she nonetheless looked inside. Her gaze went down the first page of many inked ones. This book started two years previously: 1871. And then she saw the notation. *Sam McClary. $1,000.* A year later, another one, this time for $1,500.

A drawer was partially opened, the lock broken, and it looked as though someone had started to sort through it, then stopped. Papers on top were mussed, but those underneath seemed undisturbed. She looked through them, and her hand found something heavy. She stared at it incredulously. A tintype of her mother. Sara looked beautiful, a lovely smile on her face. Shea had never seen that particular smile. A letter lay next to it. It had obviously been handled repeatedly.

Her conscience warred between her respect for Jack Randall's privacy and the need to know why her mother had hidden his existence from her for so long.

She didn't know how long she stood there, holding the folded page. She finally unfolded it and recognized her mother's handwriting. She looked at the date. August 1863. Just weeks after Rafe Tyler's court-martial.

She read the letter and then read it again more carefully. Feeling sick inside, she carefully folded it and started to place it back in the drawer. She hesitated, then took it with her to the bedroom she was using and slipped it under the mattress.

She went to the open window and looked out toward the mountains where Rafe was hiding. A half-moon hovered above the peaks, surrounded by stars.

How he must hate her father. How he must hate her. She had never truly understood before.

A cool wind blew on her, but she was oblivious to it. She was oblivious to everything except that letter and the utter hopelessness she felt.

Chapter 22

Jack Randall's condition improved quickly, as did his charm. If Shea hadn't read the letter, she would have been captivated by him. As it was, she found herself making excuses for him. Perhaps the letter hadn't meant what she thought it did.

She held off her anxious questions until the fifth day. The posse still went out daily, which meant, according to Clint, they'd found nothing. Clint didn't mention going to the mountains himself, but Shea knew he had, knew that he had told Rafe that his enemy still lived.

The doctor had returned on the third day and said it was not strange at all that Jack Randall didn't remember anything about the shooting. It might come back, he said, and it might not. Head wounds were always unpredictable.

But he thought infection was now unlikely and told his patient he could start moving around, though his arm was to remain strapped to his chest.

Kate visited briefly. She had dropped in several times, the first to bring some supplies and several dresses.

They needed a few tucks and were a little too short, but Shea had been grateful.

Kate was more reserved than the first day they'd met, and Shea wondered why. But she didn't puzzle over it long, because other matters worried her more: how to broach the subject of Rafe Tyler with her father.

After Kate left on the fifth day, Shea made lemonade and carried a pitcher and glasses to Randall's room. He was awake, sitting on the side of the bed. He had already walked around the room several times and now was breathing heavily, but his mouth broke into a broad grin when he saw Shea.

"You're like a rainbow every time you come in," he said. "You don't know how happy you've made me by coming here."

Shea set down the pitcher and poured them both a glass before she sat down in a chair next to him. "Why did you and Mama part?" It was the question that had been haunting her ever since she opened the box in Boston.

He leaned back against the headboard with a sigh. He took a long drink and then studied her carefully. "Didn't she tell you anything?"

"She said you had died before I was born."

Pain flickered across his face. Only after several moments of silence did he speak.

"Your mother was a city girl, gently reared," he said. "She . . . never accepted the West, or what you had to do sometimes to survive."

"I don't understand," Shea said.

"Moving frequently," he said. "We didn't have any money. Sometimes didn't even have a place to stay. Good jobs were hard to come by. I think when she knew you were coming, she needed a safe place, and I . . . couldn't provide that. Not then."

"But later?"

"It was too late," her father said. "I think she hated to admit . . . it hadn't worked out. Her family didn't want her to marry me, fought it every moment until we eloped. She might have been afraid they wouldn't take her in, so she told everyone I had died. I kept asking her to join me, but she begged me not to interfere with her life. She never told me about you."

His eyes begged her to believe him. They were full of regret and grief and longing, and she believed he really felt those things. But she also knew that Sara Randall wouldn't have been daunted by hard times. Not the Sara Randall that Shea knew.

"I . . . I found a clipping among her things," Shea said. "About a court-martial."

"There were several when I was in the army," he said, a muscle twitching in his neck.

"It mentioned some payroll robberies, an officer named Tyler."

There was a long silence. "I would rather not talk about that, Shea," he said. "It . . . was very painful. He . . . I . . . liked the young man."

Shea wanted to slow the fast beating of her heart. She had found a father, and now she might lose him. She shouldn't care if he had done what she was now fairly sure he had. But she did care. She cared desperately.

"It was . . . your word against his."

"They found some of the money in his quarters."

"Someone else could have put it there."

Her father's face changed slowly as several minutes went by, aging as if each minute added years. He took her hand that was folded in her lap. "Why? Why are you so interested?"

His fingers pressed against hers, as if it were a life-line.

"I . . . I just want to know more about you," she

said, not yet ready to give him information that might hurt
Rafe but desperate to discover the truth.

But his gaze met hers, searching. "Where were you
those days you were missing?"

"I told you. I was lost."

"You've met Tyler." It wasn't a question but a statement.

Shea didn't answer. But her heart beat even faster.
She knew he would realize she was lying if she said no.
Her interest had given her away.

"You were with him in the mountains." His voice was
sad rather than accusing. "The bastard," he said then in
almost a whisper. "He used you to get even with me."

"No." The word escaped Shea's lips before she could
think.

He closed his eyes, and pain flooded Shea. In a matter of weeks she had found a love and a father, and they
hated each other and accused each other of motives and
deeds so dark, she could barely comprehend them, much
less accept them.

"No," she whispered in denial again.

"What did he say, Shea?" he said defeatedly.

Shea rose and went to the window without answering.

"Did he . . . ?"

Shea didn't answer.

"Dear God," he said, his voice strained and close to
breaking.

Shea turned. "Did you? Did you lie during the court-
martial?"

"No," he said flatly. "And if he touched you, I'll see
him dead this time. Kidnapping a woman is a hanging
offense."

"I was just lost," she insisted.

"Shea, don't let him come between us. He's a convicted thief."

"What are you, Papa?" Shea hadn't meant to use the word. It just slipped out, and she realized she had already been thinking of him that way.

"A man who wants his daughter," he answered simply, and nothing else he could have said would have struck her so poignantly.

The letter.

I love you.

The words she had said to Rafe. Her mother's words to Jack Randall.

She put her fists to her ears, as if to block out any more sounds. And then she whirled out of the room, out of the house, and down to the barn. She had to leave. She had to escape all the voices. She even wanted to outrun herself.

There was no one in the barn. In the past few weeks she had watched men saddle a horse, and she knew she could do it. She saddled the most tranquil-looking of the horses. She didn't care that she was wearing a skirt. She didn't care about anything but getting away.

She buckled the cinch of the saddle and forced the bit into the horse's mouth, then led the horse outside. There was no one in sight. The few remaining hands were apparently still out.

She heard a shout and saw her father lean against the front door of the ranch house. "Shea, no!"

But another voice was louder. The one inside her head, which told her to find some kind of rest, some kind of peace, to sort out the warring emotions.

She swung up onto the saddle, her dress riding high on her thighs, and her knees nudged the horse. Its sudden reaction surprised her, and she held on for dear life as the horse spurted into an uncontrolled gallop.

* * *

Jack Randall wasn't dead. The words kept repeating themselves in Rafe's brain. He didn't know how he felt about that.

For a brief time, before he knew Randall lived, Rafe had felt something like relief. It was over. Clint and the others could go on with their own lives. He would continue to track down McClary, and then . . .

Christ, what then?

He had lived these past ten years with only one purpose in mind: exacting revenge and, if possible, clearing his name. He had never thought ahead. Now he wondered what was ahead if he did succeed. Emptiness. Loneliness.

He hadn't realized what loneliness really was until Shea Randall had left, until he'd had some knowledge of how it felt to be touched with warmth and tenderness.

How was she?

Had Randall charmed her as he had charmed too many others? She had been ready to be charmed. She had wanted a father so badly; it had shone in those eyes of hers.

Clint had ridden back up the night he had taken Shea home and had told him about Shea's lies, the way she had tried to protect Rafe, protect them all. How long would that last in the comfort of the Circle R?

Why had McClary shot Randall? Tried to kill him?

Clint knew that McClary had done it. McClary had been at the ranch house when Randall had returned from a three-day absence. Since Clint knew none of Rafe's men had shot Randall, it left only McClary. But Clint hadn't been able to convince the sheriff of that. Posses would be combing these mountains.

Restless beyond tolerance, Rafe decided to start his

own hunt for McClary. His business with Randall would have to wait. McClary would have left the Circle R in a hurry. Without supplies. He would have to steal them now, and the miners were still easy pickings. Some had banded together for safety, but others were just too independent and guarded their claims with fierce possessiveness, regardless of how little gold they found.

In addition to those miners who worked the creeks and streams, there were still those who sought yet another vein in abandoned mine shafts picked clean. Those abandoned shafts would make fine hiding places for someone like McClary. They dotted the area, and Rafe concentrated his search on them.

Rafe had found nothing in the four days he'd been looking. He'd once seen the posse moving below him, and he had quietly backed away and ridden in the opposite direction.

Rafe knew he was looking for a needle in a haystack, but he simply couldn't sit and wait any longer. He'd go mad if he did. He returned to the cabin each night in the event there was any message for him from Clint, Ben, or any of the others. Abner, who seemed content enough there with the crumbs Rafe left, would always creep out and welcome him, begging for an affectionate touch. And Rafe would remember Shea's delight with Abner, with the cub.

Today he tried to dismiss memories of her as, once again, he scoured the mountainside. His horse tied behind a thick clump of berry bushes, he skirted the ridges of the steep mountain gulch, looking below at the stream where several miners still panned for gold. He wished he had a spyglass, but he didn't.

His gaze stopped roaming for a moment, fixed on a bush below him. It seemed to move, but there was no wind stirring this day. The sky was cloudless, the sun bright, the air still and dry. Farther on down the mountain sat a miner's cabin. There was a figure standing in the creek, obviously panning for gold. A rifle lay on the ground nearby.

Rafe turned his gaze back to the moving bush. A glint of silver shone among the dull green leaves. Someone was there, someone who was also watching.

Could he be this damn lucky for once?

Rafe cautiously moved down, snaking through the underbrush. He wondered whether he should use his rifle to warn the miner below. And then he saw the barrel of a rifle sticking through the moving bush.

Hurriedly, Rafe aimed at the barrel of the rifle below, realizing he had little chance of hitting it. He pulled the trigger just a fraction of a second before the other man shot. Rafe missed the rifle barrel but kicked up a cloud of dust. The other man's bullet also went astray, missing the miner.

The miner below spun around, his hand going for the rifle as he darted for the cover of nearby rocks.

The unseen man took another shot at the miner, then turned the rifle upward, toward Rafe. The miner aimed his rifle upward, too, then fired at . . . Rafe.

The bullet winged Rafe's arm, right where the bear had clawed him, and he dropped the rifle and clutched at the pain shooting up his arm. More shots peppered the ground around him, coming from two rifles this time.

Rafe rolled behind a boulder, damning himself, damning his luck. The miner evidently thought Rafe was his assailant. Rafe realized he should have shouted out a warning, but his first instinct had been to take the man who had been doing the killing, the man he believed was McClary. Now Rafe was pinned down. He tried to crawl toward the horse, but a bullet ricocheted off the boulder, slicing along his thigh.

He sat upright behind the rock and looked down. The miner had taken refuge behind a tree; the man below him was nowhere to be seen.

Then he heard a shout, followed by another, and the sound of hoofbeats. A lot of them. The posse!

There was no time for explanations. He heard horses scrambling up the steep incline. More shouts, orders giving directions. He looked around. There was no escape except to run out in the open toward the berry bushes where his horse was tied. He knew he wouldn't get five feet.

He had six bullets in the Colt. He pulled it out of the holster and aimed at the closest member of the posse, but he couldn't pull the trigger. He'd thought he could. He'd thought he could do anything to keep from going back to prison. He could have easily killed the man below him, the man who had been killing the miners and framing him. Probably he could even kill Randall. But he couldn't kill an innocent rancher.

He thought about trying to escape and taking a bullet. But he wasn't ready to die. He hadn't finished his business with Randall. And there was another reason, one that he kept trying to push away.

Rafe threw out the Colt and slowly stood, both hands raised. His arm was bleeding badly, and the leg of his trousers was drenched in blood.

The men forming the posse approached cautiously, holding guns on him. One man, whose dull tin star pinned to a well-worn leather vest identified him as the sheriff, dismounted and walked cautiously toward Rafe. "The miner said there were two of you."

"Did he also say one was firing at me?" Rafe said dryly. "I was trying to help that miner."

"By sneaking around up here?" the sheriff said with obvious disbelief.

"Go down to that bush below," Rafe said. "See for yourself. A man was hiding behind it."

The sheriff shrugged. "An accomplice?"

"No, dammit. I saw him taking aim at the miner, and I fired my rifle in warning," Rafe said, knowing his explanation was futile.

"And who are you?" the lawman asked.

Rafe hesitated. He was wearing his gloves. Once the posse saw his hand, he'd have no further chance to explain.

"Dammit," he said. "The real gunman will get away. If he hasn't already."

The lawman stared at him for a long while, then looked at one of his men. "Go down and look around that bush. See if you can pick up any tracks. Take a couple of men with you."

He turned his attention back to Rafe. "You didn't tell me your name or what you're doing here."

Rafe lowered his hands. "Thinking about doing some mining, looking for a part of the stream that wasn't taken, when I saw this fellow showing an undue interest in that miner," he said.

"Is that so?" the sheriff asked. "Unbuckle that gunbelt and let me see your hands."

Rafe felt his whole body tense. "Why?"

"A miner has calluses on his hand. Calluses different than those come from riding."

"I haven't mined much before."

"I thought as much," the man said. He leaned down, picked up Rafe's rifle, and checked the magazine. "One shot fired," he said to the others. He turned back to Rafe. "Unbuckle that gunbelt."

Rafe did as he was ordered. When the belt fell, the sheriff leaned down and picked it up, checking the number of bullets. He then picked up the pistol and spun the cylinder, finding all the bullets in place. "You could have fired at us."

Rafe remained quiet, very aware of the three guns still leveled at him, at the hostile, disbelieving stares.

"Maybe you're what you say you are. Maybe you're not," the lawman said. "But with all the robberies and killings around here, I'm not taking any chances." He went to his horse and took handcuffs from the saddlebags. Rafe stiffened.

"I'm Russ Dewayne," the lawman said, and Rafe remembered the name. Clint had liked him, thought him a fair man.

Dewayne set the handcuffs down on a rock and took off his bandanna. "Roll up your sleeve," he said. "Let's take a look at that arm."

Rafe nodded and the sheriff turned his attention to the bleeding wound that had torn open the still-stitched ragged tear from the bear. "What in the hell happened to you?"

"A bear," Rafe said.

His eyes narrowed. "You seem to have bad luck, Mr. . . ."

"Tyler." It seemed useless to give another name, particularly with the brand that would soon be discovered.

The lawman said nothing else but tied the bandanna around the wound and then checked the leg. It had already stopped bleeding. "Just a crease, but it needs to be looked after. I'm taking you into Casey Springs. There's a doctor there."

"Do I have a choice?"

"No. The miner down there claims you shot at him. And there've been a lot of robberies. I'll be real interested to see whether they'll continue once you're locked up." He picked up the handcuffs, then looked at the arm he'd just bandaged and hesitated. Rafe realized what the lawman was thinking. It would be damned difficult to get down the mountain with the wounds and the handcuffs.

"Where's your horse?"

Rafe deliberately put a hand over the bandage as if it bothered him more than it did. "Up above."

"How far?"

"Quarter of a mile."

The lawman signaled one of his men to go find it. "Let's go on down," he said. "Talk to that miner." He tucked the handcuffs in his belt. "After you . . . Mr. Tyler."

Rafe carefully made his way down the slope, very conscious of the guns still on him. His leg hurt, and his arm felt like fire, but he was damned grateful to the man behind him. He had a chance, a slim one, to escape. Or convince the miner he hadn't been trying to shoot at him.

They reached the bottom of the slope. The miner stood there, rifle in hand, glaring at him, taking several threatening steps toward him.

The lawman stopped in front of the miner. "Take it easy, Charlie. He says he was just trying to help you. You see anyone else up there?"

"Yes, sir. There was two of them. Saw the sun hit the barrel of their rifles. That's how I hit him," he said with satisfaction. "Figure they was together."

"Then why in hell do you figure he was shooting at me?" Rafe said.

"Well, now, I didn't see that," the miner said. "I just knew the dust was jumping up around me."

"That first bullet," the lawman said. "Do you know where it came from?"

The miner squinted back up the slope. "I don't know. I just heard it coming from my back and grabbed old Herman here," he said, lifting his rifle. "Saw the sun on the rifle up there and shot. Then a bullet hit real close, and I dived for the woods and started shooting."

"So it could have been like he said?"

"Ain't likely," the miner said. "Why would he just happen along at the right time? More likely he's one of them that's been killing miners up here."

Rafe saw the trap closing just as it had years ago. No one was going to believe him, especially when they saw his hand, and that, he knew, was just a matter of time, maybe even minutes.

He schooled his face to indifference. He had one chance now, and that was to keep those handcuffs off, to make a run for it, once he was on his horse.

One chance in a million.

He thought to test his captors, to see how closely they were watching him. He walked over to a tree and leaned against it as if too weak to stand any longer. The wounds had kept his hands free thus far.

Two men followed him. They holstered their guns, but their eyes didn't leave him. Neither did the sheriff's, although he continued to speak to the miner in a low voice that Rafe couldn't hear.

Two men rode in with his horse in tow, then the three men the sheriff had sent out earlier to trail the missing man. "There's tracks, Russ, but whoever made them got plumb away."

"No loyalty among thieves," one said with a grin as he glanced at Rafe.

Rafe kept his gaze cool, but he was dying inside, piece by piece. He wouldn't see her again. Shea. Pretty Shea. Randall's daughter.

Randall was winning again.

The sheriff walked over to Rafe. "I'm sorry to do this with those wounds," he said, "but I can't take any chances. Hold out your wrists."

Dewayne was standing in front of him, the irons in his hand.

Rafe felt a muscle in his cheek twitch, and he concentrated on controlling it. He wouldn't show the bastards how familiar he was with irons. How much he flinched at the thought of them. Not again, dammit. Not again, something inside him screamed.

"Tyler." It was Dewayne again, his voice insistent. "Your wrists."

Slowly, Rafe lifted them. He felt the iron close over the left wrist and then start to enclose the right, but the glove got in the way. Dewayne pulled it down, stared, and Rafe heard the hiss of indrawn breath.

Dewayne's hands hesitated and then snapped the lock shut on the right cuff. "God in heaven, I've never seen one of these before," he said, pulling the glove back up over the brand as if he'd revealed someone's nakedness.

Rafe shrugged. He'd known this was coming; still, he could barely contain the rage and frustration he felt. They would watch him like a hawk now, and with eyes that proclaimed him guilty.

But he wouldn't let them know how much it hurt, how very much it hurt. He had tried to help the miner. Christ, he *had* helped. And now he most likely would hang for it because of the brand he carried. The brand burned on him because of Jack Randall.

His only satisfaction was that Clint and Ben and the others were safe, uninvolved. Somehow, he had to keep them that way. He might hang, but he would hang alone.

Rafe looked up at the sky, at the sun peaking over the mountains. He thought of the past few months. The beginning of his being able to feel again. To hope once more. Fool!

Shea. The image of her face flashed through his

mind. It had been there, hovering in his consciousness ever since she'd left. He wondered where she was now.

One of the men brought his bay over to him and waited for him to mount. He clenched his teeth together as he stretched his arm for the saddlehorn and cascades of pain roared through him. Another man took the reins of his horse and started leading it across the creek and down toward Casey Springs.

Chapter 23

Shea dismounted gingerly. She was trembling as much as the horse, which was frothing at the mouth and sweating all over. Shea had barely clung on during its wild dash over the ridges and gulches near the ranch, and now her body stung from a dozen scratches by scrub bush, and her thighs and posterior were sore.

Holding on to the reins, she sank onto the pine-carpeted ground. Her legs simply wouldn't hold her up any longer.

She didn't have the faintest idea where she was.

She held out her hand, trying to steady it, but it shook.

Her mind was still muddled with that terror she'd felt. How far had the horse run? He'd headed toward the mountains, toward the area Rafe had been hiding.

Rafe. She wanted him now. She wanted him to hold her, wanted to feel that protectiveness that had enveloped her the rare times he'd lowered that barricade between them. She wanted to feel his arms around her, his mouth against her cheek.

She heard the heavy breathing of the horse. Its head

was lowered as if it were thoroughly exhausted. She needed to find the animal some water. She looked around. She had no idea which direction to take. In front were the sharply rising mountains. The Circle R Ranch was someplace in back of her. The Circle R and her father. His frantic yell echoed in her mind.

But all she wanted now was to see Rafe, to beg him to leave now and take her with him, to forget his quest for vengeance that would destroy him as well as her father. Rafe was up there someplace. Up in those mountains, in a blind valley she had no way of finding. She knew Clint wouldn't take her, but perhaps Ben would. She had figured out that Ben was in some way involved with the miners. That meant he might be living somewhere along Rushton Creek.

She stood slowly, her legs still weak. She looked back from where she'd come. She looked toward the beckoning mountain. She knew its dangers now. Bears. Cougars. Snakes. She knew how easy it would be to get lost.

Behind her was safety. Her father.

Ahead was danger. And Rafe. Perhaps her last hope of seeing him again. Perhaps her last chance of keeping him from destroying himself and, as a consequence, destroying her.

She knew how slim her chances were of finding him. How foolhardy the search was. Until she'd come West, she'd never taken risks. And this was the biggest risk anyone could take.

She thought of the letter she'd found, the sincerity of her father's denial of any involvement in framing Rafe. And she knew she couldn't go back to his home.

The ride on Clint's horse several days earlier hadn't taken more than a few hours. It had all been descent, just as getting there had been nearly all climbing.

It was midday now. She had seven, eight hours left of daylight.

Why did she think she could find him if no one else could?

Because during her captivity she had studied every peak, every hill, had drawn the landscape from so many different angles. She had only to find the right juncture, the right angles.

Remember how you got lost that first day. But then she had been inexperienced, distraught, afraid of Rafe Tyler but even more afraid of herself.

And there were miners in the hills. It shouldn't be hard to find one, to locate Ben, if she had no luck in finding the trail up to Rafe's valley. But she had no supplies, only a box of matches she'd stuck in a dress pocket after lighting the stove this morning.

Eight hours until sundown.

Go back! The practical part of her kept ordering her to do the safe thing.

Rafe! The need to reach out to him was stronger. Stronger even than the instinct for self-preservation. Stronger than her instinct to protect her newfound father. She kept seeing the concern on Rafe's face as he'd held the small bear, as he'd watched the mother and cub play at the pool, the stunned wonder when they'd made love. Those fleeting moments that revealed everything he tried so hard to disguise, to deny.

She started walking toward the mountain, the horse trailing wearily behind.

Sam McClary slowed his horse to a trot. He knew he'd been damned lucky to avoid the posse. The miner's taking aim on the man above him had been pure good fortune, giving McClary a chance to escape when the posse showed up.

He wondered who that man above him was. He hadn't been able to see the face, but something in his bones told him it was Rafe Tyler.

He didn't hang around to see what happened, but somehow he had to find out. Everyone in Rushton knew his face, but Casey Springs might be safe; he hadn't stopped there on his way to the Circle R weeks ago.

He could get some supplies there, too, and decide whether to go on to Denver or Mexico. Too bad about Randall. He had always been good for a stake. But he'd picked the wrong time to suddenly find a conscience.

McClary rested his horse for an hour as he ate some jerky he'd found in the cabin of one of the miners he'd killed. Their gold dust was in his saddlebags. Enough for a good meal and fresh supplies in Casey Springs with some left over.

He wanted some distance between him and that posse before he headed east. He rested, stifling his impatience. He would stay until dark and enter Casey Springs in the early morning hours.

Jack Randall nearly fell from his horse several times before reaching the Dewayne ranch. Unable to saddle a horse with only one good arm, he had ridden bareback.

He had barely managed to get a bit in the horse's mouth and had to mount from a stump. Though his head had stopped throbbing, his shoulder felt as if someone had stabbed a hot spear through it.

But he had to get help. He had tried to follow Shea, but she seemed to have disappeared completely, and so he had set off for Dewayne's place. Damn Tyler and his robberies. Because of Tyler, he was alone. Believing that

McClary was long gone, he had sent Nate and the other remaining hands off to check on cattle. He had even sent Clint out on the range to keep any more stock from wandering into the hills. Every last head of cattle was so damn important now.

He had to save the ranch for Shea.

Summoning every bit of strength he had, he kicked the horse into a canter. The ten miles seemed like a million, but the ranch finally came into view. Several horses were tied to the hitching post inside, with men milling at the front door.

They turned almost in unison toward him, two running over to him to grab the horse. He leaned over. "My daughter . . . her horse bolted with her."

One man nodded. "A number of us just got back. We caught someone shooting at Charlie Sams up on Rushton Creek. Russ is taking him into Casey Springs."

Jack tried to straighten. "Who?"

"Said his name was Tyler. Had a brand on his hand. Has to be the one responsible for the robberies around here . . . could be the one who shot you."

Randall closed his eyes for a moment. It didn't make sense. Tyler? Shooting at miners? Blamed for shooting *him*? But it had been McClary . . .

Had McClary stayed? Had he somehow managed to frame Tyler again?

Jack couldn't think about it now. The most important thing was Shea.

Men were already saddling fresh horses. Michael Dewayne came over. "Which direction?"

"Toward the mountains."

"What happened?"

Jack wished he knew why Shea had bolted the way she did. "She . . . wanted to see something of the ranch. No one was there to saddle a horse, and she took Hooker.

I had just gotten to the porch when the horse took off. I couldn't saddle one fast enough, and no one else was there."

"We'll find her. You stay here with Kate."

Jack shook his head. "She might . . . come back."

"Then Kate will take you home and wait with you."

Jack nodded. One of the men helped him down, while Michael strode back inside the house to call Kate. He returned and told Randall, "Kate will be out in a moment." He hesitated. "We'll find her, Jack. At least we got the bastard behind all this trouble."

No, Randall wanted to say. But he couldn't delay the searchers now.

He watched the men ride off in a cloud of dust, and in just a moment Kate was beside him. "Michael will find her," she said with confidence. "He'll pick up the tracks at your place. Wait here, and I'll hitch the buggy."

But Jack couldn't wait. He couldn't sit and do nothing. He walked with her to the barn, wishing the clamoring in his head would stop so he could think. Too much was happening. Shea gone. Tyler captured. McClary on the loose. He had hoped McClary might have left the territory, but he knew now he hadn't. Rafe Tyler wouldn't go after a miner. Jack Randall was the one *he* wanted.

Randall didn't know how McClary was doing it, but he was framing Tyler all over again.

And if Shea ever discovered . . . She would be gone just like her mother.

He helped Kate hitch the horses as best he could, and then took the reins with his good right hand. He would go crazy if he didn't do something. He had wanted desperately to go with the men, but he would only slow them down.

When they arrived at the Circle R, Kate wanted to help him back to bed, but he refused. He poured himself a glass of whiskey and went into his office, sitting back in his chair while Kate busied herself fixing coffee. He opened the drawer with the tintype of Sara and took it out. He stared at it for several minutes, seeing so many similarities between mother and daughter. The same stubborn chin. The eyes, brown in the picture, but forever a tranquil bluish-gray in his mind. His hand went back into the drawer, searching for the letter.

It wasn't there. He pulled the drawer all the way out, hoping against hope that it might have been caught someplace in the back.

It was gone.

He emptied the glass of whiskey and buried his head in his hands. He suspected now why his daughter had left.

Shea realized she was hopelessly lost. As she climbed higher, the landscape kept changing. Nothing seemed familiar. The temperature was dropping quickly. It would soon be dark.

Shivering in the dress, her legs protected only by thin cotton pantalets, she turned the tired horse downward, hoping to find Rushton Creek or some stream leading to it.

She realized how foolish she had been, how much she had underestimated these mountains, which Rafe had warned her not to do.

She rode awhile, then walked again, leading the horse up steep inclines. She reached a sheer wall of stone. Water was dripping down and had formed a small pool before running downward across rocks. She stopped and used her hands to form a bowl and drink. The horse moved eagerly to the small pool and drank greedily. Shea sat on a rock and tried to decide what to do next. She could follow the water down. Or she could stay the night here and start looking for Rafe's valley again in the morning when there was better light.

She looked around. Some nearby wild raspberry bushes decided her.

After tying the reins of the horse to a bush, she gathered firewood and picked wild raspberries. She started a fire, and in minutes the wood was burning merrily, radiating much-needed warmth. Shea leaned back against a rock and ate the raspberries.

In the weeks she'd spent with Rafe, she'd learned to appreciate the songs of the woods: the chirp of crickets, the hoot of an owl, the stirring of night creatures. Noises that he had been denied for ten years. He would listen with an intensity that silently revealed pleasure his stonily set face seldom showed.

She couldn't bear the thought of him throwing away what was left of his freedom and life. She had to find him.

Then she thought about her father and what she'd discovered in his desk. Jack Randall would recover. She wasn't sure that Rafe Tyler would.

By nightfall the men who had been searching for Shea appeared at the Circle R empty-handed. Clint returned, too, from the range and found out about the missing Shea and about Rafe being taken in. There was even talk of miners going to Casey Springs and forming a lynching party.

Kate had already cooked dinner, and as she served the meal, Clint thought of how amazing she was. She moved confidently among the men, sharing quick words about the search while dishing out a tasty stew.

Jack Randall looked as if he'd aged years. Clint knew he probably did too. He realized that Shea had probably gone looking for Rafe, that she was somewhere in the mountains. He had to alert Ben and the others both about Shea Randall's disappearance and Rafe's capture.

Shea was the most immediate problem. He wasn't sure how long she could last out there. As soon as he ate, he planned to search on his own.

He quickly finished the plate of food, nodded at Kate with thanks, and said he was going back out.

"Wait till morning," Michael Dewayne said.

"I can see in the dark as well as day," he said truthfully. Randall looked at him gratefully, and Clint stifled the guilt that was now his constant companion. He excused himself. Kate accompanied him to the door.

"What do you think?" she said.

"She's been out there before. She's a survivor, Kate, even if she doesn't look like one. She has an instinct for doing the right thing." He hoped to hell he was right. She *hadn't* been out there but the Shea Randall he knew was practical and levelheaded. At least she had been until now.

"She's had such a hard time," Kate said. "Her mother. Getting lost those weeks, and now her father wounded. I don't know if I could be that strong."

"You already are, Kate," he said, his hand going to her elbow. He wished he could lean over and kiss her, but there were too many people around, and he had no right. Still, he couldn't tear his gaze away from hers. "You're so damn beautiful," he finally said.

"Be careful," she murmured.

His fingers brushed an errant lock of hair from the side of her face. "Don't worry about me."

"Why?"

"I'm not worth it," he said, hearing the shade of bitterness in his own voice.

"I think so," she said, and there was such trust and

faith in her eyes that he wanted to shake her. After he kissed her.

He didn't do either. Instead, he turned away abruptly and he strode quickly to the barn. In minutes he rode out, never again looking toward the ranch house.

Shea slept lightly on and off during the night, aware that she didn't dare let the fire go all the way out. She had only two matches left.

And she was cold. Freezing even though she wrapped herself in the saddle blanket and moved as close as she could to the fire. When dawn broke, she was stiff all over.

Time to start again. If only she hadn't been blind-folded on both journeys to and from Rafe's cabin. But still, he obviously felt she might know enough, or he wouldn't have told her he was leaving. She had to get there before he did.

Jack Randall knew what he had to do. He'd spent a sleepless night, haunted by the ghosts of his past. By Rafe Tyler's face. Sara's. Shea's. McClary's.

He knew he could never repair the damage he'd wreaked years ago. God knew he'd tried these past ten years, but his past had caught up with him now, and it wasn't going to let him go.

Rafe Tyler would know where Shea was trying to go. Tyler knew those mountains. He had been haunting them the past months while haunting Randall.

And Jack knew he had to get to Shea before McClary did. McClary hadn't left the area after all—the most re-cent attempt on the miner proved that; it was just a matter of time before McClary knew Jack hadn't died. And he would hear about Shea and try to use her to get to him.

Jack measured each of his options. There were damn few. He could tell Russ Dewayne everything, but now Rafe Tyler was in someone else's jurisdiction and accused of several murders. It was doubtful he would be released on Jack's say-so.

And once released, why would Rafe bother to help Jack? It would be suitable revenge to watch Jack confess everything, then leave his daughter to die. Tyler had obviously seduced Shea in the mountains, holding her captive. What kind of man would do that?

What kind of man was Rafe Tyler now?

Jack had one bargaining tool. One he couldn't give away until his daughter was safe. Her safety now was the only thing that meant anything. She might hate him when she discovered what he really was, but Jack would give anything to see her safe. Anything.

This morning he watched as the men rode out again. He had not yet seen Clint Edwards, but Kate and Michael, who had left late during the night, returned, and Kate made breakfast.

By noon there was still no news, and Randall knew what he had to do. He asked a hand to saddle his horse, and he strapped on his gunbelt. Thank God, his right hand was still useful. He ignored the persistent pain in his head, the occasional moment of dizziness, ignored the warnings Kate gave him.

He left the ranch, riding toward the mountains until he reached the road for Casey Springs, and then turned the horse in that direction.

Rafe paced the floor of the small room above the sheriff's office that was his prison.

The one window had been boarded up, letting in only a few cracks of light, and a ring was bolted to the floor. His hands remained handcuffed; a pair of leg irons had been fastened around his ankles and connected to the ring by a chain five feet long. Not long enough to reach the window to try to pry the boards off. He had tried his damnedest to work the ring from the floor, but it was anchored securely.

He had a pacing range of ten feet. Five feet from the bolted ring, then five feet back to the other side. He'd soon learned to measure his steps, or he'd go pitching down to the floor.

The only furnishings were a hard cot and a slop bucket.

His wounds had been tended by the doctor, and then he'd been placed up here to await the circuit judge. He had not been comforted by talk that the last inhabitant of this room had been summarily hanged by the impatient populace.

That damn brand had convicted him in the eyes of the town. Otherwise there had been room for doubt. The men had found signs in the dirt of another man and indications he had fired at Rafe. And doubt *had* been in Dewayne's eyes until the moment he'd seen the damning mark.

Rafe lifted his right hand and glared at the *T*. His gloves had been taken as well as his boots when the leg irons were applied. The scar seemed even more stark than before. Ugly and rough and indelible. The mark of Cain. Frustration caused him to sit on the cot and yank again at the chain confining him. Pain coursed through his wounded arm, through his ankles as rough iron bit into skin.

And then he heard a noise, steps on the outside stairs that provided the only access to this room. He leaned against the wall and rested a bent leg on the side of the cot in a languorous, unconcerned pose. The chain between his ankles was just long enough to permit that.

The key in the lock rattled, and the door opened. The deputy sheriff who had taken custody of him moved inside followed by another man. Rafe tensed, and he swallowed the rush of hatred that blocked his throat momentarily.

"Major Randall," he said lazily, cloaking the fierce anger he felt at seeing his betrayer for the first time since he'd been branded. "I'm honored."

Jack Randall had aged in the last ten years. He was heavier, obviously well fed, but not fat. His brown hair was sprinkled with gray, and his face was burned dark by the sun. But a closer look showed lines in the face, a sheen of perspiration on his forehead. There was a bandage at the side of his head, and his left arm was in a sling. He licked his lips nervously as he looked at Rafe.

Randall, the tendons in his neck clearly visible, turned to the deputy: "I want to talk to him alone."

"I don't know about that," the lawman said. "He's a murderer."

"Hell, you have my gun, and I'll stay out of his reach," Randall said impatiently. "I'll take the risk."

"All right, Mr. Randall," the deputy said, obviously in awe of the rancher. Rafe felt his gut tighten. "Fifteen minutes. No longer."

Rafe's lips twisted into an ironic smile as the deputy turned around and left, closing and locking the door behind him. The sound of the key in the lock was louder than Rafe remembered, perhaps because of the silent tension that radiated in the room.

"I would offer you some hospitality, but, as you see, my resources are extremely limited at the moment. Have been, in fact, for some time." He didn't move from the sitting position, but every muscle was taut, every sense alert.

Perspiration dripped down the side of Randall's face, but he didn't seem to notice. He took a step forward, then stopped.

"Come to gloat? Or did you have another reason in mind?" Rafe was surprised at the evenness of his own voice. Christ, he'd had experience in controlling his rage, but even he was amazed at how casual he sounded when he wanted to strangle the man standing before him.

Randall didn't say anything, but Rafe felt the intensity of his gaze. It took measure of the bandages on his arm and under his trouser leg, as well as the chains.

"Oh, I'm well chained, Major. You don't have to worry about that." There was no mistaking the fury underlying in the calmly spoken words. "I can't get to you, just as I couldn't ten years ago. And *this* time, I'll likely hang for something you did."

"No." The reply held a tone of finality that puzzled Rafe.

Slowly, Rafe lowered the bent leg and placed his foot on the floor. He kept all his attention on Randall's eyes, trying to read them. He had thought Randall had come by to gloat, but now he wasn't so sure. "No, what? No, I won't hang, or no, I won't hang for something you did?"

Randall took another step toward him, his mouth opening as he obviously tried to find words.

Another step, Rafe willed him. God, he wanted to get his hands around the man's throat.

"I . . . I have an offer to make you," Randall finally said.

Rafe eyed Randall with contempt. "Say what you came here to say and get out. The sight of you makes me sick."

"Shea . . ."

Rafe quickly stood and moved as close as he could to Randall. The chain stopped him two feet away. His handcuffed hands were fisted, the brand vivid on a hand now pale with strain. "What about Shea?"

"She's disappeared. I think she might have gone looking for you."

Rafe turned away toward a wall. He didn't want Randall to see anything in his face. "Why would you think that?"

"She was . . . asking questions."

"And you gave her the right answers?" Rafe asked mockingly, trying to fight down the desperation that was swelling inside him at Randall's words.

"No," Randall said in a low voice. "And I think she knew it."

"What do you expect me to do about it?" Rafe hid his fear for Shea under a veneer of indifference. "Because of you, I'm rather occupied at the moment, and the whole damn town seems to have plans for me."

"Tyler . . ." Randall stopped and put his hands to his face for a moment, as if hiding while gathering courage. He tried again. "I can't take back what was done years ago. If you had come to me months ago, I would have given you everything I had."

"Everything wouldn't be enough," Rafe said bitterly as he turned to face Randall. "You could have come forward any time during those ten years. You could have stopped this." He held out his hand. "Look at it, Randall. The least you can do, God damn you, is look at it!"

Randall remained still under the force of Rafe's fury, resisting the urge to step back. He was losing. He knew he was losing. "So you seduced an innocent girl?" he snapped back.

Rafe smiled grimly. "Is that what she told you?"

"She didn't have to tell me. Is that how a man like

you gets revenge, Tyler?" His anger now was as great a
Rafe's.

Rafe would have killed him if he could have reached
him. He tried, dammit, he tried. He lunged toward Ran
dall, but the chain was already taut, and he fell to hi
knees.

He wanted to roar with frustration and humiliation
Instead, he froze, trying to school his emotions, refusing
to give Randall a glimpse of what he had unleashed.

Rafe felt the moments ticking away. Randall was ab
solutely still. He had not backed up, had not moved
When Rafe slowly straightened and looked into his face
he was startled to find an agony that matched his own.

"You said you have an offer?" Rafe was surprised to
find his voice steady.

"If you help me find Shea, safe, I'll tell the authori
ties what really happened ten years ago."

Rafe looked down at the chains holding him.

"I'll help you escape," Randall said simply.

"What makes you think I won't kill you once I'm ou
of here?"

"I'll take that chance."

"How do I know you won't renege on the offer?"

"You don't," Randall said. "You have to take tha
chance."

"You mean we have to trust each other?" Rafe said
with contempt.

"Up to a point." Randall turned away. "You were
man of your word."

"You weren't. It seems you get the best of the bar
gain."

"Yes," Randall said, his self-contempt obvious, "I ge
the best of the bargain." He hesitated, then added wea
rily, "Do you know where they keep the keys to those
irons?"

"Downstairs. I'm a dangerous character. They wouldn't chance a deputy venturing too close."

Randall leaned down, pulled up the left leg of his trousers and took a derringer that had been tucked in his boot. He held it just out of Rafe's reach. "Your word you'll help me find her?"

"And you'll confess your part in the payroll robberies?" Rafe said.

Randall nodded.

"And the recent murders?"

"I didn't have anything to do with those."

"But your friend McClary did."

Just then they heard footfalls on the steps. There was no time for more conversation. "In case anything goes wrong when I try to get the keys," Randall said, "go after her." He handed the derringer to Rafe, who slipped it in the waist of his trousers and pulled his shirt out to cover it.

"I'll be back in a few minutes with the keys," Randall said in a whisper just as the door opened.

Rafe didn't answer but retreated to the cot, assuming the same position he'd been in when Randall entered.

"Find out what you needed, Mr. Randall?" the deputy asked.

Randall nodded and followed the deputy out, who once more locked the door.

Rafe stared at the door. He didn't know what he felt. Except fear for Shea. He put his arm on the raised knee and rested his head on his hand. There was nothing he could do now but wait.

Chapter 24

Jack Randall knew he was out of his element. He'd never been a brave man, though he had faked bravery well enough. And now he was alone in what he was doing.

His legs shook slightly as he followed the deputy down the stairs. He thought of everything that could go wrong. He thought of the hate he'd seen in Rafe Tyler's eyes, as strong as it had been ten years earlier. The meeting had been far harder than he'd expected, but then he'd always been able to justify and minimize the effect of his actions.

It wasn't too late to back out.

And then he thought of Shea. Alone. Without warm clothes. Without a weapon. Two days now. He stiffened his backbone as they walked into the sheriff's office.

The deputy handed him his gunbelt and turned around to hang up the keys alongside another set. The key to the irons. Jack slipped his gun out of the holster and struck the deputy on the back of the head. He caught the body with his right arm and lowered it to the ground. He leaned down. The man was breathing.

Jack took the deputy's gun, then grabbed the two sets of keys. He moved quickly outside and up the steps. He had to try several keys before finding the one that unlocked the door.

Tyler was sitting on the cot, but he straightened the minute Jack entered the room.

"The deputy?"

"Unconscious downstairs," Jack said, kneeling at Rafe's feet, unfastening the leg irons.

Jack turned away.

"The handcuffs," Tyler reminded him.

"They stay on," Jack said. He pulled out his gun, holding it on Rafe, and reached for the derringer.

"What was that about trust?" Rafe said.

Jack shrugged. "Just a precaution. The handcuffs shouldn't slow you down."

"What if I refuse to go?"

"You won't," Jack said. "I'm the only chance you have."

Rafe shrugged, and Jack knew he was thinking he could overpower him later. But right now, at least, he couldn't argue. "Horses?"

"We'll have to get one at the stable. I couldn't risk taking a riderless horse from the Circle R. Too many people milling about, coming and going while looking for Shea."

He opened the door, waited for Rafe to go out ahead of him, then locked it. The tactic might stall pursuers. At the bottom of the steps he paused. "Where's your horse?"

"The livery stable."

"What is it?"

"A bay. White stripe down its face."

The last of daylight had faded. They were standing at the side of the sheriff's office in the shadows. Jack glanced down at the handcuffs on Rafe's wrists. "Stay here. I'll see if I can get your horse."

Tyler just glared at him, and Randall knew that sooner or later there would be an accounting. But Tyler needed him now with those handcuffs. He wouldn't run out on him. Not yet.

Jack walked out into the dirt street and strolled to the stable. The owner came out to meet him.

The man recognized him. "Mr. Randall, what can I do for you?"

"You have one of my horses here," Jack said. "A bay with a white stripe."

"The one they brought that murderer in on?"

Jack nodded. "That's the one. Guess you heard about all the attacks on my place. That horse was taken, hadn't even had time to brand it."

The owner looked dubious. "Deputy brought him over here."

"I know," Jack said, all his old lying skills returning. "He just said I needed to take care of your bill for boarding him." He took out some bills from his pocket. "Here's a couple of extra dollars for your trouble."

All doubt faded from the man's face. "Seeing it's you, Mr. Randall, I guess it's all right."

"Can you throw in a saddle?" Randall said. "My cinch is close to tearing, and I don't want to wait to get it fixed."

"Sure thing. Don't guess I'd better give you his. Suppose it's his property. Until he hangs anyway."

"Anything you have," Jack said, feeling impatience mixed with that excitement he'd always felt when pulling a con.

The man disappeared, then returned with a worn saddle. "Don't look like much, but it's sound. Only ten dollars," he added hopefully.

Jack nodded. "It's fine. Would you mind saddling it for me?"

The livery owner looked at the arm in the sling, then quickly saddled the horse. He took the additional bills offered by Jack, who took the reins of the horse. "Can I give you a hand?"

Jack accepted. He could exchange horses with Tyler later. He needed to get back. He grew more and more anxious about Tyler every second.

Jack was back in front of the sheriff's office in minutes, ready to bolt any moment he heard an alarm. Tyler slipped out the door, wearing the deputy's hat slung down on his forehead and boots and gloves. Randall pointed at the black horse tied to the hitching post, and Tyler mounted quickly, despite the cuffs on his wrists. They walked the horses to the end of town and then spurred the animals into a gallop.

Rafe felt exhilarated. If it were not for his nagging fear about Shea, he could almost laugh. He had found a gun in the sheriff's office, and it was now tucked in the same place the derringer had been. He could take Jack Randall any time he wanted.

He had checked out the office because he wasn't sure this wasn't a trap. Many of Randall's problems would be solved if Rafe were killed trying to escape. But only the deputy was there, lying on the floor.

Then Rafe did his own search, hoping he would find another set of keys to open the handcuffs. He didn't, but he did find a gun in a desk drawer. And his boots and gloves.

He'd half expected to find a half-dozen men in the office. Hell, it could still be a trap to discover who had been working with him, to get Rafe to lead a posse to the cabin. But it was a chance he had to take; he had to find Shea.

He sure as hell didn't have to take Randall along with him though. But for the moment, he enjoyed the fresh air, the whiff of freedom. And he savored the idea of pulling the gun on Randall and using the handcuffs on him.

Shea came first, and Rafe knew he could move much faster alone. He would leave Randall handcuffed to a tree someplace between here and Rushton Creek. It was time Randall experienced his first taste of what Rafe had gone through. As for Randall's promise, Rafe knew that was nothing but chaff in the wind. He wouldn't trust Jack Randall with a drop of water in the middle of a lake.

Shea finally found what she sought. She had kept thinking of the pictures she had drawn, and now she saw the sun flash on a familiar patch of snow. She was going in the right direction. If only she could find that opening in the canyon wall.

She had dismounted on the last climb upward, and now she wanted to stop at a nearby tree and rest for several minutes. She pulled on the reins, but the horse shied, tugging at the lead to regain its freedom. It was becoming increasingly stubborn, repeatedly trying to turn back toward the valley.

It reared, and she stepped back, stumbling, the reins dropping from her hands. The horse turned and started to head downward.

She went after the horse but soon realized she couldn't catch up with it. She stopped and looked around. The land had just leveled out after a steep climb. There was a wall of stone in front of her. Rafe's clearing had to be around here someplace. She walked wearily toward the wall, then followed it. And then she saw the opening.

Unless one was searching, it would be nearly impossible to see. She moved through it, remembering the turns when she was blindfolded, and finally she was in a pine forest again.

Satisfaction . . . expectation flooded through her. She felt as if she were coming home. Her tired legs picked up the pace, and she started running toward where she knew the cabin was. Rafe. Home. Safety.

Sam McClary had been drinking, listening to the talk around him at the saloon. It was hanging talk. And as the drinking accelerated, so did the fever for lynching the murderer being held at the sheriff's office.

McClary even bought a free round of drinks with his stolen dust. There was only one disquieting factor. Jack Randall wasn't dead. But McClary was sure that once Rafe Tyler hanged, he could again control Randall, especially now that he had a daughter.

He was betting with himself as to how long it would take the mob to drink up enough courage to storm the jail. The deputy sheriff was said to be in favor of the necktie party himself. But the ringleaders wanted to be sure the good citizens of Casey Springs were off the streets.

It was nearly dawn when the mob moved toward the sheriff's office and threw open the door. The first men in found the deputy. Several others ran up the outside stairs and shot the lock open, only to find the room empty.

McClary heard the deputy tell how Mr. Randall, the respectable Jack Randall, had apparently engineered a jailbreak. Mutters of disappointment and anger swept through the crowd, and in minutes a posse was organized. McClary knew it would be ineffective. Most of the men were nearly falling down drunk now and would be hungover in the morning.

Disgust rushed through McClary as he realized he had badly underestimated Jack Randall. For some reason he had joined forces with Rafe Tyler. The damned girl must have had something to do with it.

McClary could cut his losses and head down to Mexico, but then he would be looking over his shoulder the rest of his life. If only he could find Randall and Tyler. Ambush them. But where? Randall couldn't go back to his ranch, not after breaking a man out of jail. They would head for the high mountains.

Both men were wounded, and that should slow them down. Perhaps he could catch up with them. It was worth a try.

Jack Randall and Rafe slowed their pace to spare the horses. Randall positioned himself a short distance behind Rafe, and Rafe made no attempt to alter that order. He didn't want to ride in Randall's dust or ride apace of him. He hated the fact that Randall had been the instrument of his escape, and he sure as hell didn't feel any gratitude.

If it weren't for Randall . . .

His horse stumbled, and he knew it was tiring. They had moved fast to get as far from town as possible, and they had taken a high, rough route, away from the road, to Rushton. Rafe had gone this way before, and he knew a stream ran nearby where they could stop for water. He also wanted to get rid of the damned handcuffs.

They stopped at the stream. Moonlight filtered through the trees, providing some visibility. Randall almost fell as he dismounted. He went immediately to the stream and drank water he scooped up into his hand and then splashed some on his face. When he turned around, he saw the pistol in Rafe's hands and stiffened.

"Drop the gun tucked in your belt, and then your gunbelt," Rafe said coldly.

Randall smiled. It was a disarming smile, one Rafe remembered from ten years earlier. Charming and wryly amused. Only the slightest line of strain showed. "I should have known."

"The guns," Rafe repeated.

Randall withdrew the deputy's gun, dropped it, then slowly unbuckled the gunbelt, letting it fall to the ground.

"Now the derringer."

Randall shrugged. "It's in the saddlebags."

"You wouldn't have left it there."

Randall reached down and slipped it from his boot.

Rafe grinned wolfishly at him. "I really do appreciate your concept of trust, Randall. Now throw it in the creek. I don't like those little guns."

After Randall did as he was told, Rafe aimed at Randall's knee. "Now the key to the handcuffs."

"What about Shea?"

"The key, Randall," Rafe said. "I would take great pleasure in putting another hole in you if you don't think one is enough."

Randall put his hand in his pocket and withdrew the key.

"Throw it in front of me and back away. See how high you can raise that right arm."

Jack Randall threw the key, then raised his arm, taking several steps backward.

Rafe held the gun on Randall while he unlocked the right cuff with his left hand, then switched the gun to the other hand, feeling the heaviness of his arm, the dampness of the shirt. He knew it had started bleeding again. He also knew he couldn't allow Randall to see that weakness.

He allowed the iron cuffs to drop, and he stood there

hesitantly. He had intended to use them on Randall, but now he questioned that intention. Randall's left arm was in a sling.

"What now, Tyler?"

"You stay here. You aren't worth killing. And now you've broken a dangerous prisoner out of custody, you'll go to jail," Rafe said harshly. "Enjoy it."

"Shea?"

Rafe wanted to ignore the question, to let Randall worry and wait as he had done. But the sudden desperate agony in Randall's face stopped the intended mocking reply before it left his lips.

"I'll find her," he said finally. "She's no part of what's between you and me.

Randall's mouth worked. He lowered his arm and moved toward Rafe, stopping a few feet away. "I meant what I said in Casey Springs."

Familiar anger coursed through Rafe. "You're ten years too late, Randall."

Randall flinched. "At least I can clear your name."

"Can you also remove the brand?"

Randall's eyes met his. "No, I can't do that."

Rafe felt his strength fading, along with the hatred and anger that had been fueling him. He tried not to let it show, but something flickered in Randall's eyes. "Let me come with you. You might need me."

"Like I need a rattlesnake." But Randall was right, and Rafe knew it. Randall could bargain with a posse; Rafe knew he would be shot on sight. And then what would happen to Shea?

He looked down at the irons at his feet and kicked them away out of sight. He felt a sudden flash of relief when he did so, as if cool air had been pushed through the dark hot hell of his soul. When his eyes met Randall's in the moonlight, he knew Randall realized exactly what Rafe had intended.

"I meant what I said," Randall said. "I'll tell what happened ten years ago."

"It doesn't matter anymore," Rafe said wearily. "They were ready to hang me back there because of the brand. There's no place I can go on earth without questions, suspicions, accusations." He turned around. "Go ahead, pick up your guns. We'd better get moving."

They reached the valley at dawn. Rafe didn't think there was any chance that Shea might have found it. But it was a starting point. The only one they had.

He didn't even care now that Randall knew its location. The only thing that mattered was Shea. They would rest their horses, then move down, hoping to find some sign of her.

The door of the cabin was open. Rafe didn't pay any attention to Randall at all as he galloped to the front door. No one was inside, but a wildflower lay on the table next to some broken crackers. For Abner, he knew.

Rafe smiled. He didn't know how she'd done it, but she had. And he knew exactly where she was now.

Randall came into the cabin and looked around curiously, anxiously.

"She's safe, Randall," Rafe said.

He whistled softly, and Abner crept out from under the bed, then streaked toward Rafe and ran up his trousers. Rafe took the mouse in his hand, stroking him as Randall stared at him with amazement.

"How do you know?"

"Wait here," Rafe commanded.

"Why? Where's my daughter?"

Rafe threw him a cold stare. "Remember trust," he

taunted. "Think about it." He turned around and went out the door, not waiting to see whether Randall had obeyed him. He would have broken out into a run if his leg allowed it, but he knew he'd lost enough blood in the past forty-eight hours. His arm had bled continually throughout the night, and his leg was raw and burning.

He found her huddled against the rock overlooking the pool at the bottom of the waterfall, just as he knew he would. She was sound asleep, her brown hair tumbling over her cheek.

Relief, tenderness, something very close to love, assaulted him with such strength, he could only stand there, trying to comprehend the power and complexity of those feelings. That she had even tried to make it here alone humbled him, filling him with bittersweet anguish for what could never be.

That she had succeeded astounded him and spoke eloquently of that strength of spirit she had.

He didn't want to wake her. He just wanted to watch. To relish the fact that she had risked everything for him even though it caused him an equal part of pain.

The morning birds started their sweet songs, and her eyes fluttered open, looked confused, then found him and flew all the way open. "I was looking for your fawns," she said, though her eyes said something else altogether.

He opened his arms, and she rose and went into them, her own arms going around him, her head resting against his chest. He lowered his own head and let his cheek rest on her hair.

That was all they needed.

Jack Randall had followed Rafe at a distance. He stopped as he saw Shea go into Rafe Tyler's arms. He remained frozen, half-hidden by raspberry bushes and pines.

He had thought Rafe Tyler had used Shea for revenge. He had thought that every moment, until Tyler had kicked away the handcuffs and allowed him to retrieve his guns. Until he understood that Rafe cared about nothing but his daughter's safety.

Now he watched like a peeping Tom, unable to retreat from watching a moment of such exquisite tenderness that tears formed in his eyes.

He leaned against a tree. How many times in the last ten years had he pushed aside the image of Captain Tyler's arrest, his court-martial, the morning he had been taken to prison? Even then, he had done nothing to stop McClary, knowing as he did that the sergeant would make every mile hell for his prisoner. He had been afraid of McClary. Afraid of prison, of the disgrace that would separate him forever from his Sara. The irony had been that his cowardice had done exactly that, and had designed a torture chamber of his own making.

But even then, he knew it wasn't as bad as the one he'd made for Tyler.

Jack bent over in agony, dragging his eyes from Rafe Tyler and his daughter, the daughter who looked so much like Sara. He tore them away from the man from whom he had taken so much and yet who remained capable of such obvious love, even for the daughter of the man who so wronged him.

Nothing could be worse than this pain. Not prison. Not a noose.

He turned slowly and walked with dragging steps back to the cabin.

* * *

McClary picked up the blood trail. He probably wouldn't have found it if he hadn't had a general idea of where Rafe Tyler had been hiding these months. The Casey Springs posse, he thought, would head directly for Rushton and Randall's ranch. He hadn't counted much intelligence among the lynch mob, or for that matter, from the deputy sheriff, and the sheriff was out of town.

Who, he wondered, was bleeding? It could have been either one, although Tyler had been the most recently wounded.

They were no longer being careful as Tyler had been in the past. The trail, once found, was not difficult for McClary to follow.

He came to where they had obviously paused at a creek. The ground was trampled in several places. His eyes caught the glint of metal, and he found a pair of irons lying partly under a bush.

He reached down and hid them much more efficiently, then wiped away signs of disturbance just as he had covered up the traces of blood he'd found. He didn't want anyone following him. He didn't want a posse reaching Randall before he did.

McClary wondered briefly about the strange alliance and what had brought the two men together. Tyler hated Randall, and Randall had great fear of Tyler.

McClary shrugged. It didn't matter. He would kill both men, and whoever else was with them.

Chapter 25

Rafe didn't know how long he stood there, alongside the lake, holding her. He just knew how good it felt.

She snuggled there in his arms, as if he were all she wanted in the world. He tried to breathe through the knot in his throat, the constriction of his chest.

He hadn't realized how completely he cared until this moment. He hadn't let himself.

He couldn't let himself now. But there it was. Sometime in the past few weeks she had snaked her way into his heart and taken it over. Wholly and forever.

Yet nothing had changed. If anything, circumstances had worsened. Not only was he an ex-convict now, he was also wanted for murder. The sigh that came from his mouth was ragged, and she looked up at him, those eyes of hers so full of light.

"How did you ever find this place?" he finally asked. Anything to break the spell that wrapped them in what he knew was a false cloak of safety. If she had found this valley, others could.

"I remembered those peaks," she said, and he recalled those drawings he'd destroyed, afraid they would lead others to him. He had not considered her own ability to re-create. She moved slightly, and he couldn't stop the ragged breath as she touched the wounded arm. Her gaze went to his shirt, red and still damp with blood.

"What happened?"

He shrugged, and her eyes narrowed. She backed a few inches away and rolled up the sleeve of the shirt, revealing a crimson bandage.

"What happened, Rafe?" she said insistently.

He sighed. "I'll tell you later." He felt himself swaying. He had been moving on pure nerves, on fear for her. But now his body was failing him. "I think I need to get to the cabin."

She nodded, taking his good arm and putting it around her to give him some support. But he hesitated. "Shea . . . Jack Randall's at the cabin." He still couldn't tolerate thinking of Randall as Shea's father.

He felt her stiffen. "Why? How?"

"Posse . . . found me. I was taken to Casey Springs. He . . . Randall helped me escape so we could find you."

Shea's face paled.

"Why did you leave the Circle R?" His question was soft.

Shea hesitated. "Because . . . I knew . . . you were right. He did what you said he did." Her voice dropped to an anguished whisper. "How can someone do that to another person?"

Rafe didn't ask how she knew. He didn't care now. He only cared about the hurt that had driven her away from comfort and safety, that had made her risk these mountains.

He dropped to the forest floor, unable to stand any longer but not willing to go on and make her face what she obviously didn't want to face.

She stood above him, and his hand guided her down. She moved stiffly, like a stick figure. "Shea, he risked everything to free me because he figured I was the only one who could find you. He risked being shot, being accused of being one of us, and allowing the truth about the past to be revealed. He risked my killing him, and by God I considered it. He bartered with me. He would tell the truth if I helped him."

"Is that why . . . ?"

"Hell, no," Rafe said. "What's between him and me has nothing to do with you. I never wanted it to have anything to do with you. I never wanted you hurt by it, not from the moment I saw you. I came because I had to come."

Her eyes were fringed with tears now, and he didn't know why or for whom. He felt so damn helpless. He felt foolish defending the man he'd hated so long.

Foolish and angry. And tired. So very, very tired.

She appeared to see some of that, and the strain on her face was replaced by that damned determination that so aggravated and attracted him.

"Can you get up, or should I go and get . . . ?"

The very idea of being in debt any more than he already was to Jack Randall gave Rafe strength. He used a tree to help get himself to his feet and then reluctantly put an arm around her.

It was going to be a damned long walk.

And it was. He felt he would fall at any minute. He hated his weakness, hated not being able to think, to reason.

Finally, they were there. Randall was outside, waiting, his face anxious as he saw them coming, particularly when he darted a look at Shea's face. He hurried over and offered his good arm, but Rafe shrugged it aside, straightened, and made it the few steps into the cabin before collapsing on the cot.

Shea watched Rafe sleep. Abner had curled up in the crook of his arm, obviously content to have his friend back. Her father had taken the horses down to the stream to water them. He had anxiously tried to help, fetching a bucket of water to wash Rafe's wound, watching as Shea had sewed it again. The skin had broken loose from the doctor's stitches.

But Rafe's soothing comments to her had obviously not affected his feelings toward the man who had fathered her. Raw hostility radiated from his eyes, and Jack Randall had used the horses as an excuse to disappear.

He had not returned.

Shea was relieved. She had to sort out her own ambivalent emotions toward Jack Randall. In those several days of nursing her father, she had reveled in the warmth of his obvious delight in her, and now, as Rafe had observed, he had risked everything for her. But Rafe's unforgiving attitude made it clear that she would have to choose between the man who fathered her and the man she loved.

Rafe moved restlessly on the cot, and Shea instinctively reached out a hand to soothe him. Perhaps her father had risked much to find her, but Rafe had risked just as much in trusting him in this one desperate thing. She knew how much that must have cost him: accepting Jack Randall's help.

Because of her.

She moved from the chair and sat on the floor next to him, resting her head on his hand, wanting that closeness, that small intimacy, for as long as she could have it.

Shea closed her eyes, comforted by the nearness of

him. She didn't want to think about anything else. He was here. Safe. And that was all that mattered.

Jack Randall finished rubbing down the horses, grateful for the respite from Rafe's dislike and Shea's awkwardness. It had been a very long time since he'd had any sleep now, and his head still ached, but not as it had. His shoulder also ached, but he was almost grateful for the distraction.

There were a couple of sacks of oats, and he fed the horses. Then he walked slowly back to the cabin. The door was half-open, and he peered inside. His daughter was asleep, her head on Rafe Tyler's hand. Tyler himself was asleep, his body naked to the waist, a . . . mouse curled up on his shoulder.

He watched for several more moments, wondering at the love inherent in Shea's gesture. Because of what he had done ten years ago, it could be a very tragic love. But he would fight for it, as he hadn't fought for his own so long ago.

Quietly, very quietly, he backed away and gently closed the door.

Sam McClary finally found the opening in what looked like sheer cliffs. He had followed the blood trail to stone walls and then started feeling his way around them. It was late afternoon. The sun was beginning its descent toward the western peaks.

After an hour he saw another red splotch and then the crack in the wall. He followed the winding path and saw the opening into a pine forest. He smiled. The perfect hideaway.

He wondered if anyone other than the two wounded

men was in the valley. He led his horse downward to where the trees and thickets provided cover. He took the rifle from the saddle and checked his pistol. Staking his horse in good cover, he snaked through the woods until he saw a clearing and the rooftop of a cabin. He circled the area silently and finally found what he was looking for: a stack of flapjacklike rocks with an excellent overview of the cabin. He would wait until the occupants came out and catch them in the open.

He took a piece of jerky from a pocket and started chewing on it. It was just a matter of time.

The first thing Rafe saw when he woke was Shea, her head resting on his hand. She looked so peaceful, his heart quaked with strong response. She was so incredibly lovely with that sun-tipped hair falling over her shoulder and down the side of the cot. Tenderness swept over him like tidal waves, and his hand reached over to touch the silkiness of that hair. He longed to touch the smooth skin of her cheek, but he didn't want to wake her.

The second thing he saw was Abner, who, startled, ran down his chest and trousered leg to the end of the bed and disappeared.

He tried to sit without disturbing Shea, but her lashes fluttered open, then her eyes. They found him, and she smiled, a slow, warm, delighted smile that made him smile in return. One of his hands went to her hair and smoothed it back.

He felt so damn good with her so near. Weak as a kitten, but still filled with all those electric responses she always created in him.

Her hand smoothed the back of his hand, the hand with the scar, and she brought it to her mouth and kissed it. When he tried to pull it away, she shook her head.

Rafe winced.

"Don't," she said. "It's nothing to be ashamed of. You're not at fault. I just hate the pain you endured because of my . . ."

Rafe sat up and put his finger to her mouth. "Where is . . . ?"

"I don't know. The last I saw of him, he was taking care of the horses," she said.

"How long have I been asleep?"

Shea rose from where she'd been sitting and went over to the door, opening it. "It's almost dusk."

"Do we have any food left?"

"Not much," she said. "Two cans of peaches. Raspberries I gathered last night." She hesitated. "What are you going to do now?"

Rafe realized he damn well didn't know. He had put every bit of effort he had into reaching this place, and then he'd collapsed. He remembered Randall's promise to clear his name, but he felt damn little joy in it.

He wasn't sure he believed it. Even if he did, the prospect left him feeling hollow.

Rafe hadn't allowed himself to consider what Randall's confession would mean to Shea, the disgrace, the notoriety, the loss of a father she'd just discovered.

And what, really, would it accomplish? His conviction might be reversed in military records, but that was of precious little comfort when the brand would continue to mark him in the eyes of whoever he met, just as it had several days ago.

He had thought revenge would be sweet, that justice would be soothing, but now he was realizing that neither was true. Somehow, he would have to learn to live without them. And without Shea.

He stood. "I'll check on Randall," he said. He went to a hook where his extra shirt hung, pulled it on, and then picked up his gun from the table where he had placed it last night. He supposed his gunbelt was still in the sheriff's office someplace. He simply hadn't had time to look for it. He tucked the gun into his trousers, realizing he was still wary of Randall. He always would be, despite what happened last night. The man was a coward and a thief; the old anger bubbled inside him, though not to the heated degree as before.

Rafe saw Shea's anxious expression and shrugged. "Habit," he said, but as he went from the door, she followed as if afraid to leave him alone with Randall.

The hours of sleep had helped immensely. The arm still hurt, but his legs didn't fail him as they'd done earlier. He checked the stable first and found Randall there, sitting against one of the walls. He also looked better, as if he had been revived by sleep, and he stood as Rafe walked in followed by Shea.

His gaze went from Rafe to Shea and hesitated there, then flickered back to Rafe. There were several questions in his eyes, but Rafe ignored them. "I wasn't sure you would be here," Rafe said.

"I didn't want to disturb you," Randall said haltingly. "Your arm . . ."

The tension filled the air like heavy fog. Anger and regret whirled like eddies between them. Randall took a step forward, then stopped. He turned to Shea, and his mouth worked slightly. "I'm so damned sorry I'm not what . . . you deserve," he said finally, his voice breaking.

Rafe saw the distress on Shea's face, the conflict, the need she always had to comfort, yet she was holding back that comfort because of him. She trembled, her eyes wide and the blue-gray of them misted with tears. He felt her uncertainty, her confused pain, as if it were his own.

He tried to make his voice matter-of-fact. "We need

something to eat. Randall, you help Shea with a fire, and I'll see if I can't catch some trout."

The gesture cost him. But he was promptly rewarded by the stark gratitude in Shea's eyes. Randall simply nodded.

From the wall of the stable Rafe took the long pole he had fashioned and started out the door, heading for the stream. He knew that Randall and Shea were behind him; he felt her presence as he always did.

Rafe turned toward the stream when he heard the first shot. Automatically, he turned around toward Shea and saw Randall throw his own body over hers as a second rifle shot came, barely missing her. It would have hit her, he knew, if Randall's movement had not thrown them both a foot to the left.

In one quick movement Rafe threw down the fishing pole and swept up the pistol from his waistband. He threw himself to the ground, rolling as the rifle turned toward him and a bullet spurted dirt, barely missing him.

Pain numbed Rafe's arm as his shoulder struck the ground, and the gun fell from his fingers as he kept moving, hearing the bullets following him.

Did Randall have a gun now? He couldn't remember as he slid behind some brush that gave little cover. He looked out. His gun was several feet away. He saw Randall's back disappearing into the stable; apparently he was ushering Shea inside.

The sound of the gunfire changed, and Rafe knew whoever was shooting was now using a pistol. He must have run out of rifle shells. The accuracy would be less. He decided to take a chance, to go after his gun. Just as he left the cover, the door of the stable opened, and Randall stood there in full view, aiming toward the direction from which the shots came. He fired, and the shots turned toward him just as Rafe spurted for his gun, grabbed it, and fired rapidly. He heard a scream, and there were no more shots.

He waited a moment, then looked toward Randall, who was in a crouch. "You all right?"

Randall nodded.

They cautiously approached the group of rocks, one from each of two directions. Rafe saw him first, the thin, long form crumpled on the ground. It was the first time in ten years Rafe had seen Sam McClary, but there was no mistaking him. The same lanky blond hair, the familiar pale blue eyes staring sightlessly above. The malice was gone from them, but not the lines of dissatisfaction that marred the thin face.

"How in the hell did he find us?" Rafe didn't even realize he was speaking the thought out loud.

"He must have followed our trail," Randall said. "We weren't being that careful."

Rafe nodded. "That means others can do the same."

"He would have covered his own tracks. He always does," Randall said bitterly.

"Shea?"

Just then the barn door opened, and Shea came running out, straight into Rafe's arms. Her hands moved over him, as if to confirm he was all right. He winced as she touched his arm but smiled wryly. "No additional holes, Miss Randall, thanks, I think, to Mr. Randall."

She looked down at the body. "Who is he?"

"A man named McClary," Rafe said.

Randall looked at Rafe and then Shea, holding her gaze. "The man who helped me frame Tyler ten years ago. The one who's been killing the miners in hopes of doing the same thing again."

"Why?" she whispered.

"Because"—Randall's body stiffened as if expecting a blow—"Captain Tyler suspected McClary and I were behind the army payroll robberies." His face was set. "I thought if I had enough money, your mother would come back to me." He hesitated, then continued. "And then I was afraid of being discovered." He didn't spare himself, and Rafe felt fleeting respect.

She stared at Randall as if he were a monster. Rafe understood. She had come to believe her father had been responsible for what had happened ten years ago, had admitted as much to him, but he also realized now it must have seemed unreal to her before. She had fought hard to find reasons, an excuse. "You let them . . . brand him for something you did? Go to prison?"

Jack Randall's face grew visibly older, but he didn't try to avoid her gaze, or her outrage. "Yes," he said, not trying to excuse himself in any way.

Shea's own face seemed to break. "I kept thinking, hoping there was some mistake, that you didn't really know he was innocent, that someone else . . ." She stopped, then continued in a trembling voice, "I wish I never found that letter, that I never found you." She turned and ran toward the woods, stumbling, then regaining her balance and continuing on.

Randall's shoulders slumped. "You'd better go after her."

Rafe didn't feel an ounce of sympathy. Maybe in a few weeks, months. But not now. He turned to go.

"Tyler!" Randall's voice stopped him.

Rafe turned back.

"I'll take McClary down to Rushton, tell Russ that he's the killer . . . and that I knew about it. And," he added, "I'll tell him what happened ten years ago."

Rafe had once thought he would feel elation, relief, some kind of emotion, at such an admission, but he didn't. There was already too much pain. He didn't, couldn't, take pleasure in the agony on Randall's face, though he couldn't forget or forgive what had happened, either. "I won't hold you to your bargain," he replied. "When you protected Shea . . . you erased the debt."

Randall shook his head. "No," he said carefully. "I did that for her. She's my daughter." His mouth worked silently for a moment, then he continued. "As for telling the truth about the past and about McClary, I have to do it. For myself."

"What about Shea? It will hurt her."

"It will hurt her worse if I don't. She's too much like her mother. It took me a long time to realize that all Sara wanted was . . . what I couldn't seem to be. She would have forgiven anything if I'd just owned up to it and tried to change. I don't think Shea will ever forgive me for what's happened, but at least she'll know that once in my life I tried to do something right."

Rafe was silent a moment, then simply said, "You'd better wait until tomorrow morning. The area around Rushton will be full of riders tonight, and they probably won't ask too many questions. After losing their prey last night, they'll be shooting first, asking questions later." He hesitated. "We still need something to eat. You any good at fishing?"

Randall looked grateful for the change of subject. "I can manage."

Rafe looked toward McClary. "And get him out of sight."

Randall nodded.

Rafe knew Shea would be at the pool. At their rock.

She was sitting, her knees bent and her head resting on them. He approached quietly, but she knew. She looked up at him, her eyes desperately unhappy. "How can you even bear to look at me?"

He smiled, the first real smile in a long time. "It's easy. It always has been."

"I don't understand how he could have done it."

"He just saved your life, maybe mine."

"It's too late," she said. "I don't think I can ever forgive him for what he did to you."

"I'm finding out," he said, "that you can't allow the past to rule the future."

"How can you ever look at me and not see him?"

"Because you're not him. Because what happened years ago had nothing to do with you."

She took his hand and held on for dear life. "Then . . ."

Grief seeped through him. He was slowly letting go of that life-draining hate, but he knew he could have no life with her, or with any woman. He would always carry that brand. He would always be suspect. Just as he had been here.

He wouldn't subject her to that kind of life. But he needed her now. He needed her more than he knew it was possible to need anyone. He had almost been killed twice in the past twenty-four hours: once at the hands of a lynch mob, the second by McClary's gun. He was surprised to discover that life was still precious to him.

He leaned over and did the worst possible thing. He kissed her and tasted the saltiness of her tears. Tears for him. It was still incredible to him that anyone would care that much, that a woman would risk everything that she had risked for someone who had so little to offer.

Her arms went around him, gently, careful of his arm but with a certain desperation, as if she knew exactly what he was thinking. He felt that desperation straight through to his soul. He ignored the pain in his arm. He ignored all the warnings in his mind. He even ignored the conscience that was finally making itself known after being quieted, dampened, hidden away. He would send her away tomorrow with her father, and then he would disappear to some faraway place and live haunted by her for the rest of his life.

Their lips met with such tender wistfulness that Rafe felt an exquisite agony that surpassed any other feeling. It filled him, cleansed him, renewed him. It made him feel like a man again, a whole being worthy of being loved.

The kiss deepened, his tongue roaming deep in her mouth, seeking to possess her in an elemental way. He wanted to live at this moment, to throw off the last of that intense hatred that had maimed him even more than the scar had. It was seeping from him now, like sand from an hourglass, and he felt the first real freedom since he had been accused all those years ago. That hate, he knew, had been a more brutal prison than the one of bricks and iron.

Her hand was roaming, and he stopped thinking. He only felt.

Her fingers teased and loved as they roamed along his skin, stopping and taking special liberties here and there, like the back of his neck and muscles along his shoulders. They tensed under her touch, just as he felt the growing arousal in that least-disciplined part of his body. He groaned with the growing expectancy there, with the glorious heat that burned in him with such insatiable need.

Her hands unbuttoned his shirt and slid up and down his chest, until he felt as if he'd been struck by a dozen lightning bolts. Piercing streaks of need sliced through him, and he sensed her desperate urgency; he knew she suspected this was a good-bye. His heart slammed against its rib cage as he felt the love flowing from her, the giving, wordless plea that he give more than he had any right to give. She wanted forever, and he had no forever to give.

He could only give this moment, and he was desperately afraid that he would be doing more damage if he did that, but he needed it so badly. He needed her warmth. He needed the knowledge of being loved. He needed love itself.

Shea sensed the battle waging inside him, his sudden hesitation even as his body strained toward her and hers toward him. She saw the raw, naked longing on his face and knew it was far more than the physical hunger that also ran violently between them.

"I need you now," she whispered. She needed his strength, even that odd and unexpected compassion he'd just showed toward her father, a compassion that, at the moment, was lacking in her. She needed a grounding when all the ground beneath her had been swept away, the foundation of trust and honesty she had thought her heritage had been made into mockery.

Shea's hand went up to his face, traced its outlines with tender possessiveness, and then his mouth returned to hers with a fierce need. His kiss deepened, his tongue moving slowly and sensually inside, each caress prolonged before proceeding to the next one. She knew he had surrendered, in this one moment at least, and she intended to make the most of it. Her own hand moved to the back of his head, her fingers entwining in his thick hair. To touch and be touched was enough at first, but then each movement fired the urgent expectancy inside her, the rising need that was exploding between them.

His right hand moved along her cheek and to the back of her neck, so delicately for such strong fingers. And then they moved to the front of her dress, slowly unbuttoning the front before moving inside the chemise and cradling her right breast. Her skin was alive with feeling, with wanting, and the core of her was a mass of writhing nerve ends, the pain sweet and exquisite in anticipation.

She helped him take off her dress and underclothing, and then her own fingers started unfastening his trousers. Without actually taking them off, he pulled her body close to his, and the combined friction of cloth and skin against her own naked body caused her to shudder with anticipation. She felt herself trembling with a need that went beyond the fierce passion she also felt. She wanted him inside her. She wanted him a part of her. She wanted to make him understand that they were one, could always be one if only he would allow it.

Their bodies came together, and he entered, deep and throbbing but still carefully, tenderly, as if each touch was to be savored and treasured and remembered, every movement like a sensual dance of love. Her legs went around his as she answered that dance with one of her own, moving with him, helping him to reach the very core of her, giving him every piece of her body and heart and soul. "I love you," she whispered, knowing he didn't want to hear those words but unable to hold them back.

He stilled a moment, a moment that seemed suspended in time, but then his urgency became greater and his movements turned wild and uncontrollable, and she joined him in a majestic journey, rocketing to places unknown in flashes of white-hot splendor.

He rolled over on his good shoulder, carrying her with him. Holding her close. Holding her as if he never wanted to let her go. She relished that hold, even as her body shuddered with the aftershocks of sensation. She sighed with a honeyed contentment, and he gave her a crooked smile that cracked her heart, his good hand resting on her breast.

She took his hand in hers, fingering the scar. "What happens now?"

"I don't know," he said slowly, painfully. "I've . . . never thought beyond this point."

"If he admits what he's done? . . ."

He withdrew slowly, gently, from her body, not wanting to let her go but knowing he must, lest his resolve weaken anymore. This had to be the end of it.

"I've been robbing stagecoaches," he explained gently. "And the express office. I'm still an outlaw. I'm wanted in Casey Springs. And wherever I go, I'm a marked man. There will be the law, bounty hunters."

"But you can explain. . . ."

"There's no good reason for what I've been doing," he said, "none the law will accept." He hesitated, trying to find the next words. "I'm discovering there's damn little satisfaction in revenge. I spent ten years thinking about it, and now I know I've done more damage to myself than your father ever thought about doing. Even worse, I've . . . damaged you, and I won't ever forgive myself for that."

There was so much sadness in his voice, Shea felt a penetrating loneliness drive through her, for him and for herself. He *was* saying good-bye, and she knew she wouldn't change his mind, but she had to try. She had to.

"I'll follow you," she said determinedly.

"Not if you care for me," he said, using the one weapon he knew might dissuade her. "I have to find some kind of life, Shea. I can't do it with reminders everywhere, with memories."

"Because I'm Jack Randall's daughter?" Her voice was an agonized whisper.

"Yes," he said, his throat constricting. His heart seemed to shatter as he saw the realization, then acceptance, in her face. The one thing that would dissuade her. Saving him from pain.

The one and only thing. He stood and looked away from her stricken face. He dressed silently and waited for her to do the same. He wanted to grab her and tell her that Jack Randall didn't matter. That she could be the daughter of the Devil and he would love her.

But then she might die in a hail of bullets meant for him. Or be forced to live in isolation the rest of her life. He wouldn't do that to her.

He turned away as she dressed. He waited until she rose silently. And together, but separately, they walked back to the cabin.

Chapter 26

Rafe took several blankets and spent the night at the pool. He watched as the bears came, the cub managing very well on three legs. The wounded leg seemed to be healing, the cub testing it now and then.

The cub came up to him as the she-bear held back, and Rafe looked at its leg. The splint was gone, but then he'd expected that. He knew Nature had her own way of healing.

If only this sharp ache inside him could be healed. But he had boxed himself in readily enough, and he couldn't see his way out, nor could he continue to blame Randall for everything, not any longer.

He watched as the she-bear fished, slapping several trout out of the pool for the cub, who attacked them with ferocity. Rafe had to smile at how fast the little animal had returned to normal. And then he remembered Shea's intent face as they had worked over the cub together days ago. Or was it years?

Supper had been a nightmare of strained emotions. Randall had brought back one fish, which Shea had cooked over fire without comment. Rafe had simply taken a can of peaches and the last of the hardtack and gone outside to eat, taking Abner with him for company. It was time that Randall and Shea somehow sort out their problems, come to some kind of truce as he had.

Rafe no longer doubted that Randall would do as he said he would. He even thought about trying to change Randall's mind because of what the revelations might mean for Shea, but he sensed it would do no good. It was something Randall had to do for himself.

Abner crawled up into Rafe's hand, and he wondered about his own future, what he had to do now for himself. Nothing was left here. McClary was dead. Randall would in most likelihood go to prison, if not for the payroll robberies of years ago, most certainly for his knowledge of McClary's activities here. At the very least the rancher was guilty of accessory to murder.

Rafe had accomplished exactly what he'd set out to do, and now he could lose himself in some far piece of earth, just as he had planned. Too bad, he thought ironically, that triumph was so damned bitter. In gaining his "justice", he was losing the most precious gift he'd ever been given: love.

And Shea. He would return the money he'd stolen from Randall. She would have enough money to go wherever she wished and do whatever she wanted. She would be fine. She would find some upstanding proper gentleman who could give her the family and life she deserved.

He looked up at the sky, at the three-quarters moon and the millions of stars that made it into a jeweled tapestry. He would never again take it for granted or lose his wonder at its beauty. But its very vastness and majesty made him feel incredibly alone.

Where would he go? And Clint and Ben? The others?

Would he run the rest of his life, like Jack Randall for the last ten years, if not from the law, from himself?

A decision started forming in his mind, and he didn't, couldn't, sleep. He didn't want to lose this night of freedom, the lonely but magnificent power of such a bright clear sky. He wanted to memorize the brilliance of every star, to retain in his mind the delicate silver of the nearly full moon.

He knew he wouldn't see the heavens again in a very long time.

Shea wanted to go to the pool. She wanted to be with Rafe, but he didn't want her, and with good reason. She had just heard the whole ugly story, told with unvarnished frankness.

Her father had stolen from the army; and it hadn't been the first time, he'd admitted. He had been stealing since he was a boy. Her own grandfather had been shot by someone he'd tried to cheat.

He'd tried to quit, Jack Randall told her, when he'd met Sara, but it had been too easy to continue, especially when he'd wanted so much more for his wife. He'd winced when he said that, knowing it for the excuse it was.

"But consciously framing another man for something you did?" she asked. "Lying about it in court?"

"I was a coward, Shea. I always had been. I never meant anyone to be killed, and troopers were. I've always been able to rationalize what I did, and then I convinced myself I'd just given away information anyone could have. I was still hoping your mother would come back to me, that with the money, I could buy a ranch, become what she wanted. . . ."

"Then McClary discovered Captain Tyler was asking

questions about me, and I knew it was a matter of time. McClary offered me a way out, and I took it. I did manage to save Tyler from being hanged. I'd thought I could do more, but the officer in charge believed Tyler was a traitor because he was a Texan."

"You just let him be branded and spend ten years in prison instead," Shea said bitterly.

He was silent.

"Why come forward now?" she said sarcastically. "The damage is done. Do you really think it will change how I feel now?"

"No," he replied wearily. "I know it won't. But at least I can clear him of these recent murders." He was sitting, and now he stood. "I know nothing I say now can excuse the past, but for what it's worth, I've lived in my own hell these past ten years."

"But you let . . . that man stay with you . . . knowing. . . ."

"He's been blackmailing me for years. He shot me because I told him I was going to the authorities. Too late, of course."

There was so much self-loathing in her father's eyes that Shea felt the first vague stirrings of sympathy.

But Rafe's anguished face kept coming back to her. The first time he'd shown her the scar, the way he always wanted to sleep outside so he could see the sky, the words of Clint Edwards: *He loved the army. He was the best officer I've ever seen.*

And then Rafe's face a few moments ago. That closed, tight look when he said, "I have to make a life for myself somewhere. . . ." Even as he knew how difficult it would be with that brand marking him.

She swallowed hard and looked up at the man who had fathered her. "I love him, you know, and I can never be with him because of you."

"I'm sorry," he said in a gruff, broken voice. "If there is anything . . . God in heaven, I'm so damn sorry." His shoulders slumped. "I'll stay in the barn tonight and start down in the morning. Will . . . you go with me?"

No, she wanted to scream. I want to stay here. I want to be with Rafe. But that was impossible. She nodded, tears edging her eyes.

"Shea . . . I didn't know about you until just a few weeks ago, but I . . . love you. I would do anything, anything at all, for you. I want you to know that. I also want you to know I . . . don't expect anything from you. I know you . . . can't love someone like me. Or even understand." He went wearily to the door and started to open it.

"Papa." Her voice was low, so low she wondered if he even heard it, but he turned and faced her. There was no hope in his face. "Mama never stopped loving you. There was a picture of you . . . I saw her looking at it until the day she died."

He stilled, his face like stone, then he silently left the room, leaving Shea utterly alone.

Shea lay awake all night, so many emotions battering her. Part of her wanted to hate Jack Randall, but she couldn't. She kept seeing those sad eyes with so much regret, and she knew that he, too, had paid a desperate price for the past and would face another kind of punishment in the coming days. She'd learned enough about him to know how much he loved the ranch, the position of respect he held, and now he would give all that up.

And Rafe? Dear God, what would Rafe do now? She'd sensed a difference in him tonight. Some of that deep, dark bitterness was gone, but none of the determination. He would leave her because he thought . . .

She remembered the words, each one of them, and suddenly she realized how hollow they were. The words that said he wanted a new life, that he didn't want memories of the old one.

She had believed them then because she had been so distraught over her father's confession to her, over her own guilt of somehow being a part of it because of the blood tie. But now she remembered the tenderness with which he touched her, the wonder of those intimate moments, and she suddenly knew that they would never have been possible if she'd been a reminder of Jack's treachery.

He had said them for her sake. How could she forget the number of times Rafe Tyler had tried to protect her in just this way?

Her mother had left her father. She wondered now what would have happened if Sara Randall had stayed with her husband, had told him of the coming child. Would he have changed? She would never know, but she realized now that her mother had run away from something she couldn't face. She had thought it had taken courage to leave a man you loved. Now she wondered if perhaps it wouldn't have taken greater courage to stay.

She didn't know, and the questions were all agonizing and unanswerable.

Just before dawn, she rose. Her clothes were still there, in the valise. She changed into a clean dress and pulled a shawl around her shoulders and started toward the pool as the first rays of the morning sun lightened the night sky.

She saw Rafe at the same time he apparently heard her. He had been sitting cross-legged near the rock, and he stood as she approached.

Without saying anything, he just held out his arms to her, as if he, too, had made some kind of decision. She walked into them and felt them close around her, and she laid her head against his chest, just standing there, comforted by his closeness.

She didn't know how long it was before they moved. She didn't want to move, to break this moment that somehow spoke of love more than words she'd wanted so badly.

He finally moved a few inches away, and she looked up at him, at those vivid sea-green eyes that were now alive with emotions he'd never allowed to show before. He put a finger to his mouth and guided her away, up in the rocks where they had watched the bears before.

Shea didn't know how he knew, for she had heard nothing, but in several minutes a doe approached the pool and looked cautiously around, and then a fawn followed it out into the open, and with a grace Shea had never seen before, the two bent their lovely heads and drank from the clear blue water. Her hand tightened around his. The deer he had promised mornings ago.

She breathed deeply at the utter enchantment below: the mist from the waterfall, the peaceful pool, the deer, the streaks of light above now casting a golden glow over the scene as if blessing it. She wished she had her drawing pad, and the most wonderful paints, but even then she knew she could never re-create the complete tranquillity of the moment. Nor the joy of sharing it with the quiet, complex man beside her. A man capable of the exquisite gentleness required to gain the trust of animals, and yet who could harbor the most violent of emotions. She was beginning to understand, though. For a time she had hated her father for what he had done; there was a residue of that anger left, though it was tempered now with his own pain and regret.

They watched as the sky lightened and the deer retreated into the woods, blending almost immediately into their surroundings as if they had never been there.

She turned and looked up at Rafe, and she knew her heart was in her eyes. "No matter what you think," she said haltingly, "I'll never be whole without you."

A muscle in his cheek worked. "You don't understand," he said.

"I do," she said, willing him to believe. "I know that you think leaving is best for me. It's not. I'm not a child, Rafe. I never . . . have felt this way before, and I won't ever feel this way again about someone else. You can go, but you will still carry part of me with you, and the part that remains won't be worth much."

"I'll be going back to prison," he said, having finally made a decision during the past few hours. He had thought it would be the hardest he'd ever made, but leaving Shea was even more difficult.

"You said you would never go back."

"Your father has taught me you can't run from what you've done," he said slowly. "I've been trying to come to terms with that tonight."

"You had reason," she said fiercely.

"Not for involving Clint and the others. Or for the deaths of those miners. That never would have happened if I hadn't come here."

"You had nothing to do with that."

"Didn't I? Hate begets hate, Shea. Violence begets violence. I should have taken my freedom and enjoyed it."

"Then I wouldn't have met you."

"No. You would have settled down as Randall's daughter, been courted, and married." He hesitated. "Have a family."

"I don't think so," she said softly. "I've been waiting all my life for you, I think. No one else would have done."

He smiled wryly. "You must like lost causes."

"You're not a lost cause," she said indignantly.

"Ah, Shea. I've been alone all my life. I don't know how to live with anyone . . . even if I had a chance."

"There's never been . . . anyone?"

He hesitated. "Once. I was . . . to be married. She returned the ring . . . by messenger . . . after I was charged."

Shea felt indignation and jealousy rush through her. "She didn't believe you?"

"She never even asked," he said with a shrug.

"Then you were well rid of her," she said, but the dry tone in his voice didn't quite hide the wound behind it. No wonder he didn't trust anyone.

He smiled slowly but without warmth. "I finally reached that same conclusion, but . . ."

He didn't have to finish the sentence. It *had* hurt. And she hated that unnamed woman who had made him so suspicious now. "And you think I might do the same?"

"I don't know," he said with stark honestly. "I stopped expecting anything a long time ago."

"Is that why you're giving up now?"

He glowered at her.

"Fight, Rafe," she demanded. "Don't give up. They can't send you to prison, not after my father. . . ."

"They can do any damn thing they want, and I don't want to trade my life for your father's."

"I thought that was exactly what you did want," she retorted, suddenly angry beyond caution.

The anger seeped from his eyes. "Christ, what have we done to you?"

Her hand went up to his face. "You've given me a great deal, Rafe Taylor, and so . . . has my father in these past few days. He has to do . . . certain things now, and I need your help. I need you."

He turned away from her. He'd never been able to help anyone who needed him. Never. He thought of that six-year-old boy, held by a Comanche, as his mother was raped, then killed. He had felt so damned helpless, as if there had to be something . . . anything . . .

And then the army, and it had happened again. He had been transferred, and the unit he'd trained had fallen under the command of an arrogant glory hunter, and he'd watched it decimated. He managed to save Clint and Ben, but so many others had died. And then those men guarding the payroll . . .

If only he'd acted sooner . . .

Now Shea Randall needed him, and he was so damned scared he would fail again.

"Rafe? . . ."

He turned. She was standing there in a green dress, slender and strong. Stronger, he thought instantly, than either he or Randall. She was willing to take chances. She always had been, from the first moment she came here, from the moment she'd left Boston to find an unknown father.

"What do you want me to do?"

"Go with us, but let my father do what he needs to do."

"I could still go to prison."

"I'll wait for you."

"I have damned few prospects."

She moved toward him and leaned into his body. "You have friends. Very good friends. You have me." She searched desperately for some hope to hold out to him, some prospect. "We can find a little piece of land someplace and . . . you're so good with horses, we could raise them. You and Clint and Ben."

The idea was more than a little appealing to Rafe. He knew he *was* good with horses, always had been. They could round up some wild stock, break and sell them. Perhaps find a little valley someplace. The image was so good, it scared him. It had been so long since he'd permitted himself to dream, to hope. . . . He put his arms around her and pulled her close. "I don't know how long . . ."

She looked up at him. "I love you. I've never loved anyone before, and I know I'll never love anyone as I love you. It's worth the wait."

He leaned down and kissed her. Slowly, yearningly, heartbreakingly. A good-bye. Yet a promise too. For the first time a promise, and Shea felt a quiet, bittersweet satisfaction. He'd had so many failed promises, so many hopes broken. What if she was guiding him toward yet another one? Yet she couldn't believe justice would fail him again. Not if she had to go see the governor herself.

She wanted to say something, but she couldn't. Her throat was choked with fear, her heart constricted with love. What if he did go back to prison? Could he stand it again? She meant what she'd said. She would wait. But could he be caged again and remain the man he was, the man she knew had just barely survived the past ten years?

Shea was almost ready to throw her words to the wind, to ask him to run away with her, to risk being hunted, but she didn't have the chance. His jaw set and rigid, Rafe took her hand and guided her back to the cabin with firm, determined steps.

Jack Randall had wrapped McClary's body in a blanket and placed him next to the gelding he had found not far away in the woods. He'd known McClary must have brought a horse with him, and he'd searched for it after finding Shea had left the cabin. He'd surmised she was with Tyler.

Disregarding the pain in his shoulder, he'd shunned the sling he'd been wearing and had awkwardly finished saddling his own horse when Tyler and Shea emerged from the woods, but he hadn't been able to lift McClary.

His daughter was clutching Tyler's hand as if it were a lifeline. Tyler's own face was weary and drawn.

"I'm going with you," Rafe Tyler said, turning toward Shea. "Perhaps you'd better get that valise." He hesitated. "I want you to take Abner."

Jack watched his gaze follow Shea to the cabin. Tyler was as obviously in love with Shea as she was with him. He swallowed, afraid for them both. He no longer cared about himself.

He swallowed hard, then asked, "Abner?"

Rafe's gaze turned cold as it moved from the cabin to Jack. "A mouse. A companion from prison."

Jack averted his eyes, unable to meet the direct, challenging glare. He remembered the small creature several hours ago when Tyler was sleeping. A mouse. And his daughter had reacted so naturally to Tyler's request that she retrieve her valise and . . . Abner. He felt so damned much the outsider. He wondered whether he would ever have a chance to learn more about his daughter.

To cover his sudden awkwardness, he lowered his gaze to Rafe's bandaged arm. "Can you help me . . . get McClary on the horse?"

Tyler nodded, and together they managed to hoist the body onto the saddle and tie him there.

Jack moved away. "Is there anything else I . . . can help with?"

"No," Rafe said curtly, and disappeared inside the stable after his own horse. Minutes later he led out his horse and stood waiting for Shea.

Jack gathered up the reins of McClary's horse and

mounted. He knew Shea would ride with Rafe Tyler. He watched as she came from the cabin, holding a valise, her hand cuddling a small gray mouse that she tucked into a pocket in her dress. She glanced at the body tied to the horse, then at Jack Randall, and gave him the slightest uncertain smile, and he felt a tingle of hope.

Tyler swung into the saddle, then helped her to mount behind him. Without looking back, Tyler urged his horse into a canter toward the opening in the canyon walls.

They had been riding an hour when they spotted the first of the posse. Jack recognized Michael Dewayne, Russ's son, with relief. He had been afraid they might run into some of the posse from Casey Springs before he could explain.

Michael saw them at the same time and drew his gun, shooting it once in the air, an obvious signal. He then turned it toward Rafe and then Randall and back toward Rafe, obviously uncertain as to what to do.

Jack raised his hands. "We're turning ourselves in, Michael," he said. "Where's Russ?"

"That shot should bring him," Michael said. "What's going on, Jack? The deputy sheriff from Casey Springs is mad as hell, said you broke Tyler out of jail. You're damn lucky we found you first. They're out for blood." Then his eyes went to the horse carrying the blanket-wrapped body. "Who is that?"

"Sam McClary. The man who's been killing the miners."

"Your friend?"

"He was never my friend, but it's a long story."

"I've got to ask you to unbuckle that gunbelt. And throw down those rifles."

Jack unbuckled his gunbelt with his right hand, then threw down his rifle. Rafe dropped the gun tucked in his belt, then took his rifle from the saddle and gently lowered it to the ground.

Just then a group of men rode up, Russ at its head. Clint was with them. He looked sharply at Rafe, who almost imperceptibly shook his head, warning him not to say anything.

Russ Dewayne glared at Rafe, then looked toward Jack. "I thought it was something like this—he had your daughter. That's why . . ."

Jack shook his head. "No. He didn't have my daughter. And he isn't responsible for any of the killing. I helped him escape because the good citizens of Casey Springs were going to hang him for something he didn't do."

Michael broke in. "He said that's McClary on the horse, that it was McClary who killed the miners."

Russ looked at the weapons on the ground. "Michael, you pick those up. I think I'd better get these three out of here before that fool lawman from Casey Springs arrives."

"Where do we take them?" Michael asked.

"To our ranch while I try to sort all this out. Then we'll decide what to do." He leaned over and took the reins from Rafe's hands. "Jack, just how far can I trust you?"

Jack glanced over at Rafe's face, the sardonic look that replaced the rigid mask that had been there.

"I was coming to your ranch. There's some things you should know."

"Such as?" Russ Dewayne's voice was doubting.

Jack looked at Shea and seemed to gather courage. "I knew what McClary was doing. He was blackmailing me."

"Damn it, Jack. Why . . . ?" He stopped. "We'll talk at the ranch."

They rode hard for two hours. It was easy to see that Russ Dewayne did not want to be intercepted by the Casey Springs posse. When they arrived at the Dewayne ranch, Russ dismounted and motioned to Randall and Rafe to accompany him inside. Russ's two sons went with him.

Kate, who had come out on the porch at the sound of so many hoofbeats, ran to Shea. "We've been so worried about you. Are you all right? What happened?" The questions came so quickly that Shea just stood there as she watched the men disappear inside.

"Who *is* that?" Kate asked, and Shea knew she had followed Rafe's every move with her heart in her eyes. "Oh, Shea," Kate said, obviously recognizing Shea's distress. "What can I do?"

"Nothing," Shea said. Then she saw Clint standing aside his mount. "Perhaps something to drink . . ."

"Of course," Kate said. "Come inside with me."

"In a moment. I would like to speak with Clint."

Kate hesitated, looking from Shea to Clint and back again. "Of course," she said finally, and disappeared inside.

Shea went down to where Clint stood. "I wish I knew what the hell was going on," he said in a quiet voice that was barely audible. "I've been looking for you . . . and him."

"You . . . heard that my father helped him escape."

"Hell, yes. Everyone in the territory is looking for them. I was searching for you up in the valley night before last, and then we found your horse and figured you were dead . . . or lying hurt someplace. I was riding with the posse to try to steer them away from the valley. . . ."

"My horse ran away just as I got to the valley," she said. "My . . . father went after Rafe, thinking he might know where I was. McClary followed them and tried to bushwhack us last night. Rafe killed him."

"And now . . . ?"

"My father says he's going to tell what happened ten years ago."

Clint smiled slowly.

"I hope that Rafe will be allowed to go, that we can start a place of our own. That you and Ben will come with us."

"That's a lot of hopes," he said with a wry smile. "And your father?"

"I don't know," she said. "I don't know how I feel about that."

Clint shook his head. "I never used to think Rafe was lucky. I do now."

"He had you and Ben. Someday I want to meet the others."

He grinned at her. "Someday you will."

She smiled back at him and turned around, anxious now to go inside, to discover what was happening. "Thank you for being such a good friend to him."

Shrugging, he turned back to his horse.

When Shea turned around, she saw Kate watching them, a glass in her hand. Shea went up the stairs and took it, realizing for the first time how dry her mouth was.

"Where are they?" she asked.

"In my father's office."

Shea started to go inside, then turned to Kate. "Don't let him get away, no matter what."

Now it was Kate's turn to flush. "I thought . . ."

Shea suddenly understood Kate's coolness of late. "Oh, no. Clint's . . . just been a good friend. I love . . . the man inside. Rafe."

"Rafe?" Kate's face screwed up as she concentrated

on Shea's words. "Rafe . . . Tyler? The man my father took to Casey Springs? The outlaw? Oh, Shea."

"Don't judge," Shea said. "Don't make that mistake. Sometimes people do wrong things for the right reason. I've discovered in the past weeks that black is often white and white black, or shades of gray." She was thinking about Clint, about everything Clint had done in the name of friendship. But she was also talking about Rafe.

Kate put her arm around her. "I'm sorry. I didn't mean to judge. If you care about him, I'm sure . . ." Her voice trailed off, and Shea felt as protective as that mama bear, even though she knew Rafe didn't need that protection.

If only she knew what was going on inside.

She turned and walked inside, noting two men standing guard at a door. "I want to go in," she said.

"Orders, ma'am. The sheriff says to keep everyone out."

She thought about barging in, but she would probably be stopped and perhaps hurt Rafe's cause. She had to let him handle it. He'd been waiting long enough.

She ignored Kate and sat down, opposite the door. And wished. And willed.

And waited.

Chapter 27

Rafe watched Russ Dewayne's brows furrow, the lines around the eyes grow deeper. Some of the warmth he'd initially showed Jack Randall faded away as he listened intently.

Every once in a while the sheriff's gaze flickered over to Rafe, as if weighing the impact of the words being said. Dewayne listened in silence as his two sons swore several times in low voices.

When Randall had finished, Dewayne turned to Rafe. "Why in the hell didn't you say something about this several days ago?"

Rafe shrugged. "Once you saw that brand, you weren't going to believe anything I said."

Dewayne turned back to Jack Randall. "Why are you telling me this now?" His tone was suspicious, as if there was still something Randall wasn't telling him, some excuse for Randall's actions, which clearly offended the lawman.

"I . . . was going to, I told McClary as much. That's why he shot me. He thought he'd left me dead."

"Why should I believe you? McClary is conveniently dead."

Randall looked at Rafe, then back to Dewayne. "There's no reason I should incriminate myself if it weren't true, damn it."

"Your daughter, perhaps. We know this man had others working with him. Maybe they threatened her."

Rafe felt his jaw tighten. Dewayne would obviously rather believe anything that would excuse Randall. To hell with the truth. He stood restlessly, his anger explosive.

"Sit down!" Dewayne ordered.

"Why in hell don't you just hand me over to that mob in Casey Springs?"

The sheriff's face grew grimmer. "I'm sorry about that. If I had known, realized, I wouldn't have taken you there."

Rafe snorted, his bitter disbelief obvious. "Sorry? Why? I'm just an ex-convict who's threatening the daughter of your leading most respectable citizen."

"You also admit you've been robbing stagecoaches and the express office. Now sit down."

Rafe balled his hands into fists but sat back down.

Dewayne sat back in his seat, studying each man carefully. "What a damn mess," he said. "Jack, you say you knew McClary was committing those murders and you just let him go on doing it. You know that makes you an accomplice."

Randall nodded grimly. "I wish I had an excuse other than cowardice, but I don't. I wanted to protect what I'd built."

Russ Dewayne shook his head. "I thought I knew you. And you," Dewayne said, turning his attention to Rafe. "You were going to prove you were innocent by robbing stagecoaches?"

Rafe smiled wryly at the ironic tone in the sheriff's

voice. "I just wanted Randall exposed. I thought if I pushed him hard enough, he would resort to his old ways of getting cash."

"It seems you managed that. You can share the same cell together."

"That wasn't exactly what I had in mind," Rafe said.

"No, I don't suppose it was," Dewayne said, staring at both of them with distaste, and then fastened a stare on Rafe. "Why in the hell did you come in with him, anyway? Wanted to make sure?"

Rafe shrugged. "I guess I reached the same conclusion you did. Stealing those payrolls was a pretty damn stupid thing to do, and I didn't want to keep running the rest of my life."

"Because of the girl?" Dewayne asked shrewdly.

"That's . . . part of it."

"What about the others who worked with you? Where are they?"

Rafe's body stiffened. "They . . . are gone. I have all the money. They just wanted to help me. It was all my doing, my planning. No one was hurt."

"Strangest damn bunch of outlaws I've seen," Dewayne said, "giving up that kind of money. But do you really think it's that easy? Forget armed robbery because you and your friends were doing it for what you considered a just cause? The law doesn't work that way. I want to know who they are."

"No."

"You want to go back to prison real bad, don't you?" Dewayne said.

Rafe's lips thinned into a hard line. He didn't answer.

The silence in the room was suddenly punctuated by the sound of hoofbeats outside. Michael Dewayne went over to the window. "It's Quarles from Casey Springs with about twenty men."

Dewayne looked toward his sons. "Ed, go out the back and get what's left of my men over here. Michael, you stay with these two."

He left the room, Ed behind him, and Michael went to the door, keeping it open just enough to hear as Russ opened the front door.

"Quarles?"

"I heard you captured the two men who escaped from my jail and my goddamn dumb deputy. I want them."

"They're my prisoners," Russ said. "They're going to stay here until I can take them to Denver. I heard you almost had a lynching there the other night. I thought you had more control over your town than that."

"I want them, Russ," the sheriff from Casey Springs said. "You don't have anyplace to keep them."

"It appears you don't either. I can guarantee they won't escape from here."

"It's my jurisdiction."

"Hell it is. The crimes occurred in my territory. I voluntarily took a prisoner to your jail, thinking he would be safe. I was mistaken. Now take your men and get out of here."

"Not without those prisoners. No one escapes from my custody."

"Nor is anyone taken from mine," Russ Dewayne said coolly. "And don't even think about trying." He looked out. Men were coming out of his bunkhouse, rifles in hand, surrounding the mounted men.

"You haven't heard the last of this," Quarles said.

Dewayne shrugged. "Take your complaint to the governor. I never wanted this goddamn job, but now I have it, I'll do it my way."

Rafe could hear every angry word from the sheriff,

every calm one from Dewayne. He sensed the simmering fury in the visitor's sudden silence.

Rafe's estimation of Russ Dewayne continued to grow. He knew Dewayne had been right. Neither he nor Randall would have lasted the night in the Casey Springs makeshift jail.

"You'll pay for this," the sheriff blustered as he made his retreat.

"Maybe," Dewayne said calmly, stepping out on the porch. Rafe couldn't hear any more. Several minutes later Dewayne returned, chomping down on a cigar.

"Now where were we?" he asked.

Rafe paced back and forth across the bedroom he now shared with Jack Randall. A guard sat outside the window, and another outside the door. Dewayne had obviously meant exactly what he'd said when he'd predicted Rafe and Randall would share a cell.

This room was a damn sight more comfortable than a cell at the Ohio Penitentiary, but it was a cage nonetheless.

He wished to hell he knew what Dewayne thought, but the lawman had been uncommunicative, and his expression poker-faced. Rafe had not the slightest hint of what to expect of him, not after he refused for the second time to give Dewayne the names of the men who rode with him.

He had been given several minutes alone with Shea, just to hold her, to feel her strength and faith. He hadn't dared kiss her, because that invariably led to something else he couldn't afford at the moment.

She had looked at him with questions in her eyes.

"Your father did everything he said he would," he

said gently. For her own peace he wanted her to forgive her father, even if he never could.

"Why don't they let you go, then?"

"I still robbed those stages," he said, "and then I'm not entirely sure Dewayne believed everything . . . your father said."

"What . . . will happen to him?"

"He'll probably stand trial."

She leaned against him, and he knew she was seeking his strength, when all the time she was his. He finally said the words that had been in his mind and heart. "I love you, Shea. I have no right to . . . tell you that now, but . . ."

Shea looked up at him with those damn expressive blue-gray eyes that always seemed to reach inside and see what no one else had ever seen. "You didn't have to tell me," she said. "You've told me in so many other ways. But . . . but I'm so glad you did."

He gathered her closer to him, wondering how anything so . . . perfect could have happened to him, wondering whether it had come too late.

And then the knock on the door, and Dewayne stood there, waiting for him. . . .

Randall had been silent ever since he, too, had been incarcerated in this luxurious jail. He had taken a chair and placed it where he could look out toward the mountains and had directed his gaze that way. There was nothing left to be said between the two men. Their enforced proximity did nothing to alleviate the tension between them.

Rafe took the bed, pillowing his head on his hands. He was too tired to even think any longer, which was a blessing. His eyes closed and oblivion took over his thoughts.

* * *

Russ Dewayne took three days to check out the stories. He knew he couldn't take much longer. Quarles would be hammering at the door of anyone with any influence.

He'd sent a telegram to the Army Department for details of the court-martial. He checked with the remainder of Randall's hands to make sure Randall couldn't have killed the miners, and he questioned Shea at length to make sure that Rafe couldn't have committed the murders. She'd finally told him she had been with Rafe, but that he had in no way kidnapped her.

To avoid throwing blame on Ben or Clint, she said that part of her original story was true, that she had become lost and Rafe had found her. She told Dewayne about the bear and said that was why she had stayed with Rafe, to nurse him after he had rescued the cub at her request.

She also told Dewayne about finding the box with the letters and the money, and the clipping about the court-martial.

Russ finally decided that Sam McClary had been behind the killings, that he had been killed in self-defense by Rafe Tyler. The other matters were more complicated. It worried him that he had been so wrong about Jack Randall, and that he had jumped to conclusions about Tyler because of the brand. If Tyler had been lynched . . . .

Russ spent an afternoon writing ten pages of explanation and sending them to the territorial governor. He asked for a deputy marshall, since he didn't trust the authorities in Casey Springs. He made several recommendations. And then he sent Michael with the package to Denver.

* * *

If the Devil ever devised a torture, it couldn't be more agonizing than the one Russ Dewayne provided. Five days with the man Rafe had hated for ten years.

Poetic justice?

Exquisite irony?

But for whom?

They were eventually forced to confront one another. Silence could last only so long.

After those five minutes alone with Shea, Rafe had been allowed no more. He had been asked additional questions. Mostly about who had ridden with him. It was a question that seemed to haunt Dewayne.

After the first day he understood that Shea had returned to the Circle R. So had Clint, he imagined, since he no longer saw his friend from the window.

He was a prisoner. No one tried to hide that fact. Both he and Randall were kept under constant guard, their meals delivered to the room by one of Russ's sons and the slop pail emptied daily by one of the hands.

There was one bed. But blankets and sheets had been delivered for someone to sleep on the floor. Randall was intent on Rafe taking the bed after that first day when he'd slept for several hours; Rafe was just as intent on sleeping thereafter on the floor. He damn well didn't want any favors from Randall.

It was the third day before they exchanged any words.

It was Rafe who initiated it. "What in the hell does he think he's doing?"

"Russ is careful," Randall said. "He's discovered I'm obviously a liar. He'll check everything before he decides what to do. You won't find a fairer man."

Rafe grimaced, thinking of his first encounter. He

felt as if he were going crazy, waiting on someone else's moves. He wondered whether he'd made a mistake coming here.

Randall watched him carefully. "Take care of Shea for me," he finally said. "Take care of the Circle R."

"I don't want anything from you."

"It's not for you. I know there's nothing I can ever do to compensate you. But do this for Shea. She so obviously loves you, and the Circle R can give you a beginning. I'll never come back, if that's what you want. The deed is yours. No conditions." He gave Rafe a wry smile. "I suppose you have the money to pay the notes."

Rafe turned away from the plea in his face. "It's up at the valley, in a hole in the stable. I didn't want to lose it in case the wrong people found us. But it's yours . . . and Shea's. And I might well be in prison with you."

"I don't think so. Russ will do his damndest for you. He'll help you with the Circle R."

Rafe looked at him with startled amazement. "Why?"

Randall shrugged. "After eight years I know him. He'll feel guilty about what happened in Casey Springs."

"I don't want pity," Rafe said in a voice much like a growl.

"He won't give you any. It's a matter of justice to him, like sending me to prison will be. He didn't particularly care for the way you went about obtaining your justice, but he understood it, and I sure as hell don't plan to press charges against you. I take it I'm the only one you stole from?"

Rafe nodded.

"Think about it, about the Circle R," Randall pleaded.

"I think about Shea tied to a man who's forever marked as a thief," Rafe said. "She deserves more than that."

Randall winced. "Once everyone in this valley knows what happened, they won't give a damn. It will be a badge of honor, so to speak. A war hero unjustly treated. I'll be the dishonorable one, the one who disappointed them."

Rafe leaned against the wall, wishing he didn't feel sorry for the man, but he did. A little. "They'll forget."

Randall shook his head. "No. I fooled them, and that's one thing they won't forgive." He swallowed hard, and Rafe saw a wetness in his eyes. "I have no right to ask you, I know that, but Shea obviously loves you. Don't let what you feel about me hurt her. People here will give you a chance once they know what happened. Take the Circle R. Make it into what it can be."

Rafe hesitated. He didn't want anything of Randall's, but if what the man said was true, if the people in this valley could forget about the brand, accept him and Shea . . .

But what if he was wrong? What if Shea would wear the double burden of a father in prison and a husband who was an ex-convict and outlaw?

What if he did go back to prison himself?

"Just consider it," Randall repeated. "Please."

Rafe stood there. "I'm giving the money to Shea, all of it. She can do whatever she wants."

"I know what she wants," Randall said. "And she has all the signs of being as stubborn as her mother."

"Her mother left you," Rafe said pointedly.

"I drove her to it," Randall said. "You're a good man, Tyler. You always were. I think that's why I went along with McClary. I was jealous of you. You were everything I wanted to be: brave, a natural leader, so damned honorable. You're everything Sara wanted me to be, the kind of man I want for Shea. Even if she . . . never wants to see me again." Randall's last words were almost strangled, and he turned to the wall.

Rafe turned away to give Randall privacy. He realized how much courage it had taken for Randall to say what he said. He didn't know, however, that he agreed with him, that he, Rafe, could ever be good for Shea.

So he was silent, wondering at the sudden empathy he felt for the man he'd hated so long.

Clint Edwards no longer had a choice. He knew from Kate that one of Rafe's remaining problems was his refusal to name the other men who participated in the robberies.

He also knew he could no longer lie to Kate and her family. She hadn't understood his quick departure that day when Randall and Rafe had been brought in, and he'd forced himself to stay at the Circle R. But then Kate rode in to see Shea, and they had almost smashed into each other as she was leaving the ranch house and he was going in.

His arms automatically went around her protectively and lingered there. He didn't want to go, especially when those green eyes studied him with protective reserve. He knew he'd hurt her by avoiding her so obviously.

He wanted to kiss her now, to kiss away that reserve and that hint of sadness. But he had to talk to her first. He took her elbow and led her from the ranch house, out to the horse tethered to the hitching post. "I'll see you home," he said.

"That's not necessary," Kate said. "I'm very able to take care of myself."

Clint grinned at the independence he'd come to respect and admire, but the smile quickly disappeared. "I

know. But I want to. There's something I need to tell you
. . . and, later, your father."

She looked at him curiously but allowed him to help
her mount, and she waited as he mounted his own horse.

Clint waited until they were halfway there, until they
reached a small bluff that looked over the ranch to the
east and the mountains to the west, and then he stopped,
dismounting and holding out his hands to help her down.
She hesitated a moment and then slid into his arms, resting in them for a fraction of a second before moving away.

Clint reached out and took her hand, pulling her
back. "You don't know how much I've been wanting to
hold you," he said.

She looked up at him with puzzled eyes. "Then
why . . ."

"Because I had no right," he said. "Because I was
lying to you and to your father."

"I don't . . . understand. . . ."

"I've . . . been helping Rafe Tyler. I took part in
those stagecoach robberies," he said, watching shock replace the puzzlement.

"But . . . why?"

"He was my commanding officer for a time during
the war," Clint said slowly. "He saved my brother's life,
and mine. He violated orders to do it and was disciplined
for it. After the war I heard about the court-martial, and I
went to see him. I knew he couldn't be guilty. Not the
man I knew."

"And the others . . ."

"All men who served with him, who thought he got a
pretty raw deal. We . . . thought if we pushed Randall
enough, the truth might come out."

"All these months . . ."

"All these months," he confirmed as he watched her
green eyes cloud.

"Is that why . . . you . . ." She couldn't say the rest, but Clint knew what she was asking and it hurt— God, it hurt. She wanted to know whether he had kissed her, partly courted her, because he wanted to know what her father knew.

"Hell, no," he said. "I hadn't counted on . . . falling in love with you, and I knew . . . Christ, I knew I would hurt you, but I just couldn't keep away."

She looked up at him solemnly. "You fell in love with me?"

His hand went up to her cheek. "Oh, yes, pretty Kate, I fell in love, God help me."

Kate was already tall, and now she stood up on her toes until her mouth could reach his. Slow to believe she could forgive his duplicity, he hesitated at first, and then his lips met hers with a yearning and hunger he couldn't control.

Her arms went around him, and he pulled her against him, feeling for the first time he had a right to do so. He felt his independent Kate cling to him, and he knew that whatever came, they could survive it.

He took his lips from hers and brushed them against her cheek. "I love you, Kate," he whispered.

"It took you long enough to say it, Mr. Edwards," she whispered. "I've loved you for such a very long time."

"Then will you wait . . . ?"

He didn't have to say anything else. Their kiss did it for him.

Led by Clint, the six men rode into Russ Dewayne's ranch at sunset.

He'd found the five men up at Rafe's cabin. They had gone there when they'd learned, one by one, about Rafe turning himself in. They'd known that Clint would eventually return with some kind of word.

Clint had told them what he planned to do, and why, and advised the others to move on. Their job was over. There was no reason to risk being somehow identified with the band of outlaws. There was nothing more they would do.

Ben had been carving an animal out of a block of wood, and he looked up. "You said that lawman is demanding to know who helped the captain, and he's not saying. We all know he won't, that he would go to prison again first. Something ain't right about that. We all knew what we were getting into, and he's not taking the blame alone. I'm going with you."

One by one the others agreed. . . .

Russ was at the corral, unsaddling his horse, when Clint and the others rode in. He walked over to Clint, took one look at his grim face, and then he saw the man next to him, a man who was a younger version of Clint, except the eyes were harder. The expression was just as grim.

Russ sighed, knowing he probably wasn't going to like what he was about to hear.

Clint didn't mince words. "You wanted to know who was riding with Rafe Tyler. We were."

"The governor's here!"

The announcement, made by Michael who had just ridden in ahead of the governor's party, stunned those sitting around the kitchen table. Rafe and Jack Randall had been allowed downstairs for supper. Both were told that Russ had sent information to Denver, to the territorial governor, and was waiting for an answer. Russ didn't want to take his prisoners through the adjoining jurisdiction where they might well be stopped by Quarles, and he had asked for a U.S. marshal, whose authority would supersede both his and Quarles's.

Shea had also been invited to supper by Kate, along with Clint. Shea had moved back to the Circle R to try to keep the ranch going with Clint, the loyal foreman, Nate, and three other remaining hands. To Rafe she had looked devastatingly pretty in a green dress, though her eyes were tired, as if she had not been sleeping well. He hadn't been able to take his eyes from her. Neither had her father.

But now their eyes turned toward the door as Russ Dewayne quickly rose and went to greet his unexpected guest.

Governor William Tate was a tall, robust man who apparently enjoyed making entrances. He came in like a tornado, robust and smiling, followed by a lanky man with a marshal's star pinned on a leather vest.

"Kate, just as pretty as ever," he said, heading for her and bending over her as she quickly rose to her feet, along with the men. "And who is this lovely lady?"

"Shea Randall," Kate said with a smile.

The governor turned toward Jack Randall, and his smile faded slightly. "Can't say I wasn't shocked at what Russ here had to say," he said. "Couldn't believe it of you."

Randall's face flushed.

But the governor didn't give him an opportunity to say anything. He turned toward the other two men he didn't know, Rafe Tyler and Clint Edwards.

"Which one of you is Tyler?"

"I am," Rafe said.

"Hell of a thing that happened. But I have some good news for you. We'll talk about it after dinner. I'm hungry as a bear just coming out of hibernation. You got two more plates, Russ? You know Marshal Kettler, don't you? Evan Kettler?"

Russ smiled. "Hell, yes. Take a seat next to Clint Edwards here."

"Edwards," the governor acknowledged, and looked at Russ for more identifying information.

Russ gave it to him. "He and five others just confessed to being Tyler's gang," he said with bemusement. "I've never heard so damn many confessions in my life." He paused for a moment, then added, "My daughter also tells me he's to be my son-in-law."

The governor arched his eyebrows. "I gather this is going to be an interesting evening," he said as he sat down and, for the rest of the evening, dominated the table and the conversation, ignoring the rising tension of those at the table and the fact that no one else, other than Russ and the marshal, appeared to have any appetite.

"I didn't expect you to come all this way, Governor," Russ said. "I just wanted a marshal."

"Too intriguing not to," the governor said. "Made some inquiries after I got your information. Have some friends in the military. If what you say is true, they're going to be mighty embarrassed." He said it with glee, as if nothing would make him happier. "And it's been too damn long since you and I played poker."

All his joviality, however, disappeared an hour later when he met alone with Russ and Marshal Kettler. "I wanted to get this all settled," he said, "before the newspapers get wind of it. They would have a field day. I want to do what we can quietly. The army doesn't want news of this getting out, and we can accomplish more with their cooperation. But I need Tyler's cooperation. If he doesn't demand a pound of flesh from the army, I've been promised that they'll quietly reverse the findings of the court-martial and give Captain Tyler ten years of back pay. He will be completely cleared. It will end there. Otherwise, it could take years, with a number of noses bloodied."

Russ stared straight ahead. "I don't know if that's enough. It wouldn't be for me."

"But you aren't in love with Randall's daughter," the governor said. Then added as he saw the surprise on Russ's face, "Hell, I have eyes, Russ."

"I don't know what he'll do," Russ said quietly. "But I'd think he'd do almost anything to protect Shea Randall and those friends of his."

"And you would too, I imagine," the governor probed.

Russ hesitated. "I was angry as hell at first when Clint came to me. I felt betrayed, but then I thought about Tyler, and I was damned glad after what he went through that he had friends like Clint. I can't say I approve of what Clint did, or Tyler, but their loyalty to each other says a hell of a lot about them."

The governor chuckled ruefully. "Men to have as friends but not enemies."

"As Jack discovered," Russ said.

"At least he came forward now. That took some guts," the governor said carefully. "But I can't save him. I can help if he pleads guilty as an accomplice in these murders, but that's all I can do. I can pardon Tyler; God knows he's already spent ten years in prison for a crime he didn't commit. I can take that in account for this last . . . transgression."

"And the others?" Russ asked the question carefully. Kate's future depended on the answer.

"No one's been harmed. If the money's being returned, I think I can negotiate a little deal with the express office as long as the damages are paid. Casey Springs, after all, is trying to become an economic power in this area. Won't help the city none if there's word of lynch-mob activities. A small bit of blackmail."

"And Quarles?"

"He's appointed by the town council. I can exert a little influence there, too."

"And what can I do for you?" Russ smiled.

"A poker game, right after I have a little chat with Mr. Tyler," he said. "And," he added, "you can lose."

Rafe took Shea home. It was a strange word for her. It was a stranger one for him.

So was something called hope. For the first time in years he dared to dream again.

But a residue of sadness remained. He never thought it possible, but he'd felt regret when he'd left Jack Randall. Randall would be going to Denver the next day and would face a prison sentence, possibly a long one.

Rafe felt none of the satisfaction he once thought he would.

They were silent as they rode in the buggy Kate had insisted they take. Shea, however, had moved close to him, and sometime during the ride, his arm went around her. He was damned glad the horses were tame, for his left arm still hurt and lacked any strength.

The moon was nearly full now. Gold and bright, rather than pale and delicate-looking. There were enough stars to light the world, he thought, and they seemed to have a special glow tonight, lighting a future that was so promising, it hurt.

Rafe would never forget that brief meeting in Russ's office, the one in which he had been handed the sun and moon and admonished not to waste them. His name would be cleared. He would be pardoned for the most recent offenses. His companions wouldn't be charged.

And Clint was being welcomed into the Dewayne family. Randall had been right about Russ Dewayne. It had been made clear he could make a home here in the valley, and he would have Dewayne's friendship and support.

It had been almost too much to accept. It had surprised him as much as Dewayne and the governor when he had pleaded for Jack Randall's future as well, but there had been no give on that issue.

Shea had spent an hour with her father, alone, and when she joined Rafe, she had a kind of peace in her eyes, but also a question. "He told me he wants you to take care of the Circle R," she said. "Is that . . . possible?"

She was thinking about him again, as she always seemed to do. "What do you want?" he asked.

"I . . . like Colorado," she said. "I met you here . . . and I . . ."

He could give her this. Because she had given him so much. He could give her her father's heritage: a home. Until her father returned, and then there would be another decision to make.

And so now they were on their way to the Circle R.

Home. It was odd. Difficult to comprehend. He'd never had a home, not since he was six years old. And now . . . Jack Randall had given him one.

But he still had some reservations. He had to make sure that Shea knew what she was doing. That those days in his valley hadn't been a mistake, nothing more than emotions heightened by danger. He wanted to court her, as an ordinary man courted an extraordinary woman, not as a bandit took a hostage.

He would stay in the bunkhouse, no matter how difficult it would be.

Freedom had responsibilities. He had been so consumed by anger, he hadn't realized that until now.

They arrived at the Circle R. There was a light in the

bunkhouse. Nate was probably there. Nate and the few ranch hands. Both he and Shea had already agreed that those loyal few would be paid tomorrow, paid extra for their loyalty, and then the Circle R would have to hire more hands. Clint would join them, at least for a while. And Rafe knew of five other men. Extraordinary men.

His hand took Shea's, and he helped her down. Her fingers tightened around his as he walked her to the house. He wanted her so damned bad. He wanted to hold her, kiss her, make love to her. He craved it, but he also convinced himself she needed time.

They reached the porch, and he leaned down and kissed her lightly, keeping himself from grabbing her and kissing her the way he wanted to. He started to move away, but her hand held him.

"Don't go," she said. "Please don't go."

"I want to give you time."

"I don't need time. I need you. Tonight. Tomorrow. Forever. Don't you know that yet?"

"You should have everything," he whispered. "Everything that comes with courtship. Roses and trinkets and parties."

"I like short courtships. And I don't care about roses and trinkets and parties."

He closed his eyes and bent over, letting his lips play over hers, feeling the softness, the welcome, the invitation.

"I want you to be sure," he said painfully, his body straining toward her. After the loneliness of the past ten years, the uncertainty of the past few days, he needed her warmth, that total faith she had in him. The faith that had been so lacking in himself.

Shea smiled, a smile made so lovely in the moonlight. Luminous. Luminous and sure. And so full of love.

"I am so very sure," she whispered. "Come in with me. I need you so much."

There was something to be said, he thought as he reached down and picked her up, for a very, very short courtship.

And a home, his first home, after all, was waiting.

Epilogue

August 1878

Jack Randall was returning today.

Shea was in the ranch house, changing Sara's dress for the third time. Sara, at three, was always into something. Her latest adventure had been in the chicken yard, where an angry hen had knocked her into the mud.

Rafe had had to grin at the mud-caked little girl with the mischievous eyes and big, sheepish smile. Nothing daunted Sara. Particularly not the prospect of meeting her one-and-only grandparent.

Rafe wished he could regard the upcoming meeting with as cavalier an attitude.

He had not seen Randall in five years. Rafe had taken Shea to the Colorado prison for visits four times a year, but he'd always waited outside, and Shea had never questioned it. She knew it wasn't her father as much as the idea of being back inside stone walls. To this day he kept the windows in their room wide open and still occasionally went up to the valley and stayed overnight. Shea sensed when those spells of restlessness were coming and, until the babies came, she went with him. Sometimes now they would take the children, all three of them. They would sit on the rock above the pool and watch, just as they had in the beginning. For three years the she-bear and cub had come to the pool, and then the she-bear stopped coming. Shea had worried and wondered and worried some more, but they never saw it again.

Deer would come, the fawns growing into adults, and then one day the cub brought another bear, a young female, with him. Seasons. Everything had a season.

Just as he had. Now he was a father with three active youngsters: young Clint, who was four; Sara who was three; and the baby, Megan, who was eight months old. They were Rafe's season, just as Shea was. He loved them all desperately, too much sometimes, he feared. He didn't want to crush them with it, but he had waited so long and found he had so much love and tenderness stored in some hidden place.

And now Jack Randall was coming back. Rafe had offered to meet him, but Randall said he wanted to come alone. He wanted to savor freedom, and no one understood that as much as Rafe did.

Little Clint came running out of the house. "Papa, I want to go riding."

Rafe caught him and lifted him up. He was such joy, a bolt of energy and curiosity. "We have to wait on your grandpa," he said.

"Why?"

"Because he's been waiting a long time to see you."

"Why hasn't he come before?"

Rafe had known the question was coming. He and Shea had discussed it and decided not to lie, never again if they could avoid it. "He couldn't, Clint. He was in prison."

"What's prison?"

Rafe lifted his son up on the railing of the corral, which held a dozen horses. The Circle R was fast becoming known for its fine horses.

"You know when you do something wrong, I punish you," Rafe said carefully. "Like going too near the horses without your mother or me with you."

Clint nodded. That was his greatest sin. He loved the horses.

"Well, prison is how adults are punished."

"Did Grandfather go too close to the horses?"

Rafe had to smile. "No. He made a mistake many, many years ago, but he owned up to it, and now he's coming to meet you."

"To stay?"

"I don't know," Rafe said. Jack Randall's future had never been discussed. And truth be told, Rafe didn't know how he felt about living in the same house with the man he'd hated for so long. Yet without Jack Randall, there would be no Shea. No little Clint, or Megan, or Sara.

The thought was excruciating.

Clint was still trying to understand, his small face screwed up into a frown, and Rafe knew that the child sensed something of his mixed emotions. But then Clint had always been instinctive, more so than the girls. "Do you want him to stay?" the boy asked.

"I'm not sure," Rafe answered truthfully.

"You always fo'give me when I'm bad," Clint said.

Rafe grinned. Smiles came so easily now. And Clint with his serious, solemn probing usually brought one. "So I do," he said.

"Then why not Grandfather?" he asked.

"You always ask too many questions," Rafe said, deflecting that particular one.

"Will I like him?"

"I suspect so," Rafe said. "You look a little like him,

you know." It was the first time he'd acknowledged that. Just then, Shea came out of the house, holding Megan in one arm. Sara danced alongside her.

Motherhood had made her lovelier than ever. He had always thought her beautiful, but now she had a glow about her, and there was an excitement in her eyes. Excitement and trepidation as she glanced quickly at Rafe and smiled.

"Shouldn't be long," he said.

Shea handed him Megan and tipped her head as she studied him. He had come so far in the past five years. He never wore gloves anymore, never felt awkward about the mark. He had been completely accepted in Rushton and Casey Springs. The Circle R had grown prosperous under his management, and his horses brought the top prices. He was often consulted by other ranchers about horse stock, training, and breeding, and was respected for all those qualities of leadership she had always known were there. Clint, who had married Kate, was his closest friend and had a spread of his own now, as well as twin boys. Ben had grown restless and had moved on, as had two others of the original group. The other two worked for Rafe.

But Rafe had seldom talked about Jack Randall, and she wasn't sure about the homecoming. Nor, she knew, was her father. He had already told her he would probably move on after seeing his grandchildren. He'd said it without self-pity, but in the stark, bleak visiting room of the prison, Shea had sensed his loneliness. Still, she couldn't force Rafe, not when he was finally getting over his own ghosts.

Young Clint was looking out toward the drive into the ranch, and now he announced, "Is that Grandfather?" Rafe could hear the excitement in his voice, even if the boy wasn't quite sure what a grandfather was. He knew only that his friends Tim and Taylor Edwards had a fine grandfather who always brought them presents and took them fishing.

Rafe stiffened and turned, watching the lone rider approach slowly to where they were standing. He saw the uncertain smile on Shea's face and put his arm around her. "It's all right," he said.

Jack Randall rode to where they were standing and dismounted. Rafe thought he had aged considerably. His hair was white now, and the lines around his eyes deep. The face had character now, a dignity it didn't have before. Shea went to him, reached up and kissed his cheek. His arms went around her for a brief moment, and then he stooped to greet the children, his blue eyes suddenly sparking with the charisma he'd always had.

They swarmed around him, accepting his tentative hug, asking him a dozen questions. He finally stood and walked over to Rafe.

"Thank you," he said. "Thank you for my grandchildren. Thank you for letting me come."

Rafe found himself holding out his hand and taking Jack Randall's. The grip was strong.

"Welcome home, Jack," he said. And he found he meant it.

He felt Shea's hand replace Randall's and saw the sheen of tears in her eyes. He gripped her hand tightly.

"Come inside," he added. "We find ourselves in special need of a grandfather."

He saw a hint of tears in Randall's eyes, heard the excitement of the children, and felt the love in Shea's fingers, which had tightened around his.

And he had never been so free.

ABOUT THE AUTHOR

PATRICIA POTTER has become one of the most highly praised writers of historical romance since her impressive debut in 1988, when she won the Maggie Award and a Reviewer's Choice Award from *Romantic Times* for her first novel. She recently received the *Romantic Times* Career Achievement Award for Storyteller of the Year for 1992 and Reviewer's Choice nominations for her novel LIGHTNING (Best Civil War Historical Romance), and the hero, Lobo, in LAWLESS (Knight in Shining Silver). She has worked as a newspaper reporter in Atlanta and was president of the Georgia Romance Writers Association.

Thrill to the passionate romance and
breathtaking adventure
in Patricia Potter's next historical romance

Wanted

on sale in November 1994 from
Bantam Books

They were twin boys, separated at birth, re-
united as men. One was a lawless con artist, the
other an unbending Texas Ranger . . . and between them was an amber-eyed woman with
the face of an angel and the seductive charm
that would tempt the devil himself.

Here is the opening of this exceptional romance. . . .

West Texas, 1846

A scream of agony came from inside the adobe building.

John Davis felt the cry vibrate through him. Rivulets of sweat ran down his body and soaked the back of his rough cotton shirt.

He wasn't a praying man. But as he searched the hot, dry country outside the way station compound, he prayed as he had never prayed before. A few hours, God. Only a few hours.

He looked toward his friend, Ranger Callum Smith, who had galloped in on a horse now heaving with exhaustion.

"The Comanches are raiding this whole area," Cal said. "You have to get the hell out of here."

"Susan . . ."

John didn't have to say anything else. Another scream did it for him.

"Christ, John, but she picked a poor time for birthing."

John wiped his forehead with his bandanna. He had to do something. He didn't like feeling this helplessness.

He had quit rangering because of Susan, because Susan had worried herself sick about him. Ten months ago the Overland Stage Company had offered him the job of managing this way station on the mail route. It was a chance to build a home and a future, and he had taken it because he could finally spend time with his wife, and the children who were at last on their way.

And now . . .

The Comanches hadn't come this way in over ten years, not since the Ranger post had been established twenty miles away. But its manpower had been drained in the past months, most of the Rangers having been pulled down to the border, where Mexican bandits were laying waste to the new settlements there.

"I've got to go," Callum said. "I have to warn the settlers. But I'll get back as soon as I can."

John nodded. "I'll saddle you a fresh horse. You get some water from the well."

Callum nodded as another scream came from the house.

"How long . . . ?"

John shook his head. "Labor started late yesterday. Month early. Thank God, some woman on the stage agreed to stay over." He hurried to the barn, remembering how he had planned to take Susan to El Paso in three days, to the nearest doctor in a hundred miles. But then the pains had started just as the stage arrived. The lone woman passenger, a pretty but sad-looking woman dressed in black, offered to stay and help. Fleur Bailey, she'd said her name was, and she was returning home to Ohio after having lost her husband and two-day-old child.

Now she was in danger too. John cursed the Comanches, cursed himself for bringing Susan out here to this desolate place, as he finished saddling the pinto. He decided to get the wagon ready, too, so they could leave for the Ranger post as soon as the baby was born.

He watched as Callum mounted the pinto, gave him a brief salute, and spurred his horse into a gallop, disappearing quickly in the endless tall grass of the prairie. With any luck, John thought, by the time Callum returned from alerting the Kelly and Marshall families, he and Susan and the baby would be gone.

The baby. His child. He prayed again, then went back to the barn for two horses to hitch to the wagon. He set the other horses loose. He didn't want them trapped inside if there was an attack.

He heard the loud plaintive cry of a child.

Thank God, he thought gratefully. Perhaps prayers were answered after all.

He hurried to the cabin and opened the door. Fleur was holding a small bundle, a look of possessiveness on her face. He felt sudden apprehension, but then the woman smiled so sweetly at him, he immediately dismissed the momentary fear.

"A boy," she said as she cleaned him with a

wet cloth. Then she handed him to John, who stood awkwardly, feeling like a giant holding a baby bird.

When Susan screamed again, the woman stooped down over her and then looked up at John with a wondrous expression. "Dear heaven, there must be another."

Astonished at the unexpected news, John held his child as he listened worriedly to the continued groans and cries of his wife. Then there was one last scream, part agony, part triumph. Fleur, a stranger no longer in this most intimate of all dramas, straightened, holding a child. "Another boy. Twins."

John leaned down and kissed Susan, placing the first baby in her arms as Fleur cleaned the second one. She stopped in the middle of wiping one of the tiny feet. "Birthmarks," she said. "Almost like hearts on their feet, one on the left, one on the right."

That observation meant little to John Davis. All that mattered was that his children were healthy despite the fact that they had come early. Now he had to make sure they stayed that way. He took Susan's hand and grasped it. "Are you strong enough to move?"

Her blue eyes widened slightly in question.

"A small renegade bunch of Comanches," he said. "Probably nothing to worry about, but you and the babies would be safer at the Ranger post."

She swallowed, looking so tired. Her face

was smudged from sweat and tears, but she gave him a weak smile and nodded.

"I'll put a mattress in the buggy," he said, watching as her fingers ran over the older twin.

"Morgan," she whispered. They had already settled on that name if the baby was a boy. But the other? They hadn't expected that. Something to brag about at the Ranger post. Papa. At forty-three, he had become a papa twice over!

He knelt next to the bed and moved aside the brightly colored rug there to reveal a trapdoor. Below was a room he had made himself. Eight feet long, six feet wide, and five feet deep, it served several functions: a fruit and cheese cellar, a storage area for mattresses for those occasions when stagecoach passengers stayed overnight, and a hiding place in case of Indian or outlaw attack. The wood trapdoor was underlaid with layers of tin to protect the occupants from fire.

He carried two mattresses to the buggy, a double layer to make his wife more comfortable on the jolting ride.

When he returned, Fleur had diapered one of the babies. "You take the twins," John said. "I'll bring my wife."

But Susan refused to relinquish the child in her arms. "I want to hold him," she insisted.

He nodded to Fleur. "Can you take your valise and the other child?"

She nodded and quickly grabbed her valise. She had caught John's urgency. In the two days she had been here, she had learned that he was not a man who frightened easily. She had lost one husband and a baby. She didn't want to lose the one she held in her arms. The child felt so good. Just as her own son, Nicholas, had such a short time ago.

She nearly ran to the wagon, where she set the baby down and stowed the valise. She'd barely climbed in when the horses stamped nervously. She lost her balance and fell, just as she heard the sound of hoofbeats and a godforsaken yell.

She gathered the infant in her arms and ducked down underneath the seat. The wagon moved as the horses tried to pull loose from where they were hitched. She thought about returning to the cabin and peered through a crack in the wagon. A dozen or more painted Indians were racing toward her. She would never have time. She could only hide here and hope they didn't find her.

"Don't cry," she whispered to the child. "Please don't cry."

There were shots then. So many shots. They seemed to surround her as she huddled deeper under the seat. And then she heard the snorting of the horses, felt the jerking of the wagon, back and forth at first, and then wildly. Somehow the horses had gotten loose.

With one hand she clutched the seat while with the other she held on to the baby. The wagon swayed and rocked as it hurtled across the prairie, and Fleur desperately tried to keep from rolling over the infant. The shots faded behind her, and she concentrated her whole being on protecting the child, the little boy so much like her own.

She didn't know how long the wagon plunged across rocks and indentations. It seemed forever. And then there was another jolt and the wagon careened even more wildly. She knew the horses had broken free of the traces and that she and the child were passengers aboard a runaway vehicle.

The wagon hit a deep rut and stopped abruptly, and she was thrown against one of its sides, but the baby was pillowed by her body. Agonizing pain stabbed through her shoulder, but she managed to lift herself slightly to look up. The way station was no longer visible, but she saw smoke coming from its direction. So much smoke that the sky was dark with it.

She saw no savages, but they might be coming soon to look for the wagon, for the horses. That was what they wanted. She'd heard the Rangers talk about that.

She took the baby and crawled from the wagon. They were in the middle of nowhere, but there was tall prairie grass here. She could hide. She and the baby.

He whimpered and she pressed him to her. Nicholas. "I'll take care of you," she whispered, knowing that the others in the cabin must be dead. This baby was a gift, sent by God for her to protect, to take the place of her own boy.

* * *

John Davis knew he was going to die. His blood had turned cold when he heard the first Comanche yell. He ran to the door, estimating whether he could reach the wagon; more than likely, he would be caught in the open and Susan and Morgan would have no protection. He had to leave the woman and the other child in the wagon. Thank God, she had moved out of sight.

He slammed the door and went for one of his two repeating rifles. It was too late to hide in the cellar; the smoke from the chimney and the wagon told only too well of someone's presence.

He broke the glass in the window, aimed, and fired. He hit one of the Comanches, then another. They drew back, and as they did he looked over at Susan, who was now sitting up in the bed, clutching the baby. He laid the gun next to the window, moved swiftly to the trapdoor, and pulled it open. He reached for her.

"No," she said. "Put the baby in there, but I won't go. I can load for you."

He hesitated, then saw the determination in her eyes. He knew that look. If he forced her down, she would be back up immediately. He simply nodded, thinking how lucky he was, how lucky he had been to be loved by her.

Maybe that luck would hold. If he could only hold out for an hour, if Callum could gather others . . . He put the small wrapped figure of his child in the cellar, holding him tightly for a moment first. Morgan. His firstborn. He rubbed the small dark fuzz at the top of the baby's head, and then shots intruded on that very short time of tenderness. He lifted himself up, closed the door, and replaced the colorful rug.

He turned around and saw that Susan had taken the other gun and was trying to aim it. But her hands trembled. John took it from her, his blue eyes holding hers for an instant before he looked out the window once more.

He saw the wagon horses pull free from where they were hitched and watched as the wagon went careening across the prairie. His distraction ended immediately when a bullet plowed into his chest. He heard Susan's cry, felt her arms go around him, and then there were more shots. He felt another pain, then the weight of Susan's body as it slumped on his, her blood mixing with his.

His last thought was of the babies. "God keep them safe," he prayed, as his life emptied on the floorboards.

Callum Smith found the baby in the cellar. He had warned the two remaining families and accompanied them to the Ranger station, where one small unit of Rangers had returned from the border.

Five of them rode hellbent for John Davis's place, only to find ashes—and two corpses burned beyond recognition. Disregarding the lingering heat from the fire, Callum went to the trapdoor, hoping against hope that he would find someone alive.

His glove protected his hand from the heat that remained in the tin. He and another Ranger pulled until it finally came off, and he heard a weak cry from within.

He lowered himself down and found the tiny mewing bundle. The air was hot and stuffy, and he wondered at the newborn's will to live.

Callum picked the child up awkwardly. John had told him he intended to name the baby Morgan if it was a boy, after one of their old commanders in the Rangers. He swallowed. Neither John nor Susan had any family. What would happen to the little tyke? He handed the baby to one of the other Rangers, then climbed up.

If only they had arrived sooner, he thought as he took back the baby. If only . . .

He looked at the two embracing bodies. What had happened to the other woman? Probably taken by the Comanches. She had been pretty, blond. The kind the savages preferred in white women. The Rangers would look for her, but he didn't hold much hope. White women didn't last long with the Comanches, and he suspected this small group of renegades would head to Mexico now that the Rangers were back.

The baby. Callum felt responsible. He had let down his friend. His fellow Ranger. He couldn't let the child go to an orphanage. He owed John and Susan. He would take the baby and somehow raise it. Maria, his housekeeper of sorts, could take care of the child whenever he was gone. He would raise him as John would have liked.

As a Ranger.

Two days. Maybe three. Fleur Bailey stumbled along the rutted road. Her milk was drying, the milk that had remained in her after her baby died. The milk that kept Nicholas alive.

She was thirsty and hungry. Her left shoulder hurt like the devil, but she had to keep going. She had to find help.

She heard the sound of a wagon, and she dropped to the ground. She had become wary, afraid that the Comanches would come, or that someone who would take her child from her. Her Nicholas.

She listened as the heavy wagon came closer and she could see the words on the gaudily decorated sides. DR. CAREY'S MIRACLE MEDICINES.

A doctor. She crawled on the road, clutching the baby, and heard a shout, heard the sound of a team being pulled to a halt. She was tired, so tired. And safe.

Her eyes closed, her body finally succumbing to the shock and exhaustion and fear of the last few days. She didn't even wake when a small man, less than four feet tall, scrambled over to her side. Nor did she feel the arms of the taller man, his dark eyes curious and compassionate, as he picked her up and carried her inside the wagon, while the small man followed behind with her son.

She wasn't aware of her mutterings, of her scrambled words about Comanches and a dead husband. All were dead, she said. All but her son, Nicholas.